About th

Matt Thomas grew up in Port Talbot, South Wales. He worked for fifteen years in the computer games industry all over the UK and now runs a successful computer graphics business. He's one of the top all-time sellers on 3D data stock-site Turbosquid.com. If you ever need to digitally simulate the Chinese Navy, he's your man.

He's the author of two previous books, *Before and After* (1999) and *Terror Firma* (2001), both published by Harper Collins/Voyager. His work has been compared to the likes of Douglas Adams and Terry Pratchett. *Anthracite* is his first new fiction in 18 years. Just where that time went is anyone's guess. He now lives in Berkshire with his wife and three sons, a cat and a dog. No sheep.

Find Matt on Twitter: @MattT_Author

Anthracite

Matt Thomas

I've seen things you people wouldn't believe...

unbound

This edition first published in 2021

Unbound
TC Group, Level 1, Devonshire House, One Mayfair Place, London W1J
8AJ
www.unbound.com

© Matt Thomas, 2021

This book is a work of fiction and, except in the case of historical fact, any
resemblance to actual persons, living or dead, is purely coincidental.

ISBN (eBook): 978-1-78965-148-5
ISBN (Paperback): 978-1-78965-147-8

Cover design by Mecob

Printed and bound in Great Britain by Clays Ltd, Elcograf S.p.A.

This book is dedicated to
Sergeant Norman Jones, RAF

1921 – 2008

Thank you for showing me what is possible

Super Patrons

Miles Adams
Kirk Annett
Martin Baines
Eugene Battini
Betsy Bearden
Julian Benton
Gay and Bob Brooke
Dan Brotzel, Martin Jenkins & Alex Woolf
Etho Burrow
Bernardo Cervantes
Chris Chubbs
Alina Congreve
Kevin Copinger
Tracey Corbett
Steve Corley
Gillian Cranston
Barbara Davies
Joshua Davis
Chris Dobson
Mark Duddridge
Janice Goble

Eleanor Goldsmith
Mike Griffiths
Geoffrey Gudgion
Karin Harris
Rhiannon Harty
Cheryl Henshaw
Peter Hobbins
Amy Hudson
S Hudson
Daniel Ieuans
Ben Innocent
Billy Jarvis
Tristan John
Julie Jones
Olive Jones
Peter Kelly
Melanie Leach
Laurel Lindström
Harriet Lockett
Jacqueline Lockyer-Barrett
Ava Mandeville
Susan Mansell
Stuart Mitchell
Duncan Moore
Freda Moore
Stephani Morancie
Ben O'Neill
Diana Osborn
Ron Perry
Michael Preston
Gary Pyke
Naiara Rubio
David Saul

Keith Sleight
Peter Sleight
Eleanor Smith
Nic Smith
Mark Stahlmann
Alan Thomas
Barbara S. Thomas
Daniel Thomas
Doreen Thompson
Adam Tinworth
David G Tubby
Arjan Visser
Alun Watkins
Alexandra Welsby
Elaine Wharton
Anwen Ffion Wynne Williams
Matt Wisdom
Nastassja Wiseman
Julie Zeraschi

1

Slightly Different

The sound of the samba drifting up from Aberdare's Latin Quarter filled the bar with its contagious rhythm. It was hard to stop my feet matching the beat, but this was no time for dancing. Someone was trying to kill me.

Breathing deeply to calm my pounding heart I studied my surroundings. The bar was all greasy neon and steam-shrouded duct-work, dingy and dark despite the swarm of plasma screens overhead. They pumped out a bewildering torrent; W-Pop, sports news and frenzied Welshperanto coverage of the mardi gras below. On one big screen a holographic Tom Jones gyrated, as a line of dancers in shawls and stovepipe hats twerked themselves into a frenzy. For once I had to disagree with Uncle Tom – this whole thing was most definitely 'unusual'.

The bar's patrons appeared unimpressed by the show. Not big fans of the samba, blurry X-rated tattoos and thatched body hair seemed more to their liking. They sat nursing kaleidoscopic drinks and perfecting an air of suppressed menace. Some of them were very good at it.

In one corner a group of druids in full ceremonial dress sat hunched over their mead, muttering through thick beards. One of their number must have been communing too intimately with the spirit world – he lay face down in an ornate cauldron bubbling over with green foam. No amount of mistletoe-waving by his sniggering friends could seem to revive him.

A group of gaudy partygoers stumbled through the doors, clad in nothing but feather boas and jaunty smiles, blowing whistles and clicking castanets. How they managed in this climate I didn't know. The rain tumbling from the granite sky was the only familiar thing from home. Gwen had told me the mardi gras was an annual event, the biggest this side of Fishguard. It celebrated the Revolution, and the liberation of Patagonia which came soon after. That didn't make it any easier to accept – that it took place at all, here amidst this nondescript dead-end town. Except of course, it wasn't.

I don't mean the carnival wasn't carving its colourful, nipple-strewn path along the boulevard somewhere far below. As I sat in the towering jungle of steel and glass that comprised the gleaming Upper-City, I was only too aware of the delirious fiesta taking place beneath my feet. I only had to glance up at the plasma screens to witness the vast beached whale of an event, driven by explosive sexual tension and crowds resplendent in bulging Lycra and dayglo face paint. And the ladies weren't much better. What I mean is this wasn't *the* Aberdare I'd grown up in. In fact it wasn't anywhere I'd grown up in, or ever hoped to visit. I'd never understood the term 'culture shock', but it seemed I'd signed up for a crash course. This place would do that to you – *Under Milk Wood* meets *Blade Runner*, but with more rain and sequins. No, this wasn't the Aberdare I was familiar with. This Aberdare was slightly different.

In a vain attempt at distraction I cast my eye over the cocktail menu. I didn't like the sound of the Tonypandy Hand Shandy, so had ordered another Leek Daiquiri instead. At least four parts Brains Bitter, to which I'd developed a passable tolerance, it came with a real leek stirrer, and a miniature parasol in the shape of a witch's hat. Gwen got it for me, before disappearing into the night to 'organise the next leg of our journey'. Where had my mysterious guide vanished to? The first drink had left a ringing in my ears and a coating on my tongue like industrial disinfectant. At least it took my mind off the surroundings.

In a nearby booth a fight broke out. Insults were thrown, then drinks, finally punches – the traditional sequence of escalation. The drinks were likely the most dangerous part. Few other patrons paid the brawlers much heed; just another day in the life and death of Aberdare. Some things never change. With a start I realised I had company.

'Here ewe goes dalin.'

Suddenly my frothing drink had a twin. The waitress was built like a brick privy and wearing traditional bonnet and shawl. The fishnet stockings and basque were no doubt traditional too, but I couldn't think where – maybe Sodom or Gomorrah, which if I remembered were up just past Brecon. She gazed at me cow eyed and grinned a jowly grin. Some of her teeth might have been her own. I hoped she only wanted a tip.

Before I could fumble in a pocket for a coin (which would likely get me locked up over here), her eyes went wide with fear. She gazed at the opposite side of the booth. Her puffy face grew paler still, before she bolted, leaving just a whiff of stale sweat and a hint of eau de Cwmbran. Slowly, I turned to see what had spooked her.

3

'We meet at last, Señor Jones.'

The guy opposite was dressed to kill, no doubt for my sake. But I hardly noticed his razor-sharp lilac suit and matching feather-adorned hat, tilted at a rakish angle. Even his rapier-thin moustache and blazing indigo eyes barely registered. What drew my attention was the unfeasibly large gun he had pointed at my head, a cluster of barrels each as big as a sewer pipe and as menacing as the grave.

'Wait, you've got the wrong man.'

'Amigo, I am thinking I definitely have the right man.'

'No, I'm just…'

His face creased in a smile which got nowhere near his dead shark eyes. He must have shared a dentist with the waitress. 'You have no idea what you are. How significant your death will be.'

'Wait… please…'

He cocked the hammer with a ring-encrusted thumb. 'You die today for the greater good of mankind – well… some of it, anyway.'

I closed my eyes and the carousel parade of my life flashed by. I had been working on getting this movie up to an 18 rating, but have to admit it barely stretched to a PG – a straight-to-DVD release over before it began. When I met my maker I intended to have a few choice words. That meeting might be very soon. Before I could compose myself my world exploded in a bolt of blinding light and a deafening roar. Everything went black.

2

The Quiet Life: Aberdare Zero

Today was not turning out to be a good day – at all. I won't lie to you, I'm the sort of guy who puts a big emphasis on his own survival. Some might mistake this for cowardice; I prefer to say I have a well-developed sense of my own preservation. I like the quiet life – more la dolce vita than la vida loca. Not exactly risk averse, but why leave the safety of your home unless strictly necessary? Much like me, you're probably wondering how I got into this mess. My first meeting with Gwen would have unbalanced the best of us. If you think you would have fared better, please let me know. Perhaps I need to backtrack a little.

I'd been living back at home with Mum for a while, getting my thoughts together after college and planning the next stage of my career. The stepping stones to greatness were proving slippery and covered with moss. Courageously I'd not gone gently into that dark night – of paid employment – instead raging against the dying of my right to do whatever I wanted. Five and a half terms at Telford Art School could take their toll on anyone and, despite what some might say, I was no different to most. I was due some well-earned downtime.

Perhaps this preparatory stage had stretched longer than intended, but I'm nothing if not thorough. Sure, Aberdare was a quiet town, but its dreaming spires and derelict shops let me get to work on my graphic novel with none of the distractions you get from big shot agents or salivating Hollywood producers. Recently I'd begun to think I was doing too well in this respect. But I was finding the gentle rain, which washed in off the hills every day, watered the rich loam of my imagination in ways California sunshine never could. Plus Mum wasn't asking for any rent.

Our lives had settled into a comfortable routine. Mum went off to work down the council offices and I'd hold the fort at home, conserving my strength at keeping abreast of popular culture through the mediums of daytime TV and classic film. Us creative artists work best when our feet are grounded firmly in the rich manure deposited by the common man. I was diligent in this respect. It wasn't easy, but we all have our crosses to bear. Mine was to be a sophisticate amongst simpletons. If I felt adventurous I'd stretch to a trip to the library. As you can tell I'm not one to complain, unless, that is, I've got someone to complain to and they sit still long enough for me to unload.

Several times a week I'd visit Grandad up at the nursing home. Gafr Rhywiol was a pleasant enough place, but basically a warehouse for those on their way out. It sat atop the hill behind our row of terraced houses, overlooking the valley and smelling faintly of disinfectant and evaporating hope. When Gran died Mum moved Gramps up from the coast to be nearer to us. He wasn't as with-it as he used to be, but enough of his old personality remained to keep the nurses on their toes. He'd tell me endless tales of his time in the Air Force and what he'd done in The War. It was sad to see him go downhill, but I owed it to the old fella to give something back for all the time he'd spent with me growing up. He seemed happy enough. Only problem was we had no idea how we'd pay the fees once the money from his house sale ran out. We'd have to think of something fast.

Most days by mid-afternoon I was ready to start work. And what work it was. There is a deep abiding satisfaction which comes from knowing you're engaged in your finest labours, maybe the finest of your life. *The Windy Ninja* wasn't my first venture into the graphic novel market, but I knew with a certainty bordering on the divine it was my best. I've always had a deep respect for Japanese culture and, despite what my philistine schoolmates might say, this didn't begin and end with my massive collection of hentai tentacle porn. There is a profound spiritual meaning at the heart of Japanese civilisation which combines deep universal truths about the human condition with compelling images of young ladies in knee socks and tartan skirts. I'm unsure which elements first drew me, but I knew my contribution to the canon was coalescing daily at a heart-warming rate.

The Chronicles of the Windy Ninja, 'twas a tale of darkness, betrayal, redemption, hope and yet more betrayal, set in Muromachi Era Japan (1336–1573). Betrayal and extreme flatulence played a big part in the plot. It was as if Sergio Leone and Akira Kurosawa had spawned a bastard lovechild who got betrayed and chopped people into bits while farting a lot. Through this the gassy protagonist gained redemption, whilst propelled on a uniquely ballistic character arc. The work was packed with symbolic meaning, intense bloody violence, body parts and betrayal. And redemption.

Marketing could wait until my baby was fully formed, but Mr Watkins who ran the church newsletter promised to take a look as long as it wasn't 'too packed with filth', as I freely admit my previous efforts had been. Every auteur is destined to encounter censorship – small-minded roadblocks on the path to creative nirvana. If anything these made me more certain of my convictions. Exhausted after a long day at the creative coalface I'd pack up my pens and ink at 4.30 ready for Mum to cook my tea when she got home. I'm lucky enough to have inherited her sense of humour. She was always joking and pulling my leg.

'When you going to get a proper job you lazy scrounger?' she'd shout, before heading off down the bingo. But I knew she loved me really, maybe too much. Like all our family, apart from Gramps, she disguised her feelings behind insults and jest. Most nights, I'd continue my research down the pub. That's if my Jobseeker's Allowance would stretch to it.

Just as back in my schooldays, I remained a fish out of water in Aberdare. When I explained my plans to people they just stared at me in wonder, perhaps unused to meeting someone as driven and focused as myself. Some of my peers were still around, those who hadn't hit the big time and moved to Swansea. The good-natured ribbing had changed little from our younger days.

'Kevin, you're full of shit, you are!' they'd shout from across the street, before running back to their safe, mundane lives of quiet desperation and forlorn hope.

'Sticks and stones,' I'd call back, before avoiding the inevitable barrage of actual sticks and stones. But I cared little once the bruises had faded. They'd laugh on the other side of their bloated, tear-streaked faces when I collected the Oscar. Revenge is a dish best served cold, while sat in your Malibu condo. It was ironic considering the central themes of my magnum opus. Okay, so I hadn't *technically* suffered much in the way of betrayal, but I sensed the fates were already carving me a big slice of redemption pie from the bulging feast of life.

So those years were the best of times, and the worst of times, as they often are in situations like this. Admittedly, they'd been mainly 'the worst', but they must have wrapped back around, at least a little. Aberdare wasn't what it had been, and it hadn't been much to begin with. Our house had recently been broken into, but the intruders couldn't be arsed to take much of anything – seemed more like they just wanted to turn the place upside down. Even the care home had been raided, causing Grandad to speculate some reverse tooth fairy was building a castle made out of dentures and soiled surgical trusses. But Aberdare was the town I called home and it was into this heady, bittersweet mix Gwen first crashed unbidden – a beautiful iceberg in the path of my surging Titanic.

Like most afternoons when I wasn't with Grandad I was reading in the library. It was a vast Victorian pile in the centre of town, built back in the days when the local miners' collective harboured dreams of liberating the masses through the works of H.G. Wells and William Morris. It was run with Stalinist efficiency by Mrs Abergavenny, a fearsome old trout who'd rolled in out of nowhere the year before and swept away the *ancien régime* in a blaze of lavender breath mints and punitive late fines. She was small and compact, a geriatric pit bull who dressed like an Edwardian jumble sale and swore like a Milford Haven docker. Ours had been quite a first meeting in its own right.

'Boils my piss, it does – bloody kids, always on your phones! Hand it over before you disturbs the peace of my serene ffwcing establishment.'

I'd cast a sceptical eye over the dusty halls around me. The only one disturbing the peace of this deserted tomb was the smouldering pocket battleship in front of me. Still, I'd handed over my phone without a fuss: she was scary. Like I've said, I'm no fool.

For many weeks this was the procedure on arrival – I had to check in my mobile at the desk. It was draconian, but I learned to play the system. As long as you avoided overdue charges you were safe from the gulag. I became her favourite; perhaps she sensed a fellow seeker for the tree of knowledge, a burgeoning man of letters. Either that or I was her only customer. After a while she even let me keep my phone, as long as I kept it quiet.

Not long after that, the fateful day arrived.

It was a slate-grey afternoon at the arse end of a wet and dismal summer. My spirits were low. I'd hit an impasse with *The Windy Ninja* and couldn't think of any fresh ways for my protagonist's unruly bowels to land him in hot water. To cap it all Mum had gone AWOL without even so much as a note – probably off with one of her bingo mates again – and I was having to cook my own meals. Little did I know it, but destiny had me in her sights and was about to pull the trigger. I sensed a presence and looked up.

And there she was, backlit in the doorway and the pouring rain. An angel amongst devils, moisture clinging to her short chestnut hair as if it couldn't bear to be parted. I could see the attraction. She was the type of girl who fires an exploding harpoon through your heart before slowly reeling you in. Luckily I'm more resilient to such charms than most ruggedly handsome, yet sensitive guys my age.

She shrugged water from her short leather jacket then reached inside with a fingerless gloved hand. Tall and lithe, maybe a few years older than myself. I was put in mind of a hunting panther crossed with an ancient goddess. She looked down at her oversized smartphone, some weird foreign brand, then carefully back at me. You could have lost continents in those big brown eyes. I wanted to warn her about Mrs

Abergavenny and the library Gestapo, but my lips had stopped working along with my legs. The newcomer had a modulated lilting Valleys accent, as if local but well travelled.

'Kevin Gwydion Jones?'

I couldn't take my gaze off her. 'Yes,' I think I managed to whisper, my mouth very dry. 'Are you here for *The Windy Ninja*? It's not finished yet.'

She looked at me blankly. 'I know nothing of ninjas, windy or otherwise – but you have to listen if you want to live. We have to get going. We don't have much time.'

I was more than ready for pretty girls asking me if I wanted to live. I won't lie to you, I had been wondering for some time if my life in Aberdare constituted any sort of living at all. And here she was, my saviour, ready to whisk me away to a life of A-list parties, loose drugs and hard women. I pondered her proposition sagely, as was my way.

'Too bloody right I am! When do we leave?'

This seemed to be the reaction she was looking for. My new friend nodded, her eyes sweeping the room – perhaps she'd been warned about rogue librarians after all. She needn't have worried – as usual the place was deserted. Satisfied we were alone she turned back to me.

'Tidy. But there's no time to explain. You need to come with me now.'

'Now in a minute, or proper now?'

'Proper now.'

'But what about –'

'No time for that.'

'But –'

'No time for that either.' She gripped my forearm. Her hands were warm and soft but oh so very strong. It didn't strike me as a grip which it would be easy to wriggle out of. Which was beside the point – I would have followed her to the very gates of hell if she'd asked. I couldn't have resisted if I'd wanted to. I didn't want to.

I thought at first she might take me to a waiting limousine, or a helicopter – either that, or at least the bus station. Instead, she led me deeper into the musty depths of that ancient library. It was the first time she took me by surprise; it wouldn't be the last.

'So what's your name?' Time to turn on the charm.

She walked fast, scanning all around as if in search of danger. 'I'm Gwendolyn, but we don't have time for any of that nonsense right now.'

I had so many questions – chief amongst them being: was she single? What did she look for in prospective boyfriends? But before I knew it we were at the dented service lift doors – the ones the pearl-necklaced Taliban used to bring trolleys of age-worn books up from the Stygian depths below. Perhaps foreshadowing later events, I found myself mightily confused.

'Are we looking for inspiration downstairs? I can tell you now the manga collection here is not extensive. They'll order books in, as long as they're not filled with smut.'

She looked at me stunned, no doubt impressed at my ability to think three steps ahead. 'Something like that, yes.'

Gwen slapped the big red lift recall button. With a creaking and a groaning that made my teeth vibrate the elevator arrived like a bicycle passing through a mangle. The door clanked open and she bundled me inside. Just what Mrs Abergavenny would say at this breach of procedure, I shuddered to think. The lift wasn't for use by the great unwashed, or any lacking the mystic sacrament of a senior librarian. Inside twinkled an oddly modern control panel mounting just three buttons. The library had a ground floor, a first floor and a storage cellar I was dimly aware of as a concept but had never visited – a bit like Nando's. The antique doors clanged shut.

Gwen took great pains to position herself in front of the panel, then cracked her fingers like a concert pianist warming up for a performance. I'm unclear what she did next, but it involved pressing the buttons in a bewildering sequence interspersed with carefully timed pauses.

'Doesn't do to get the programming wrong,' she muttered.

'Programming? How hard can it be, there's only three floors.'

Her job done, Gwen pinned herself against the back wall. 'Brace yourself.'

'Brace?'

My stomach joined my heart in my mouth as we plummeted like a stone – a stone attached to a cord of elastic stretched taut down a deep mineshaft. My rising scream couldn't get past the logjam in my throat. I don't know how far the cellar went down, but we must have passed through in the first few blistering seconds. In defiance of all logic, not to mention laws of physics, we kept accelerating hellwards. I don't like lifts at the best of times, and this definitely wasn't the best of times. My feet lifted gently from the floor.

'What have you done, you mentalist!'

Gwen looked at me sideways but otherwise remained calm. 'You might want to suck one of these. It will help with the nausea.' Straining against the G-force, she offered me a mint.

'What nausea?'

Okay, I'm sometimes a slow learner. The lift didn't so much come to a shuddering halt as squirt sideways through a crack in reality, bungeeing between this world and the next like an unfortunate conjoined twin. It felt like my constituent molecules were stripped, then randomly reassembled by some mad laughing demigod. The fillings in my teeth hummed and my eyeballs itched. I could taste my breakfast, but not in a good way.

Gwen helped me to my feet. 'Next time, take a mint.'

'There won't be a *next time*, not if I have any say in the matter.'

She looked at me coolly. 'You don't have any say in the matter.' She handed me a packet of mints.

Only one thing was certain – I needed some new trousers. As if that wasn't enough Gwen pulled a large gun from inside her jacket and held it at the ready. She looked at me and smiled.

'Some reckon diamonds are a girl's best friend, but I prefer .357 hollow point ammunition.'

'Is that really necessary?'

She just winked at me. 'We're not in Kansas anymore, Dorothy.'

Placing an elegant finger beneath my chin she eased my mouth shut. The creaking doors slid open, revealing the new improved reality I've already begun to describe; Aberdare+1 – the version with the mardi gras, levitating cars and freelance cathedral enthusiasts. The familiar library was gone, we were in the bowels of some vast high-tech hotel. Things only went downhill from there. Typically I soon found myself in a bar. Ah yes, we must get back to the bar, and my new moustachioed, gun-toting friend.

3

Dial M for Merthyr

The roar subsided, I opened my eyes, surprised I still could – and instantly wished I hadn't. The guy in the hat was smeared across the booth, a Jackson Pollock of blood, brains and smouldering moustache hair, an oily stain where his head should have been. His unfired weapon spun lazily on the table. Of his hat there was no sign. The feather which had been tucked into the band rocked down through the drifting smoke to land on his gun. Behind me Gwen's voice cut through the febrile air.

'Run you numskull – there'll be more than one!'

She was soon at my table, lithely charging for the exit with her smoking sidearm drawn. I staggered to my feet. A golden sickle tossed by one of the druids whistled past my head and embedded itself with a *thunk*, quivering in the wall beside me. But you don't play as much Counter-Strike as I have without learning something about courage. I got up and ran after her, glad to leave the steaming leek daiquiri behind.

The cold wet air hit me like a slap as we emerged onto the

street. At least it had stopped raining, which had to be the most microscopic of small mercies ever recorded. Gwen reached backwards and pulled me through the teeming crowds.

'I thought I told you to lie low, to stay out of trouble.'

'I was. I've no idea how they found me!'

We barged past a line of tourists and saffron-clad Hare Krishnas. Anthropomorphic chrome robots scuttled from our path. Polystyrene punnets of half-eaten chips in curry sauce were trampled underfoot like high-calorie confetti. Gwen picked up the pace.

'Well they found you, all right. Are you a magnet for chaos? Now we've got to lose them all over again – this way.'

She led me along a wide esplanade enclosed by a metal rail, thick with sightseers. Beyond the barrier the city spread out down the valley like a casket of jewels discarded by a careless giant, the emergent late sun rendering the forest of sinuous towers in molten gold. But that wasn't even the half of it. The sky was filled with aircraft of bewildering size and shape, each bereft of wings or rotors. What on earth was keeping them aloft? The small ones whizzed along in neat lines at breakneck speed, while the big ones drifted serenely with their own purpose and design. I gawped awestruck as a huge oil tanker sized craft glided silently overhead, magenta Saint Elmo's fire rippling playfully across its hull. If I hadn't been running for my life I would have appreciated stopping to admire the view, but of course Gwen was having none of that.

'Will you stop lagging behind, this is no time for sightseeing!'

'But that –'

'Come on – or you'll get us both killed!'

As if hearing her words, the gods of fate chose that moment to prove their perverse sense of humour. Before us the crowds dissolved like the Red Sea parting, as one small flying craft came in for an unscheduled landing. Its doors opened, revealing a team of faceless black-armoured men. Fear gripped me – they were heavily armed and looked like they meant business. I was certain they weren't accountants.

The shooting started before they reached the ground, which was fortunate, in a way, because the craft's motion must have thrown off their aim. Exploding rounds peppered the pavement around us. Gwen grabbed my arm and pulled me towards cover. The shelter she had in mind didn't look up to the job, but it was the only option – a street vendor's fast food stall abandoned by its operator. A garish cartoon rabbit adorned its metal frame, under a hoarding reading 'The Big Cheese'. The rabbit was munching a piece of toast covered in thick orange goo. A loudspeaker on a loop sprung to life advertising its wares.

'Rarebit! Rarebit!'

This was a situation both surreal and deadly in the extreme, Salvador Dali in a suicide bomb vest. We cowered behind the grill's steel bodywork as the fusillade intensified. Chips of white-hot metal spalled off the leeward side and drummed against my cheek. I could smell cordite and broiling cheddar.

'We're done for – whatawedo?!'

Gwen coolly reloaded her gun, then popped up to return fire. It did little good. Our assailants stepped up their attack. The cart was all but swept away in a tsunami of blazing lead. Even Gwen must have sensed our position was futile. They had us overmatched for firepower by at least ten to one.

'Rarebit! Double Gloucester and Preseli Blue!'

'Is this the end? I'm not cut out for this!' My stomach felt like it had a better place to go. You might think me a coward; I prefer to say I have a healthy commitment to my own survival. Either way, for the first time on our journey, Gwen looked genuinely annoyed – almost peeved.

'It is the end – for them. This calls for a change of plan.' She reached into her jacket and pulled out a small silver case, flipping it open as if to check her make-up, which was doing a better job of staying composed than me.

'Are you out of your mind? This is no time for blusher!' The indignity of it – it seemed I was to meet my doom while being serenaded by a cheese-fixated rabbit.

'Scarlet Harlech, Crumbling Crumlin… Rarebit!'

But Gwen was busy fiddling with the device. When she had it to her satisfaction she snapped the lid shut and weighed it in her hand, before tossing it with practised ease over the cart towards our attackers. There followed a pause so pregnant it might have been having triplets. I think our assailants suspected what was coming next.

The world dissolved into a sheet of electric blue flame. No sound intruded, as if the very air had been ripped from around us. Black armoured limbs and lumps of air-car went sailing past our stall, which skidded, pushed across the tarmac by the blast, taking us with it. For a moment all was still.

With a strength that belied her slim physique Gwen pulled me to my feet, checking me over as she did so. 'Are you okay, are you hurt?' She ran her beeping hand-help over my limbs and face.

Dazed, and for once not at my rational ice-cool self, I swayed in her arms. 'Michael Bay called, he wants his explosions back.' She shook me back to sense. I had a long way to come.

'I'm getting out of here and you're coming too.'

'Rare… b I t… r a r e… b b b…'

It seemed the fast food stall had toasted its last cheese-based snack. Gwen led me around its mangled carcass. Nearby, the assault team's vehicle had fared even worse. Little more than a blackened husk, its bonnet popped and its interior smouldered. As we passed I couldn't help but look inside. What magic powered these silent craft? Even by the standards of that dreadful day my breath caught in my throat. Where you might have expected some complex engine of bewildering design was nothing of the sort – just a smallish black box, of a size to hold a pair of shoes; sheared-off wires trailed into it and a beefier cable trailed out – but that was it. The device stood out as the only part of the craft still in one piece. Printed on its lid were bold red letters; **Jones Corporation J-Drive, Anthracite^2 Anti-grav+ Model, 34–38 Gigawatts AC**. Somehow I felt cheated. I was dimly aware of the wail of sirens fast approaching. Gwen all but yanked me off my feet.

'Gawping again? We need to split before Pwllheli Five-O turn up and start asking awkward questions about dead hitmen. Come on – there's bound to be others!'

The street was empty, but maybe not for long. I shifted. Like I might have mentioned, personal safety is high on my list of priorities. Soon we were bounding down a flight of steps away from the deserted esplanade. Gwen half turned, glancing over her shoulder.

'We've got to get to the next gate before they shut it down.'

'Shut it down – can they do that? What gate?'

'Not likely, but the way these jokers are behaving they might just think so. This is where we need to go.'

At the foot of the steps was a wide tree-lined boulevard, just as empty as the one above. A little way down the street was a '*tacsi* rank'. At least that's what the glowing neon sign arching above it said. But these weren't your average black cabs. Sure, they were small and yellow, and decorated with a checkerboard design, but these had had an upgrade. Red and green navigation lights twinkled on stub wings in the moisture-laden air. A whiff of ozone reached my flaring nostrils. Like most of the vehicles in this bedlam, these craft seemed able to fly.

Gwen pulled me through the door of the first in line. The pilot was another of those mechanical marvels, burnished to a high shine and punchably cheerful. Its head rotated the full 180 and its latex face broke into a forced smile. 'And where do you great folks want to go to today? Special rates to all the major Tenby Casinos. Why not visit the world famous Penscynor Velociraptor Gardens?'

I didn't get the feeling we'd be hitting the tourist traps. Gwen checked our tail for pursuit, then her eyes went wide in sudden realisation. Turning to me she slapped her hand to forehead. 'You've got a mobile phone on you?'

It seemed an odd question – I didn't think my old Nokia would cut it in this technological paradise. The phone was in my pocket, on silent but still intact. Gwen snatched it from my grasp and threw it into the footwell of the tacsi.

'Holyhead Spaceport, Terminal 5 – and make it snappy,' she shouted to the pilot, before bundling me out the opposite door.

'What the hell? My phone – took weeks to save up for that!'

But with a sub-audible hum, which stood my hair on end, the VTOL craft was already rising. I watched it leave in dismay, along with my phone.

Meanwhile Gwen was moving down the line of air-cars. 'You'll pay with your life if they've got a trace on that thing. We're heading south – follow me.'

I reflected this whole day had been heading south from the word go. Two minutes later we were safe inside another of the flying tacsis, after sending a host of the others to all points of the compass. Gwen set the satnav to the Shane Williams Expressway and we settled back to enjoy the ride. It would be a short flight to the next gate.

4

Isaiah the Flyer

After escaping the carnage in Aberdare we sped south through the darkening sky. The passenger hold of the tacsi was cramped but comfortable enough. A sign inside the windscreen advised clients a cleaning surcharge would apply on any vomit. Gwen said she had cash to pay for chaff and flares, but didn't want to attract undue attention. She judged stealth mode an extravagance, unlikely to help against sophisticated opponents. What the hell sort of taxi was this? My companion seemed content our shenanigans with the phone had thrown off pursuit, at least for the time being. My stress levels eased a little, and I began to almost enjoy the ride. Gwen set the terrain-following altimeter to a conservative 500 feet of ground clearance and took the opportunity to field-strip her gun.

'There are old pilots and there are bold pilots, but there are no old bold pilots,' she said, by way of explanation.

I heartily approved. 'My Grandad is always saying stuff like that. He was in the Air Force you know.'

After locking her weapon back together Gwen checked the

radar for signs of pursuit. 'That's nice. We can go back and get him if you like.'

'Very funny. Isaiah the Flyer, they used to call him. Qualified on Spitfires, he did. Served as an engineer mostly after that.'

No answer broke the awkward silence. I noticed Gwen giving me a strange look. In the short time I'd known her it was the first time I'd seen her thrown by anything we'd seen or done. It didn't fill me with confidence.

All of a sudden she was doing too much blinking. 'Your grandfather was named... Isaiah?'

'Yes.'

'And your family name is... Jones?'

'You already know that – from the *real* Aberdare. Aberdare Zero, as I've decided to call it.' I half expected a debate about which was the real Aberdare, but she seemed distracted. My stress-ometer began to twitch.

'And he was in the RAF?'

'Yes, in World War Two, at least. Left soon after – didn't think much of jets.' I didn't like the way Gwen was looking at me; she was starting to make me nervous, which considering what I'd just lived through was quite an achievement.

I felt I was missing something. 'You don't *know him*, do you?'

Such a long pause followed it seemed she might not answer. I could almost hear the gears turning behind those bottomless dark eyes. At last Gwen shook herself out of her daze and made an effort to compose herself.

'I won't lie to you – I don't exactly *know* him, but I do know *of* him – the local version at least.'

'What do you mean? He's not famous or anything.'

Gwen studied me closely, as if gauging if I was extracting the urine. She was starting to freak me out. 'Perhaps you need to learn a little about the Isaiah Jones from this world – the *real* Isaiah Jones. The one who gave his name to the J-Drive.'

I was getting a bad feeling about this. 'You what?'

Gwen licked her lips and took a slow, deep breath. 'Maybe the most famous man who ever lived. *That* Isaiah Jones.'

'My grandfather?'

'I don't know about grandfathers, but Isaiah Jones was the last of the old-school inventors – Edison meets Tesla, but on a good day. Isaiah was the real thing – a certified genius. Working on the weeping edge of anything he turned his hand to, but his real passion was zero-point energy.'

I must have looked blank – perhaps even more vacant than usual.

She continued slowly, 'Zero-point energy is getting power from a vacuum.'

I couldn't help but scoff. 'I'm no scientist, more your *tortured creative genius* type, but even I know you can't get more out of an engine than you put in.'

'Zero-point is different. It pulls free energy from the very fabric of space – the Holy Grail of quantum physics since before Schrödinger murdered his first cat.'

I was still sceptical. Grandad had been good, he'd built me some great soapbox go-carts and epic *Thunderbirds* dioramas, but this was seriously out of his range. Yet inconveniently the huge ore freighters filling the surrounding sky required some explanation.

Gwen went on. 'Isaiah wasn't just a theoretical physicist, he was an engineer. As soon as he had thrashed out the theory, some claim scribbled on the back of a fag packet, he retired to his shed and hammered away. He got an account at B&Q.'

I had to admit this sounded like my grandad, but I still wasn't buying it. 'This can't be happening, I feel faint. This can't be an alternative universe. I must have taken a bang to the head.'

Gwen looked unimpressed. 'Would a pi test convince you?' She seemed even less impressed by my blank expression. 'The ratio of the diameter of a circle to its circumference. One of the constants that varies from universe to universe due to fluctuations in the shape of space-time. Course, you need plenty of significant figures to spot a change. Look at this.'

She tapped away on her smartphone and showed me a long string of glowing numbers. 3.14159265357...

'I've got an app for it – very precise. Comes in handy in my line of work – like a compass, or a GPS.'

I still wasn't convinced. 'Like I said, I'm not much of a mathematician, you'd need Grandad for that. I wouldn't know pi if it bit my bum. You'll have to come up with something better than that.'

Gwen gritted her perfect teeth and seemed to count under her breath. She thought for a moment, before reaching into her jacket to produce a thick wad of cash, handing me a bright orange bill. It looked like Monopoly money on crack, or maybe I'd been slipped some LSD. 'This is a hundred dragon note – currency of the Welsh Republic and legal tender in most of the civilised world, even in what's left of England. Recognise the guy on the back?'

I flipped it over, and stifled a gasp. Sure enough, there was Gramps, smiling back at me and brandishing a slide rule. He was pictured sitting at a drawing board packed full of bewildering schematics and plans. The inscription woven around the banknote, in elaborate Celtic scrollwork, read, *'National Bank of Wales – In Isaiah Jones we trust. Pay It Forward.'*

I was experiencing a horrible sinking feeling, and for once it had nothing to do with cocktails or kamikaze lifts. It wasn't just the image of Gramps – the inclusion of one of his pet phrases gave the whole nightmare a bizarre air of believability. Gwen saw my expression and brightened. 'Good to see I'm getting through to you, sport. You've got a lot of catching up to do. Best I fill you in.'

'Please don't hit me!'

Exasperated, she just shook her head in contempt. When I'd finally calmed down, Gwen got on with her story. For no good reason I could think of she'd taken to speaking in hushed tones.

'You've got to understand, this is the corporate PR version. I'm sure reality was messier, but after years of trials and false dawns Isaiah produced the first prototype. The Jones Drive Mark 1 was born – he codenamed it ANTHRACITE.'

'He built it in his shed?'

Gwen wrinkled her nose. 'Technically, yes. But by this stage he had employees – it was basically a small factory. From day one these things were so good he sold them straight off the production line. The world rolled up to his doors with wads of cash, and flew away powered by J-Drives laughing their heads off. Civilisation was transformed overnight.'

This wasn't easy to accept, but neither were the wonders I'd witnessed back in Aberdare, before being almost obliterated. Could a single leap in technology ripple out through so many fields? I was being asked to think the unthinkable, at a time when most guys would have struggled to think the thinkable. Lucky I'm not *most guys*. But still my brain was numb. 'So how do the gates fit in?'

Gwen tapped away at her handheld and looked worried. 'Oh they came much later, and that tech is still hush-hush. Just a few groups know the trick of rigging J-Drives in parallel to hack yourself a stable portal. My employers control the most extensive network.' She saw my expression. 'Still having a hard time believing me? Take a look.'

She handed me her smartphone. It showed a picture of

Grandad in pristine lab coat, standing proudly in front of a gleaming factory. The headline above it read 'Modern Anthracite Solves World Power Needs'. Gramps looked thirty years younger, but there was no denying it was him. Behind Isaiah stood a gaggle of faces I recognised from home – uncles and aunts aplenty, all of them benefitting from a significant wardrobe upgrade, and in several cases, plastic surgery. Grandad was being handed a huge medal by a guy in a suit. The caption said it was the UN Secretary-General. The medal was the Nobel Prize for Physics and Peace, combined for one year only. I began feeling a bit faint.

'One from the archive, but that factory is still the biggest. We should catch sight of it in a jiffy. They say you can see it from space.'

I had a lot of reading to do. It wasn't going to be easy, not with the way my hands were trembling.

Before I tell you what else I learned that fateful day, perhaps my family tree needs a little explanation – some might say a little pruning. My grandad Isaiah was the youngest of five brothers, from an early age held up as a paragon by his parents to which the others could only aspire. By all accounts they struggled to reach the mark. Can't have been easy in depression era South Wales. Times were hard. Often there wasn't enough to eat. A favoured child would only cause resentment in such situations, no matter how great they did at school.

The oldest was Nebuchadnezzar (I'm hoping his mates called him Neb). I know what you're thinking – the names. Long ago some long-forgotten Jones family forbearer concluded that when you have a surname as egalitarian as ours, you need some other way to stand out. Perhaps they went a bit too far, but it soon became a family tradition.

Neb was as different from Isaiah as could be, as were all the other brothers. While Grandad was diligent and studious, his older rivals were coarse and mean, hustling the weaker kid's dinner money and blackmailing the teachers. His parents packed Isaiah off to Air Force Academy at eighteen – about as close, in that time and place, as any could get to a seat of higher learning. University was a distant dream.

Years passed. Roles were played in the momentous events of the day. Somehow all the brothers conspired to avoid getting torpedoed, bombed, shot or blitzed by Hitler's panzers. Some had better wars than others. At least one got locked up for selling ration books off the back of a lorry. Grandad came back in one piece, but changed – scarred by the things he'd seen and done. He was also deeply convinced of everyone's duty to leave the world a better place than they'd found it. Plenty of his peers didn't make it back at all.

But for all their faults Isaiah's older brothers were also fertile to an alarming degree. Balthazar, Ezekiel and Herod might not have left much of a mark on the world but they left it populated with a horde of useless bastards – in every sense. Theirs was the DNA which launched a thousand shits. Neb's shady intrigues finally proved his undoing, falling off a boat running fags and booze to the monks on Caldey Island. Any passing sharks likely had chunks bitten out of them on his way down.

Meanwhile his relatives kept up the naming tradition. But the biblical theme proved restrictive. They started going off piste while, it seems, marching off pissed to the registry office. These weren't proto-hipsters – this was provincial Wales, where the 60s didn't start till 1982. This was decades before celebrity baby name inflation. But woe betide any who mocked this growing clan. Some families have one bad apple, mine was a whole festering orchard. After Grandad and Mum I was the lone snowy white lamb amongst a whole flock of black sheep. They were small town criminals; gangsters straight outta Trumpton. But no one laughed if they wanted to keep their teeth.

Neb's eldest, my mum's cousin, was the notorious 'Uncle Genghis', *uncle* to everyone, whether they liked it or not. He was a chip off Neb's flinty old granite block, but twice as mean; and much like his Mongolian namesake a deranged psychopath to boot. He'd played openside for Pontypridd until getting banned for life for headbutting a referee. Rumour was the fool made some joke about a yak. As far as I was aware Genghis had never laid waste to the Greater Middle East, but I wouldn't have put it past him – it was surely only a matter of time. He was a 'local businessman', in the Sicilian sense; of limited talent but limitless ambition, forever touting get-rich-quick schemes, long cons and short sells. He had his fingers in lots of pies, none of which would have got past environmental health – not until the inspector fell down some stairs.

'Genghis Can' as the saying went round our way. And in the end he probably would. He scared me to death growing up, and his kids Pryderi and Blodeuwedd were even worse. Family gatherings would end in smashed toys and bruises, sometimes broken bones. Unfortunately for me he seemed to be always round our house when I was growing up – he was very close to my mum.

I vividly remembered the last time I'd seen Uncle Genghis – he'd come round to borrow Mum's foot spa. He had a theory, for once maybe somewhere near the mark, that millions of these things were gathering dust in cupboards all over the world. Why not turn these unwanted gifts into something useful, something people would pay for? So Genghis proposed a kit to repurpose them as vaginal steamers – the Vaginator 5000 was born. Uncle wanted to utilise my design skills, free of charge, of course, to draw up the plans. They say there's a cigarette paper between genius and insanity, so I told him in no uncertain terms on which side this idea fell – for this reason I was 'ooout'. He told me to shut my cakehole and fetch my mam. I was lucky to escape another beating.

And then of course there was my own beloved mother. She was intelligent enough, but sometimes a smidge out of touch. For example, all that summer she'd been fretting about Genghis's kids' inevitable descent into a life of crime. It was obvious to the rest of us where that crude brood were heading, but somehow Mum still held out hope they'd better themselves, just like I'd done.

'They say young Pryderi is one of those medicine donkeys.'

Not for the first time I squinted at her in confusion. 'A what, Mum?'

'Been breaking bad with that Harri Heroin round the back of the Youth Club, helping 'im out like. You know – a *medicine donkey*.'

My tired brain struggled to translate, I stared at her in wonder. 'Mum, do you mean a drugs mule?'

'Yeeeeees, that's what I was bleedin saying. Pass us the milk.'

We seemed to have lots of conversations like this. It was almost enough to make we want to leave home. Almost.

So the upshot of all this was, despite being a sensitive and sheltered only child, I was beset by a plague of relatives every bit as egregious as anything Moses had to put up with. And I don't mean my third cousin Moses (aka 'Jones the Cones'), who ruled the ice cream trade in Tenby with a nut-sprinkled rod of iron. My family were the Borgias without the charity, the Mansons without the music. It's a miracle I turned out as normal as I did.

I told Gwen all this as we sped along through the darkening sky. She looked at me sadly, as if a horrible realisation was dawning. By the end of my tale she held her head in her hands. After an uncomfortable silence she began massaging her temples, as if beset by an avalanche of woe.

'And yet, they chose to call you... Kevin?'

This, I had to admit, was a good point. 'Mum always liked to think we were a breed apart from the rest of the clan –'

'Yeah, who calls their mam Mum, the Duke of Twatshire?'

'Maybe she just saw me and thought, *that's a Kevin, that is*. At least I don't sound like I massacre newborn babies for fun.'

'No, I'm sure you wouldn't do anything so memorable.'

It was then that the thought hit me. You're likely wondering why it hadn't occurred to me sooner, but it had been quite a bad day – I had reason to be distracted. If there were analogues of all my family over here, merrily counting their money and running this world, where was the local version of me? Gwen got there before I did. I've got to hand it to her, she was fast in more ways than one. My new friend passed me her handheld again.

'Sorry kiddo, I've already checked. No dice.'

The screen was small, but glowed with breathtaking clarity. It showed my family's extensive Wikipedia entry. A small footnote at the bottom caught my attention.

Isaiah Jones was unable to have children of his own due to injuries sustained in World War Two. He died without a direct heir.

It seemed I wouldn't be meeting my twin any time soon.

5

Getting My Tea On

Ah, the glory which was Greece, the grandeur which was Rome, the smouldering wasteland which was Port Talbot. Mordor by Sea, some called it, but without the magic volcanoes. Except of course the version I now gawped at open mouthed, wasn't. This version of Grandad's home town could have given Greece and Rome a run for their money; it could have thrashed them, picked them up off the floor and thrashed them again just for shits and giggles. To use a local idiom, this place made the Hanging Gardens of Babylon look simply *hanging* by comparison.

For starters ancient Athens lacked the bustling space port where the docks should have been, giant twinkling passenger liners floating through the dusk. And instead of the grimy steel works, the gleaming halls of the massive Jones Corp J-Drive factory stretched for endless miles into the blue-grey distance. All the way, in fact, to Kenfig Hill, where the gleaming spire of the Howard Marks World Trade Centre thrust through the crimson clouds like a glittering needle shooting-up the sky.

On the western horizon across the bay Swansea's skyline was busy putting Florence to shame. Vast pyramids of crystalline glass sprawled in profusion, nestling amidst clusters of domes and burnished spires, all vying in their brilliance with the setting sun. I didn't know where to look. Wherever my gaze fell exotic craft filled the sky, drifting through the dusk in a complex kinetic ballet. How they avoided a pile-up I'd never know. Our tacsi was in a holding pattern, circling high above Bryn, as we awaited a slot in the city's busy air traffic gyratory system. The supercomputers running the show must have been very good. I cast my gaze far out to sea.

'Are those oil rigs on the horizon?'

Gwen chuckled. 'No need for oil anymore. Not with J-Drives shipping by the ton. That's where the refugees are housed – the poor sods fleeing the war in Patagonia. For all the talk of liberation, it doesn't seem the Government wants them rubbing shoulders with us natives.'

My mouth did fish impressions as we received our traffic slot and dropped to a lower altitude. 'So where is it we're heading?' Years ago Grandad had lived down this way and I knew my way around, more than a little.

Gwen pointed to a small grotty building, out of place amidst the glittering metropolis. Even by the standards of that day I was taken aback. I squinted in the direction she was pointing.

'But that looks an awful lot like Taibach Rugby Club. The version I know from back home.'

She seemed to think I should be impressed. 'Yes, *I know*. Don't stress, I can get us in – we're on the VIP guest list. I've got a few tricks up my sleeve.'

Gwen clambered into the pilot seat and took manual control, against the shrill protests of the onboard AI. Seconds later we were coming in for a hair-raising j-hook landing on the green next to St Theodore's Church, as the hysterical autopilot squawked about the dangers of 'unauthorised landings'. My companion paid the fare with a thick wad of Monopoly cash, before bundling me out the clamshell doors. She remembered to yell the traditional 'Thanks Drive' behind her, but I think the generous tip went further to placate the jabbering machine. The robotic voice was still wittering on about 'no change being given' as it lifted into the gathering dusk. I didn't get time to study my surroundings. Gwen grabbed my arm and pulled me towards a dark line of trees.

'That was risky, but it's best we avoid municipal landing pads. Besides, there's never anyone around here – can always trust a churchyard to be quiet in this sleazy town.'

But I'd had enough of being pulled around like a bag of spuds. I was sure this wasn't the way it was meant to be. Catching her by surprise I struggled out of her grip. It was time to stamp my little foot down in authority.

'Look luv, I appreciate what you're trying to do.'

Gwen's gaze would have stopped me in my tracks, that's if my feet hadn't already been planted to the floor. Her answer was ominously quiet. 'Do you really know what's going on – what's at stake?'

I let out a weary sigh. 'Thanks for saving me from those nutters back in Aberdare, but I didn't sign up for this. I'm very much a stay-at-home type of guy. Need to get back – Mum should be getting my tea on about now. That's if she puts in an appearance today. Fish fingers on a Tuesday.'

What she did next took me by surprise. Too fast to follow, Gwen stepped up into my grill and grabbed me by the throat, her hand jamming around my windpipe. What she did with the other could have been interesting under other circumstances, but here was just excruciatingly painful. Looking deep into my eyes she whispered, 'Bull me no shit, you blathering bag of wank – without me you wouldn't last a second, not here or anywhere else in this crazy mixed-up world. If I'm curt it's because time is a factor. I don't want us both ending up dead. I get no bounty on a corpse.'

I was sensing a touch of push-back at my very reasonable suggestion. Momentarily something flickered in her eyes, as if she'd said too much. Struggling to regain my breath I was just able to rasp, 'Perhaps it's best I *do* let you take the lead, after all.'

Her grip loosened just a little. 'I've tried to be polite, thus far. But let's just remember this is not a democracy. Think of it more as a…' She strained to be diplomatic as she struggled for the right word.

Ever the gentleman, I helped her out. 'A kidnapping?'

Her face brightened. 'Yes, that's right – a kidnapping – means you do as I say. Capisce?'

I nodded fast. 'Can you at least tell me where we're going? I respond better to gentle persuasion.'

Her eyes narrowed, as if sizing me up. She must have come to a positive conclusion, at least partly, because she let go of my windpipe. 'There are… some people who want to keep you safe. They learned you were in imminent danger – mortal danger. They sent me to help.'

I loosened my collar as my feet once again took my weight. 'I noticed that back in Aberdare.'

Gwen went on, never once taking her eyes off mine. 'These… *interested parties* badly want to meet you. They've contracted me to take you to them. I'm a courier.'

She sounded more like a people trafficker to me, but I kept this observation to myself. 'And you do this for a living – pick up unsuspecting guys from libraries? Why didn't you just email? My diary is not exactly bursting.'

Now it was Gwen's turn to scoff. 'Come off it – I think we both know you're not the sort to spring into action without a massive kick up the jacksy. Think of me as the boot gently parting your cheeks.'

I did my best to look hurt, but Gwen didn't seem to notice.

'Besides, you can't get emails through a gate, nor telephone or radio for that matter. Sensitive messages, or commodities' – she actually had the nerve to nod in my direction – 'need a courier to take them through. When you have a delicate job you hire the best.'

I was a tad unnerved by her nailing my character after so short an acquaintance. 'And that's why your friends sent you – you're the best?'

Her answer held no trace of doubt. 'Yes, I'm the very best – totally elite.'

There was a pause, in which I decided I could well believe her. Gwen continued, 'And they're not my friends – *clients* maybe, for the time being, at least.'

This was all too much to take. I was rapidly developing one of my headaches. How I longed for the safety of my bedroom and a nice quiet lie down. 'So who were those guys back in Aberdare – the ones with the attitudes and Kalashnikov loyalty cards?'

My mysterious, smoking-hot kidnapper turned away as if to go. She didn't look happy; I knew how she felt. Gwen's voice was flat. 'There are other forces at play. We were jumped by more than one faction, as I'm sure you noticed. Could be the Newport Triads, or the Russian Mob out of Tredegar. Every hitman and bounty hunter between here and Blaenau Ffestiniog seems to want to use you for target practice – well, not on my watch.'

I sensed she didn't really believe what she was saying. There was more to this than she was letting on. Never mind, for now. Perhaps we both needed a fresh start.

'Well, if I've not had time to say it yet – thanks for keeping me safe. I appreciate it.'

Gwen half turned and shrugged. 'I'm a professional, just doing my job.'

'You do it very well.'

She forced a smile. On cue the sun broke from behind the evening clouds, bathing us in pale golden light. For some reason her eyes wouldn't meet mine.

'Those bad guys want to stop you meeting my clients – stop you with extreme prejudice. I'm not going to let that happen. Come on Nogood Boyo, we really have to go.'

Meekly I followed her towards the shadowy hedge line. What other choice did I have? Some unseen hand had lashed me to this mad roller coaster – might as well try to enjoy the ride.

6

The Revolution Will Be Televised

Ten minutes later I stood in the saloon bar of the Rugby Club, admiring the glass-encased shirts hanging on the walls, trying not to let my feet stick to the swirling orange-brown carpet. The floor was tacky in more ways than one, an ancient sponge soaked in a cocktail of fluids beyond human understanding. Beneath my feet whole unique ecosystems of strange bacteria lived and died in their millions, struggling through countless generations, evolving towards sentience but unaware of the parallel universe playing out within easy reach. Maybe we weren't so different after all. It was a comfort to know some things hadn't changed from home.

Gwen was busy conferring with the barman, who she insisted on calling 'The Gatekeeper', arranging the next leg of our journey. Seems he'd been expecting us. I was hoping for at least a bag of nuts out of the negotiations, maybe a pickled egg. I was destined to be disappointed.

A mix of Japanese tourists and glowering locals crowded the bar, the visitors snapping photos of the memorabilia and doing their best to contend with the devastating leek daiquiris. Several were already prostrate, frothing at the mouth, writhing comatose on the floor – *Bridge on the River Kwai* in reverse.

Above the bar a large TV carried the evening news. Welshperanto was disorientating at first, but easy to follow once you got used to it. Lead item was the terrorist attack on the mardi gras in Aberdare. It was a minor relief to see the grainy CCTV footage didn't show our faces. I could recognise the blurry forms of Gwen and myself but that was only because I'd been there. Huw Edwards said the images were being rushed over to the CSI lads in Treorchy for analysis, but I reckoned we were pretty safe. As we all know, you can't just zoom in on digital images and get more data. Phew, close one. What stripped my gears was how swiftly the news moved on – maybe such wanton destruction wasn't that big a deal. Well, it was a big deal to me.

It seemed the election campaign was in full swing. Apparently President Barry Island was behind in the polls to Llywsiffer Pendragon and his ultra-nationalist Gorsedd Party, but *El Presidente* was expected to claw back support after tomorrow's major speech. In other news the war in Patagonia was not going well, each day increasingly becoming the Welsh Vietnam. Meanwhile representatives of the local Vietnamese community were picketing major news outlets, tamping at the continued overuse of the phrase. The United Nations Security Council was only prevented from passing a resolution condemning the war by use of the Welsh veto. I don't know which detail shocked me most.

Meanwhile the Jones Corporation was increasing the cash bounty paid on returned J-Drives. For some reason they were stepping up their recycling programme, which judging by the intense sneer seemed to strike old Huw as a tad odd. None of it made sense to me. Exasperated I turned back to study of the decor. Amongst the faded shirts from assorted internationals and nicotine-stained photographs was a blue plaque that seemed strangely out of place. It was the sort which commemorates the birthplace or home of notable celebrities. I studied it with increasing dismay.

Here in September 1986 did Isaiah Amlawdd Jones and the Steering Committee of the WRU first foment the seeds of FREEDOM. Through an impassioned call to the forces of BLOOD AND IRONY, lying dormant in the Brythonic bosom, was the elixir of REVOLUTION stirred. Be sure to purchase your commemorative beer cauldron at the bar. Cash or Bitcoin only. No cheques.

I stood there staring at it for a moment, my current worries forgotten. This was too much to take. What had Grandad always told me when presented with a perplexing conundrum? *Least hypothesis* – always the simplest answer which fits the facts. I tried to apply Occam's razor to my current situation, but it left me bereft of answers and smoother than a Llandudno stripper's va-jay-jay. What on earth did it all mean?

'I wouldn't take it too literally if I were you,' said a voice close beside me. I almost jumped out of my skin, but it was only Gwen, peering up at the plaque.

I slowed my breathing. 'Shouldn't they be making more of a fuss – what with the anniversary and all? I mean, they're holding a mardi gras in Aberdare, for Christ's sake. Here it's just kamikaze Russian roulette with leek daiquiris.'

The girl shrugged. 'Every pub from here to Abertillery claims the same thing. It's good for business. Just means the Founding Uncles had a drink here once or twice. Those guys got around. There's a tea shop in Machynlleth reckons they've got the Constitution scrawled on a beer mat. Who knows, maybe they're right.'

If a suitable response existed it didn't spring to mind. My floundering brain was rescued as Gwen grasped me by the elbow. 'I've got what we need – time to go.' She brandished what looked like a light bulb.

There was the unmistakable sound of my feet ungluing themselves from the carpet. 'Not back to Aberdare, surely?'

Gwen looked at me aghast. 'Don't be mental. We're taking a trip across the Atlantic.'

'America? But why didn't we go straight there?'

She sounded weary. 'That's not how gates work. They're strictly fixed focus, only linking a single time and place. Multi-use, but you can't change the destination.'

I muttered what was fast becoming my catchphrase. 'I don't understand.'

She sighed and led me down a dingy passage. A group of Japanese took pictures as we squeezed past. 'Think of the Multiverse as a massive tower, where each floor is its own reality.'

'A Dark Tower amidst a field of roses?'

'If you like – but the lifts only work between adjacent floors.'

'Don't mention lifts.' I shuddered, remembering my last trip in one of the hideous contraptions. She ignored me and went on.

'There's no central shaft connecting all the levels – at least not that anyone's yet found. Some gates keep you on the same floor, but just teleport you around. That's the type we're heading for right now.'

I stopped and instantly stuck to the floor. 'God, I'm not going through that again.'

Gwen jerked me forward with that familiar wet crunch. 'Don't worry, kiddo – won't be so bad this time. You'll only need a half a mint.'

We turned a corner and arrived at what looked like a large

storage cupboard set back into the wall. At the risk of stating the obvious I pointed out, 'This is not a lift.'

Gwen checked the corridor to make sure we were alone. The tourists had moved off in search of alcoholic oblivion. 'Not all gates are lifts, any enclosed space will do. You were too dazed to notice but we came out in a hotel room when we jumped in Aberdare. But lifts work well as a metaphor, as well as on a practical level.' She took out a key and slid it into the lock. There was a loud click.

When I'm nervous I tend to chatter too much. 'Are we going to Narnia this time? I have no desire to meet the Snow Queen, or any of her furry-legged friends. Mr Tumnus does not float my boat. Despite what my cruel schoolmates claimed, I'm no pansexual.'

Gwen rolled her eyes in exasperation. 'Just cut the yap and get inside.' She shoved me into the uninviting-looking metaphor and quickly followed, locking the door. The room was dark and full of boxes, mostly crisps and pork scratchings. A single bare light fitting swung from the ceiling. In fact the place looked remarkably like a storage cupboard.

'Scotty from *Star Trek* would not be impressed – and neither am I.'

I could hear Gwen gritting her teeth. 'Get one of those chairs and put it beneath the light.'

The cupboard was bigger than it first looked. Ziggurats of cheap plastic chairs were stacked around the walls. It was quite a squeeze, but I did as she had bidden. Gwen positioned the chair beneath the empty fitting. She climbed up and screwed in what looked like a 50 watt bulb. It dangled there naked and forlorn.

'Get up here with me and hold on.'

I clambered up onto the chair. Her hair smelt of woodland flowers and unexploded cordite.

'Put an arm around my waist and grab the cord.'

I liked where this was heading, even if I couldn't say the same for her. Our faces were very close. I raised an eyebrow and tried to sound suave.

'These people you're taking me to meet – they have my best interests at heart?'

Gwen turned her face away, suddenly interested in our surroundings. Maybe my breath still held a trace of leek daiquiri. She was too long in answering. 'They strike me as very... professional.'

'But I'll be safe with them, right?'

She looked up into my eyes. 'It will be *safer*, yes.'

This didn't exactly put my mind at ease. There existed an uncomfortably large gulf between *safe* and *safer than imminently dead*, which was where I found myself at the moment. It was a chasm I didn't want to fall into.

Gwen got out her handheld and thumbed across the screens. 'I've got an app which can control the gate.'

'Why doesn't that surprise me.'

'You ready?'

'Don't I even get half a mint?'

'You'll get a knee somewhere delicate if you don't move your hand.'

With regret I complied. 'I guess I'm as ready as I'll ever be. Do your worst, boss.'

Gwen touched the screen. There was a blinding arc-flash of electrical light, seeming to X-ray the room. Then everything went black. I tasted ozone and wished I'd had that mint.

7

Alternative History 101

So now we have a quiet moment perhaps I can tell you what else I read on Gwen's smartphone, as we sped south towards south-central Port Talbot in that tacsi on the verge of a nervous breakdown. The device was a wonder to behold: it patched into the local internet with a speed and efficiency I never could have imagined. It could sense your thoughts through your fingers, filling out search bars with text before you knew what you were thinking – a seamless fount of information. Plus it came in a nice colour.

The local interweb was full of details on Grandad. A whole industry of books, magazines and research papers offered themselves up to tell the story of his momentous life. It seemed over here he had got quite a lot done. I found a sober documentary covering the pertinent facts – *Birth of a Nation: The Corporate State of Jones*. It had grossed millions and won two Oscars. Best Film and Best Visual Effects, even though no CGI had been needed.

It explained this was not the only Golden Age this region

had enjoyed. The first had been briefer and less intense, but back in Victorian times South Wales had been booming. The first Industrial Revolution rode on wheels of coal. Maybe the wheels were made of steel, but they were powered by coal, the original black gold. Places where it was available in abundance became cradles of new technology, white-hot blast furnaces of progress.

But not all coal was created equal. Some seams were more equal than others. The best coal, the hard stuff, which burnt brighter and hotter and drove the wheels of industry faster, could be found in only a few hallowed places – spots on Earth touched by the smouldering finger of the God of Hellfire. Which is to say, millions of years beforehand a bunch of ancient trees rotted in just the right way. One such fortunate location was South Wales. This magical stuff was called anthracite, the crack cocaine of coal.

While it lasted it was glorious. Great men made their fortunes in the crucible of the new industries, iron and coal at their heart. Tens of thousands of workers flooded in; boom towns boomed; there were jobs and money aplenty. It might have been dark and satanic, underneath the hills, but it was better than starving to death on a farm – which had been the main form of employment up until then. The coal poured out, to drive the pistons of the world's great railway expansion, and to power the boilers of the dreadnoughts of the Royal Navy, the global policemen of the day.

But like all Golden Ages it couldn't last. The easy coal near the surface ran out. The coal masters took their profits and moved to Hampstead. Other fuels proved easier and cleaner to work with. Oil was the new kid in town; it slid in and nicked the best parking spots. The miners all got nasty coughs. Smoke got in their eyes, and their weeping washed tracks of sorrow down their blackened, chiselled faces. It was a moment lost in time, like tears in the rain. I think Rutger Hauer did the voiceover.

The film went on to document the sad fate of the region. South Wales did not do well in the later twentieth century. The legacy industries struggling to compete, the chronic lack of investment. The strikes, the closures, the call centres. It was a tale familiar to me – I had lived through the arse end of it. But then came the point of departure, and it came with a recognisable face.

Grandad was portrayed in this slick piece of corporate PR as your standard wild-haired boffin, straight out of central casting. It didn't tally with the man I knew and loved, but it was close enough – no denying it was him. What was so different over here to result in such divergent outcomes? A question for another day, perhaps. The documentary went on to discuss Isaiah's invention itself.

Unless you had a PhD in integrated field dynamics you wouldn't even grasp the terminology, and even then it sounded like some serious pseudoscience woo. Put simply, and for most people it could be put no other way, the J-Drive was an infinite energy source in a box. Anthracite v2.0 required no input, no fuel, just turn it on and get the electrical power of a small star, without the heat and pesky radiation. A happy side effect, with a few configuration tweaks, was an anti-gravity field. No one knew for sure, but it seemed to mess with the fabric of reality, bending it creaking to a new will. There were rumours of even more esoteric secondary effects (the gates?), but such was the rush to make use of so useful an invention few stopped to question the theory. Humanity found world-changing uses for the J-Drive aplenty.

Significantly, Isaiah Jones never patented his device. When you file a patent you have to describe what makes your process unique – give away its secret so it can be protected by law, to the poor extent it can. Isaiah trusted in the obscurity of his methods more than he trusted in lawyers. Time would more than prove him right.

Vested interests formed a disorderly queue to buy him out. Oil companies and car giants offered billions for his research. Tesla and Microsoft offered him a seat on the board, even the table itself. Saudi Arabia put a fatwah on his head, claiming he peddled in witchcraft. But Isaiah rose above it all. He stuck to his guns, and to his all-conquering invention – the little black box that could.

The Powers That Be weren't about to take this shafting lying down. MIT tasked a top-level research team to reverse-engineer one of the first production examples – to get under its hood and learn what made it tick. They set to work unscrewing the chunky bolts. Their results were a less than resounding success.

When the first emergency responders felt safe enough to approach the crater they found no sign of the research team, nor most of the Harvard campus. Of the J-Drive itself there was just the mangled empty case, smouldering and humming quietly with an ethereal turquoise glow. These things were tough, if not indestructible.

After that people just accepted what they'd been given – the greatest gift horse ever presented to mankind, so why punch it in the mouth? J-Drives were cheap, they were plentiful, and they solved so many problems. Pollution and fuel poverty became things of the past. Travel became cheaper and faster than ever before. OPEC was told to take a long walk off a short pier into the Persian Gulf. Splash.

Of course the Jones family became immensely rich. Isaiah brought in his extended clan to help him run the show and built a massive mansion in the hills. He was no fan of the Welsh curse of nepotism, but events unfolded at such pace he had little choice. The family proved to have a head for business, providing the ruthless streak Isaiah lacked. The Corporation controlled all production and never sold shares, the most private of private companies. Security around the final stage of manufacture was eye-wateringly tight, limited to Isaiah's laboratory deep under the Port Talbot factory. Not a single J-Drive left the dustless halls without first receiving his personal seal of approval, some said a squirt of his *special sauce*.

Research continued at YIT – the Ystradgynlais Institute of Technology, the foremost engineering university on the planet, set up with funds bequeathed by Isaiah. But it was all *applied* research – practical uses rather than theory. Despite his modesty Isaiah paid for a nice statue outside the front steps. He had liberated humanity almost overnight; few begrudged him his billions. Isaiah continued to focus on production, while the natural-born hustlers in his family grew the empire. Weyland-Yutani was gobbled up in a leveraged buyout, The Tyrell Corporation consumed so fast its synthetic feet didn't touch the floor. Soon J-Corp owned half the world.

The Revolution came next. With all the money flooding into Wales and all the new-found power flooding out (in every sense), there was no way the political status quo could hold sway. Scotland was already long gone and London a virtual city state. The UK splintered into chaos and its economy imploded, creating a leadership vacuum men of action were destined to fill. J-Corp joined forces with the Welsh Rugby Union to declare the First Republic. Resistance from what was left of the British state was futile. On the fifth day the elite Barry John Armoured Division reached Westminster and the War of Independence was over. Roadblocks and AT mines had little use against hover tanks. The underdog had turned out to be an underdragon. Nothing would be the same again.

When Isaiah passed away, well into his nineties, he was

lauded as a secular saint – a genius inventor, liberator of mankind, and hero of the Revolution to boot. As per his last wish, his remains were loaded on board *The Prince Madog*, the first J-Drive colony ship, and blasted off towards Alpha Centauri. The colonists planned to build him a shrine. With him lacking direct heirs of his own, control of the Jones Corporation passed to his nephew, Genghis 'Can' Jones, who as usual no doubt would. By the sound of it the local version was much like the one I knew on steroids. The mere mention of his name sent a shiver down my spine. The sight of his gap-toothed grin brought me out in a cold sweat. Thoughts of vaginal steamers had me squirming in my seat. At least in the pictures he was wearing a better suit.

The documentary caught up to the 'present', which seemed to be a dozen years ahead of where we were (where we when?) back home. Colour me confused. But however you want to slice it, say 'hiya' to the new undisputed global hegemon – The Welsh Republic – powerful and prosperous like no nation which had gone before. An empire on which, if the sun ever set, none would notice thanks to the phosphorescent glow. Nominally an egalitarian democracy, in practice a juggernaut corporate state. Every president since independence also sat on the Jones Corporation Board. Some said Wales was no better than a benign dictatorship – which worked, as long as you could keep finding benign dictators.

The film closed with an eye to the future, hinting at tantalising new uses peeking over the event horizon for the ubiquitous J-Drive. Functions so outlandish they made what had gone before seem mundane. I guessed the gate technology would not stay secret for long. The future was bright, the future was Anthracite.

8

Thanks Drive

We awoke on the floor of a deserted warehouse. Of the small storeroom back in P.T. there was no sign – not so much as a bag of pork scratchings. The bare concrete was cool and hard against my cheek. A shard of sunlight from a greasy skylight pierced the mote-laden air. All was quiet and still. I had that vile metallic taste in my mouth again. Once they get that fixed teleportation will be a breeze. As usual Gwen was first to her feet, gun drawn, scanning for danger.

'Let's go, cowboy. Best not hang about.' She made for a half-open set of roller doors thick with graffiti.

I hastened to catch up. 'No Gatekeeper this end?'

She shook her head. 'There's no infrastructure to maintain. This spot is just a focal point, a nexus of standing waves.'

'A teleportation landing pad?'

'If you like.'

'A node for ley lines?'

She flattened herself against the prefab wall next to the doors. 'You been talking to any druids lately?'

'Not if I can help it, those guys freak me out.'

'You're not alone.' Gwen checked the parking lot outside. I could see a loading ramp and behind that stacks of disused shipping containers, piled high like shabby Lego. Faded grass grew from cracks in the crumbling concrete.

'No one about. Let's split.'

She made for a hole in the fence behind the nearest crates. The whole place had a derelict and run-down air. It felt like we were ten years into a zombie apocalypse, just without the shuffling extras. The thick undergrowth made me wary as Gwen led us along the line of the tatty fence. We emerged onto an equally shabby street, the only movement a scrawny dog hurrying across the shimmering tarmac halfway down the block. Gwen took a deep breath, holstered her gun and began moving briskly down the sidewalk.

'Mind telling me where we're going?'

'To find a bus stop. Walking's not the best idea in this neighbourhood.'

I struggled to keep up. 'And after we're on the bus, what then?'

'We have an appointment downtown, with my contact.'

'He's the guy who wants to meet me?'

'No – enough of the questions. Just walk.'

I knew better than to push my luck. From the faded bullet-riddled signs we passed I learned we were in Allendale, a suburb on the western edge of Jacksonville. It was five miles into the city. The air was scorching hot and I needed a drink – I'd have even settled for a leek daiquiri. When I stopped to peer at one of the squat, gloomy houses set back from the street, thinking I'd seen movement behind the shuttered windows, Gwen snapped at me to keep up. This neighbourhood gave me the creeps. I didn't sense the locals were friendly.

Five minutes later we were on the bus. I say 'bus' as that's the best analogue for the cobbled-together contraption we were riding. It had no wheels but wobbled two foot off the ground, as if unsure of the laws of physics. That was about as far as it went in terms of similarity with the high-tech tacsis we'd used back in Wales. The bus moved like a drunk whale, slewing across the litter-strewn highway whilst emitting a tired groan. It was piloted by a surly human driver. Gwen handed him a single banknote and he motioned us into the hold with a grunt. It seemed everyone accepted Welsh currency.

The bus was only half full. The other passengers shifted out of our way, avoiding eye contact. The smell was less than ideal, and the bars on the windows were not putting me at my ease. Some empty seats seemed to have sustained bullet holes and blast damage.

'Is this the best they've got over here?'

Gwen's head held still but her eyes scanned our travelling companions. 'What do you expect? We're not in *Pax Cambria* anymore.'

'But they've got J-Drives?'

'Everyone's got J-Drives. Cheap as chips and twice as useful. Watch out for that roach.'

We soon left the shabby neighbourhood behind, but the view from the grease-smudged windows didn't improve; if anything it got worse. Shortly we floated through what looked like a South American favela, but not the friendly, jovial kind full of plucky community spirit and limbo dancers. This place was a teeming shanty town of tin shacks and ramshackle hovels, cobbled together from anything the inhabitants could find to hand. What mostly seemed available was rusty corrugated sheeting, sun-bleached driftwood and burning barrels. Suddenly there were people everywhere, dressed in jumble sale profusion. Grubby children sat crying at the roadside, the main sewer running at their bare feet. There were a lot of dogs that looked scrawnier than the people. We wobbled past a plethora of street food stalls which seemed intent on curing the dog problem.

Several times we stopped to let on more passengers. Quite a few seemed to lack the required fare, pleading with the driver until he waved a brutal shotgun at them, chasing them away. Soon it was standing room only. A forest of armpit hair sprouted next to my face. At one point a kid in a faded Ospreys rugby shirt and mismatched flip-flops clambered up the bars outside our window shouting something about cheap watches. The driver seemed to intentionally swerve into the bush to brush him off. The youngster's cries faded into the distance as he cartwheeled through the humid air. At the next stop passengers scrambled onto the roof. I thought the bus's straining motors might give out at any moment. This was my first trip to North America, and I was feeling a tad let down – not what I'd been expecting at all.

'Who are all these people?'

Gwen looked sad. 'Refugees from the Confederacy, mostly. We're close to the border. This is where the lucky ones wash up.'

'And the unlucky ones?'

She shrugged. 'There are a lot of alligators between here and Georgia. They rarely want for a meal.'

'Unlike these poor sods.' This wasn't the Florida I'd seen on *Miami Vice*. The locals weren't wearing socks, but I didn't think it was a fashion statement. It looked more like desperate poverty to me.

'And they'd prefer to live like this than stay at home?'

Gwen shook her head. 'I guess what they're escaping from is worse. Apartheid 2.0 is not for everyone. Those charming funsters north of the border are busy building their utopian ethno-state – these folk didn't pass the melanin test.'

I gulped down the ball in my throat. Suddenly my empty stomach didn't feel half so bad. I'd lost my appetite.

Downtown Jacksonville was a major improvement. I mean, it wasn't Aberdare, but at least the streets looked clean and they weren't barbecuing family pets to ward off starvation. These things are relative. There were people dressed in suits and normal-looking cars. Flying craft too, but far less than back in Wales. The buildings looked like they might withstand a strong breeze. We stopped at a busy intersection. The lights changed to green and we were about to pull off when a wail of sirens blared from our right. A column of police cars and SWAT trucks hurtled past, a neon light show hurtling at full speed.

'Riot, most likely,' said Gwen in explanation.

As we arrived in what looked like the financial district, passengers started getting off. Gwen told me they were employed as cleaners and servants – low wage service workers holding up the tottering pillars of civilisation. All possible thanks to the massive workforce on hand night and day. Every cloud had a silver lining, and this one was buffed to a high shine by cheap immigrant labour. The favela dwellers cost less than robots and were less prone to psychosis. The final stop was outside an impressive tower block of glass and steel. We were the last people on the bus; I was glad to get off. Gwen turned to our host as we climbed down.

'Thanks Drive.'

I guess old habits die hard. He just looked at us in wonder, spat out a wad of tobacco juice and cycled shut the doors.

We strolled across a wide tree-studded plaza, sirens blaring in the distance. Business people hurried past, paying us no heed. As usual I was full of questions.

'So what happened to the USA?'

Gwen's eyes never stopped checking the square. 'Balkanised

to within an inch of its life. But with none of the quaint folksy charm of the original – just the ethnic cleansing and internment camps.'

'The US split up?'

'Split up and fell apart. It was one messy divorce. California got the music collection and Texas got the kids – shame they're all psychos. Just as well the nukes were sold off to pay the legal fees. Those are the last things you want clanking round when you've got two hundred mutually antagonistic micro-states arguing about where the money's gone. There's a lovely religious dictatorship in the Midwest. New England's nice, if you're a billionaire. Don't ask about Nevada.'

I wasn't about to enquire. Besides, we were already at the tower's massive main doors. Above the entrance a camera on a spherical gimbal slewed to scan us up and down. It seemed to contemplate us for a moment, before the smoked glass doors glided open with an impressive swish. This was more like it – the cool air was a welcome relief after the heat of the streets. We entered a spacious atrium decorated with tropical plants. A fountain bubbled somewhere nearby. Two of the biggest men I'd ever seen stood before us, kitted out in dark suits and darker glasses – like a couple of testosterone-filled black holes. They had the same air of deadly wariness that seeped from Gwen's every pore. I thought it best to let my companion take the lead.

We halted before the pair of gorillas, who inspected us as if we might be trouble. Gwen carefully raised her arms to head level and showed them her open palms, and then *very* slowly reached into her jacket and removed her gun. She held it between finger and thumb, as unthreatening as could be. One guard held out a clear plastic bag, into which Gwen dropped the weapon. I realised I'd stopped breathing. We were all professionals and it wouldn't do to have any misunderstandings. Gwen went through the same rigmarole with her smartphone. Then they scanned her head to foot with a beeping baton, which sounded the all-clear. I was ready to get searched the same way, but they didn't even bother. I guess I have an honest face – either that or they knew who wore the trousers. Scowling, but a fraction more relaxed, they led us over to the lifts.

Next to the buttons was a series of burnished copper plaques. Apparently 'Sentinel Private Security LLC' took up the first five floors. 'No conflict too big or small. Combat air support available. Tyrants toppled, democracies stabilised (or combinations thereof).' Above that was the consulate of the Welsh Republic, this one with special responsibility for 'Cultural Affairs'. I guess *Gavin and Stacey* reruns weren't going to syndicate themselves.

Gwen saw me reading this last plate. 'Just a local branch office; the main embassy is down in Tallahassee.'

I didn't know what to say, so read the final plate instead. 'Holden, Holden and Finch – Attorneys at Law'. There were no offers of air support, combat or otherwise. I was past feeling any relief. The lift arrived with a ping. We got in and Gwen pressed the button for the top floor. The gorillas watched us depart and got back to their guard duty, as impassive as ever.

I've never been that keen on lifts, even when they don't lead to alternate dimensions full of psychopaths trying to kill me. Maybe that's why I was sweating profusely. 'So you're handing me over to these lawyers? They'll keep me safe?'

Gwen looked at me for a long time. I could hear the gears turning behind those brown eyes. 'These lawyers represent my clients. This is just to ensure you're the right guy.' She seemed to think for a moment. 'I won't be handing you over today.'

I sighed with relief. The thought of saying farewell to Gwen left me strangely empty inside. 'That's good news. Anything else I need to know about these jokers?'

She tilted her head from side to side, stretching tired neck muscles. 'Only that to them I'm known as Wanda Sevastopol – don't even ask.'

I was beginning to suspect there was more to my multi-talented kidnapper than met the eye. And what did meet the eye could have kept you busy for weeks. Interrupted by that familiar surge of weightlessness the doors pinged open. We exited into a plush lobby where a nervous underling ushered us to a well-appointed conference room. The handful of functionaries we passed fell back and stared in awe. The atmosphere in the place seemed thick with tension.

Inside the conference room stood a couple of corporate types – suits so sharp you could have used them to shave. An open medical case lay atop the long table in front of them. The man on the left was staring at me with an intensity bordering on fanaticism. He had an oily face and wet, bulging eyes. He motioned for his companion to close the full-length blinds masking us from the outer lobby. Whatever was going down they had no desire for an audience.

'Ah, Mr Jones, you have no idea what a privilege – no, an honour, it is to meet you at last. You can't possibly know what you mean to our organisation.' With an excess of enthusiasm he pumped my hand up and down, until, fearing he might damage the goods, he stopped in a panic. Goggle eyed, he checked my arm was still in one piece.

'Er... thanks. I think. And who are you?'

'My name is Finch, I'm the senior partner here. But at the moment I'm the happiest man on earth.'

'Really – why's that?'

'We've hit the jackpot with you, Mr Jones. We just need to confirm your identity. A formality I'm sure.' He turned to his companion. 'Doctor, please administer the test.'

The other half of the reception committee retrieved a small

plastic cup from the case and came round the table to join us. He seemed less enthusiastic than his boss, not that it was hard.

'We need a sample of your genetic material.'

I unbuckled my belt and eyed the container sceptically. 'You're going to need something bigger than that, chief. And a bit of privacy wouldn't go amiss. There's a lady present.'

'We only need you to spit in it.'

'Of course, I knew that. How stupid do you think I am?'

The doctor looked to be preparing an answer, before Finch bundled him into a seat with a menacing glare. My host was all smiles when he turned back to me, nodding for me to continue. I hacked up a good one and slid the cup over to the doctor, who pulled a beeping probe from the case. The sensor was linked by a long curly wire to the apparatus; he plunged it into my offering and swirled it round. The machine whirred for a moment, as whatever strange magic it contained weaved its spell. After a few seconds it beeped, and several coloured lights flashed. The doctor looked up at Finch, adjusted his glasses, and nodded. The lawyer had been bobbing from foot to foot, but now hooted and raised both fists in triumph.

'Hit the jackpot! We're going to be rich! Well, richer than we are already.' Finch performed a strange little dance of joy.

The mood of jubilation was interrupted by Gwen clearing her throat behind us. She lay sprawled over the conference chair nearest the door, outwardly relaxed but as menacing as a lounging tiger.

'Maybe we are – but I've still got to get him to your boss first. And need I remind you, gentlemen, the first instalment of my fee is now due.'

Finch waved his hand as if this was a mere trifle. 'Of course, of course. This is a momentous day. When the analysts get to work we can start taking back control from those jumped-up sheep-worriers across the pond.' He turned to Gwen. 'No offence, Ms Sevastopol.'

'None taken, I'm sure. We're just the Irish who couldn't swim.'

Finch's smile didn't get anywhere near his eyes. 'A true professional – you're the best there is. Our employers have authorised me to make the first payment.'

'And the rest of the fee?'

'– will be paid when we hand him over. I need to speak to you about that.'

A dark cloud seemed to gather over Gwen. 'We agreed I'd handle that end of the deal. Right up to handover.'

Finch licked his blubbery lips. 'The situation has changed. Our masters are keen to begin work on the subject right away – very keen indeed. You can't imagine what's at stake.'

Gwen's eyes held a hint of steel. 'You'd be surprised how good my imagination can be. I'll keep hold of *the subject* until the rendezvous, thank you. Like we agreed back in Langley.'

The pair glared at each other for an uncomfortable moment. It fell to me to lighten the mood before bones got broken.

'Can we get anything to eat around here? I'm sure you don't want *the subject* starving to death.'

9

France is Bacon

I pushed the last piece of bacon around my plate. We sat at the counter of a downtown diner just two blocks from the offices of HH&F. I was reminded of something Grandad was always saying to me – 'Knowledge is Power, France is Bacon'.

I could well believe the first part; I could see how information was key. But bacon? Surely if France was any comestible it would be some sort of liquefied cheese, either that or a baguette. There was so much I could learn from Isaiah – a lifetime's experience I needed to rediscover. Would I ever get the chance again?

Gwen also seemed to have a lot on her mind. She was quiet and lost in her thoughts for most of our meal. The only time she showed any emotion was when a news report flashed up on the TV behind the counter. A blue-helmeted, flak-jacketed reporter was embedded with the Welsh forces that had just retaken Puerto Madryn. He explained its significance as a major logistics hub helping supply the Expeditionary Force and the rebels they fought alongside. Argentine government sources were making no mention of what CNN and S4C were claiming as a significant Welsh victory. Gwen seemed troubled by the news. She looked away as a silent tear rolled down one perfect cheek. I badly wanted to cheer her up.

'So where are you taking me next? Not that I'm not enjoying this random world tour. I'm looking forward to wearing the t-shirt with the list of gigs down the back.'

My companion sniffed and composed herself. 'The handover is arranged for the client's head office in Virginia. Don't worry, it's not part of the Confederacy, it falls inside the Sovereign District of Columbia – all that's left of the Federal USA.'

'Gee, will I get to meet the President?'

Distracted as she was, Gwen didn't seem to think it an unreasonable request. 'I'm sure they'll wheel him out if you ask them. It's not like he's got much else to keep him busy these days.' She didn't appear to be joking. The joint's proprietor took away our empty plates. Now it was my turn to look sad.

'So how long do we have left together? I'm going to miss you.'

Gwen signalled for the tab. 'The Consortium needs to wait for several stakeholders to arrive. There'll be delegations flying in from Moscow and Beijing – not the types of hombres you'd want to keep waiting. It's a fragile coalition. We can get a commercial flight up to Dulles. It will take a few days.'

I supposed it was better than nothing, but I still had nagging doubts about my future. 'And when I'm with these guys I'll be safe? No more ambushes and random hit squads?'

Gwen seemed mesmerised by the dregs of her coffee, a moment too long in answering. 'There'll be no more random hit squads.'

I let out a sigh of relief. 'Thank Christ for that. I'll be glad when all this fuss is over and I can get back to normal.' Subtly

I reached out for her hand across the counter. She pulled hers back, but then leaned in closer.

'Kev, don't look around, but there's a guy sitting near the door who's been following us.'

It took all my considerable self-control not to check him out. I tried hard to sound nonchalant. 'Yeah, I was wondering if you'd noticed him too.'

Gwen toyed with a sprinkling of salt atop the counter. 'He's been with us since we left Finch's office. He's just a tail keeping tabs on us – no threat, other than to my professional pride.'

I tutted. 'That Finch was a bit of a slime-bag. I didn't think he was going to let us leave.'

Gwen smiled and her tone remained neutral. 'I wasn't about to give him any choice. No one backs me into a corner and lives to tell the tale. So you know about the others?'

'What others?'

Gwen looked taken aback. 'That little old lady along the counter with the dog. *Puddles* is likely a cyborg relaying real-time video back to Finch's office. And the kid who just came in for coffee to go – he was speaking into a radio mic hidden up his sleeve – bloody amateur.'

'Oh, yeah, I spotted them too.'

'The point is Kev, I'm good –'

'You don't need to convince me of that.'

'– but there's no way I can keep you safe indefinitely. We can't run forever. There are powerful forces... interested in you. You have a unique set of experiences. These guys can make or break nations – even worlds. The stakes are very high.'

Why did I get the feeling she was trying to justify herself? 'What experiences?'

She looked away, if not a thousand-yard stare then at least halfway there. 'You should expect a thorough debriefing when my employers get hold of you. Very thorough. Too many factions want a piece of you.'

I could only nod by this stage. If I was honest I didn't have a clue what was going on. Gwen was looking very sad.

'And I don't just mean the Consortium, or the other lot who want you dead. There are other players in this game. It's like multi-faction tag team three-dimensional chess, played by touch in a dark room, and someone's just ripped out the light switch.'

I realised I'd stopped breathing again. 'Who is it who wants me dead?'

Gwen sighed. 'My best guess is the Gorsedd – everyone's favourite sheet-wearing, sickle-waving ultra-nationalists. Then of course there's the Jones Corporation –'

'What, my own relatives! Uncle Genghis would never –' but of course, before the words passed my lips, I knew that he would – most likely with bells on, and a raucous celebration.

'So you do see,' Gwen continued, her moist eyes big and brown, 'the best thing for you is to be handed over to the Consortium. You do see that, don't you?'

What a mess this whole thing was turning into. After all she'd done for me, the least I could do was put her mind at rest. I forced a smile. 'Sure, I understand. It's for the best. I'll be safe with the Consortium. Protective custody and all that.'

Gwen didn't seem convinced. If I'm honest, neither was I. Our sombre mood was broken by the tinkling of the diner's entry bell. The place went deathly still. A familiar voice cut across the silence.

'Ah, Miss Sevastopol. Stand aside please, we can take things from here.'

It was Finch, and he was not alone. The two gorillas from the lobby stood behind him, filling the doorway like a pair of black-clad monoliths – *2001* but with more existential menace.

Next to them the tail we'd spotted earlier had risen too, one hand resting inside his jacket.

Gwen turned on her stool, moving with the careful precision of a cat under pressure. 'We've been through this, Finch. He stays with me until handover.'

The old lady with the dog had taken up a flanking position. A small whirring satellite dish unfolded out of the top of the animal's head. One of its eyes was flashing red.

The lawyer broke into an oily grin. 'I've been in touch with our employers. They've instructed me to take charge. You will be fully paid.'

'This isn't about the money.'

Finch's grin slithered into a sneer. 'It's always about the money, for the likes of you. Don't worry – he'll be safe with us.'

I sensed Gwen go tense by my side. Her muscles seemed to quiver; it was like standing next to a human tuning fork. She let out a long, measured breath, then whispered so only I could hear.

'Kev, do you trust me?'

'Yes.' My voice seemed to have gone up several octaves.

'Tidy. Then follow my lead.'

I didn't like where this was going. Meanwhile Finch seemed too relaxed, teetering on the verge of slapdash. 'There's no need for this to get unpleasant. We're all professionals here. If we're smart we can all leave this place smelling of roses rather than splattered in shit.'

An all-too-familiar click sent my stomach reeling, then I felt the cold barrel of Gwen's gun thrust against my ear.

'We don't want to mess this up – the merchandise I mean.' Dismayed, I realised she was talking about my head.

Finch's eyes went wide; it looked like he might faint. Suddenly everyone had a gun. The little old lady's was the biggest of the lot – it looked like it might be for shooting elephants, or maybe tanks. I felt naked, like I was in a dream, sat at my school desk missing several vital pieces of uniform. When I got up everyone would point and laugh, either that or open fire. It was a Mexican stand-off with no Mexicans. Maybe the little old lady's dog was a chihuahua.

Even at a distance I could see Finch was perspiring. He licked his rubbery lips. 'Let's all be cool here.'

Now it was Gwen who sounded relaxed. 'Yes, let's be cool.' She moved to place herself behind me, her human meat-shield. 'I'm not being funny, like – but we're leaving now, and you're going to let us go.'

She edged us backwards, as Finch made strangled gurgling noises. Gwen continued. 'Unless, that is, you want to explain to your bosses why all their precious data is smeared around this diner's walls. Have you ever tried scraping brains off a ceiling fan? I have and it's not easy.'

Finch's complexion, not the best to begin with, was currently cycling through some interesting shades. Gwen gripped my arm and edged us towards a gap in the counter. The proprietor had long since departed. We slid behind the bar. I felt I should help play my part in the show.

'SHE'S MAD ENOUGH TO DO IT! You don't know what she's like – the perverted things she's made me do!' Gwen accidentally kneed me in the hamstring, quite hard.

Finch and his goons inched cautiously into the establishment. 'Oh we know what she's capable of, all right. We've closely studied her file. But she must know she can't get away with this. Who's paying you off, girl? You double-cross us at your peril.'

Gwen backed us towards the doorway to the kitchens, careful to keep me between herself and our foes. Behind us I glimpsed a narrow passageway leading to a jungle of

Matt Thomas

galvanised pots and pans. In the cavernous barrel of her gun I could hear a sound like the distant ocean, calling me to deep, sweet oblivion. It disturbed me how good Gwen was at this charade. She spoke with calm assurance.

'I don't expect you to understand, Finch, but some things surpass narrow self-interest. I can't let this happen again.'

He opened his mouth as if to reply, but we never got that far. His eyes darted behind us, distracted for an instant. In one smooth motion Gwen dropped behind the counter and pivoted, pulling me down with her in its lee. The coffee delivery boy with the sleeve mic had blindsided us and snuck in through the kitchen. His shotgun was raised and at the ready but Gwen was much too quick. Her weapon roared and the poor sod danced a lead-fuelled fandango, his limbs thrashing against the passage walls.

Instinctively Finch's accomplices opened fire. The counter behind us exploded in a haze of wood and glass, fragments ricocheting this way and that. Thankfully enough metalwork had been built into it to deflect the fusillade. Gwen released me and crawled away, scampering crab-like down the length of the bar. 'Stay put!' was all the instruction I was given. I reached for her, but she was gone.

Even above the din Finch bellowed with rage. 'CEASE FIRE YOU IDIOTS! If we kill him we're all dead!'

Here was a sentiment I could relate to. I lay dazed for a second, shards of glass and splintered wood covering me in a glittering scree. Moments later a huge hand dragged me up from the floor, then none too gently over the counter. Soon I stood quivering amongst Finch's motley team of desperados – the five of them forming a wary cordon around me.

The lawyer's eyes bulged with fear, spittle flying from his lips. 'Where did the mad bitch go!'

I don't know what came over me – I'm not always so good

65

under pressure. Trembling, I pointed back towards the kitchen, where the unfortunate coffee enthusiast was busy being dead. All five cast their gaze down the passageway, its air still clouded with lingering smoke. The cyborg dog growled, its satellite dish whirled. If I'm honest I wet my pants.

As I'd suspected, this was all the distraction Gwen needed. Five shots rang out in quick succession, the reports echoing off the walls like thunderclaps. None of the targets had time to turn round, let alone return fire. Five bodies thudded to the ground around me, the sole bowling pin left standing. I might have screamed a bit, but I couldn't hear it for the ringing in my ears. I think the dog got away, but I'm not sure.

Gwen scanned the scene of destruction from her position at the end of the bar, calmly reloading her gun. Pleased with her handiwork she strode up to me and put a hand on my trembling shoulder, until I stopped shaking. Reaching into her pocket she produced a handful of banknotes, which she slapped down on what remained of the counter. I'm not sure if it included a tip. Next she took me by the hand. 'Come on, kiddo – time we blew this joint.'

10

Live Free or Dai

Three hours later we were hidden in the cargo hold of the huge container ship *Spirit of Fishguard*. It wasn't the fastest way back to Wales but Gwen assured me it was the safest. The Consortium would be watching all known gates and airports – we didn't want a run-in with Finch's employers. I got the distinct impression they made our friends back in Jacksonville look like boy scouts in comparison.

Gwen had used this method of travel before. After reaching one of her contacts at the docks we were ushered into a dingy back room and introduced to the laconic captain. A big wad of money changed hands. It was made clear we were stowaways, strictly off book, and told to stay out of the way of the crew. Half of them were robots anyway. A short time later we were spirited aboard the vast ship lying at anchor in the harbour. Just another consignment lost amidst the rows of steel shipping crates filled with industrial components and spent J-Drives heading home for recycling.

With the esoteric power sources driving the vessel the

crossing could be made in well under a week. Not ideal, but it gave us time to think and plan our next move. Gwen took the opportunity to catch up with her fitness regime. The rest of the time she was lost in thought – some thorny problem playing on her mind. On our third day out I had more practical concerns on mine.

'Do you want the last enchilada?'

She pushed her plate towards mine. The food wasn't great, but it was hot and there was plenty of it. Our meals were left near our hiding place, the only sign we saw of the ship's tiny crew.

'So I guess this means you're done with the Consortium. Who the hell were those guys, anyway?'

Gwen looked glum; it didn't suit her delicate features. 'Not the sort of people you'd want to cross in a hurry – powerful people. This won't be great for my career prospects. We can assume I'm off their Christmas list. The global deep state doesn't forget a slight in a hurry.'

I did my best to sound sympathetic. 'I feel bad for you. What did they want with me anyway?'

Gwen lay back and stared up at the cavernous ceiling far above. 'In your world, what happened? I don't mean the grand sweep of history – I mean, what happened to you and your family?'

That was an easy one. 'I won't lie to you: not very much if I'm honest. My relatives are small-time crooks, for the most part. I did five and a half terms at Telford Art School before heading home to look after my mum. We hardly set the world on fire. Maybe in time one of Uncle Genghis's schemes could have –'

Gwen waved me into silence. 'Exactly my point. While in this world your rellies run the greatest corporation known to man; transforming the lives of billions, saving mankind from an environment-wrecking fixation with fossil fuels, reaping untold profits in the process. What's the difference between these two worlds, apart from that trifling detail?'

I struggled to come up with an answer, instead settling for letting rip with a heroic enchilada burp.

'It's you, Kev.'

'Me?'

'Yes. Here, Kevin Gwydion Jones was never born, never to darken this dusty Earth with his shadow; never to graduate from Telford Art School. Isaiah never had any children. Neither you nor your mam ever existed.'

'It was five and a half terms, and I didn't *technically* graduate, but I still don't get your point.'

Gwen sighed. 'There's something about your existence which stops the Jones Corporation becoming the global juggernaut it is in this here and now; something which stops Wales's ascent to its position as global hegemon.'

'Hold on a sec. It's funny you mention Mum – I've not seen her for a few days. You don't think...?'

'In my line of work it's best not to speculate. Who runs your world, Kevin? Who calls the shots?'

I thought for a moment. 'Some say it's the corporations or global bankers, maybe the Illuminati. I guess the Americans and Chinese still hold some sway.'

'Don't you think those same people in this world want to know what went wrong? How a bunch of rain-soaked sheep worriers wound up running the planet. We're just learning how to move between worlds using gate technology. Every single reality downstream of your date of birth, apart from the one where your mam actually pops you out, ends with Wales as the dominant superpower. It's a deterministic multiverse trend which seems inevitable, like death and taxes, but in a shawl and funny hat.'

Anthracite

'Wait, what – there's more than two worlds?'

She looked at me as if I was a bit *twp*, a fair reflection of how I was feeling. 'Of course there is. Think about it – if there's more than one universe there's bound to be –'

'Five or six?'

'Don't be daft. There're untold millions. Billions. They're finding more every day. Some ahead of us in time, some behind. Why do you think they call it the Multiverse?'

I got that sinking feeling again. Talking to Gwen could do that to a guy.

She went on, 'So far the only world anyone's discovered where Wales does not end up dominating is the one you come from. The one where you exist. Don't you think the CIA, KGB, both Popes, Google, Standard Oil, Big Pharma, Grand Duke Henri of Luxembourg-and-all would want to understand why? Of course they would – of course they *do*. Kevin, you're the key.'

No matter how much blinking I did it didn't seem to make things any clearer. 'So that's what the Consortium is – a syndicate of shitheads?'

She nodded. 'Plus a few others. The Scientologists never like to be left out. Together they believe they can weaponise your existence. Maybe not fix this world, but help alter the others we're finding every day. These lovely chaps think on a bigger scale than you or I.'

Blubbering a bit, I tried to take it all in. 'But if it's already happened here, what good will having me do them?'

Gwen lined up our cutlery in four neat parallel lines, then pushed one knife an inch ahead of the rest, moved a fork back a smidge. 'All worlds are parallel, right – but they're not temporally in phase.'

'I think I might have gone temporarily insane. Please explain.'

'Time moves on a consistent vector, but out of sync in each reality. When we jump between worlds it doesn't stay the same date, not even the same year. We keep finding major differences.'

'I think I need a stiff drink. Just not one of those leek monstrosities.'

'Explorers have gone through gates that lead back to 1492, but it's not *our* 1492 – torpedoing Columbus doesn't do any good. Looks like time travel, but it's not. They're just altering a non-synchronous parallel universe. Simples.'

'And they know this how?' I had to admire Gwen's patience.

She spoke slowly. 'When they come back, everything's the same here. They've just altered the destiny of some other world.'

I thought back to every time travel book or film I'd consumed. 'That's good, because I'm guessing if you changed your own past it wouldn't be pretty.'

My companion's face darkened. 'What's known as a paradox. Not something you'd want to mess with.'

I was on more familiar ground here. 'Yeah, cos if you handed your grandfather a rubber johnny you'd wink out of existence, right? That's a bad day at the office.'

Gwen shook her head. 'I'm afraid it's worse than that. Current theory predicts any sort of entropy inversion, however minor, would fold space-time in on itself, triggering the heat death of the local universe. The stars would turn black in a shockwave of destruction rippling out through your galaxy and beyond. *Messy* doesn't begin to cover it.'

I think Gwen was a little concerned at my sudden change of complexion. She brightened. 'But don't worry, sport – paradoxes are not possible. All the boffins anyone pays attention to agree. Our past always stays the same because if you mess with one of those other streams you're just messing with an alternate universe. Time travel is not possible. Any other outcome wouldn't make sense. Capisce?'

From where I stood none of this made much sense. 'So let me get this straight – The Consortium wants me to give them a detailed breakdown of my life story? For clues and whatnot.'

Gwen grimaced again. 'Nothing so benign. I imagine *enhanced interrogation* and deep hypnosis play a big part in their plans. How do you feel about large needles full of Sodium Pentothal? You wouldn't come out the other side in one piece. Not that they'd care. You're just a source of data to them.' She rapped me on the skull with a knuckle, a little too hard.

It might have been in slow motion but the penny was finally dropping. 'And these are the good guys, the ones who want to *rescue* me?'

'They're the ones who don't want you dead – at least not right away. There's some ugly fish at the bottom-most depths of the deep state ocean – ugly horrors that never see the light of day. Angler fish in suits and ties.' She shuddered.

Bravely I made a supreme effort to regain control of my breathing. 'So this other faction, the ones *actually* trying to kill me – we've still got those jokers on our tail?'

Gwen nodded. 'I believe pro-Welsh forces – perhaps the Gorsedd, maybe J-Corp itself – want to thwart the Consortium. Easiest method is for you to end up with a thoroughly ventilated head. Llywsiffer Pendragon has put a fatwah on your head. Your existence is an embarrassment to too many people.'

If only this was the first time I'd heard those words spoken. I began to appreciate the sacrifice Gwen was making on my behalf – this wasn't her fight. 'So now we've got this world's most deranged power-brokers hunting us down, and their rivals trying to wipe us out to boot? We're not doing things by half.'

Gwen looked as sick as I felt. 'That's about the long and the short, sport – yep.'

There was a long, glum silence. Weirdly there was one small detail in this volcanic eruption of woe that troubled me more than most.

'Everyone says you're such a professional – why didn't you hand me over? You could have been counting your fee right now.'

My companion got a faraway look in her eye. 'That's a story for another day.'

I knew not to push it when she got that glint in her eye. Perhaps best to change the subject. 'So what are we going to do when we get to Wales? We stand no chance. Best to put me out of my misery now.'

Gwen reached out and squeezed my hand. 'Don't worry, it's not over yet, kiddo. You've got me on your side now – we outnumber them.'

For a moment I could almost believe her, then the ship's deck rolled beneath us on a mighty Atlantic swell and the spell was broken. Something flickered deep in Gwen's eyes and she looked away. She sprang to her feet and went for another run around deck. I went to sleep and tried not to think about elite corporate hit squads and large needles full of truth serum.

The next day I wasn't feeling any better. I'd spent an exhausting night tossing in my sleeping bag, dreaming about parallel universes and mad druids bent on my destruction. The floor had been as cold and hard as a sacrificial altar. I awoke with a scream on my lips and an icy sweat clinging to my body like a shroud. My nightmare's parting shot was the image of a ceremonial sickle plunging towards my waiting chest. Not the best way to start the day.

I rubbed my eyes and wiped the dribble from my chin. Gwen was fiddling with one of the video screens mounted around the cavernous compartment; she'd told me they were used for relaying messages to the crew. With some tinkering she managed to switch it to a satellite news channel. Was there no end to her talents? President Barry Island was giving a major speech as part of his re-election campaign. It seemed to be a cry for national unity.

'... *No man is an island, and as we all know, Barry Island isn't one either. And neither is a Nation...*'

Gwen snorted; she didn't seem impressed. 'What about Fiji?'

'... *We must never forget the fine principles for which this great Republic stands.*'

'Good luck with that. Liberty, Equality, Fraternity and Profit.'

'*Let us ask, not what this country can do to them, but what our enemies can do to us... if they stop squabbling and get their act together...*'

Gwen shook her head. 'Bless him, but he's more Bill Clinton than John Kennedy.'

'*We all know world opinion looks unfavourably on our regrettable police action in Patagonia. That's why I stand before you today, to promise to bring the boyos back home...*'

'Fair play to him, maybe he has balls of steel after all –'

Gwen's commentary was cut short. Something small and fast fizzed across the screen. The camera trained on President Island was zoomed in from far away, so it was hard to get the bigger picture. A moment later the device was back – it looked like a small quad-copter drone. It plunged towards the stage, as the crowds in the front row scrambled for cover. A swarm of security personnel dived for the President, trying vainly to bundle him from harm's way. With sickening inevitability the drone dissolved in a blinding flash. The screen filled with smoke and dust; there were screams and sound of panic. If the President had been trying to channel JFK this was taking it too far.

Gwen stood up and put her hands on her head. 'Well, looks like the nutters finally got to him. All bets are off now.'

'The nutters?'

'Our friends in the Gorsedd. They don't take kindly to talk of winding down the war in South America. That's ethnic nationalism for you. One minute it's all folk dancing and language revivals, the next it's armoured divisions rolling across the pampas on a crusade for lebensraum – arse cancer for the human soul.'

Gwen got over the shocking news quicker than I did. She did some star jumps then went for another run around the deck. This was a girl who certainly liked jogging.

11

Homage to Patagonia

Within the hour Fox, CNN and S4C were reporting nothing else but coverage of the attack. Miraculously President Island had survived the blast and was in a critical but stable condition in hospital. A bewildering range of previously unknown groups had come forward claiming responsibility for the bomb. Assorted 'security experts' wheeled out for the cameras took turns looking bemused, claiming never to have heard of such organisations as the Daughters of Glyndwr, or the Sons of Penderyn. *Russia Today* tracked down the drummer from the rock band Sisters of Mercy for comment. He made more sense than most of the rest.

A constant theme running through the bulletins was talk of the President's political opponent. Behind each newscaster glowered the gaunt, bleak face of Llywsiffer Pendragon, leader of the Gorsedd Party and Barry Island's electoral nemesis. Even in a still image his eyes seemed to flash with hellfire, his bushy grey monobrow casting them in permanent shadow. No pundit seemed ready to go on record – perhaps they didn't want to wake up to a sheep's head in their bed – but you didn't have to be Sherlock Holmes to read between the lines.

Safer to stick with the terrorists' outlandish demands. Some were sent in by fax, others posted on social media, and at least one was scrawled in crayon, wrapped around a lump of coal and thrown through the window of the *Western Mail*. Taken together they made an extensive list. Chief amongst them was the demand the war in Patagonia be stepped up so the Welsh side actually had a chance of winning. For too long, so they claimed, the Expeditionary Force had been fighting with one hand tied behind its back. The time for political niceties was over. After that the demands got more outlandish. Some highlights included…

An end to the use of an 'Area the Size of Wales' as a unit of international measurement. Degrading and disrespectful – ATSOW no more!

The Australian state of Queensland to change its name immediately to New North Wales.

All international diplomacy to be carried out through the medium of YouTube comment threads. I didn't think this last one would end very well.

Gwen watched the reports roll in, stony faced. All she'd say was it smelt like a false flag attack – someone was trying to muddy the already murky waters. I was already too confused to speculate.

Our compartment ended in a set of heavy bulkhead doors. On the other side was a narrow walkway recessed into the hull of the ship. From the rail it was a hundred-foot drop to the broiling waters of the North Atlantic below. This balcony was our one chance to get a lungful of fresh air. I followed Gwen outside to watch the sunset, trying not to wonder how many I had left.

There's a unique palette of colours you only get when the

sun goes down behind a thousand miles of ocean, a range of shades paint manufacturers struggle to invent names for. We gazed at the spectacle in silence for a while, as beneath us the swell crashed against the hull of the enormous ship, racing away to points unknown.

'Are you going to tell me why you're risking your life for me?'

Gwen was a long time answering. I sensed the moisture in her eyes wasn't just down to the brisk, salty breeze. When she spoke her voice seemed changed somehow, distant and smaller.

'I knew this girl once, she was young and naïve, but full of hope; thought she could change the world.'

'Don't we all. What happened to her?'

Gwen inhaled deeply. 'She signed up for the military. Seems weird now, but back then we all believed we were fighting for a just cause. The Revolution was young, just like us, and the principles of the Founding Uncles resounded in our ears like thunder round the hills. If only we could give the world a big *cwtch*, everything would be all right. Of course, we might have to invade it first.

'Turned out that girl was more than cut out for army life. Went through basic on Bardsey Island like shit through a sheep. Truth was it was easy after growing up in the orphanage. Her drill instructors gave her a standing ovation when she graduated. She was transferred to Special Forces – the legendary "Raspberry Berets" – and fast-tracked through OTC. That was where she met the Colonel.'

'The Colonel?'

'Yes. He was already a legend by then, a true hero of the Revolution. The only ranking officer in Welsh Special Forces with one wooden leg but two real feet.'

Gwen took a moment to extract a troublesome eyelash and sniffed. 'He was a hoary old soldier who had seen it all before, but he'd never seen anything like her. He took her under his battle-scarred wing, taught her things few men ever learned, becoming the father figure she'd never known. They had a special bond, stronger than steel and deeper than a drift mine.'

'Wow.' I have to admit I was rapt by the story. 'Did she get sent to the war?'

'Oh yes. She might have had a tear in her eye the day she shipped out for Patagonia, on a transport much like this one. She was with her unit, as elite a team of badasses as ever set sail, but still the closest thing she'd ever known to a family. As the politicians were at pains to point out, they weren't an invasion force, but "military advisors", sent to help the brave rebels throw off the Argentine yoke.

'They were heading south, much like the situation on the ground in Chubut Province. Turns out the rebels were just as bad as the Argy Junta – freedom fighters to us back home, but terrorists to everyone else. Atrocities were committed on both sides. Not least being Max Boyce going out on a non-stop tour performing for the troops. And as it goes, not all the locals were thrilled to be liberated. They were quite happy without the benefits of Welsh Civilisation – they threw that cheese on toast and hymn-singing right back in our faces.'

I could see she was welling up, but Gwen's tale had taken on a life of its own. Once started it had to be told. Like that point of no return in a really big poo.

'The war dragged on. The politicians back home fed yet more troops into the fray, but never enough to tip the balance in our favour. The world was watching, and it didn't like what it saw – an Argentine Dafydd pitted against a Welsh Goliath. A generation of young lives scarred forever. Wars these days are fought as much on social media and in news rooms as they are on the battlefield, and Wales was losing this one.

'At the end of Black October her unit found itself in Puerto

Madryn, surrounded by the Argies on three sides. Outnumbered twenty to one, they put up a desperate fight, but it was no use. It was like Rorke's Drift, but without the racism and close harmony singing. They ate nothing but corned beef for days. She saw her friends fall one by one. After a week of fighting it was just the girl and the Colonel left. After rigging a fake rearguard of jangling defenders from spent Fray Bentos tins, they slipped silently into the night. She shed bitter tears for her fallen comrades but at least she could still save her mentor. Half-carrying him they hopped along; luckily it had been his wooden leg which was blown off. They were soon in a hellish three-legged race for life itself.

'The Argies sent their Mapuche Indian trackers after them through the bush. The girl could have escaped on her own, but there was no way she was leaving the Colonel behind. They were run to ground at a long abandoned farmhouse above a desolate, dry river bed. The whole place reeked of death.

'Their pursuers hung back, wary of the destruction they'd already seen her reap. They were happy to let her go, the *Ángelita de la Muerte*, soon to be enshrined in legend. It was her CO they wanted. One amongst them called out from the night, "Don't worry – he'll be safe with us." Those fateful words would come to haunt her dreams.'

Gwen slumped against the ship's rail, her body wracked by dry sobs. Feebly I patted her on the shoulder. I was taken back to the diner in Jacksonville, where Finch had uttered those self-same words about yours truly.

Gwen regained her composure and continued the tale. 'She would have died for him a thousand times over, but he commanded her to go. *He'd be a prisoner of war*, he told her – *parcels from the Red Cross*, he said, *escape committees and sing-songs; prison camp dirt down trouser legs*, they'd all seen the films.

Against her better judgement she followed his orders and fled into the night. The Argies descended on him like a pack of wild dogs, their howls ringing in her ears. She was safe back behind Welsh lines by morning. For him there was another fate in store.'

Gwen grew silent and stared far out to sea. The sun had set and the sky was bathed in a breathtaking indigo twilight. Salmon-tinted clouds skittered off in search of a place to spend the night. I badly wanted to hear the rest of the tale, hoping for a happy ending.

'So they treated the Colonel well – Geneva Convention and all that?'

She looked at me in wonder, the first starlight glinting off her eyes. 'Of course not – they horribly tortured him.'

'Oh.'

'They broke him on a wheel. They put him back together again then broke him on another wheel. They kept going till they ran out of wheels. They moved him next to a wheel factory. They'd never heard of Geneva, or any conventions. They fed him the Tears of the Puma, and other stuff just as bad. They only had that coffee that's been passed through the gut of a cat. Sent his mind to places no sane man should ever visit. Not all of it came back.'

My mouth moved but no sounds emerged. Perhaps it was for the best.

'He was released two years later in a prisoner exchange. They'd given up trying to get information from him. He might have been howling at the moon by then, but the Colonel was as tough as old boots and twice as leathery.'

I stood in silence as I tried to take it all in. 'So this girl from the story – where is she now?'

Gwen regarded me for a good while, her head slowly

shaking. At last she muttered, 'Er mwyn ffwc. Lord preserve us.'

'Pardon me?'

'That girl WAS ME! Try to keep up!'

Gwen stormed off back inside. There was a series of hollow thuds as I banged my head against the ship's hull in frustration. Who amongst us would ever understand women and their mysterious ways?

12

The Green Grass of Home

Two days later we caught sight of Milford Haven. The low grey landscape slid into view like it was sneaking home after a night out on the town, trying not to rattle the milk bottles and scare the cat. Gwen had been quiet and withdrawn since telling me her tale; I suppose I couldn't blame her. She'd not be drawn on what our next move should be. To tell the truth I don't think she knew herself. This struck me as a worrying development.

I started having paranoid thoughts she would dump me at the first convenient opportunity – far from convenient for me. I was less than no use to her and my presence painted big cross hairs on her back. She'd already saved my life more than once; why should I expect her to do so again? As we stood at the rail watching the muddy banks of the Cleddau estuary draw closer, like the jaws of some massive trap, Gwen seemed to sense my thoughts.

'What are we going to do with you, Kev?'

'I don't know. I'd like to go home now. Back to the real Aberdare.'

She peered out at the mud flats slipping by. 'I'm afraid it's not that simple. Home is the first place they'll look. You've got too many big players gunning for you.'

I didn't like this talk of guns. 'Can't I go back and we just – I don't know – block the gate, burn the library down? Nobody would notice.'

Gwen shook her head. 'Easier said than done. The Consortium would move heaven and earth to open another portal; it's always possible at that site. These people will never give up. They've got the resources to keep trying until they hit the jackpot. Whammo! Kevin's brains go splat.'

I shuddered at the thought. 'So what do we do then, any ideas?'

She drummed her fingers on the cold rail. 'Perhaps we have to hide you.'

'Hide on this side?'

'Why not, there're worse places to live? You've not yet sampled all we have to offer.'

This thought hadn't occurred to me. Perhaps Gwen would see me right after all. She placed a hand gently on my shoulder. 'I've got a friend who might be able to help. There're no guarantees, it won't be easy, but he's our next port of call.'

I chewed it over, unsure if I liked the taste of this idea. It would be hard, adjusting to this mad world, but was it any madder than the one I'd left behind? 'Where does this friend of yours live?'

I felt her hand go tense. She hesitated. 'You'll see soon enough. Time to get to our positions.' She was gone before I could quiz her further.

The captain had told us that when we reached port we should shut ourselves in a specific cargo container. This unit would be unloaded in the first batch and left in a quiet part of the vast port complex. He'd ensure it was left open so we could make good our escape. The idea terrified me, but Gwen assured me she had used this method before. Not for the first time I was putting my life in her hands.

We found the container and clambered inside. It was full of large boxes filled with computer equipment. There was just enough space to wedge ourselves in a hole left vacant by the mismatched packages. Gwen kept the doors ajar until the last moment, when we heard the ceiling covers grind open far above. The next few hours were some of the worst of my life, which considering what I'd recently been through was quite an achievement. Confined spaces have always made my pulse race and lately I'd had several suboptimal experiences with lifts. I'd always put my claustrophobia down to race memory – a perfectly rational fear of suffocation carved into my DNA. I wouldn't have made a good miner. People are quick to condemn Mrs Thatcher but at least she'd spared me a life underground. Herding trolleys around a supermarket car park would always be much more my sort of career. Fresh air and sunshine.

Gwen wasn't going to let me get away with whining about my predicament. She told me I would have to toughen up if I wanted to cut it, in this world or any other. Apparently I'd been mollycoddled too long; I was a special snowflake yearning for the security of the drift. The cheek of it. I was about to highlight my long list of achievements when I thought better of it. Perhaps she had a point.

It was dark inside the container. The clanging and banging from every side seemed to last a lifetime. Silently I cursed the careless programming of robotic port cranes. Gwen passed the time meditating and told me not to worry about things over which I had no control. Very Zen, but what good would it do if we were dropped from a great height? At last the ordeal came to an end and all was still. I was shaken and traumatised but seemingly still in one piece. Waiting in the silence was almost as bad. An unknown time later, maybe an hour, maybe a few minutes, I jumped out of my skin as the locking mechanism of our metal coffin disengaged. A ghostly arm tossed a package inside. Gwen put a restraining hand on my shoulder, as if fearing I might flee at the first opportunity – did she think me that much a fool?

We waited in silence for what seemed a lifetime. At last Gwen slipped from her hiding space and peeked out the crack in the doors. When she was sure the coast was clear, she beckoned me down. 'Here, put this on.'

The package contained a pair of hard hats, luminous yellow vests and clipboards. There were also a couple of lanyards, bearing what looked like electronic keys – LEDs rippling across their surface. Gwen was soon kitted out in the gear; I followed suit.

'I don't think we've got time to conduct a survey.'

Gwen slipped her head through a brightly coloured loop. 'A hi-viz jacket is the best camouflage known to man. Take the clipboard and walk like you know what you're doing. It's all about looking the part.'

We were soon out of that cursed box and striding through alleys of steel. We saw no people. In the distance robot shuttle carriers glided by on errands of their own. I'd never seen so many ISO containers in one place, stretching as far as the eye could see. The towering stacks hid the sky. We were like ants lost in an unending maze of brightly coloured children's blocks. At each intersection Gwen paused to peer at her notes. 'Left at the next junction. Almost there.'

'What is all this stuff?'

'Milford's the biggest container port in the world. Wales

seems bent on buying all the consumer crap the rest of the planet can produce. Got to find a use for all that foreign currency.'

We turned the next corner and caught sight of the fence. It was a good half a mile away across a vast expanse of concrete. Above us drifting craft carried containers in every direction. As usual Gwen seemed to know where she was going. 'Don't rush. Walk like you've not a care in the world. There's a personnel gate set in the fence.'

I followed her lead. It wasn't easy, I felt terribly exposed sauntering across the tarmac. We reached the fence and found a small booth blocked by a turnstile. Gwen slid her security card into a slot and pushed against the bars. A light flashed green and she was through. Seconds later I'd joined her beyond the barrier.

We ditched our disguises in a convenient bush. I had to admit they'd been a success. Twenty minutes, and a spot of light jogging later, we were in downtown Milford Haven. Gwen was better at the jogging than me. It wasn't Aberdare, but the place was still an impressive metropolis. The highest skyscrapers barely peeked through the skittering clouds. No rain was falling, but it looked like the sky might open at any moment. It felt good to be – sort of – back home in Wales. We grabbed some cheese on toast from a roadside café and asked directions to the nearest tacsi rank.

Just as we were leaving the rarebit joint Gwen pulled up short. A group of locals were clustered round a glowing screen set behind the bar. Gwen caught the proprietor's eye. 'What's going on?'

He wiped his hands on a greasy apron and looked glum. 'Damnedest bit of bad luck you could ever imagine. Seems a small asteroid slammed into North America. Completely levelled an office block in Langley, Virginia. No survivors. Makes you think, donnit.'

Something about this news troubled me, but I couldn't quite put my finger on it. 'Jeeze, this world is so random. What are the odds?' The TV pictures showed nothing but a glowing crater picked over by rescue crews.

Beside me Gwen had gone very pale. It was far from a happy news story but her reaction struck me as over the top. Without a word she bundled me out of the door and onto the glistening pavement.

'What's up with you?'

She checked the street in both directions. 'That office housed a CIA black facility in the basement. It was our rendezvous – where I was scheduled to hand you over to the Consortium's top hombres. Someone very badly wants you dead. Someone powerful enough to lob rocks from orbit.'

My recent meal felt like it wanted out of my stomach. I started seeing faceless assassins lurking in every shadow – there were plenty nearby to choose from. Perhaps sensing a panic attack, Gwen took my elbow and led me briskly down the road. Minutes later we were clambering into another of the bright yellow tacsis, Gwen counting out the cash. We were soon airborne and heading into the darkening night. What fresh nightmares would it bring? All that cheese I'd eaten wasn't going to help.

13

To Live and Die in Swansea

Just like ancient Rome, Swansea was built on seven hills, one for each of the deadly sins. Trouble was they needed some new hills – they'd been busy enough inventing sins. But while in the Eternal City it was only slaves at the auction block who could be bought and sold, in Swansea every man had his price, and some were pretty low. It was a bubbling pressure cooker brimming with human flotsam, a fetid stew on the verge of boiling over; packed full of disgraced butchers, renegade bakers, erotic candlestick makers; pimps and pounces, whores, bores, freelance druids and traders in bodily fluids; sheep rustlers and bingo hall hustlers. There wasn't much you couldn't buy before midnight, and absolutely nothing you couldn't get after. The shops shut early on a Tuesday so they could try to remove the stains. There wasn't enough disinfectant in the world. Some said *an ugly lovely town* – but only if you wore industrial-strength beer goggles. Fortunately most of the inhabitants did. The indoor market sold excellent cockles. Just don't ask what they fed on out in the bay. And that was the Swansea from my world – just what the place would be like over here I shuddered to think. I was about to find out.

We tumbled from the tacsi, yelling our thanks to the oblivious robotic driver, into a world of blaring neon and burning chrome. My heart was in my mouth, but what I really needed were eyes in the back of my head. As usual it was raining, but this rain had the good sense to vaporise before reaching the ground, filling the ozone-laden air with a swirling kaleidoscopic steam. Gwen took me by the hand and led me from the landing pad. 'Come on. I know the way to go.'

We hurried down a busy commercial thoroughfare. Folk from every corner of the globe rubbed shoulders with burnished androids, diligently going about their business. Far above, glittering spires punched holes in the night sky as vast advertising holograms danced against the ragged clouds. Welshperanto, Korean, Cyrillic rippled and morphed before my wide eyes.

We passed a beggar with no arms and legs, a sign around his neck claiming they were back in Patagonia along with his innocence. Gwen tossed him a coin without breaking stride. A kid in thick NHS specs with a plaster over one lens tried to sell me a deep-fried rat on a stick. I politely said I'd eaten. Music blasted from an all-night nail emporium across the street, staffed by an army of tiny Chinese women and Shiva-armed robots. The local answer to George Michael knocking out 'Wake me up before you go-go-goch' like his heart depended on it. Maybe it did.

By my reckoning it was way past 3am – my watch had stopped somewhere along the line, and it seemed the dimensional time jumps had given it a nervous breakdown – but every shop we passed remained open. Unlike the false promises made in songs, this really was the city that never slept; shame it was locked in this walking nightmare. I'd already tried their cocktails; I didn't want to think what their espressos might be like. We passed seedy all-night laverbread dens, fronted by scantily clad hawkers, and the biggest Greggs I'd ever clapped eyes on, complete with roped-off VIP area. At least the bouncers here were making a vain effort at chucking-out. I tiptoed through a minefield of shattered pasties and sausage rolls, while ahead of me Gwen picked up the pace. My legs ached and my ears throbbed.

I called after her. 'Why the hurry? Unless you're finding me a proper bed for what's left of the night.'

In a flash she was in my face, pulling my ear down to mouth level against the din. 'Don't think for one moment we're safe. The Consortium has spies everywhere. Be on your guard.' She was gone again as fast as she'd arrived. It was all I could do to stumble in her wake.

Ahead of us a group of heavily armed cops were shaking down a gang of druids, who must have overstepped some local by-law. The swelling crowd of onlookers were growing restless, equally divided between supporters and detractors. Several ugly scuffles broke out. Overhead a police gunship hovered like a praying mantis, dancing spotlights fashioning a hideous disco on the rain-slick tarmac. Nervous bystanders stood around filming the floor show. Gwen gave the skirmish a wide berth. I struggled to keep up.

'There's just one thing I don't understand?'

'Really, just the one?'

I sidestepped a drunk barfing a torrent of glowing mucus onto his shoes. 'Okay, there're lots of things I don't understand. But there's one bothering me in particular.'

'What's that?'

'This is the richest, most advanced country in the world –'

A hovering ball of LEDs and whirring gyros regarded us

with a cyclopean eye as it pitched us life insurance – did it know something we didn't? Gwen brushed it aside.

'– but why is it all so… sordid?'

My companion carried on her way. 'This is the sophisticated part of town – you should see the Under City.' She saw my look of dismay. 'On second thoughts, maybe not.'

I wasn't deterred. 'You know what I mean. Why does it have to be this way?'

She paused for a moment to check her bearings. A warbling ice cream van trundled by, horribly out of tune. 'The more wealthy a society becomes, the more the inequality – it's always been the way. If power corrupts what do you think ultimate power does to the soul of a nation? Come on, it's just down here.'

We arrived at what must have been Castle Square, turning the corner at the base of a 500 ft skyscraper bedecked in giant wraparound screens. The brightness blasting forth could have knocked the unwary off their feet – I think it might have been giving me a tan. The huge bank of shimmering pixels showed international rugby highlights – The All Blacks getting pounded, looking decidedly black and blue. Few of the revellers paid it much heed, our lot clearly winning so hard it had lost any sense of satisfaction.

The castle itself was still there, complete with eerily realistic holographic dragon gyrating in the throbbing air above, but the rest of the place had changed quite a bit. Gwen navigated a course through the crowded plaza, around the fountain – as ever foaming with drunken students. We zigzagged towards a plush parade of shops. There was a Tibetan wholefood takeaway – *The Deli Lama* – and what looked like a fancy nightclub – *Crystal Tips Topless Ice Bar* – come-along girls ushering swaying marks down the roped-off entry line. Our destination nestled between these two establishments. Through the huge plate glass windows I could see a bright interior; the place seemed to be an upmarket hairdresser. The glowing sign stretching along the facade read *Celtic Fringe*. I didn't think a haircut was a priority, but Gwen seemed to know what she was doing.

We entered a well-appointed waiting room, complete with plush seating and haughty major-domo standing guard behind a podium – it was that type of joint. Even at this late hour the place was packed, evidently the most popular chop shop in town. Yet more screens set around the walls cycled images of the outlandish styles you could request. Each bore hairy testament to the powerful cantilevering effects of the local hairspray. Gwen had a quiet word with the major-domo, who looked us up and down with unconcealed disdain. I think he was about to give us the bum's rush when a commotion broke out further back in the studio. A tall man tending a client's towering ginger afro spotted us through the interior glass and dropped his tools with a clatter. Soon he was barrelling through the inner doors to greet us.

Gwen smiled when she saw him coming. 'Kevin, meet Juan Llewellyn Ramirez, the best hair-wrangler this side of the Tawe.'

Juan had the sort of tan which would have got him sent to the back of the bus in the Confederacy. He was over six-four of lean muscle, shown off to devastating effect in a tight white shirt open to the navel. Michelangelo might have sculpted his close-cropped beard, the rest of him perhaps rendered by more talented artistes. Catching sight of Gwen his green eyes flashed as bright as his arctic smile, which dazzled even in this over-bright environment. For some reason I took an instant dislike to the fellow.

'Chica Bonita! Is been too long – you finally come back to

us.' He wrapped her in his massive arms and gazed down at her in adoration. Cheeks burning, I felt my fury mounting.

Gwen patted his stubbly cheek affectionately and gazed back at him. 'Old friend, we need your help. *Code Red* I'm afraid.'

14

The Celtic Fringe

An hour later we were upstairs, sprawled in Juan's luxury apartment. He owned the penthouse suite at the top of the skyscraper towering over Castle Square, an easy place in which to relax. Basically our host lived above his shop. This fact made me feel a little better about my love rival; the guy was obviously a complete fraud. I suspected his accent was put on for the sake of his clientele, more Gorseinon than Guadalajara – guess he got to charge more for a haircut that way. I'd resisted my irrational urge to punch him in the face for two main reasons: first, I couldn't deny Juan had been infuriatingly polite; second, I was sure he could dismantle and reassemble me one handed without breaking sweat. Otherwise I would have taken him out in an instant. Scumbag.

Juan fed us a gourmet supper rustled up from a handful of ingredients tossed into a sizzling pan, before telling us to treat the place as our own. I took this as an invitation to snoop round the spacious open-plan lounge, four wall-length windows granting panoramas of the glittering city far below.

There was room for a tennis court, but apparently that was on another floor. Huge arty black and white photos of naked musclebound men sprawling with kittens hung from every wall. I was sure if I looked hard enough somewhere I'd find a dimmer switch, maybe next to the button triggering Barry White's greatest hits – clearly the bachelor pad of a try-hard bar steward.

I was drawn to a crackling fake fireplace big enough to garage a small car. A row of glittering, Oscar-like statuettes crowded the wide mantle. Gwen saw me inspecting the weird things and glided over to stand at my shoulder.

'He's a man of culture, our host. A leading light in the Welsh film industry – after retiring from his first career. That's how he got the money to buy this place.'

I didn't need to ask what sort of films Juan had starred in. The 'Oscars' turned out to be a whole firing squad of burnished golden phalluses, replete with inscriptions bearing the titles of his well-oiled body of work. I'd not yet seen *Shitty Titty Gangbang*, or had time to enjoy *Willy Wanker and the Fudge Packing Factory*, but the night was still young. Who knew where things would end? But of course, for some of us, it would only lead to bed. Despite my strange surroundings I soon found myself drifting off to sleep on one of the many oversized couches. I'd had a busy day.

As I lay drowsing Gwen and our host sat talking quietly nearby. I did some pretend snoring so as not to cramp Juan's style. If I gave him room to make his play maybe he'd crash and burn. For the life of me I couldn't understand what Gwen saw in the handsome, suave, manicured, multi-millionaire. So what if he could do her hair for free into the bargain? To top it all they seemed to be old friends, colleagues from long ago. If any can fathom the minds of women they're better men than me.

Gwen was almost purring up at the slob. 'Thanks again Juan, I didn't know where else to turn.'

'No worries, Bonita. You saved me enough times back in the day. I owe you more than a few.'

She hesitated for a moment. 'This is different. We've got some major players on our tail. I can't overstate the danger. You're risking your life just talking to me.'

Even the way Juan clinked the ice round his glass drove me up the wall. 'Gwendolyn my love, we survived our share of danger many times. Remember when we escaped from Tarkov?'

She chuckled without much mirth. 'Yeah, we gave that troll factory the full billy goat treatment. I've still got the crate of vodka somewhere.' There was a pause. 'But how are things round here? The old place feels, I don't know, different somehow.'

Now it was Juan's turn to hesitate. 'I won't lie to you, is not so good. This country, how you say, goes quickly to the dogs – and these might turn out a pack of hyenas. Prophets and madmen roam the streets – gets worse every day. The fabric of society tears like last week's pantyhose.'

'I've seen the news,' Gwen muttered. 'There's been a backlash building for years. We're heading for a crash.'

'Exactly this – so it is no time for the picking-up of the strays. Where did you find this one?'

Gwen took a while to answer. 'He's not a stray, he was... the mission. I had my doubts from the start. Guess I should have trusted my instincts.'

'What is it that has been occurring?'

Gwen let out a long sigh. 'We got to the handover and I couldn't go through with it. Sometimes your past catches up with you, and mine had been closing in for years. Like I said, the clients are not people you'd want to cross.'

'But you crossed them all the same. You don't change, my little flower. Brave and loyal, to the point of the foolhardy.'

'I was working for *The Man* – should have known he'd turn out to be an asshole.'

'And now these asswipes want their prize. Maybe figuring you want to up your price?'

'Maybe they do. But that's not how it is at all. I owe it to Kevin to set him right. You wouldn't believe who he was if I told you – and believe me, you don't want to know. He's more of a lost sheep than a stray dog.'

'And you're Little Bo Peep? I can picture you in the outfit now – cute.'

It was all I could do to suppress the urge to jump up and punch the oily git. Did he think he was funny? It heartened me that not a titter passed Gwen's perfect lips; if anything she sounded sad.

'You know I've got my reasons.'

There was a pause, no doubt while Juan caressed his chiselled jawline. 'On the subject of our old compadre, you know he's been discharged from the facility? The doctors claim they've done all they can.'

Gwen was silent for a while. 'I'd heard rumours. Can't see how it's a good thing. He still needs help.'

'Maybe you should go and see him. Might be good for both of you – silence can fester.'

'I doubt talking would help. Silence can also heal.'

What was this lunk trying to push her into? As if we didn't have enough on our plate already. Juan had some nerve, as well as, I had to admit, a voice like oak-aged sherry.

'We all have regrets, Bonita – comes with our line of work. Or rather, your line of work.'

Gwen poured herself another drink. 'Yes, I see retirement

has treated you well. Don't you miss the buzz – the sheer excitement of the game?'

Now it was our host's turn to take a while answering. 'Sometimes. Retirement has been good to me, as you can see. But we are not here to speak of my home comforts. To return to your lost sheep – who doesn't think much of me, by the way – can't you just… drop him back where you found him?'

Gwen took a deep breath. 'It's not that simple. You have no idea what an idiot he is. It would be kinder to pop one in the back of his head and leave him in a ditch. Maybe even a service to society.'

I nearly fell off the couch with shock and had to stifle a snort of derision. Was this how Gwen really thought of me? Apparently so. Neither of the lovebirds were paying enough attention to notice my convulsions, as Gwen continued.

'That's why I need to get him hidden, to buy time. Unless you've got any bright ideas how to extract us from this mess.'

Again Juan paused. 'You'll see things better in the morning. The spare room is made up. Sleep will help, it always does.'

I heard Gwen getting to her feet. I think she kissed him, and then she was gone, ghosting off to one of the many guest rooms. Juan sat there by himself for a while, swirling the last of the ice around his glass and mulling over how badly he'd just crashed and burned. Lol. I sensed his dark eyes range over me.

After a lengthy reflection he creaked to his feet and left for a moment, then returned with a blanket and pillows. I was taken aback by what happened next. He draped the blanket over me and put the pillows within easy reach. He even patted me on the cheek.

'Sleep well oveja pequeña. We'll sort you out – have no fear.' It would have been no surprise if he'd given me a goodnight kiss. Perhaps I'd been wrong about Juan's motivations, or maybe his tastes. I didn't know whether to laugh or cry. I'd been through so much lately my head was all over the place. Juan turned out the lights and then he too was gone, leaving me to my unhappy thoughts. If I hadn't been so tired I don't think I would have slept a wink. When I opened my eyes it was morning.

15

The Mumbles Quarter Mile

Looking back, I'm not proud of what I did next. While this is true for much of my life up to that point, what happened next was a particular nadir. But you've got to understand the pressure I was under – I'd been running for my life through a bizarre mixed-up world that made no sense to my fevered brain. I wasn't exactly operating at my usual cool and rational best. Once I'd had it rammed down my throat what Gwen truly thought of me, there was no way I was hanging around. I was determined not to burden her any longer. She'd saved my life countless times already, enough was enough. My pride could only take so much. I grabbed my meagre possessions and headed for the door.

At first I worried I'd stand out like a sore thumb, my every step marking me out as an interloper from a distant world. I needn't have worried. There was such an eclectic mix of people swirling through the open sewer which was Swansea I would have fitted in if I'd had two heads and wings. Some claimed they'd built this city on rock and roll – I thought an ancient Indian burial ground was more likely.

I had no clue where I was going, or what I'd do when I got there – perhaps a great summation of my life to date. I had a pocketful of cash Gwen had given me in case we got separated, and the extent of my thinking was to get plastered and eat a kebab. I intended to heroically drown my sorrows, to blow it all in a bar on leek daiquiris or something worse. Swansea is nothing if not a reliable venue for getting hammered. Before the day was out I intended to join the melancholy parade of sloshed poets honking in Cwm Donkin. Maybe not a good one, but it was 'A Plan'.

As I stumbled through the grimy rain-soaked streets, I reflected this was my long dark teatime of the soul, even if – as far as I could tell – it was about 8am. Time was fluid round these parts, much like the available consolation. Crowds of locals and tourists parted before me as if they could sense I was not a man to trifle with. I walked and I thought until my feet ached as much as my brain, and the conclusion I came to was this – much like my wanderings, my life lacked direction.

By the time he was my age Grandad had experienced more than I could ever imagine. And this wasn't even the guy who transformed this world a myriad ways for the better. Forget inventing the J-Drive, the Isaiah I knew had lived through the Second World War. I'd heard all about it because he never stopped telling me from the earliest age I could remember. Until well into my teens I don't think we had a conversation which didn't reference The War in some way. It had given his life meaning and direction. His character had been forged in the white-hot crucible of conflict. Was it this that gave his twin the potential to achieve such great things over here?

And what had stopped him doing so where I came from? A horrible realisation was dawning – it seemed the thing that held him back must have been me. A thought which went no way towards making me feel any better about my sorry existence. I was nothing but an albatross around the neck of everyone I met – only difference was no one was getting cursed if I got shot. If anything, quite the reverse.

In a perverse way Isaiah's generation had been lucky. The War had been both a blessing and a curse; a blessing, in that it gave purpose to their lives; a curse since lots of them had been shot, blown up or maimed – but hey, every cloud. When you've saved the world from fascism everything else looks tame by comparison. How was my generation meant to compete? Crafting the perfect social media presence wasn't going cut it as a life-defining experience. I thought *The Windy Ninja* was shaping up pretty nicely, but I had to admit it didn't compare to facing down Hitler. The grandfather I knew might not have created Anthracite, but he'd learned a practical philosophy he'd tried in vain to pass onto me. I'd once asked him, a few years before, why he was spending so much time with me, helping with my education – how could I ever hope to repay him?

He'd looked down at me with his watery, pale eyes and said, 'There's no need to repay me, bach. One day you'll be in a position to help someone else – not because you owe them, or because they have a call on you, but because they're in need. We all have a duty to pay knowledge forward – to leave this world in a better place than we find it. That's how you can pay me back, by helping some stranger further down the track.' He told me to *Pay It Forward*. Even without the mad inventions it was impossible to escape the conclusion my grandad was one of the good guys. How could I ever live up to that?

It was no use, I gave in. I was down by the seafront and turned into the first bar I came to. There were plenty to choose from. I'm not sure what I ended up drinking but in half an hour I was past caring. I made some new friends, a stag party down from Llandeilo. We did a bit of singing and we did a bit of drinking. I told them I was secretly the rightful heir to the globe-spanning Jones Corporation, and they lined up the drinks for us to celebrate. Some of them even made it as far as our mouths. The lads must have sensed the darkness infesting my soul because they slipped away when I wasn't looking. The bartender was less understanding when I told him of my woes.

'Get out, you mingin mochyn,' he shouted, as he threw me onto the street. 'We wants no manky piss-'eds 'ere!'

I didn't care; there were plenty of other distractions in that part of town. Even at that time of day the promenade was thick with hookers. They came in all shapes and sizes and seemed to cater to every taste – at least if the sandwich board menus carried by the touts could be believed. I was propositioned more than once.

'Hya luv, fancy a rub?'

Even if I'd been in the mood for romance I don't think I'd have been up to the job. Politely I demurred, then vomited on her platform shoes.

'Ffwcing pervert!' Her pimp appeared and chased me away.

In a park just across the road I noticed a crowd gathering, watched by a wary TV camera crew. The sign on their van read 'S4C News 24'. The congregation were there to listen to a ragged man wearing flowing robes, who moved like a drunken octopus – perhaps he'd have my answers, he had a better chance than me. I latched onto the back of the throng and strained to catch a look. In the distance I could hear the wail of approaching sirens.

The speaker had a long grey beard full of twigs and the mad, wild eyes of a prophet – Swansea seemed well stocked with these of late. His voice shook with emotion as he bobbed on his makeshift stage.

A hefty middle-aged man stood beside me wearing a 'Make

Cymru Great Again' cap. I'd spotted a lot of these on the street. He had a tub of popcorn and a beer in a plastic cup. My new friend nudged me and winked, gesturing towards the speaker. 'Iestyn von Däniken, one of the best. Bang tidy he is, mun. The sort of *manic street preacher* we actually needs, not some bloody lefty in make-up and a frock.' He settled back to enjoy the show. On the stage Iestyn was just getting warmed up.

'We live in great times, my children. Our nation is blessed like no other. Why hold back the full force of our might? The rest of the world curse us whatever we do. Might as well be hung for a sheep as a lamb, as they say up Brynamman way.'

There was scattered applause and cheering. The sirens sounded closer.

'But first we needs to drain the swamp! The Liberal Elite have held sway in Cardiff too long. They preach to us about equality, then fill our cities with immigrants and even worse abominations. In their hellish labs they spawn artificial creatures indiscernible from you or I – walking, talking monstrosities vomited forth to satiate our leader's warped carnal desires. The true Welsh stock are the lost tribe of Atlantis. We must not corrupt our sacred seed!'

'Wanker!' someone shouted from the back. Amongst the cheers there were scattered boos. A nasty fight broke out nearby, but Iestyn wasn't stopping, he was only getting into gear.

'Just as we will not suffer this witchcraft to continue neither will the Sons of Cambria be led by degenerates, feminists and even... LIBERALS! Barry Island wants to shut us down. Look what happened to that traitor – good riddance I say! When the time comes to cast your vote make it count, cast it for the Gorsedd!'

If he was looking to polarise his audience he was doing a good job. Even in my inebriated state I could detect an air of confrontation amongst the throng. Fists were thrown, as well as plastic cups full of amber liquid; I hoped it was only beer. Von Däniken wasn't deterred.

'We need to spread the wealth. The snowflake Taffia down in Cardiff can't block the will of the people for long. We can roll back their globalist agenda. We just needs a leader with the Will to Power! Vote early, vote often, vote Llywsiffer Pendragon!'

But he'd lost the crowd's attention – supporters and detractors alike seemed more intent on rioting than listening to his words. The crowd surged and milled around me like a sweaty human maelstrom. Meat pies, shattered teeth and worse flew past my double-glazed vision. Then something genuinely weird happened. Von Däniken caught sight of me and did a cartoon double take. One bony finger shot out like a wand.

'You – the Chosen One has returned!'

I glanced behind me – nothing but a scene of chaos. It seemed he was speaking to yours truly. Drunk as I was, it seemed rude to hold back now. I held out my hands towards yet another new friend. Iestyn jumped down from the stage and staggered towards me. The TV camera crew followed in his wake, recording his every move. The sirens sounded right upon us.

'The light of destiny burns bright in you, my brother! Your halo is cowing lush!'

Rambling though he might have been, this maniac seemed able to sense my budding genius. I let out a mighty burp and did my best to get him in focus. 'Have you read *The Windy Ninja*? Always good to meet a fan.'

Confusion washed across his face – looking back I can't say I blame him. I did my best to help make things clearer. 'Don't tell anyone, but I'm heir to the Jones Corporation fortune – Isaiah's long-lost grandson from another dimension. Ssssshh!' I tried to put a finger to my lips but only succeeded in poking my eye.

Iestyn opened his mouth as if to speak but never got that far. There was a loud *thunk*, like a high-board diver arriving in an empty pool. The preacher's eyes glazed over, he swayed for a moment, before face-planting before me like a felled oak. A riot policeman in full SWAT gear stood behind him, weighing his nightstick in his gloved hand.

'Move along now, sir. Best not interfere with the due process of law.'

I wasn't about to let this interloper get away with molesting my fan base. I marshalled the full might of my dignity. 'What seems to be the ociffer, problem? This man did nothing wrong.'

The cop raised his gas mask and sighed. He looked bored. 'Ewe trying to be clever with me, butt? We're taking your mate in for questioning. Move aside, unless ewe wants to join 'im, chopsy bugger.'

Drunk I might have been but I knew my rights. 'Does freedom of speech count for nothing round here? Did Magna Carta die... zzzzzz!'

I think he must have tasered me; either that or I fell victim to a localised micro-thunderstorm. Next I knew I was writhing on the floor, every limb doing its own thing, bereft of central control. What they mainly seemed to be doing was striking out for pastures new on their own accord. Through a haze of stars I watched the police cart the unconscious prophet away. The TV crew filmed as much as they could but were soon bundled from the scene. With practised efficiency the cops cleared the park of warring factions. I got the feeling they'd done this before.

As my muscle contractions eased I was overcome by a serene inner calm. I closed my eyes and listened to the sounds of nature – the tweeting of the birds, the rustling of the trees on the breeze from the bay, the departing sirens of the police VTOLs. I sensed a great shifting of internal gears, a moment of catharsis like no other. I was next to the road to the Mumbles, rather than the road to Damascus, but the effect was much the same. If I breathed deeply there was a good chance I'd avoid throwing up again.

As I lay there on the grass a vision formed before my eyes. It was the face of my grandad, Isaiah. The one I knew from home, not the turbo-charged version from over here. I was overjoyed to see those familiar features. But grandad looked far from happy, his ancient, rugged brow sad as he spoke softly in my ear.

'Kev bach, what do you think you're doing with your life? What a mess you've got yourself into.'

It made me ashamed to disappoint him. Deep down I knew he was right. I was squandering what little talent I possessed, always taking the easy path and hoping it would turn out a shortcut. 'I don't know, Grandad. Sometimes it all seems too much. It's not easy being me.'

'Dew, dew, lad – always getting your excuses in early – you've got the Welsh disease proper bad. Time to end the whining. Have a word with yourself, will you. This sort of thing can't go on.'

Stung by Grandad's message I resolved to turn my life around. Compared to the problems he'd faced mine were nothing special. Sure, I was being hunted by multiple teams of crack assassins bent on my destruction, and another mob who wanted to pick my brains apart, but Grandad had been through far worse with nothing but a fag and a cup of milky tea. Starting right then, I resolved to live up to his example. I couldn't wait to tell him the good news.

But a change had come over Grandad, he was no longer the

kindly old man I knew and loved. He shook me roughly, and his tone grew more strident – this wasn't like him at all.

'Kevin, what the hell do you think you're doing!'

His voice had changed too, gone up several octaves, hectoring. 'You trying to get us killed?'

He shook me harder, and I began to think I'd been optimistic about avoiding the sick. Something else odd was happening – Isaiah's face began to swim and morph before my unfocused eyes. His features softened and before I knew it, Gwen was staring down at me.

'Kevin, have you lost your bloody mind?'

16

Safe at Last

Gwen and Juan somehow got me back to the apartment. There might have been a bit of vomit along the way, but the streets of Swansea were no stranger to the pitter-splatter of that gentle carroty rain. By the time Juan dialled us through his fortress-like security lobby I was feeling better; maybe tasering was a good way to sober up. Gwen, on the other hand, was still tamping.

'I can't believe the trouble you've caused! Have you any idea what it's like finding another pisshead in this drunken town? You've shaved years off my life.'

I sagged in her arms. 'How did you track me down?'

She pulled back – I don't think my breath was the sweetest. 'We just followed the trail of chaos. You'd only gone 400 yards – the most pathetic attempt at the Mumbles Mile I've ever seen. Your breath is mingin.'

I could only apologise and try not to throw up in her lap. I didn't think it would help her mood. Meanwhile Juan was being the practical parent. He bundled me out of the lift, stripped off my clothes and dumped me in his shower. I don't think what he saw impressed him much, but I wasn't at my best. His bathroom was big enough for a choir, and the sound system did a great job of recreating one. There was panel to control the lighting effects, and a dial to set the wetness of the water. *Amazonian Monsoon* sounded like me. I slumped on the floor and began the long journey back to my senses as the warm water cleansed my soul.

A lifetime later I was clean and dry. Wearing one of my host's voluminous bath robes I sat at his kitchen table. A wall-sized screen silently carried the lunchtime news. We were trying to work out what to do next. It wasn't easy. Juan took the floor.

'Kevin Amigo, Gwen here has taken it upon herself to see you safe and well. Show her some respect. She is a *serious* individual.'

'Seriously stupid,' muttered the lady in question.

Juan shushed her and went on. 'When she sets her mind to a task she sees it through, to the bitter end. She has requested my aid in this matter. Why fight against us? You put us all at great risk.'

My words struggled past the lump in my throat. 'All I can say is I'm sorry, to both of you. I know I've let you down; Grandad too.'

Gwen snorted. 'That's an understatement. This is like babysitting a toddler.' She would not forget this fiasco in a hurry.

I jumped back in while I had the chance. 'I've been having a serious think about my life choices. I've not been great at taking responsibility. That will change, starting now.'

She looked at me with something close to pity. 'I'm glad to hear it, Kev. Not before time, if you ask me.'

Juan interrupted (maybe he was braver than I knew), 'Gwen

Amiga, at least he is trying. Let us be giving him a chance, no?' Her face softened just a little as our host went on. 'The question is, what is it we are doing with our guest now?'

With impeccable timing the rolling news channel, playing silent on the big screen, chose that moment to intervene. The shot cut to a close-up of the messy denouement of my earlier chat with Iestyn von Däniken in the park that morning. My eyes looked a beautiful shade of blue, if a little glazed. We didn't need the voiceover: a ribbon of text along the bottom gave the images all the context they could need. *Alt-Right Rally Throws Up New Jones Family Claimant.* We each watched the broadcast with a mounting sense of despair. There was no good way to spin this development.

Gwen sounded tired. 'Only you, Kevin, could gatecrash that nutter's latest stunt. This channel is beamed around the world.'

Juan shook his head sadly. 'That man is a living, breathing cunning stunt. *Maligno.*' He brushed his fingers beneath his chin.

Gwen rose to her feet. 'We have to assume our cover here is blown. We've got to move on, but where?'

Juan shifted awkwardly. 'Gwen my friend, there is always that other, of whom we spoke – El Coronel. I don't know if you've heard the rumours?'

Pacing the kitchen, Gwen waved him away. 'That's the last thing we need right now. I thought you told me this is no time for herding lost sheep.'

'No, Amiga. But the Old Man has been claiming some strange things. Some strangely *relevant* things.'

Gwen halted in her tracks. You could almost hear the screeching of brakes. 'Relevant how, exactly?'

Now it was Juan's turn to backtrack. 'Bonita, they are just rumours, but word is he sees visions.'

'What sort of visions?'

Juan seemed reluctant to elaborate. 'The man has gone full Colonel Kurtz. He claims a saviour is coming from another world. A hero who will reverse this nation's malaise. Most dismiss his words as the babblings of a madman. Others flock to hear him speak.'

'A saviour? If he's describing Kev then we're totally fucked.'

Juan was not perturbed. 'He says this messiah is Arthur come again to lead us – the true heir to the House of Jones.'

There was a lengthy silence. Gwen chewed her lower lip. I had to fight to stop myself biting my nails. I felt we had reached a turning point, maybe a crux in history. I thought it best not to mention the queer things Iestyn had said along similar lines. Events were already unfolding way too fast.

Eventually Gwen found her voice. 'I guess – maybe we should pay him a visit. Where can we find him?'

For a moment Juan seemed to wrestle with a dilemma. 'Some say he dwells halfway up Cader Idris, leading his flock in strange hellish rituals not meant to be performed by man. Claims it helps him talk to the spirits. Plus he likes the view.'

I could stand it no longer. 'Who the hell are you talking about – who is this prophet who seems to know so much about me? If he's anything like von Däniken you can count me out of a sit-down chat!'

'So much for taking responsibility.' Gwen rolled her eyes in disgust.

Juan put his hand on my shoulder. 'He calls himself Taliesin these days –'

'– but we knew him by another name.' Gwen had a tear in her eye. 'Once upon a time he was Colonel Frank MacIntyre, Welsh Special Forces, Patagonia Expeditionary. He was our CO.'

It took a moment for the news to sink in. 'You mean the

mad guy with the wooden leg and corned beef addiction? The one you left behind for dead?'

Juan shot me a look of reproach as Gwen looked down at the floor. She nodded. 'The very same.'

I was about to ask if seeking out another deranged lunatic was a good idea – we seemed to have a magnetic attraction for them already – when my train of thought was violently derailed. A series of thumps and bangs reverberated from the roof above, followed by an ominous silence. Three sets of eyes panned slowly to the ceiling. Juan went pale, quite an achievement for someone with his complexion.

'Something just landed on my roof. This is… not so good.'

Gwen made a dash for the floor-to-ceiling windows overlooking the square. She strained to peer first upwards, then down at the city below. I was soon by her side. Far beneath us, at the doors to Juan's establishment, a column of black vehicles pulled up in a haze of dust and scattering pedestrians. Squads of black-carapaced figures poured forth like hungry warrior ants. It appeared the Celtic Fringe was about to get a scalping of its own.

'How long will the doors hold?' Gwen began calmly checking the action of her gun. From beneath the kitchen counter Juan produced some terrifying hardware of his own – a magazine-fed shotgun complete with underslung grenade launcher. For some reason it was bright pink. I scrambled to find my pants.

'Depends how good their forced entry team is.' There was a brace of muffled explosions from above.

'That was the rooftop doors. We have to move, right NOW.'

For the first time in what felt like ages Gwen grabbed me by the arm. It seemed the Consortium, or someone equally unfriendly, had tracked us down again.

17

Cwtch-22

Our predicament did not look good. We were caught between the jaws of a crushing vice, one set of fangs biting down from above, the other grinding up from below. At least I now had my pants on. No man should face death distracted by what flaps between his legs. Gwen looked ready for a fight, no change there, but I didn't think even she fancied our chances of getting out of this one alive. She caught me watching her as she took stock of her remaining ammunition.

'Don't worry, I'll save one last bullet for you. Best not be taken alive.'

'Thanks,' I croaked. If she was trying to make me feel better she was failing spectacularly. I'm the sort of guy who's always thought it best to be taken alive – you can deal with the hideous torture later. On the other hand, self-inflicted headshots tend to be harder to wheedle your way out of. It's all a matter of timing, some things are best put off indefinitely. One day I might accept procrastination is my biggest flaw.

Thankfully Juan was still in a rational frame of mind. You

could almost see the lightbulb appear above his head. 'Wait – there is another way.'

We both looked at him, hope pipping desperation in a photo finish. Our host shouldered his gun and ran towards the balcony doors. 'Follow me, we've not got much time – *ràpido!*'

The penthouse veranda was a wide, sweeping affair, enclosing the apartment on three sides. The doors from the lounge faced eastwards, giving spectacular views across the bay. As we joined him in the fresh air Juan turned left and broke into a dead run, scanning the roof edge above for signs of attack. He led us around the balcony corner and along the length of the north facade, the glowing neon city spread out in the hazy air below. We weaved our way around expensive outdoor furniture and exotic potted plants. The broad balcony ended in a set of white roller doors – a dead end. A fitting metaphor perhaps, but I wasn't impressed.

'Great – is this where we make our last stand? It's hardly the Alamo.' Even the patio furniture had petered out. This section of the walkway was as bare and open as a runway.

The big man gave me a funny look. 'For you my friend, there will be no last stand here today.' Juan punched a button on a panel recessed into the wall. A loud whirring began from some unseen mechanism above our heads. It was not the only sound from that direction – at least one further VTOL was landing on the roof. How long before our uninvited guests gatecrashed the party? Not long, judging by the worried look on Gwen's face.

With a sickening lack of urgency the roller doors trundled open. They revealed a small parking bay, bare walls and concrete floor. Sitting quivering in its midst was a machine the like of which I'd never clapped eyes on, nor could have imagined. My gaze seemed to skid off it, such was its sleek aerodynamic form. It looked like a sinuous, perversely stretched motorbike, stubby wings and jet intakes rounding out its skeletal frame. The contraption's silhouette screamed unmatched speed. It made me travel sick just to look at.

Even at such a moment of high stress Juan couldn't conceal his pride. 'My new toy – the latest Maserati-Boeing model. J-Drive powered plasma jets and designer Italian styling. Highly illegal over the city, but today a traffic cop is the least of your concerns.'

I couldn't have agreed more. Gwen had already sprung onto the sculpted leather saddle, one hand caressing a curving armoured fairing in admiration. 'Will we all fit? There's not much room.'

Juan shook his head sadly. 'My baby is strictly a two-person rig – the leg restraints a much-needed feature. Besides, I shortly have to play the gallant host. I will not have my hospitality besmirched.' He chambered a round into his huge gun.

A sickening realisation was dawning in Gwen's eyes. 'No – we can't leave you behind.'

Juan thrust out his impressive chest. 'Go, Bonita. It is you and the man-child they want. I will negotiate my way out. Of this, you must have no fear.'

She could see there was no other way, and I for one didn't intend to argue. Not long before I would have been all for this puffed-up virtue-signalling buffoon sacrificing himself on my behalf – survival of the fittest, and all that; but now his willingness to play the hero brought a lump to even my throat. Never mind, I was soon crouched behind Gwen struggling with the complexities of the harness system. We were reclined forward at an extreme degree, my sweating face close beside her ear.

'You've flown one of these things before?'

'Not exactly, no.'

'What does that mean, not exactly?' She was doing nothing

to calm my pre-flight nerves. I didn't think even a mint would have helped.

'I attended a seminar back in the military. Should be easy enough – I learn quick.'

If there was a good answer to her stunning disregard for health and safety it momentarily escaped me. I could do nothing but watch in horror as Juan gave the sketchiest of outlines of the flight controls. The stubby, drooped handlebars and twist grips looked like something out of a fighter jet, knobs and dials close to every finger. A bright green holographic HUD booted-up inside the cowling before us, as bands of steel snapped around our legs and feet. There was no turning back now. With an animal howl the mighty engines sprang to life. The whole craft throbbed and vibrated like a volcano waiting to erupt. I wanted to get off, but I wanted to not get shot even more – a moral dilemma if ever there was one.

Above the roar Juan gave his last piece of advice. 'Easy on the throttle. Just like some others I know, she is a flighty mare.'

Gwen hesitated a moment longer. 'Goodbye, my friend. We'll not forget what you've done for us this day.'

Juan put a hand on her shoulder and kissed the top of her head. 'We will meet again, Bonita, have no fear. Now go.' He saluted, and she replied in kind.

There was no time for protracted farewells. The first black-clad figures rounded the far end of the balcony and raced towards us, weapons drawn. Juan took cover as best he could as rounds ricocheted around us. Gwen set her gaze forward and twisted one handle grip. There was a blood-chilling sound, like ripping canvas, as we rocketed from the hangar. If the first squad of assailants hadn't hit the deck we would have taken their heads off. With the merest tilt of the controls Gwen sent us banking out of the veranda and into the crystal blue of the Swansea sky.

Only hazy recollections stay with me of that dreadful flight, perhaps because the brain blocks out excess trauma. We didn't get off to a good start. While barely clear of the overhanging landing pad we grazed a strut bristling with aerials and antennae, a satellite dish shattering in our wake. It only got worse from there. Gwen banked us left and we plunged earthwards, negative G threatening to launch my innards from my screaming throat. We seemed certain to meet the jagged rooftops rushing up towards us – the chasms either side as inviting as a grave. When it came the pull-out was every bit as brutal as the gut-wrenching descent. Blood drained from my head, tunnelling my vision to near blackout. Unconsciousness would have been a relief, but my ordeal was far from over. At least Gwen was proving true to her word – she was indeed a fast learner. But could her skills keep pace with our headlong escape? She was on a learning curve even steeper than our flight plan.

At this low altitude the towering buildings were more densely packed. We hurtled between them like an unguided missile, neon signs and ad hoardings flashing by. I shrieked in panic as we plunged through what turned out to be a giant hologram, my voice lost in the churning air behind us. If Gwen thought her evasive manoeuvres had thrown off pursuit she was sorely mistaken. A blaze of tracer fire flashed across our starboard bow. Straining against the surging forces I glanced over my shoulder – an insect-black craft was upon us, armed figures hanging from it like noxious parasites. Idly I wondered how they held on, until suddenly one of them didn't – cartwheeling through space to pancake against a passing monolith of glass and steel. It seemed our escape would not be straightforward.

Gwen threw us into another eye-watering turn. Colours leached as my vision narrowed; it was like gazing into the abyss. We seemed to skid through the air, over-steering around obstacles and vaulting others with mere inches to spare. Yet more tracer fire riddled our snaking path – their aim was getting better. This mad flight couldn't go on for long, but how could we escape such a determined foe? Perhaps sensing my thoughts Gwen came up with a creative answer. I didn't like it much.

We were flying parallel to a crowded flight lane, a highway in the sky maybe half a mile distant across the rooftops. Craft of every size floated contra-ways through the crackling air. Another flick of Gwen's wrists and we were racing towards them, our collision with the crowded lines only seconds away. Two huge freighters dominated the traffic crossing our path – one heading north, the other south. Gwen aimed at the fast-diminishing gap between their snub noses. I let rip another plaintive shriek; it had no more effect than the first. My deranged pilot twisted the throttle and we accelerated towards our fate, as accurate gunfire rattled off our tail.

There was no way we could make it – the gap was narrowing too fast – any chance of aborting long gone. I braced myself for impact, but it was an impact which never came. We missed the nose of the first freighter by inches, Gwen pulling hard on the controls to get clear of its twin. There was an excruciating screech of metal against metal and a blinding shower of sparks – we'd struck it a glancing blow. Seemingly breaking every law of physics, we made it through to the other side. Our pursuers were not so lucky, if the loud *crump* was anything to go by. Elated, I looked back to see an oily explosion hanging in the air, debris tumbling down like black rain. The two huge freighters slipped past each other, serenely oblivious to the carnage.

But something was badly wrong with our mount. The bike lurched and kicked like a rodeo mule, before righting itself unsteadily. The pitch of the engines changed, and we lost speed. Seconds later we were losing altitude too, Gwen's HUD a mass of flashing red. We were above the river Tawe by this stage, its wide muddy expanse cutting through the city like a brown stain down a cheap suit. Gwen lined us up along its length. I could guess what she had in mind and it filled me with dread. I suppose it was preferable to ending our flight with a fireball amidst the densely packed streets. The dark water rushed up to meet us. I shut my eyes and prayed to the gods of emergency landings. At least I was already in the brace position, almost ready to kiss my arse goodbye.

Such was our speed and low angle of attack we skidded off the surface of the river like a skipping stone, a curtain of spray thrown up behind us. I'm unsure if this was Gwen's intention, but she must have sensed a way out. Gently she angled us down again. The second impact was marginally less jarring than the first, our speed bleeding off at a heartening rate. Was it too much to hope I wouldn't have to do any bleeding of my own? Gwen took us down once again, and this time we barely lifted from the water.

Deceleration threw me against the harness, but we were still travelling at a rate of knots. The Tawe is not a wide river; it snakes through the valley like a crooked scar, with more curves than a Tonmawr hooker. Before us one of those broad turns was fast approaching. It comprised a muddy bank rising to a shanty clutter of scruffy buildings. There was no way we could avoid it; to her credit Gwen didn't try. We departed the river surface one final time and skidded up the slimy shore, ruined shopping trolleys and car wrecks flashing by. The upward gradient helped kill our speed. I could only pray no unseen obstruction killed us first.

I should have trusted Gwen's skill. She guided us in a controlled skid which matched the curve of the embankment precisely. We came to a complete halt just yards from the top of the bluff, foul-smelling steam rising from our overheated craft. The stillness was eerie after the wild sense of motion. Stunned, I realised we were still in one piece. The same could not be said for Juan's precious jet-bike – it had seen better days. The sole remaining headlamp fell off with a wet plop and sank into the mud.

Gwen wasn't one to rest on her laurels. She slapped the quick-release mechanism on my harness and the leg restraints broke free. 'Let's move, we have to get clear of the blast.'

'What blast?' Okay, I'm a repeat offender – by now I should have known better.

Gwen pulled something from her filthy tunic and tossed it inside the bike's yawning intake. Before I could enquire she was hauling me up the slope, past a sad parade of mangled refrigerators and pre-loved sanitary wear. We'd not gone fifty yards before a deafening *thump* rent the air behind us. I turned to see the remains of the jet-bike blazing merrily with an ethereal blue light, before Gwen dragged me back into motion. 'If gawping is your superpower we need to find you a better one.'

I couldn't agree more. We were cold, wet and shaken, we were plastered in stinking oily mud, but we were alive. For the time being, at least.

18

Once upon a Time in Moriston

A short time later we sat in the back room of a ramshackle shop. This part of town was a lot less shiny and new than the waterfront. There were no gleaming skyscrapers and the robots all looked on the point of breakdown, if not breaking bad. Everything was either rusty or on fire, sometimes both – post-apocalyptic, just without the understated charm. It was like Mad Max had got just a little madder and retired to Prestatyn. There were plenty of large rats, some with four legs, many with just the two. In our mud-splattered clothing we fitted right in. I was lost, in more ways than one.

'What are we doing here?'

Gwen looked at me for a long time. 'When you're trying to hide from a murderous all-powerful continent-spanning global deep state conspiracy, what do you do?'

She had baffled me again. 'I don't know, I've not been in this position all that often – maybe try to blend in?'

Gwen seemed to think this proved her point. 'Exactly. That's why the last thing you want to do is *blend in*. In fact you want to look the least like you're trying to blend in as possible. The Russian military call it *maskirovka*, while in the Welsh Special Forces –'

'The Raspberry Berets – I can hear their marching song now.'

'– we called it *cuddio cuddliw*, the art of operational deception – hiding in plain sight.'

'Did you learn this in a seminar too, same way you learned to fly that death trap?'

Gwen looked hurt. 'I think I did a pretty tidy job of piloting, under the circumstances. And no – I learned it in the field, while under fire. Saved my skin more than once, it did. So less of the sarcasm, you chopsy bugger.'

I paused as I took stock of what I'd learned. 'Why the hell are we at war with Argentina, anyway?'

'Who knows anymore – the logic of empire, expand or die.'

'But we invaded them? I mean, I get that the place is ruled by a ruthless military dictatorship, bullying the Welsh diaspora in Patagonia, but it still seems far fetched.'

Gwen pulled a sour face. 'I suppose *technically* that's true. What folk tend to forget is that Argentina had a perfectly passable working democracy right up to the start of the war. A bit corrupt around the edges, but nothing that would make Barry Island blush. The ethnic Welsh were treated no worse than anyone else.'

'So what happened?'

'The Argentine government was toppled under suspicious circumstances. Almost as if someone *wanted* a brutal junta running the show in Buenos Aires. The perfect manufactured enemy. They've played the part very well ever since.'

'So you're saying we pushed them into it? What did we have to gain?'

She looked at me weirdly. 'So it's *we* now, is it? I don't know, I'm just a grunt – was a grunt. I was never privy to what went on in the Head Shed. The politicians make their own rules.'

I suspected she was being modest, but also accepted she knew way more about this than me. Perhaps we needed to reset.

'So we're looking for camouflage? I should warn you I don't look good in green.'

Gwen shook her head in derision. 'We're not looking for that sort of camouflage – too much like blending in. We're going to stand out. That's why we're here. This is a fancy dress shop.'

I wasted a few moments searching for a clever comeback, but was rescued by the proprietor, who stuck his head through the stained curtain behind the counter. He beckoned us through. There was something fishy about him, and it wasn't just his mullet. The back room was packed with stock; rack upon rack of outlandish costumes. You could have run several high-octane mardi gras from the contents.

'So this party we're attending – who should I come as?'

Gwen sighed. 'Do I have to think of everything? I don't know, use some imagination. Who's your favourite *Star Trek* character?'

'Surely they're not going to have Uhura?' Looking around I suspected they probably might. They seemed to have every other monster Kirk had wrestled with on countless cardboard planets from here to the Horsehead Nebula.

Gwen looked genuinely impressed. 'You know, that's not such a bad idea. Here, try this on.' She handed me a dress. 'But we're going to have to shave your legs.'

19

Dai the Flake

So that's how Gwen and I came to be mincing down the main strip of the Swansea Under City, kitted out like a pair of hippy chick Woodstock rejects. The platform heels took some getting used to and I wasn't sure spandex was the fibre for me, but at least I wasn't wearing drab olive green – just most other shades on the spectrum.

'Skid-Mark Row' was a sight to behold. I'd expected to draw my share of attention from the locals, maybe a few wolf whistles, but the denizens of the ghetto paid us scant heed. They'd seen it all before, and most likely done it too. Maybe Gwen's tactics would work after all. My confidence grew and I began throwing my heart, as well as my hips, into the role. My companion was considerably more circumspect.

'Easy, tiger. There's room for too much of a good thing, especially in that dress.'

'Can't see how – there's barely room for me in here.' I struck a pose on a street corner and twirled my purse around a finger until, misjudging the manoeuvre, it spun off into the face of a passing local. He handed it back without so much as a second glance. Gwen paused and checked behind us for pursuit. I remembered we were still on the run.

'So what's the plan, Stan?'

My companion kept it subtle but scanned our surroundings for danger. 'We've got to get out of this mad town. For us, Swansea has become too hot.'

Perhaps the first time those words had ever been spoken, but I had to agree with the sentiment. Anywhere was preferable to here right now. Even Port Talbot suddenly had its appeal. Some like it hot, but I had no desire to be the main course at a barbecue. Apart from anything else my outfit would be a terrible fire hazard.

Content we weren't being watched, Gwen led us across a busy intersection towards what looked like a scruffy mechanic's yard. Half-cannibalised vans and engine parts littered the forecourt. The sign above the door read *Dai Giovanni's Dairy Trade Supplies*.

Not for the first time I was overcome with confusion. 'Wait – what are we doing here? We don't have time for distractions.'

Gwen held open a rickety gate. 'Trust me – this is the best way out of this madhouse. The Consortium will monitor all air traffic. We're going to roll out on four wheels, accompanied by a jaunty tune and a sprinkling of nuts.'

'But no one drives anymore.'

'Exactly. This will be nice and discreet.'

I wasn't convinced. 'You know this guy?'

'We've had dealings in the past, it's true. He's a… contact.'

I didn't like the look of desolation about the place, never mind the smell. 'Let's hope *Dai the Flake* doesn't turn out to be *Dai the Death*. You trust him?'

Gwen adjusted my dress. 'About as far as you could throw

127

him, and he's a big bugger. But he's all we've got to work with. Gotta warn you now, he's so far in the closet he's almost in Narnia. Come on.'

We entered the equally decrepit office, to be greeted by that unmistakable French supermarket whiff of slightly gone-off milk. A greasy teenager slouched behind the counter reading a magazine – *Gelato Digest*. He didn't look up.

'Hiya, what's occurin?'

Zero bushes were beaten around by my companion. 'Is he in? Tell him Wanda needs a fast job – for cash. He knows who I am.'

The youth slid from his stool and pocketed the magazine. Frowning, he looked me up and down with his one good eye, the other heading off on safari round the room. The lad didn't seem impressed.

'I'll see if the boss is in.'

He disappeared through a frosted glass door behind the counter. From the workshop came the sound of thunderous banging and the occasional curse. The youth didn't try to lower his voice. 'Couple of tarts here to see you, Dai.'

'Well tell em to bugger off and ply their trade elsewhere. What do I pay ya for?'

'You don't pay me nothing, Dai. Mam said I have to help out.'

'Well, what does they want?'

'Don't look the sort to mess with – couple of real mingers. One of em says she knows ya – goes by the name of Wanda.'

There was a sudden clatter, as if a large spanner had been dropped. Seconds later Dai filled the doorway, a big-bearded man wiping his oily paws in a rag. He looked wary.

'Wanda, always a pleasure. To what does we owe this honour?'

Gwen got straight down to business. 'We need a set of

wheels – nothing fancy, but enough to get out of town in one piece. Can you deliver?'

Dai's brows furrowed, two hairy caterpillars making out. 'For the right price, I can deliver. They call me the Mail Man, and not just cos I wears shorts in unsuitable weather. Who's your cute friend, by the way?' He seemed more impressed with me than his young apprentice.

I thought it best to stay in character, even if my voice was all over the place. 'I'm Havana – Havana Goodtime, pleased to meet you, Mr Giovanni.' I fluttered what lashes I could muster. Gwen must have slipped because she kicked me in the ankle, quite hard.

'I'll do the talking, numbnuts,' she whispered.

Dai seemed to brighten. 'As it appens I've got a sweet little Bedford number just been refurbished. She's out back, all yours for 5K. Care to take a look?' He ushered Gwen through to the workshop.

I was left cooling my platform heels in the waiting room. A TV above the counter carried the latest news. The recent terrorist attack in Swansea dominated the headlines. Apparently a condo above Castle Square had been targeted in a foiled hijacking, which had turned into a kamikaze VTOL raid. Local plod was on the case, so all were sure they'd get to the bottom of events – maybe by this time next year. Meanwhile CSI Llansamlet were busy trawling the river for the last two insurgents, both presumed dead. I doubted our mystery attackers would be so easily fooled.

In other news the election campaign of hospital-bound President Barry Island continued to go badly – seemed near-martyrdom would only get you so far. Capitalising on the opportunity, his political opponents had pulled ahead in the polls, this time maybe for good. The glowering form of the Gorsedd Party's charismatic leader, Llywsiffer Pendragon, could be seen rousing a party rally packed with baying druids. It seemed certain the Republic was heading for a change of leadership.

With a start I realised Dai had returned on his own. He was standing very close to me, too close. The smell of yesterday's yoghurt and WD-40 filled my flaring nostrils. He looked me up and down ever so slowly and licked his blubbery lips. At least, for the time being, he wasn't licking mine.

'Tidy little number. Gender fluid are we?'

I didn't like the glint in either of his lazy eyes. 'I don't think so chief, but if there is any I promise to mop it up.' Backing up against the counter I wanted to make it clear I wasn't *that sort of girl*, in fact I wasn't any sort of girl at all. My questionable virtue was saved by Gwen's breathless return.

'It needs a new compressor for the refrigeration unit, but we'll take it. How much stock can you let us have?'

I was taken aback. 'Wait – we're taking ice cream? What's the point in that?'

She looked at me as if I was *twp*. 'Of course we're hauling merchandise, all part of the cover.'

Dai seemed to think it a reasonable request. 'I can throw in half a ton of rum and raisin, maybe a bit of haddock. The laverbread ripple always sells well up north.'

There was a tense pause. Gwen's tone remained level but her gaze held a hint of steel.

'What makes you think we're heading north?' The pair locked eyes for an uncomfortable moment. I was aware of a bead of sweat running down my neck to where my cleavage should have been. At last Dai flinched and looked away.

'Just a guess. Every bugger seems to be 'eadin north these days, just as the country's 'eadin south. Place is totally ffwced if you ask me. I'll go sort out that compressor.'

Dai slipped away as Gwen started counting out the cash. It

looked like we had a set of wheels, not to mention a sugary frozen disguise. Grandad's smiling face gazed up at me from the mounting pile of bank notes. He looked happier than I felt.

Within the hour we were almost ready to roll. Gwen and I helped Dai load up our new transport; I never knew the ice cream trade was so involved. Gwen explained there were still uses for old-style wheeled vehicles – ice-cream vans being chief amongst them. Apparently something in the field given off by a running J-Drive caused dairy products to go off at a rate of knots. Our machine was a relic from a bygone age, a rolling antique. Faded images of lollies, long since licked away to nothing but a stick, plastered the cracked glass beside the serving hatch. The formica counter was chipped and worn, Turin Shroud-like images of Jesus swirling across its beige expanse. The van itself was a shade of pink which made my eyeballs water. 'MIND THAT CHILD!' screamed the sign at the back – you'd be lucky to see them against the glare. We certainly wouldn't be blending in.

Before long we were ready to go. Gwen hopped in the driver's seat and I took my place by her side. As usual I had my share of misgivings.

'Are we sure this contraption will start?'

Before she could answer Dai popped up at my open window. He had been keen to give me a guided tour all day long, but I'd avoided this dubious honour, along with his wandering hands.

'As it appens this ere is the pinnacle of British engineerin. State of the art back in 1972, she was. Show some bleedin respect, Miss Havana.' He ran a gnarled hand lovingly along the sill.

I forced a smile. 'That's what I'm worried about. Will we get to the end of the road?'

He rested his big, hot hand on my bare forearm, dead casual like. 'Don't worry, luv. If you breaks down I'll spring to the rescue.' His wink threatened to curdle our precious stock. I pulled my arm back from the window, but Dai wasn't finished yet. He looked over at Gwen.

'Greatest trade in the world, the ice cream game. Beats hairdressing any day. That can be a messy business.'

They locked eyes one last time; on this occasion it was the girl who looked away first. Dai smirked. It wasn't a pretty sight.

'You pair are more *Miss Whiplash* than *Mr Whippy*. Don't reckon you'll be short of customers. Good luck up north.'

'We'll see,' said Gwen, as she started the engine. The machine coughed like a bronchitic miner, before spluttering into life. All that remained was to test the all-important musical chime. The creaking melody wound up slowly, as tuneful as a brick, before racing towards a speedy conclusion beyond my range of hearing. I guessed deaf kids and dogs would be key parts of our sales demographic.

Gwen eased us out of the workshop and onto the deserted road. In the dented wing mirror I watched Dai wave us his fond farewells. We turned a corner and glided out of sight. We were soon leaving the bright lights of Swansea far behind. Would we slip away from our pursuers so easily?

20

How Green Is My Silicon Valley

Do stainless steel rats dream of electric sheep? Maybe they do if they're built in the gleaming android factories of Pontardawe. There were certainly plenty of sheep grazing the hillsides as we drove up the winding valley road. Gwen told me the animals were kept for cosmetic purposes, living a bucolic existence amidst the picturesque pastures and fields. The gambolling lambs could bet on a life of peace and quiet; seems I wasn't destined to do the same.

We drove at a steady pace up the deserted mountain highway. I was struck by how little the bustling sprawl of the mega-city on the coast penetrated this hinterland. If you ignored the streams of silent flying craft cruising above the distant hills you could almost believe you were back in a saner time and place. Oh for the comforting embrace of my mundane version of Aberdare. Would I ever feel her suffocating arms again?

Was it possible I was experiencing a sense of *hiraeth* for my drab home town? That peculiarly Welsh form of homesickness that usually manifested through dodgy poetry and a lot of pro-level moping about. Not very likely, in a dynamic go-getter like me. It was probably just that I was missing Grandad. This evening should have been one of our regular film nights. Over the previous year I'd introduced him to a selection of classics from my DVD collection. Up at the care home, for a small fee, you could rent one of the trolley-mounted TV rigs that trundled from room to room. Grandad had sat patiently through *Aliens* and *Apocalypse Now*, oohing and aahing at all the right places. But once the shooting started invariably he'd become quiet and withdrawn. In retrospect I could now see that, given his personal history, maybe these weren't the best choices for our viewing pleasure. Gramps had said he'd order in a few movies of his own. He was going to blow my mind, he said. Next week we'd watched *Twelve Angry Men* and *Casablanca*. My head still ringing from these twin detonations, I'd had to admit maybe he had a point. Happier times. Sad that it was taking this road trip to hell to make me appreciate the old fellow. I vowed one day to make it up to him. At least Gwen was in better spirits.

'Cheer up, kiddo. Take a look at that view – magnificent, don't you think.'

I wasn't about to let myself be cheered up. 'Nice, if you like that sort of thing.'

'Well I do like that sort of thing. When life can be snatched away in an instant you've got to take time to smell the roses. You get to appreciate that in my line of work. What's eating you?'

It wasn't easy to put my feelings into words. 'I just don't see a way out of this mess. The guy we're going to visit – do you really think he can help?'

I was glad Gwen didn't take her eyes off the twisting road. 'I won't lie to you, I don't have a clue – but he'll have as good a chance as any. As we learnt back in Swansea he's been spouting some weird stuff. Seems to know a lot about you. I want to find out how.'

'Yeah, weird. Did the Colonel show any talent for prophecy before… you know –'

We picked up speed and Gwen's tone darkened. 'Not in the slightest. I've got a few questions I want to ask him of my own. Scores to settle, you could say.'

I pushed myself back in the seat as the mountain sides flashed by. 'Let's just make sure we get there in one piece, yeah.' If only the road were as wide as my eyes.

Gwen eased off the accelerator and released a deep breath. 'What harm can a little chat do, a catch-up on old times? You got any better ideas?' I shook my head furiously, afraid to say the wrong thing. Gwen wasn't letting me off the hook.

'But that's not all that's bothering you. Spill it.'

I did my best to explain. Despite what she'd told me crossing the Atlantic, I was finding it hard to accept this tiny backwater of a country had grown to dominate the world, earth-shattering inventions or no. The fact Wales had done it in 'most other universes' didn't make it any easier to accept; quite the reverse. Back on the boat the revelations had come thick and fast, I'd just accepted them one by one. In the cold, harsh light of day they were sounding far fetched, if not totally unconvincing. Gwen heard me out and pondered her answer.

'You have to understand nation states are less powerful here than in your world, though yours is heading that way too. The big multinat corporations hold all the aces. Remember we're a smidge ahead of you guys, in more ways than one.'

'Yeah, I noticed that. So why does it pan out that way?'

'Money talks, and I don't know if you've noticed but old-fashioned physical states don't tend to turn a profit. Whereas corporations…' she left it hanging. 'And if they don't like the local climate they can just pack up sticks and relocate to a lower tax jurisdiction.'

'Okay, I get your point. But what's that got to do with Wales running the show?'

'Well, Wales is basically run by Jones Corp, the most profitable private company in history. The Republic's a corporate state without even the hindrance of publicly traded shares – no pesky AGMs. The Jones family have set themselves up with a pretty sweet deal.'

'What about the election?'

'They pay lip service to democracy but the structure's basically feudal – with your Uncle Genghis sat puffing a fat cigar at the top. Presidents serve at his beck and call. Barry Island's so far in his pocket he must be in danger of running out of air.'

'He's not my uncle,' I muttered. 'At least, not the version over here.'

But Gwen wasn't listening. 'And of course Wales has certain other inbuilt advantages?'

'Really? I can't think of any off the top of my head.'

'Well for starters there's the flag. That's a massive positive right there.'

She could see I didn't look convinced. I was relieved when she got her eyes back to the road.

'Modern geopolitics plays out in the court of public opinion. It's not all about smart bombs and tanks. These days soft power is where it's at.'

'What's that got to do with flags?'

'The downside of being a superpower is you step on lots of toes. The little guys always want to bring you down. But however good their campaign against you they need something to latch onto. Angry crowds need to burn your flag in the street, all played out for 24-hour rolling news.'

I thought back to all the flag burnings I'd seen on TV. I had to admit they were pretty effective. Stamping your enemy's effigy into the dust never grew old. A double whammy guaranteed to whip your own population into a frenzy, and show the strength of your feeling to a watching world.

Gwen continued. 'Well, first you need a flag – or rather a bedsheet painted to look like the symbol of the chosen Great Satan. The problem the Yanks and Brits had was their flags were too easy to copy – too many straight lines.'

If I squinted really hard maybe I could see the beginnings of her point. 'Too… many… straight lines?'

'Exactly! Now, have you ever tried drawing a dragon? Ever attempted it on a torn bed sheet using third world art supplies? Good luck with that. You'd have more chance reproducing the Sistine Chapel.'

I thought back to my own schoolday efforts, a thousand St David's Day posters watered by bitter tears of frustration – and I was one of the kids good at art. A snarling crimson cat was about the closest I ever came to *Y Draig Goch*. How an angry Arab mob would fare I didn't want to imagine. I threw Gwen some case studies. 'Star of David?'

'Way too easy. Israel has no chance.'

'Hammer and Sickle?'

'Ditto – bye bye, Soviet Union. When it comes to Wales the opposition can never pull it off. The crowd just gives up and goes home in disgust. Nothing cools the fury of a baying mob like substandard artwork.'

I had to admit perhaps there was something here; maybe Pax Cambria wasn't so far fetched. I gazed out the window at the passing hillside, towering robot harvesters moving through the trees like graceful giants. 'But what about the English? They kept a tight boot on our neck for centuries, how did they let it slip?'

Gwen snorted. 'The Sais had problems of their own – the economic wheels came off. The UK was effectively a city state with an unusually large hinterland. When London struck off on its own the rest fell apart pretty quick. Power vacuums get filled.'

'So Wales saw its chance and was gone?'

'Precisely. Powered by the gentle hum of a million J-Drives. Plenty of unlikely nations have punched above their weight – the Dutch, Portuguese and Venetians all had their fifteen minutes of fame. Why not us?'

'But where are those empires now? They didn't last.'

'Empires never do, and neither will this one. All's not right with the mighty Jones Corporation. There's something rotten at its core.'

Now it was my turn to scoff. 'Remember I'm on first name terms with Genghis, or at least his alter ego. You don't have to try hard to convince me something fishy is going on, but what?'

'No one knows for sure. There's rumblings – some think the writing's already on the wall.'

'And what does this particular graffiti say?'

Gwen sighed. 'The usual story – when you grow too fast there's always winners and losers – and the losers aren't going to take it lying down forever. The Gorsedd have tapped into that sentiment. They've convinced plenty they deserve a bigger slice of the pie – our very own populist backlash.'

I was getting one of my headaches again. 'That's another thing I don't get. In my world the nationalists are a bunch of warm and fuzzy tree-huggers. How did they turn into the toxic variety you've got over here?'

Gwen shrugged. 'Once the stakes got raised by Wales's growing power, external influences came into play. The Gorsedd sprang up out of nowhere almost overnight. There are rumours they're backed by foreign cash, but nothing's ever been proven.'

Gwen explained how the Republic was born with the highest of ideals. How Isaiah and the other Founding Uncles tried to build a minimalist state, not perfect, but *good enough* – pragmatism winning out over dogma at every turn. Nothing quite like it had ever been tried before. They were aiming for a streamlined government, as sleek and understated as one of the new Anthracite-powered sky-ships floating off the production lines. There was a glint in her eye as she finished.

'They wanted this country to go about its business with its head down, staying out of trouble. Certainly no foreign entanglements, not even with the best of intentions. A nation without nationalism.'

'And they pulled it off?'

'They did a fair job at first, but it could never last. When the influence and money came flooding in, the state bureaucracy grew. *The Welsh Disease* – corruption and nepotism at every turn. Human nature doesn't change. The leaders we have today would make the Founding Uncles spin in their graves.'

'Barry Island and his puppet masters.'

'The very same. But it only gets worse from there. Barry's trough feeders are getting kicked out and replaced by the Gorsedd – led by their demagogue Llywsiffer Pendragon. Meddling in world affairs won't be enough for him. He wants a thousand-year Reich – without the laughs but with more leeks. Why settle for influence when you can have crushing supremacy. The druids are set to crush all opposition beneath their open-toed sandals.'

It all sounded depressingly bleak. 'And these lovely chaps are going to win the election?'

'Looks that way, yes. The Jones Corporation has brought unimagined wealth to this country, but it's never been evenly spread. Enough of those who think they've missed out can get the Gorsedd elected. Not good for the likes of me.'

I looked at her sharply. 'Likes of you? You're not an immigrant, you're as Welsh as a rain-damp sheep. What do you have to fear from the Gorsedd?'

Gwen turned her big moist eyes on me. 'Kev, I don't know if you've noticed, but I'm *enhanced*.'

Well this was a revelation. 'Enhanced? They look real enough to me, move that way too. Are you telling me you're sporting a couple of artificial milkers?'

Gwen saw where I was looking and shook her head in exasperation. 'Not those, you numbskull. Maybe we should talk about this another time.'

I knew better than to push her when she was in this mood. Instead I sat and pondered my unhappy thoughts. We sped ever northwards, but what were we travelling into? The sky above the mountains looked bleak and grey. It was starting to rain.

21

Woolly Jumper at Coelbren Falls

We laid up for the night in a picnic area just inside the Beacons National Park. Our van came with some hidden extras – Gwen found a couple of musty sleeping bags stuffed behind a box of cones. They didn't smell that great but they were better than shivering through the cold night. We arranged them on the peeling linoleum back of the cab and settled down for the evening. It wasn't luxurious, but it would have to do. We were both shattered. After the stress of the day's adventures I slept like a log, nightmares of jet-bikes and crash landings racing through my head.

I awoke to the pale grey light of dawn. There was no sign of Gwen, but a note taped to the dash told me she had gone to the village in search of wholesome food. We still had a long drive ahead of us to Cader Idris, and I was already sick of ice cream cones. I climbed out of the van and stretched in the cool morning air, a jagged line of the first proper mountains blue against the distant horizon. I told myself I'd feel better when

Gwen got back. I wasn't used to being on my own; made me uneasy.

Our parking spot was a small lay-by nestled amidst trees at the top of a tall cliff – a minor tributary of the Tawe tumbling over the rocks in a petite but spectacular waterfall. The roar filled the surrounding countryside and had serenaded us all night long, but we'd not been able to see it in the dark. Absentmindedly I wandered down the path from the car park to take a look. Gwen was right, it was best to take every chance to smell the roses – you never knew when it would be your last.

There were few people around that morning. The occasional dog walker passed me by, but other sightseers were in short supply. The snaking path ended at a metal rail close to the head of the falls, its peeling surface slick with slime and spray. I glanced over at the jagged rocks far below – I don't have a head for heights. Cold moisture hung in the glistening air. If there'd been sunshine we might have had a rainbow, but the brooding overcast sky wasn't ready to play ball.

That was when I spotted him. He was standing the other side of the railing on a broad slab of granite overlooking the falls. Something about his posture made me uneasy. I didn't get the impression he was here to admire the view. Against my better judgement I moved towards him along the rail. As I got closer I could see he was peering over the edge of the overhang at the sharp rocks below – maybe only a hundred feet, but it was enough to do some serious damage. Was he going to jump? My stomach turned at the thought.

If I'm honest I'd have to admit that I'm not always a man of action. You might not have noticed but I can be a bit of a coward at times. Hard to believe, I know, but you'll have to take me at my word. No matter how courageous I appear on the surface I'm often screaming inside. And yes, I do *sometimes* do some actual screaming, but take it from me, that's nothing compared to what's going on in my head. Maybe that's what true courage really is.

What I'm saying, in a roundabout way, is I'm not a big fan of putting myself at risk for others. So what I did next took even me by surprise. Something flipped – I couldn't stand this nonsense any longer. Perhaps my recent experiences gave me a new appreciation for the value of life, even when it wasn't my own. No matter what he'd been through this maniac had nothing on me – didn't he know what I'd been through? How dare he. I climbed over the slippery barrier determined for a chat.

I realised at once I wasn't dressed for the occasion. The cold rock ledge was slick with spray, wholly unsuited to my footwear. I kicked off my platform heels and inched forward barefoot. The guy was mumbling something repeatedly, but in the roar of the falls it wasn't easy to hear. I was going to have to get close.

'Alright mate, how's it going?'

He didn't look around. He was an enormous man, hunched at the shoulders as well as hunched inside. Silvery moisture clung to his beard giving him a magical look – a mythical Green Man turned blue at the lips.

'Gone, it's all gone. Generations of work swept away.'

I could tell this would not be easy. 'Why don't you tell me all about it – before you do anything hasty, like.' I put a hand on his shoulder. I don't know what I was thinking, but it felt right.

His reaction was immediate. He spun round and swept me up in a crushing bear hug that squeezed the air from my lungs. For a horrible second we tottered on the brink, me wheezing like bagpipes, him weeping like an oversized child. The blackness filling my vision threatened to become permanent. I tried not to think about jagged rocks and broken bones.

'Let's talk about it first,' I managed to rasp, between his wracking sobs. His grip loosened a little and he looked down at me for the first time.

'Aye, maybe we should, at that.'

He dropped me, too close to the edge for comfort, but at least I'd avoided suffocation. My new friend sank to his knees and plunged his shaggy head in his big hands. 'Gone, it's all gone.'

I won't bore you with the details. Suffice to say it was the usual sad tale of a farm fallen on hard times. One of the big agro-corporations made him an offer for his land, but it was barely enough to pay off the mortgage. Wife and kids were long gone, driven away by his drinking and bouts of thunderous depression. I couldn't say I blamed them, but kept this observation to myself. What chance did this poor guy have of starting afresh, with all the unskilled jobs done by Patagonian migrants or robot labour? I felt bad for him, but could offer no practical advice. The weird thing was it didn't seem to matter – he just wanted someone to listen. I don't think anyone had done that for a while.

We sat and talked for maybe an hour, our feet dangling over the edge of the precipice. We were both wet through and chilled to the bone but it felt refreshing. Once you got used to it the view of the drop wasn't so bad. It's amazing what the human mind can adjust to when you have no other choice. I could sense a crowd had gathered behind us along the rail, and felt their eyes upon me. Time to wrap things up.

'So you see, Dillwyn, all life is basically suffering. Any impression to the contrary is strictly temporary. As Leee John once sang, *It's just an illusion.*'

'Aye, what? Who?'

'There's always going to be winners and losers. Hierarchies are inevitable – something to do with lobsters.'

He looked at me in wonder; I don't think he'd ever met a philosopher before. 'Kev Bach, you're so wise. Where did you learn all this shit?'

I tried to remain humble. 'YouTube is a great resource. Just don't read the comment sections, they're enough to tip anyone over the edge.' Perhaps not the best choice of words considering our current predicament. Dillwyn sprung to his feet and grabbed me by the arm.

'So we're going to jump together!' he clamped me to his side. My god, but he was strong – as was his sheep dip-inspired aroma. But I didn't have time to gag.

'No!' I cried, as a gasp went up from the assorted onlookers. 'Let's not do anything rash.'

Dillwyn's brows furrowed. 'But you said all life is suffering. What's the point carrying on once you realise that?'

I wracked my brain for any distraction, some flaky bit of cod psychology to help reel him in. It wasn't easy, what with him squeezing the life out of me and the drop looming before my eyes. Inspiration came like a thunderclap.

'You've got to compare yourself to who you are today, not to who someone else was yesterday,' I just about stammered.

The big man looked down at me in confusion. 'What the ffwc does that mean?'

I took the opportunity to slip gently from his grasp. 'Come on, Dillwyn, let's move towards the rail.' I inched us backwards towards the straining crowd behind us; they were only feet away.

Dillwyn's craggy brow creased in concentration. 'How can you… surely… you *are* who you are today? That makes no bloody sense, mun.'

But now we were within range of a forest of grasping hands.

A chap in Mountain Rescue gear got hold of Dillwyn and didn't let go; another helped him onto the safe side of the barrier, the big man muttering and distracted all the while. I climbed over next, with no shortage of helping hands. No one made any comment about my flowery apparel, for which I was most grateful. There was a spontaneous round of applause. Gwen was there, holding two takeaway coffees, long since gone cold, a gobsmacked expression on her face. She might have had a tear in her eye, it was hard to tell in the mist.

A short time later I sat in the tailgate of the Mountain Rescue truck, wrapped in a silvery blanket and sipping warm, sweet tea. Dillwyn had been taken away in an ambulance, still confused but safe. I sensed a presence and looked up. Gwen stood silent, regarding me with a peculiar expression.

'Impressive, Kev. I didn't know you had it in you.'

I did my best to sound casual. 'Oh, it's nothing – I do that sort of thing all the time.'

I paused, to give space for the compliments to continue. When Gwen finished laughing I realised it wasn't going to happen, so filled in the details myself, mostly keeping the bitterness out of my voice. 'Since you ask, I couldn't stand to see another wasted life – couldn't have lived with myself if I'd done nothing and watched him jump. Just how I roll.'

She wiped her eyes and continued to peer at me oddly. I'd never seen Gwen look at me this way; perhaps it was a new-found respect. She roused herself with a shudder. 'Still, pretty brave all the same. Well done you.'

I quite liked where this was going, so turned up my smile to eleven. 'Maybe you're rubbing off on me – now there's a pleasant thought.'

She chuckled again and grimaced. 'Come on, hotshot. We need to get going if we're gonna keep the light.'

22

Fromage Frayed

What remained of that day passed on the drive up to Cader Idris, home to the mountaintop retreat of the wild-eyed prophet now known as Taliesin. Gwen knew him by another name – Colonel Frank MacIntyre, her one-time commanding officer, Welsh Special Forces, Raspberry Beret and hero of Fray Bentos. As we steadily gained altitude I fought against a growing sense of unease. We had no clue what sort of reception we would receive. Last time Gwen had seen him she'd left him shattered and broken for their Argentine pursuers to devour. Sanity was a fleeting mirage, a rare and exotic bird once flown not easily nailed back onto its perch. Who knew what the ordeals he'd suffered had done to his creaking mind. I wasn't keen to find out.

We stopped off in Aberystwyth, famed the world over for its drunken students and morose private detectives. We saw no sign of either, parked up on the windswept esplanade. What we did see was a roaring trade in laver-ripple cones and rocket-lollies, tourists and locals alike forming a disorderly queue. The only crimes we witnessed that day were against propriety, one tipsy denizen propositioning me as I leaned through the serving hatch touting my wares – *How much for a sixty-nine, luv?* I snapped his flake in half and sprinkled it over the glistening dome of his dairy-based midday treat. He shut up and moved on after that; so did we.

It was a journey like no other. As we climbed back into the hills I sensed we were leaving the thin veneer of civilisation behind, each passing mile taking us further away from the rational, and deeper into the slumbering ancient heart of darkness. We were heading into druid country.

Late that afternoon we pulled into the deserted parking lot of a quiet roadside diner. We were just past the village of Tal-y-Llyn, overlooking the watery expanse of Llyn Mwyngil. This was the closest we could get to the summit of Penygader – the majestic crown of Cader Idris – via the road. Gwen assured me it wasn't far, but this was a girl happy to jog 10k before breakfast and then do some push-ups, so I wasn't holding out much hope for a leisurely stroll through the woods and vales. The restaurant was a rarebit speciality joint, one of many around these parts. '*The Homage to Fromage*' offered a smorgasbord of cheese-based cuisine. I could feel my arteries hardening just reading the menu, as the waitress wobbled over to take our order. She might have been coming to take our souls. Undecided, I felt the need to stall for time.

'What's the Llanddewi Brefi Special?'

She cast a critical eye over my garb and took a break from her relentless gum chewing. 'Foot-long hot dog smothered in the best Caerphilly. Nestled between coupla Scotch eggs. Bloomin lush, it is mun. Should be right up your back alley, luv, by the looks of things.'

Self-consciously I adjusted my dress, it was starting to chaff in several sensitive places. 'What's the soup of the day?'

'Stilton.'

'Should have guessed.'

Gwen had heard enough. 'We'll have the Rarebit Sharing Platter for four please, extra leeks. Plus a side order of chips and curry sauce.'

'What ewe drinking, luv?'

'We'll have the Builder's Tea El Grande, three sugars apiece.'

Chewing once more, the waitress snorted and waddled off. My companion saw the way I was peering across the table at her, one eyebrow raised. She shrugged. 'We're going to be needing our carbs. Don't know when we'll eat again.'

I had to admit I was famished. Our banquet arrived and we tucked in like dervishes. It wasn't the *best* meal I'd ever experienced, but it certainly filled me up. Who knew what trials lay ahead? I suspected my next visit to the bathroom would be an odyssey all in itself. But never mind my bowels, there was something I needed to get off my chest.

'What did you mean when you said you were enhanced?'

Gwen looked at me for a long time. 'You've seen the things I can do. How do you think that's possible?'

'I don't know – good genes maybe? Training? You're the embodiment of the Welsh master race. I certainly wouldn't chalk it up to your diet.'

Gwen's expression remained flat. 'You're closer than you'd think about the genes. My genetic make-up is a carefully selected cocktail from every corner of the globe. Cherokee, Russian, Berber, Oz Aborigine, a spot of Welsh – I've got the lot.'

'Aborigine?'

'Yeah, you should see what I can do with a boomerang.'

I thought long and hard about how to phrase my next question – I didn't want to cause offence. 'Are you telling me your mum got around a bit? I know how these things are done in certain parts of Swansea. Did she live close to the docks?'

Gwen didn't bat an eyelid. 'What if I told you I didn't have a mam or a dad?'

All of a sudden the gorgonzola was repeating on me. 'I know you were raised in an orphanage, but you obviously had a mum and dad *at some point*. Everyone does.'

'Not everyone – I didn't. My mother was a test tube, my father was a knife. The childhood memories I have of growing up in the Llansamlet ghetto were implanted. I never played hopscotch in the Projects – those memories are a pit prop for my sanity.'

I tried shaking my head, but it didn't seem to help. 'I'm afraid you've lost me again. You'll have to spell it out.'

'I wasn't born, I was created at Jones Corp's Cybernetics Labs in Moriston. Timestamped the stroke of midnight, Saint David's Day. I'm what's known as an Artificial Person, or AP.'

Now this piqued my interest. 'Are you telling me you're some sort of cyborg? All silicone and latex and stuff? Can I fiddle with your dials?' This was getting seriously kinky AF.

'You can take your eyes off those, buster.' She reached across the table and put one slender finger under my chin, to raise my gaze back to eye level. 'I'm no android, I'm as flesh and blood as you are, maybe more so. I just didn't have the same start in life – that's all.'

'And this explains why you can kick the living shit out of James Bond with one foot tied behind your back?'

'Pretty much so, yes. When genes are chosen in the optimum arrangement, human potential can go quite high. I'm living proof of that. You normies are just a train wreck of bad recessives. Holds you back, it does.' Gwen must have seen the way my mouth was hanging open. 'You asked, so I told you. Put your tongue away, kiddo.'

With an effort I composed myself. 'So what did you mean when you said the Gorsedd getting elected was *not good for the likes of you?*'

She took a deep breath. 'Apart from not being great for anyone in the long run, the Gorsedd have promised to do away with me and my kind. They see us as abominations created through witchcraft. They're unclear how they'll achieve this, but I'd imagine it involves a one-way trip to the incinerator. Nice people.'

'But isn't that mass murder?'

'Well, Llywsiffer and his boyos don't think of it as murder – according to them we don't have a soul. Amazing what the mind of a religious zealot can justify, even in this day and age. Do you want that last chip?'

I pushed my plate towards her. There was little doubt Gwen ate like a human: she couldn't half pack it away. 'How many of *your kind* are there exactly?'

'Hard to say,' she muttered around a mouthful. 'We're not talking more than a few thousand – APs don't come cheap. But the technology's moving along apace, much like everything else round here.' She chased cheese grease around my plate with the last chip.

'Yeah, I noticed. Are the rest of them like you?'

Gwen shook her head. 'Not in the least. I was an experimental model – the prototype for a new military line. They really pushed the boat out with me – an expensive date.'

I thought back to all the times I'd had a front row seat to working demonstrations of Gwen's lightning-fast reflexes, never mind her unerring aim. 'So why didn't they put you into production?' I tried not to picture what destruction an army of Gwens could do.

She licked her salty fingers. 'When you make an AP with a functioning intellect you risk rendering it unusable. The brain's the hardest bit to get right. Self-awareness in a non-human entity comes with the risk of a cartload of neuroses – suicidal tendencies at best, psychotic at worst, some even end up genocidal. That's genocidal towards you meatheads, not us.'

'Beg pardon?'

She spoke slowly. 'We tend to go round the bend at the drop of a hat – mentally unstable.' Gwen rapped herself on the head with a knuckle. 'It's the same reason they keep the androids as dumb as a brick. Just barely able to do the job for which they're intended. Wastage is not good for the bottom line.'

Maybe I was beginning to understand. 'Threw away the mould,' I muttered.

'Something like that, yes. Though it was more a vat of amniotic fluid in my case. So that's why most of my crèche-mates are designed with the IQ of a houseplant. No one wants to get shot in the face for the sake of a slightly cheaper cappuccino.'

There was a long pause as I let it all sink in. 'So what are the others used for?'

Gwen looked sad. 'We're considered expendable, ripe for the sort of job no sane normie would contemplate. Many are employed in space exploration – life expectancy measured in weeks – or down here on earth for more... mundane tasks.'

'I'm guessing you don't mean the DVLC?'

She looked me straight in the eye. 'They're used as doxies – sex slaves for the rich and famous, if you must know.'

I was feeling more than a touch nauseous, and miraculously it had nothing to do with what I'd recently eaten. No wonder so many of Gwen's brothers and sisters ended up stripping their gears. A life of slavery and/or violent death didn't sound much fun. My companion studied my facial expression and leaned in close.

'So next time you go off on one about what a pain in the

arse your family is, just remember some of us don't have that luxury. Some of us are very much on our own.'

The lump that rose in my throat had nothing to do with my recent cheese-based ordeal. 'Sometimes I feel like I'm on my own.'

Gwen's gaze didn't waver. 'Well, you're not. You have a mam who loves you. From what you've told me she raised you pretty much on her own, and you didn't turn out a *complete* disaster – so I'm sure she can't be as clueless as you sometimes make out. Maybe you should try giving her a break.'

Seemed I had more to digest than the farmyard's worth of saturated fats churning in my stomach. Maybe I now understood why Gwen had felt so at home in Special Forces, maybe the only place where she'd ever belonged. So perhaps it was high time she confronted the demons in her past – at least one of us was in the right place. My musings were interrupted by the reappearance of the furiously masticating waitress, who salvaged our plates with a clatter.

Did we want to see the dessert trolley?

I never wanted to clap eyes on food again, never mind a knickerbocker glory made with real knickers. We sat in silence for a while, me with my dark thoughts, Gwen staring out the window at the slate-grey lake surface, whipped into a chop by the rising wind. As I did my best to apply the brakes to my racing mind I noticed a shadowy figure watching us intently from across the room. He had the air of a local about him – an old guy, dressed like a tramp, shifty and glowering. When I caught his good eye he staggered to his feet and shuffled over. He waved his liver-spotted hands over us as if casting a spell. His voice creaked as badly as his knees.

'Beware!'

Good advice perhaps, but a little too generic to be helpful.

'Too late mate, we've already eaten.' I let out a heroic cheesy burp.

He wasn't put off. 'You 'ere for that nutter up the 'ill. The one who talks to the spirits.' This wasn't a question – somehow he knew the aim of our quest. Gwen was instantly on her guard. In line with my new persona, I continued to play it cool.

'How can you tell – is it so bleeding obvious?'

He studied my clothing, his wandering eyes searching for a cleavage that wasn't there. 'Don't get many trannies round these parts. Those we do are always 'eading up the mountain. You can't fool me – you seeks Taliesin.'

Gwen licked her lips and scanned the empty diner, one hand resting near the bulge under her armpit. 'Maybe we does, and maybe we doesn't. Who's to say?' Her pupils flashed. 'We've heard he speaks of other worlds.'

Our new friend smiled but his eyes narrowed. 'He speaks of that and much else besides. None of it makes any bloody sense. It's a haunted place up there – BEWARE!'

'You already said that, mate.' To be honest he was starting to freak me out.

'I knows. You needs to BEWARE!'

I got to my feet, certain this conversation had run its course. We'd extracted as many relevant facts as we were ever going to from this guy. 'We'll be really careful, promise.' The man didn't look convinced.

Gwen followed my lead; neither of us wanted a scene. She paid the bill and left a generous tip. We slipped out to find our van. Behind us the old man stood in the feeble pool of light cast by the restaurant doorway and watched us leave.

'BEWARE!'

'Cheers dude. Catch ya later.' At least there was no one else around to see us go. As discreetly as we could we slipped out into the night.

23

Bonfire of the Insanities

The darkening sky was thick with clouds, racing against the coming storm. A rumble of distant thunder reverberated around the hills, heralding us as we made our way over to the van. The truck wasn't hard to find in the gloomy backlot, its bright pink paintwork the only colour splashed in a blanched world of shadow and grey. Gwen flung open the rear doors and pulled out our sleeping bags. She produced a knife from a sheath on her calf and proceeded to cut holes in the material – they'd serve as makeshift overcoats. Not the most elegant attire perhaps, but they'd keep us warm. I pointed out that perhaps a hike up Cader Idris, in the midst of a hurricane, wasn't the wisest course of action when wearing platform heels, but Gwen was eager to press on. She was keen to get reacquainted with her former mentor.

Walking was the only option. Back in Swansea Gwen had learned 'Taliesin' had set up shop in an abandoned Methodist chapel – Capel Ysbrd. It shouldn't be hard to find. A hiker's trail from the back of Homage to Fromage led up the cairn-encrusted hillside to the summit. The secluded retreat was along this track near the top. As we left the comforting safety of our familiar ice cream van the first raindrops began to fall. They were fat and swollen, pregnant with foreboding. I stifled a belch as Gwen led us into the trees at the head of the car park.

We found the start of the path easily enough. It got steeper as it broke from the foliage and began its snaking journey up the barren mountain side. We paused at a kissing gate to get our bearings. I was having second thoughts; the thunder sounded closer.

'Are we sure this is a good idea?'

Gwen stopped to peer at me in the darkness. I couldn't make out her expression; maybe that was just as well. She sounded hoarse and more than a little strung out.

'A lot of good people have made sacrifices to get you this far. We're not turning back now.'

I already felt out of breath. 'Juan meant a lot to you, didn't he?'

She said nothing, but turned to go. I followed her into the darkness. The black mass of the mountain towered over us, like some slumbering mythical beast. I was in no hurry to wake it up.

We seemed to walk for hours; the rain only got worse. My night vision wasn't the best, but Gwen had no trouble finding the way. By midnight regular flashes of lightning were illuminating our footsteps, their sudden staccato brilliance seeming to X-ray the landscape around us. A series of stark after-images burnt onto my retina, an exhibition by some mad artist working in electrons rather than paint. I was cold, miserable and scared. I prayed I'd done nothing to anger any thunder gods lately – now was not the time to be pushing my luck.

At last we crested a stony ridge and the chapel loomed into

view. It hid in a sheltered valley, steep cliffs and tumbling slate scree surrounding it on three sides. Behind the crooked structure a bleak mountain lake boiled in the rising storm, its surface lashed by sheets of rain. As if on cue a flash of lightning cast the bowl into monochromatic glare, wrecking our night vision and almost deafening us. Even above the howling wind I could hear the eagerness in Gwen's voice.

'Come on, we're almost there.'

My companion pressed on ahead. The trail meandered down a gentle slope towards the forgotten church, crooked and peculiar in design. I picked my way over the rocky ground, not wanting to be left behind. Yet another fork of lightning ripped open the sky and I ploughed into the back of my companion – Gwen had pulled up short. A lone figure stood blocking our path. I might have let out a bit of a shriek, but my companion moved forward after only a moment's hesitation. The apparition before us had the craggy outline of a man, his tattered clothing whipping in the gale. It called out with a voice as gravelly as the hillsides and as thunderous as the tempest.

'Welcome! I've been expecting you.' Neither of us wanted to ask how. Mutely we followed him down the path towards the ruined folly he called home, or maybe it was a lair.

On arrival the figure paused at the doorway. 'When you enter this place you accept my rules. Leave your preconceptions at this threshold. They might not be waiting for you on the way out. You won't depart entirely the same.'

Thoughts of any sort of departure struck me as a tad optimistic. Huddled in the shadowy porch I glanced over at Gwen, her expression unreadable. Finally she nodded, and I followed her inside. I was glad to get out of the downpour, but apprehensive about what lay ahead. There was something queerly discordant about this place.

The chapel smelt musty but by some miracle the roof was still intact – no small mercy in this pouring rain. In front of the altar an impressive bonfire blazed merrily, the remaining pews set around it in a haphazard circle. A peal of thunder crashed above us and the stained glass windows flared. I caught half-glimpses of the grisly scenes they depicted – a horror movie rendered in frozen disjointed frames. I was glad not to get too close a look at them. Our host led us towards the flames, Gwen following with me behind.

I was dimly aware of others moving through the shadows, disciples who no doubt helped their master meet his modest needs. I didn't get the impression he darned his own socks; don't even think anyone washed his clothes. The scuttling figures kept their heads bowed, but one shuffled forward and handed me a steaming mug. If nothing else it thawed my frozen fingers. It smelt peculiar, but glad of the warmth I took a sip.

Our guide turned and regarded us with cool detachment. 'Noswaith dda, Gwendolyn. It's been too long.'

The girl gazed back at him, her face a sea of emotion. In the dancing shadows I studied our host. He was a tall, thin man, gaunt to the point of emaciation. He looked as old as these ancient hills, but reborn in some ageless way. His long grey hair was unkempt and dangled to his bony, cloak-wrapped shoulders. A scrawny beard might have been home to as yet undiscovered forms of life. I sensed he'd been round the block a time or two, maybe lapping people twice his age. He had the eyes of a man who'd seen too much, and the aroma of one who showered too little. He made a lasting impact, a bit like cholera.

Gwen's voice held a hint of reverence. 'Colonel MacIntyre, you look... well, all things considered.'

Back in Swansea Juan had told us the old soldier had gone *full Colonel Kurtz*, but the figure now standing before me looked more Dennis Hopper than Marlon Brando. He smiled, crevasses of leathery skin starkly lit by the flickering flames.

'A name I've not heard in a long while. Have no fear child, I couldn't be better. You could say I'm a new man. They call me Taliesin now.'

Gwen cleared her throat, for once not her assured self. 'Yes, we heard. That's why we came –' She seemed apprehensive, as if uncertain what next to say next.

Taliesin tilted his head in reproach. 'We of all people should be able to be honest with each other, Gwendolyn. Cymbrogi, who've faced the gods of war together, companions in arms. Is that really why you've come?'

My partner looked very young as she gazed down at her hands. Her eyes glistened in the firelight. 'It's just... I wanted to say – I'm sorry I left you behind. I don't expect forgiveness.'

Taliesin waved her words away. 'Fenyw, there is nothing to forgive. All things happen for a reason – you helped me discover mine – my new mission. For that I am forever grateful.'

Gwen looked bewildered, not at all convinced. Our host continued. 'But it's not simple forgiveness you seek. I sense anger too – let it out, girl.'

She took a deep breath. 'Back in Puerto Madryn you told me to leave you behind. Told me everything would be all right. You knew that wasn't true – knew what they'd do to you. How do you think that makes me feel? I lost the only family I've ever believed in.'

He shook his head serenely. 'None of us can be responsible for another's feelings. All we can do is live our lives in truth, content that time will bear us out. That other-I-once-was told you to go for the best of reasons. What good would your suffering have done beside his? He was right for other reasons too. Not everything is always as it seems.'

Gwen was almost pleading. 'What reasons? It's been hard living with myself ever since.'

Taliesin placed two fingers to his forehead. 'At the time the Colonel couldn't know it, but I've been granted the gift of vision. The Tears of the Puma will do that to some men, we lucky few, those who it doesn't send round the bend. If you hadn't escaped you wouldn't have played your role in the great events which now unfold. Everything happens for a reason, girl. You've played your part in it very well.'

I was just thinking this was some high-calibre happy-clappy new age bullshit – at least no one had suggested a group hug yet – when Taliesin turned the full force of his attention towards me. It felt like I was being probed by ultrasound – his gaze omniscient, penetrating my very soul. It tickled the back of my brain; it was all I could do to suppress a giggle.

Taliesin's face was enigmatic as his eyes played over my clothing. I was conscious my legs needed shaving; my personal grooming standards had slipped. With a start his eyes went wide.

'Behold – the Chosen One will come in the guise of a harlot. This moment has been foretold, written in the stars!'

Not this horse excrement again. 'That's nice,' I said. 'When are they arriving? It's going to get crowded round here.'

For the first time Taliesin's serene smile slipped. One of his eyes twitched in spasm; he looked uncertain. I thought it best to change tack – any subject would do. I gazed around at the cobweb-shrouded tomb. Beside us the fire crackled, casting shadows with its dancing orange light.

'What is this place?' I muttered.

The old man composed himself with a visible effort. He seemed more than happy to fill me in. 'It's known as Capel Ysbrd – the Chapel of the Spirits.'

'Sadly not the alcoholic kind?' I could have done with a

stiff drink, maybe more than a few – the herbal tea had tasted terrible, tiny bitter leaves clustering at the bottom of the mug. Suddenly I felt light headed.

Taliesin ignored me and went on. 'There was never such frivolity here in days gone by. Legend says a Methodist minister led his flock up here over a century ago. Crazed he was, and raving like a prophet. They were trying to get closer to heaven. They found that other place instead. They called him Organ Morgan.'

'Was he blessed in the trouser department?'

Our host peered at me oddly, but was warming to his tale. 'Better than that, he was blessed in the House of the Lord. His congregation hailed him as a holy man – turned out he was wholly mad. Built this chapel with his own bare hands, he did, its stones hewed from the living rock of the mountain. When it was done he turned the bloody stumps of his fingers to attending his massive organ.'

Taliesin looked at me expectantly, but I wasn't playing ball. 'Best let that one pass,' I said. 'What happened next?'

Taliesin seemed a little disappointed, but carried on all the same. 'Huge it was – his mighty organ – the greatest instrument of pleasure this side of Bala. The pipes could blast out a hurricane of sound. When Morgan caressed his organ God stopped what he was doing to listen; some claimed Jesus wept; the Holy Ghost held his lighter aloft and swayed.'

I was transfixed. 'What about the angels?'

'The Hosts of Heaven danced, but not just on the head of a pin. And that's what Morgan's congregation did, on a night much like this over a hundred years ago – danced like demons, they did. Couldn't have stopped if they'd wanted to, and they didn't want to. They danced all night like there was no tomorrow and, for them, turns out there wasn't. Slaves to the rhythm, they kept going until sunrise, when they danced right into the lake behind us. Some say it goes down forever. Some say they're dancing still.'

The silence which followed was broken only by the crackling of the fire. Outside the wind howled. Nearby one of Taliesin's shadowy coven jabbered and coughed. Come to think of it the place was as noisy as hell.

'Nice story,' muttered Gwen, as she appeared by my side. My companion looked like she had a lot on her mind. Taliesin's eyes grew distant.

'A story which should be more widely known, studied perhaps. A parable – considering the place our nation finds itself, at this precipitous moment in time.'

'What do you mean?' I'd had enough of these riddles. 'Can't you simply tell us what you're driving at?'

Taliesin looked directly at me, his intensity returning. Tiny flames flickered in his growing pupils, a reflection of the bonfire, or maybe something worse. 'This country is much like Morgan's congregation – hedonists to a man and woman, dancing to our doom. We've forgotten our true purpose.'

It was hard not to scoff. 'What else is new? Tell me something I don't know.'

The prophet seemed to swell in size. 'Wales needs a saviour who can break this death spiral. A crash is coming, and when it arrives it's going to be hard. We needs us a human air-bag.'

My head was swimming. 'What on earth does that mean? Why can't you just be clear. Cut the riddles.'

Taliesin's tone went flat. 'The Jones Corporation can't build new J-Drives anymore. They've lost the knack.'

24

Out of the Fire

There was another one of those tense silences. I glanced over at Gwen, ready for her to refute this ridiculous claim, but she just looked numb – as if another horrible truth was dawning. I knew the feeling, but that wasn't all I was feeling. I swayed a bit, unsteady on my feet. Why was the hall spinning like that, the walls and floor tilted at eccentric angles? Gwen grabbed my arm to prevent me falling.

'Kev, are you all right?'

I was so far from all right I couldn't have found it on a map. It felt like my skull had been opened and my brain licked clean by an enthusiastic puppy. 'My head hurts,' I mumbled.

Taliesin seemed untroubled. 'Pain is nothing but weakness leaving the body. He'll be fine.'

'What have you done to him? What was in that drink?' Gwen sounded panic stricken as she eased my body to the floor. But it was a body I no longer inhabited. I watched events unfold as a disembodied spirit, my mind hovering above the scene like some invisible drone. I could see the bonfire, and

Taliesin's skulking disciples. Gwen cradled my head in her hands. The prophet himself towered above us.

'Have no fear, child. The procedure is unlikely to kill him. Just like me the Cauldron of Rebirth will spew him forth once it's had its way – probably.'

'What was in that drink?'

'Not easy getting hold of the Tears of the Puma. Customs officials can be such sticklers for their silly rules. I had to substitute the best local equivalents.'

'Tell me what was in it, right now!'

'Certain unusual mushrooms grow in these valleys. They sprout nowhere else on Earth – which might be for the best. Mix them in the right way and you can go on a real journey, a trip to other worlds. He needs to be prepared, anointed for the trials which lay ahead.'

'This is crazy, bring him back!'

But I'd already started to drift heavenward. My point of view rose up through the rafters of the chapel, past the nests of birds and small, timid creatures, up into the thunderous night sky. But it didn't end there. Before I knew it I was gazing down at the roof of the storm, silent and cold on my unending ascent into space. It was a long way down. Somehow Taliesin was beside me, but also all around and inside me too. It would have been weird if it hadn't been up against such stiff competition.

'Nice view, isn't it,' he said.

'Looks so peaceful from up here.'

'Well it's not. There's some things I need to show you. Follow me.'

We continued our journey away from Earth, gaining speed all the time. The Moon sped past, a silver blur. Mars and the gas giants were next. I had time to wonder why planets were always so narrowly missed in flypasts like this, almost as if some unseen hand arranged things for dramatic effect. There was a lot more space than planets – a fact which was becoming increasingly apparent. Our nondescript local star soon receded into the glowing orb of the Milky Way. Next our home galaxy was nothing but a shrinking speck, one of millions scattered like grains of sand amidst the velvety blackness of interstellar space. Finally our entire universe dwindled to an insignificant crimson singularity, adrift in a profound void incomprehensible to any mind remaining within. At least I seemed to have got over my fear of heights.

Taliesin was still with me. 'Impressed, boy? You should be. That's my special effects budget blown for the foreseeable.'

For once I was almost lost for words. 'Why are we here?'

'Perspective. Look at this.'

Suddenly our universe was not alone, the tiny pinprick of red light joined by a myriad of others, spreading out in all directions as far as the mind's eye could see. But somehow I knew these realities weren't separated in space. Each was layered on top another in a towering lasagne of existence. Taliesin clicked his fingers and the scene changed again. Now each universe was a twinkling node on a fairy light chain, looping around itself in a Gordian knot of mind-shredding complexity – a wool ball plaything of some cosmic kitten. Scientists had string theory all wrong.

Even at this great distance, or perhaps because of it, I could sense differences between each point on the thread. All universes downstream glowed bright scarlet, much like our own – somehow I knew these were worlds where Wales dominated. The endless queue of those behind were yet to reach the stitch in time where Isaiah made his great discoveries – these blazed in rainbow shades beyond imagining. I realised our grasp of the spectrum was highly parochial. Patterns of colour emerged, but it would be an endless life's work to make sense of them.

'What are those weird-coloured ones over there? They look... sort of sickly black, but... wrong.'

Taliesin frowned. 'Best not to talk of the Shadow Dimensions, lad. Universes so alien to our understanding that no mortal man has set foot there. But that's not to say they're not populated. And what lives there likes to sneak and slither out sometimes to pay us a visit. *Ych a fi!*'

I suppressed a shudder. 'Are they in our past or future? I can't tell in this tangle of neon spaghetti.'

'Neither and both.' Taliesin sounded impatient. 'Restrict your attention to the realm of man. There's more than enough to keep us busy.'

I couldn't argue with that. There was so much I wanted to ask, but I didn't know where to begin. I was mesmerised. 'What separates each reality along the line?'

Taliesin slipped his arm around my disembodied shoulders. 'Mere fractions of a second, lad – for those worlds which are close. When you jump between two such realities you'd never spot the time shift. They're parallel, for all practical purposes.'

If I'd had eyes they would have been wide with wonder. 'The universe I came from...'

'Look over there, just a little way back.' How had I missed it? My home reality stood out, a sad dot of dull grey amidst a stream of blazing ruby. Taliesin whispered in my ear. 'It's a dozen years behind this one – close, but there are a billion worlds between – Pax Cambria in every one. Your home earth bucks the trend.'

Perhaps now I understood why the Consortium had wanted to probe my brain. I'd just prefer if their instrument of choice wasn't an ice pick. Steeling myself I got a grip – I knew how these metaphysic revelation scenes were meant to go. I gestured towards the plethora of realities tangled beneath us.

'Let me guess – you need me to save the Multiverse from

unravelling? In the Shadow Dimensions there's a Dark Lord with scissors, or worse yet, a pair of knitting needles?'

Taliesin gazed at me pityingly. One of his eyes started to twitch again. 'Were you born this *twp*, boy, or did you have to practise? Quite the reverse – I'm trying to convince you of your insignificance. With you it's an uphill struggle.'

I wasn't buying this for an instant. 'Come off it. The fact I'm here at all has to count for something. You said I was the *Chosen One*.'

My disembodied guide let out a weary sigh, seems I was trying his patience. 'Yes, yes – *locally* chosen, perhaps. But trust me, *bach*, there's nothing significant about you on the cosmic scale. Save that you exist in only one reality – rare in itself, I grant you.'

I grasped this admission like a drowning man reaching for a life ring. 'Ah ha! So that makes me special, right?'

Taliesin pounded his palm against his forehead. 'No! Almost everyone gets to live in two or three. Your existence on only one plane is a pure fluke. You're the fly in the ointment of the cosmic plan – an aberration against gods and nature.'

Growing up in Aberdare I'd heard words to this effect too often for it to be coincidence. 'So I *am* part of the Cosmic Plan? Interesting.'

There was a sound a lot like the grinding of teeth. Slowly Taliesin got his frustration under control. 'There is no master plan. You are an insignificant speck lost amidst trillions inhabiting just one universe amongst billions. We clear on that?'

This was always the problem with these tree-hugging new age mystic types – you could never pin them down on specifics – always talking in riddles. I would have thrown my hands up in despair, but I didn't seem to have brought my arms. Taliesin wasn't finished yet. He sounded tired.

'I brought you here to make this clear. Perhaps it was a mistake.'

Was this a chink of light? 'So you're far from infallible?'

'Apparently so.'

There was an awkward silence. I just wanted to clear this up once and for all. 'So you're not sure about me being sent to save the Multiverse? Maybe I'm like Jesus with better hair?'

Taliesin looked at me for a long time. 'There's not much I'm sure about anymore, but I am sure of that, yes.' I think he sensed my disappointment. 'Lower your expectations, boi. I'm here to crucify your messiah complex.'

I mulled this over for a moment. 'Okay, I *think* I get it. Tell me more. I guess I can settle for being *locally* special, after all. Better than nothing.'

My host seemed to roll his eyes. 'Progress at last.' His relief was palpable. 'You do have some part to play in coming events – the future destiny of your homeland, for example. Would you settle for that?'

This was more like it. 'What do I have to do? Any swords need pulling from stones? Any maidens need rescuing from their virginity? Got special rates for that at the moment – I'm your man.'

There was another pregnant pause. Trailer park Gandalf sounded vexed. 'That's the thing. I don't *exactly* know what it is you have to do, just that the odds are stacked against you. Your mettle will be tested to the limit. We're talking a million-to-one chance of success.'

I was far from impressed. 'I thought you were meant to be a visionary, a prophet. Is there some ombudsman I can complain to? Don't you have any clue?'

Taliesin sounded a bit embarrassed. 'Well – my guess is…

you learn to make more J-Drives. Something like that. That's what this country desperately needs. When the secret gets out, we're screwed.'

I let out a strangled laugh. 'Forget it, Einstein. I got straight Fs in science. Try again.'

My host regained his composure. 'I won't lie to you, I don't yet know the details – only that it will almost certainly end in your painful death. Let's face it, you're not exactly hero material.'

'Oh thank you very much, pound shop Nostradumbass.'

'Sometimes the mists of foresight take time to clear. But you've arrived at an auspicious moment. Soon your fate will be revealed to me. I sense *that* in my bones.'

Who did this joker think he was? 'Oh well, that's all right then. Can't wait to hear the details of my inevitable death. When will this revelation take place?'

'Now, in a minute.'

'I never know what that means.'

'Christ on a pedalo – maybe this very night, maybe tomorrow, who knows? You can't rush these things. Time is different over here. Which reminds me – get back home we must.'

'Lead the way, Yoda. Omniscience makes me giddy. I'm keen to discover the details of my imminent demise.'

The trip home was faster than the journey out. There was a hairy moment when we skirted Uranus but we managed to just miss ploughing through the place – what were the odds of that? As the local version of Earth raced up to meet us, Taliesin shared one final pearl of wisdom.

'There's only one thing that gives me hope.'

'What's that?'

'To become the master you first have to play the fool. And you, my boi, are uniquely qualified in that respect.'

'I think you're just trying to wind me up now.'

'You've been granted the gift of self-reflection – use it well.'

We were soon plunging back through the Earth's atmosphere. For once the weather above Cader Idris had cleared, tattered clouds tearing away to the east. Shards of sunlight glinted off the surface of the lake, which from up here was so blue it hurt the eye. My consciousness crashed back into my head like a falling meteor, I just hoped it wouldn't leave a crater. After an instant of jarring deceleration and profound disorientation, I realised I was back – spreadeagled on the cold, hard floor. I had a splitting headache, but my mind seemed bigger somehow, expanded. Maybe my skull just needed adjusting.

From somewhere at the back of the chapel I could hear the throaty bellow of organ music. Had our host been here the whole time? The music wasn't doing my head any favours, seemingly played exclusively on the black keys. It seemed Morgan's fabled organ wasn't so mythical after all. It took a while to place the tune. The Colonel formerly known as Frank was hammering out a spirited rendition of 'Raspberry Beret', marching song of the Welsh Special Forces. It didn't make me feel like dancing, never mind romancing. Despite my clobber I guessed I'd never make a Nolan sister. My eyes fluttered open; a pair of big brown ones peered back. I lay with my head in Gwen's lap. Relief swept over her face.

'Kev, you're back. You've been gone for hours. I'd begun to give up hope.'

Squinting against the brightness I struggled to get up. Daylight streamed in through the chapel's open door. The storm had passed and outside dawn was breaking, really knocking itself out. It felt like parts of me were broken too, but quickly reassembling. I was uncertain if they were going back the same way as before. Struggling onto my elbows I gingerly sat up. My mouth felt like a cheap pub carpet, my head felt like it was rammed with cotton wool. There was movement all around. Taliesin's disciples were stumbling towards the exit, vacant expressions on every grimy face.

'Where are they going?' My voice was a harsh croak.

Gwen got to her feet. 'Just be grateful they're not dancing. I don't think we'll like it, but let's go take a look.'

After the gloom of the chapel the morning sunlight was intense. I shielded my eyes with a trembling hand as Gwen supported my other arm on her shoulders. As their spiritual leader played on, Taliesin's flock filed out along the hiker's trail we'd travelled up the night before. The congregation were heading over the ridge to some unseen destination. We staggered after them, until Gwen pulled up short.

The chapel and lake sat at the bottom of a broad depression, stony ridge to the south, soaring cliffs on three other sides. Ahead of us, a line of hooded figures emerged over the crest of the ridge. They wore robes of white and grey, stained and patched in haphazard fashion. Their hair and beards were bedraggled and matted; they clearly weren't patrons of the Celtic Fringe – even Juan's clever fingers would have struggled to whip them into shape. Yet more figures appeared from the rocks and cliffs behind us. Golden sickles glinted in the dawn sunlight, others held twisted clubs and sprigs of mistletoe. I could only pray none of them wanted a kiss. Fear gripped my vitals, and threatened to tear them off.

'Who are these dudes?' Sick, I realised I already knew the answer.

Gwen's tone was flat. 'It's the Gorsedd. We're surrounded.'

My stomach sank towards my toes. There was no escaping this one. These druids didn't look like they'd come to dance.

25

Into the Flames

'So your scumbag mate sold us out.' I had no doubt who'd tipped off the new arrivals.

Gwen said nothing in reply. Organ music continued to blare from the chapel behind us as the line of druids closed in. Seemed Taliesin preferred to keep playing rather than greet his new guests. The druids were now close enough for me to get a whiff of their fruity aroma. Apparently washing wasn't a bardic priority. Our own priorities were a more pressing concern.

'What do we do? We can't shoot our way out of this one.'

Gwen took a deep breath. 'We… negotiate.'

'They don't look in the mood for palaver!'

No sooner had these words left my lips than a gap opened in the massed ranks. A hooded figure emerged and strode purposefully forwards. With a scarred, calloused hand he pulled back his cowl and looked us up and down, frowning. It was Iestyn von Däniken, my friend from the park back in Swansea. His face bore fresh bruises, but he looked no worse for wear after his recent run-in with the cops. The nail at the end of the finger he thrust towards me was long and yellow. Maybe the blow to his head had knocked some sense into the chap.

'Behold brothers, the Chosen One!'

Or maybe not. I stood up straight and squared my shoulders, just like Grandad had always told me to. 'Nice to meet you again, sir. Why does everyone keep calling me that?'

No answer came from his blistered lips; instead they creaked into a sinister grin. Dental cover didn't appear a perk of joining the Gorsedd. 'Ere he is lads, *Jones the Messiah*. Grab 'im and don't let go.'

A squad of minions surged forward. I felt an urge to warn them about my companion, but I needn't have worried. I sensed Gwen go tense by my side, but even she could see the time for violence was over. We were surrounded and outnumbered hundreds to one. One sneering underling took her gun, and we were grabbed by a swarm of hands. Like it or not, it seemed we were going on a hike with the druids. Iestyn turned on his sandalled heels and led the way, shouting, 'Let's get this party started!'

We backtracked along the rocky path we'd climbed the night before. Just over the ridge it forked – I'd failed to spot this in the darkness and storm. One path led back down the hillside to the cheese joint, the other ascended the rim of the sheltered valley. The upper trail narrowed and climbed to the summit of the mountain, twisting between rocky outcrops. It was this lonely path we now took – a road less travelled, if ever there was one. I didn't expect I'd like the view.

We were pushed and shoved into following Iestyn up the slope. Catching up with him I felt the urge to at least get some answers. 'What is it with you nutters? Can't you see you're bringing this country to its knees?'

The bard snorted but didn't bother to look round; he was too busy setting a fearsome pace. 'This country's run for the benefit of a tiny elite – your family and their cronies in the government. They hoard the wealth for themselves. We're going to share it with the people – a holy cause.'

Put like that I had to admit it didn't sound so bad. 'Maybe you have a point. Like you said, I'm part of that Jones clan – even if from a little far afield. Maybe I can get them to change their ways.'

Iestyn threw back his head and laughed. 'Rubbish! You have no idea what Genghis Jones is like. Driven mad by wealth and power, he is – half Midas, half Judas, total knob'ead.'

It was all I could do to keep up, never mind win him round, but I had to try. 'I might know him better than you think. And I have it on good authority Jones Corp has problems of its own. They're keeping massive secrets – I know where the bodies are buried.'

Iestyn stopped in his tracks and looked at me oddly. Was there a flicker in one twitching bloodshot eye – maybe I'd struck a chord? But the crumpled prophet shook his head and snapped out of it. He clipped me around the ear, quite hard. 'Shut your gob! I've got my orders from a higher authority. I play my part, you play yours. Now get crackin up this bloody 'ill.'

So much for negotiation. We marched on.

I hoped Gwen was devising some cunning plan, because I was out of ideas. My companion seemed lost in a trance, not her usual kinetic self at all. The lake and chapel were now far below, like the discarded toys of some careless giant. We were approaching Penygader – the mountain's brooding peak – soon to be lost in a world of blazing sky and racing cloud. The strains of Taliesin's organ were faint but still clear, carried up like an offering on the crystalline breeze. He was getting his money's worth from those black keys.

As we crested the final ridge many of the druids were out of breath – I couldn't say I blamed them, and gasping I dropped to my knees. At nearly a kilometre above sea level the air was as thin and scrawny as our captors, but Iestyn was driven by a higher force. He loomed above me as I took a sneaky breather.

'Keep moving, you mincing lady-boi – we're almost there.'

'What happened to the *Chosen One*? And where are we going? There's nothing up here but rocks and madness.'

Iestyn looked down at me with sneering contempt. 'Oh, you've been chosen all right. What you've been chosen for is a great honour. Many would die to be in your place. Get to your feet and you'll be able to see her – look, ain't she a beaut!'

He pulled me upright. The summit of the mountain levelled off in a windswept plateau, dotted with tumbled boulders and clumps of bleached grass. Central to this barren expanse a monstrous contraption was taking shape. Workers busied themselves with hammers and nails, fastening planks to the towering structure. More druids stuffed bundles of kindling into its timbered frame. It was fully forty feet high, a pagan idol not seen in these parts since the last Roman legions snuffed out the old ways. The sight of it chilled my blood – it was a wicker man, stark and cruel. Just looking at it gave me splinters.

Iestyn seemed invigorated by the sight of the crooked thing. 'Let's get you ready, we haven't got all day – Boss is arrivin soon.' A hand shoved me roughly forward and I stumbled in a daze. Gwen let out a strangled gasp. We were led to the foot of the looming effigy. I could guess what hellish rites our host had in mind. We were having a picnic – a barbecue with us the guests of honour, not to mention the chargrilled main course.

The wooden cage was wrapped in chicken wire. We were bundled up a crude ramp leading to an opening in the figure's chest. This was the point of no return; did my companion have even the most basic plan? Gwen continued to play it cool – a temperature she'd struggle to maintain once this thing got going. Iestyn's underlings rolled forward enormous barrels of paraffin.

Despite the wind I was covered in a cold sweat. 'You do know real druids never conducted human sacrifice, don't you? It was propaganda dreamt up by the Romans.'

Iestyn threw back his scruffy head and laughed. 'Authenticity is no concern of ours. The greater good dictates that you die. Get in and cut the yap, you preening man-child.'

There was no talking our way out of this one. Without further ceremony we were pushed inside. The iron grille clanged shut behind us and its rough bolt was thrown. The wooden kindling didn't make for comfortable seating. I sensed our predicament was about to get even more uncomfortable still. Gwen reached out and I felt her fingers searching for mine – I took that as an ominous sign. Was this really the end? Iestyn at least seemed in high spirits.

'We burn your kind in offering to the gods up here, lad. And you degenerates look like you'll go up a treat. Ready the torches!'

Considering the man-made fibres I was wearing I didn't think they'd struggle to set me ablaze – I was already a walking fire hazard, my flowery dress a rhapsody in polyester, prone to catch light at the slightest spark. The petrol being sprayed over us wouldn't hinder my combustion in the slightest. Valiantly I struggled against the coarse wooden bars.

'Why do you want us dead? This is beyond a joke!'

Iestyn smirked as he emptied the last jerry can. 'You're a heretic, a misfit, with no place in this world or the next. Your very existence threatens to condemn our nation to a place of servitude. We can't let that 'appen.' He took out a match, struck it on his stubble, and threw it into the thicket of twigs beneath us. There was an audible *whoosh*, followed by cheers from his congregation.

Through the thickening smoke a long white air car glided in for a landing – a flying limousine. It alighted on the crown of the hill and one blacked-out window slid down for the occupant to observe our fate. Had the Gorsedd started selling tickets? Iestyn was certainly hamming up his role in this infernal show.

'By Bran's Brambly Beard, and Nudd's Silver Left Nut, I set these faggots ablaze!'

Gwen squeezed my hand. 'Kev, I just wanted to say – I'm sorry I dragged you into this mess. It's a real bummer.'

There was no sense making her feel worse than she already did. The tears in both our eyes weren't just down to the smoke.

'Oh, not to worry – we all have to go in the end. It's just…'

'What?' She looked at me forlorn.

I struggled to put the sheer irrationality of our predicament into words. What a way to meet your doom; it was too much to bear. For once my emotions got the better of me and I cried out, 'What a way to go – who could imagine dying this way?'

Gwen winced. 'I hate to say it, but Edward Woodward would.' At least she had the decency to look embarrassed.

If there was an answer to that I wasn't the man to oblige. All I could do was stare at her in wonder – distraught that these should be the last words past those lovely lips. Gwen deserved better. But the flames had already begun to lick my toes. At least my athlete's foot would not be a problem for long. I tried to tell her of my true feelings, but all that came out was a raking cough.

Maybe it was my less than salubrious surroundings, maybe it was my recent jaunt with Taliesin, but whatever the reason I was hit with a sudden flash of memory. Ever since this road trip to Hades had begun I'd been wondering why I'd turned out the way I had. Trying to understand my crippling aversion to risk, or even anything so hazardous as leaving home. What had made me this way? Not that it had done any good.

I was taken back to a family gathering, lost in the mists of time. Long forgotten or, perhaps more accurate to say, edited out – too traumatising for my young brain to comprehend. It had been Uncle Genghis's birthday, attended by all the clan. Mum and my four-year-old self had been in attendance, nervous to be amongst such a boisterous, braying mob. As a special present for the birthday boy, I'd drawn him a lovely picture, poring over it for hours with crayon and felt-tipped pen. Completed the night before, way past my bedtime, it showed our whole extended family dancing and celebrating merrily at his barbecue bash.

Only problem was the real party wasn't running so smoothly. Uncle G was having a hard time lighting his grill. The hordes of wound-up kids and pissed-up adults bouncing round the small garden weren't helping at all. Hungry, frustrated and humming of firelighters, Genghis was at risk of looking a fool. Maybe it hadn't been the best time to try to give my special uncle his present, but it was the first chance I'd got.

Looking down at me, maybe noticing me for the first time ever, his eyes had lit up. He'd plucked my masterpiece from my podgy little fingers and squinted at it, crying, 'Just what I needs, boi!' before lighting it with a match and plunging it into the coals.

Not long later he was munching a charcoaled burger, while burp-singing 'Cwm Rhondda' with his drunk brothers and their drunker wives. I'd sat huddled in a corner, hugging my knees and rocking gently as I bawled my eyes out. Mum had to take me home, inconsolable and traumatised, still in tears, never to speak of that day again. Weird how these small events can shape our lives, rippling down the years like toxic shockwaves. Still, all academic now – looked like I'd reached the end of my line. Pungent smoke filled my nostrils as I reluctantly gave myself up to oblivion. Goodbye cruel worlds.

'STOP!'

A roaring voice reverberated around the hillside, drowning even the crackling flames. Every head turned to see who had the temerity to gatecrash the party. An angry growl went up from the assembled host – it turned into a gasp. Taliesin stoop at the crest of the hill, his scrawny arms thrown aloft, a blazing staff held in his hand. He looked for all the world like some avenging Old Testament prophet – Moses reborn, with a Valleys accent, looking to kick Egyptian butt. Just as well, as I could already smell my very own burning bush.

'Stop this defilement, my brothers, you know not what you do!'

He seemed to shimmer with a mesmeric light that shone from within. A sparkling multi-hued aura danced around him as his hair stood on end, floating twigs and leaves forming a profane halo. A fearful groan went up from the congregation. Taliesin obviously held no small power over this conclave of druids. At the foot of the effigy Iestyn looked torn, struggling with some momentous inner battle. At last, with a snarl, he nodded, and squads of his underlings sprang forward to douse the flames. I could have kissed Taliesin, despite his rancid breath. Our salvation had come not a moment too soon.

Our saviour strode forward to converse with Iestyn, whose head sank as he listened in meek submission. Taliesin spoke in animated fashion, before turning on his heels to march up the slope to the parked air car. He climbed inside, the window closed – not a conference suitable for the riff-raff.

Gwen and I were handed down from our wooden prison, relief flooding over us in waves. Iestyn looked pained as he stood before us, disappointment oozing from every pockmarked pore.

'There's been a change of plan. You've been summoned to meet the Boss. Be on your best behaviour.' Unable to meet my gaze, he slunk away into the crowd.

We were marched up to the waiting limo as the clamshell door opened with a hiss. It was dark inside, but I could make out a well-appointed interior – video screens and communication terminals nestled around an antique drinks cabinet. Every surface was padded in red velvet. Taliesin sat on a crimson leather seat, his face unreadable and his staff thankfully less apocalyptic. Across from him lounged a tall and elegant figure, who I recognised from the TV news. It was Llywsiffer Pendragon, Chief Bard of the Island of the Mighty and leader of the Gorsedd. With a long, bony finger he beckoned us inside. He wasn't someone it was easy to resist.

26

Sympathy for the Devil

Something struck me as queer about Llywsiffer from the start, like he was less a man than an elaborate illusion – a living disguise masking something far worse. If you glimpsed him out of the corner of your eye the facade slipped just a little, and you got a terrible indication of the hideous creature beneath. His true visage didn't lay still, but writhed and slithered like something pale you might find under a rock. I tried looking directly at him, but that was worse. Somehow we'd found ourselves sprawled in the back of his limo, sipping cognac while trying to ignore the stench of woodsmoke pouring off us. It was a step up from being burnt alive as a sacrificial offering, but not by much.

Llywsiffer cleared his throat and fanned the air with a silk handkerchief, lewdly decorated with hypnotic astronomical symbols. His voice was oddly sibilant. 'Welcome, my young friends. So good of you to come.'

Trickery it might have been but our host cut a dashing figure – tall, gaunt and immaculately dressed. His tweed suit and elaborate cravat seemed from a bygone era, but I knew he must be a cunning political operator – Nosferatu with better PR; a dark conjurer who really did saw pretty girls in half. He regarded us coolly from beneath a bushy grey monobrow. His eyes were sunken and dark rimmed, but a crimson light flickered within. His piercing gaze ranged over us, making my skin crawl and my mind itch. The presidential candidate continued.

'Our mutual friend here,' he gestured languidly towards Taliesin, 'informs me some fresh information has come to light – information which has a bearing on our plans. Experience has taught me to have faith in his visions.'

Gwen seemed in a mood to be difficult. 'That's nice of him. Did he also tell you there are laws against murdering innocent people? Even up here human sacrifice is frowned upon.'

Llywsiffer tittered, a sound like some monstrous cricket chirping. 'Oh, come, come, young lady, let's not be melodramatic. Don't play the special snowflake with me.'

My companion's lip curled in anger. 'Enough snowflakes can form a blizzard. We know what you've got planned for this nation. We're gonna freeze you out.'

Our host inspected his obscenely long manicured nails. 'I very much doubt that, my girl. None of us here can claim to be innocent. Don't climb on your moral high horse with me – I'll have it boiled down for glue.'

While this exchange was taking place I couldn't help but notice Taliesin slouched in a dim corner. He was tinkering with what looked like a smartphone, for all I knew posting a status update. Weird, I wouldn't have had him down as a social media addict. Perhaps he was right – people are not always what they seemed. But this was no time for idle speculation; courageously I could see I would have to play the peacemaker.

'I think what my friend here was *trying* to say,' I shot her a withering look, 'is that we're very grateful you called off the ceremony. I love quaint cultural traditions as much as the next man, but I was a little too intimately involved to enjoy that one. We're confused about what you plan next. What do you plan next, by the way?'

The full force of Llywsiffer's attention fell on me like a cartoon piano. Whatever the reverse of charisma was, he could broadcast it on all channels. If I'd not been frozen to the spot I would have flinched right off the hand-stitched leather seat. Our host arched one bushy eyebrow; it reared up like some monstrous caterpillar.

'What we plan next, my boy, is nothing less than the total overthrow of the corrupt globalist elite who have lorded over us for too long. The Jones clan have fleeced this country to the bone, then tucked its legs in their wellies better to administer a rogering of eye-watering proportions. We will bring the whole corrupt edifice crashing down, lower Genghis to his scabby knees. Their days are numbered, their nemesis has stepped down from the train. Pleased to meet you, hope you guess my name.'

'That's nice,' I gulped. 'And what do you want with me, Mr Pendragon?'

Llywsiffer's eyes blazed. 'You, my lad, are going to help us do it. Think of me as Barnes Wallace – and you are my bouncing bomb.'

Gwen and I exchanged a glance. I had a bad feeling where this was heading. 'Look, I'll level with you –'

'A wise course of action.'

'– I can only apologise for causing all this fuss. There's been some terrible misunderstanding I'm yet to get to the bottom of, but I would never spill my guts to the enemies of our nation. I'm as patriotic as you are.'

With a sneer Llywsiffer regarded my attire. 'I doubt that very much, but carry on.'

'Five minutes ago your henchmen were all set to flambé us alive. Why should we trust you?' This struck me as a reasonable enough question, but our host seemed to disagree.

Llywsiffer ground his pointed teeth. It seemed a struggle for him to get the words out. 'Yes, I'm… sorry… about that.' Perhaps not a man practised at delivering apologies. His sour face looked like it might crack; I shuddered to think what might come out. 'Consider it from my point of view. Wales's enemies think you are the key weapon in their plan to halt our dominion. It would be easier for us if you became… permanently indisposed.'

'Yes, I get that. But now?'

Llywsiffer leaned in. 'That was before we learned you had… other uses.'

Choking on his sulphurous deodorant I coughed the words out. 'What other uses?'

Mercifully Llywsiffer leaned back to pour himself a stiff drink. The dispensed ice cubes gave off a thick acrid smoke. 'Taliesin's sight has proved infallible in the past. The old ways are strong in this one.'

The mystic looked up from his phone and nodded modestly, as Llywsiffer carried on. 'He tells me the Jones Corporation can no longer manufacture J-Drives. The secret of their construction died with their founder – your illustrious grandfather. These past months your family have been recycling old models, shipping out existing stock – shysters and conmen the lot of them.'

I nodded stiffly; he'd get no argument from me. 'Taliesin told us the same thing. But you're no friends of Genghis and the Jones Clan – they're the cornerstone of the government you're trying to overthrow. Barry Island sits on their board. Wales is their personal fiefdom.'

Our host steepled his long fingers. Yellowing nails, which were almost talons, clicked together. I hoped they were only stained with nicotine. 'Very true, my boy. But when news gets out of this sad state of affairs, as it surely will, J-Corp stock will plummet. Our country's economy will crash. We're going to overthrow the degenerate liberal order – we don't want to inherit a wasteland.'

I found it helped a bit if I rubbed my temples. 'Okay, I think I understand. But where do we fit in?'

Llywsiffer leaned closer, again that whiff of brimstone. 'That's the new information Taliesin learned while you were Iestyn's pyrotechnic guests – he has foreseen that only you can unlock the riddle of Anthracite construction. Only you can acquire this vital information – only you, Kevin.'

With an effort I snapped out of his hypnotic gaze. Now it was my turn to laugh, a little too manically. 'I hate to disappoint you, but I'm no scientist or engineer. Taliesin's been on the magic mushrooms again.' I caught Gwen giving me a pained look. Perhaps it wasn't wise to ruin Llywsiffer's delusions. The image of the wicker man loomed large, still smouldering not far down the hill.

Gwen interrupted. 'I think what my friend is *trying* to say is that he's well up for giving it a go. Isn't that right, Kev.'

I nodded as enthusiastically as I was able. Nobody looked convinced, least of all me.

Taliesin wasn't about to have his reputation as a soothsayer besmirched. 'You can believe what you like, boi – but I know what I saw in the flames. Only you can save this nation. Destiny is calling, and it sounds a bit like Huw Edwards.'

I slowly massaged my aching head. 'And how am I meant to pull this miracle off?'

Llywsiffer looked at Taliesin; the mad prophet only nodded in reply. Our host continued. 'We believe you must travel back to Aberdare – the strangely primitive version you hail from. There you must talk to your grandsire, who abides in that reality. There are many important things he must tell you, wisdom to impart. This is what Taliesin's vision has foretold.'

It took a moment for it to sink in. I could hardly believe my singed ears. My heart soared at the prospect of heading home. I didn't like to point out the Isaiah I knew had about as much chance of explaining an infinite free energy source, to me or anyone else, as I had of building it from egg boxes and string. Most days he was lucky if he could wipe his own bum. Trust Llywsiffer to derail my happy musings.

'And I know what you're thinking, boy – that your version of Isaiah never built the Anthracite device in the first place, only the Isaiah over here. Perhaps I should let Taliesin explain that part.'

The prophet put down his phone and drew himself up in his full height. It would have been more impressive if his robes hadn't been torn and stained. 'This is what I witnessed in the flames. Isaiah experienced the same events in both worlds, give or take. Something happened to him years ago, when he was a young man, which led to the invention of Anthracite. These memories lie dormant in the mind of your own grandfather, back in your universe.'

Everyone looked at me as if this should have made things clear. Perhaps my confusion showed. Llywsiffer leaned in one more time. 'We can't bring him here – the gate journey would kill him. We need you to go back and get the information out of the old chap. Any clue to what occurred would be a start.'

I clapped my hands together decisively; this was more like it. 'Right, take me to the portal. I'm well up for a chat with Gramps.'

Llywsiffer lay a cold hand on my forearm, his grip like a vice. 'I also know what you're now thinking – that when we've sent you home you can do a runner, never to be seen again.'

My eyes went wide. 'Really? That honestly hadn't crossed my mind.' I was hoping my face didn't betray this whopper; my hopes were soon cruelly dashed.

Llywsiffer's thin lips pulled back in his version of a smile, a sight which could have soured milk. 'Disavow yourself of any such notions forthwith. We'll be keeping hold of your young friend here,' he waved an elegant hand towards Gwen. 'Her safety depends on your swift return. Fail to come back and she will meet not her maker, but mine. And believe me, he's far worse.'

With a lump in my throat I gazed at Gwen. She gave a brave smile, confident in my abilities. 'You've got this, Kev. I put my trust in you.' I only wished I shared her optimism.

Seemed I was being cornered into these hare-brained heroics. Best play up to the role everyone was keen to foist upon me. 'If I do this for you, then you'll let us both go – we're quits?'

Slowly Llywsiffer nodded. 'You'll just have to trust me, boy. You have my word of honour.'

Trust was a bit of a stretch, but as usual, what choice did I have? Gwen's fate depended on my mission. The hope in her eyes was almost too much to bear. 'Okay,' I muttered, 'I'm in.'

Llywsiffer smiled again. Outside any passing birds likely fell from the sky stone dead. 'But I warn you now, boy. Attempt to betray me and the fate you've avoided thus far will seem luxurious compared to what lays in store. We are not an organisation you want to cross. Terrible is our fury.'

I could well believe it. I swallowed hard, but played it cool. 'There's just one problem with your plan. How am I meant to

get this information from Grandad? He has – how can I put it
– good days and bad.'

Now it was Taliesin's turn to speak. He leant forward and
handed me a small flask. 'Give him some of this, boi. It will help
perk him up.'

I was appalled. 'Not the Tears of the Puma? I can't give him
that, it will finish him off.'

Taliesin shook his shaggy head. 'Have no fear, this is a milder
concoction. It's made from rare seaweed gathered on the rocks
down Aberdyfi way – flowers of the lost kingdom sunk below
Cardigan Bay, plucked by mermaids – magical it is.'

Against my better judgement, which had been overworked
of late, I reached out to take the bottle. Taliesin pulled it back.

'Just a little, mind – it can take a while to work. But when
it does…' His eyes went wide, he mimed an explosion
blossoming forth from his temple. 'Optrex for the third eye.'
The vial stood balanced on his open palm.

I looked at it dubiously, but took it all the same. Trying to
sound more confident than I felt, I said, 'Let's get on with it
then.'

Llywsiffer clapped his hands. They made a sound like
mausoleum doors slamming. When he rubbed them together
they gave off a fine grey dust. 'I love it when a plan comes
together!' He stabbed a bony finger at the intercom panel.
'Driver, set a course for the Aberdare Gate.'

27

Gateway Plaza Hotel

Along with Iestyn, Gwen and a team of heavily armed druids, I huddled in the back of the unmarked VTOL truck belonging to the Gorsedd. We'd transferred to this more discreet mode of transport, rather than travel south in Llywsiffer's ostentatious limo. Best we weren't seen in the company of the front-running presidential candidate. Llywsiffer had to keep his distance from what we planned next – apparently it offered 'terrible optics'. Which was a fancy way of saying the cheeky bugger didn't want to be seen with us plebs – something about having a knife-edge presidential election to win. There was likely to be a fair amount of shooting. Some dying wasn't out of the question, either. I just hoped it wouldn't fall to me.

We parked across a busy commercial street from the Gateway Plaza in Aberdare, the same spot where I'd first entered this crazy batshit world just over a week ago. It already seemed like I'd been here a lifetime – a lifetime in danger of screeching to a shuddering halt. Somewhere nearby was that seedy bar where I'd survived the first attempt on my life. I had no desire to pay it a second visit, I could almost taste those infernal leek daiquiris. Aberdare itself seemed none the worse after last week's terrorist attack. The mardi gras was another matter – body glitter and rainbow ostrich feathers still clogged the kerbs and gutters. Much like home, a soft rain was falling from the leaden sky. Some things never change.

It was tantalising to think the gate in the basement across the road led back to my own familiar version of Aberdare, the one with living grandfathers and no Cambrian New World Order. I was hungry for a slice of home, however brief. Iestyn meanwhile wasn't letting me forget my mission. He peered at the front of the hotel through a thermal imaging scope. He sounded nervous, as well he might.

'Every faction gunning for you will have agents watching this gate. Our best plan is to rush you through before they can react. This op will be more *crash bang wallop* than *sneaky, sneaky*.'

I scanned the faces passing on the bustling street outside the hotel – the usual seedy crowd. Nobody stood out as a trained killer, but this was Aberdare, so they all looked pretty mean.

'Sounds incredibly dangerous,' I said. 'Perhaps we should call it off.'

The druid looked at me in horror. 'There's no turning back now, mun. You don't want to face the wrath of Llywsiffer empty handed. Nothing's worse than that. We'll go in hard and fast to overpower the gatekeepers. The girl will program the control panel and we'll send you through.'

I looked over at my companion. Gwen was sporting a new piece of hardware – a golden torc snapped tightly around her neck. But this was no ordinary piece of cosmetic jewellery. The collar was linked by radio to a switch hidden on Iestyn's person. One touch of the button and Gwen could be reduced to quivering jelly, nerve impulses from brain to limbs fried in a blazing short circuit. Llywsiffer had given us a demo back at the mountain. I was in no rush to see it used again.

Gwen ran a finger around the snug torc. 'Even with their leadership scrubbed, what's left of the Consortium still runs this gate. If you take it they're sure to counter-attack. This is a suicide mission.'

Iestyn scoffed. 'Those wet foreskins are in meltdown since the meteor strike. The Old Gods can be trusted to smite our foes. We've got a window of opportunity, and we're pushing the Chosen One through.'

The Chosen One gagged at the image, but Iestyn didn't notice, too busy wittering on. 'Besides, I've been coming back from suicide missions all my life. I have my orders. We have to hold the gate for as long as it takes lover-boy here to get back with the goods. We'll just have to hope he doesn't take long. That's why we've brought plenty of ammunition. We're good to go when you are, chief.'

I realised everyone in the van was looking at me. My mouth had gone very dry. They were looking at me for some stirring words of encouragement – I wasn't up to speeches. 'Let's do this,' I just about stuttered.

Seconds later we piled out of the van. It was like someone had fly-tipped a truckload of the Mafia's dirty laundry onto the pavement – the Taffia had come to town, and we weren't here for the shopping. Passers-by dissolved wide eyed as we marched across the street. Traffic screeched to a halt as glaring druids held up fire-blackened hands in warning. The robes we wore might not have been the cleanest, but they were great for concealing the artillery we were packing. Onlookers gawped in awe. Lamp posts were crashed into. Subtle we might not have been, but we were a primordial force of nature. I was terrified, but Christ, it felt good to be part of such a team. We were agents of destruction, come to kick butt and take names, and we didn't even have any pens. We strode into the hotel lobby like the lords of creation.

A smartly uniformed concierge stepped into our path and looked us up and down. 'Can I help you… gentlemen?'

I smiled at him. 'Yes, we're looking for –'

Iestyn appeared by my side and punched him hard in the face. The poor man crumpled to the marble tiles like a house of cards. We stepped over his body and continued our advance through the lobby. Guests and staff alike shrunk in our wake. Clearly we weren't guys to be messed with.

Despite traversing this route before, the layout of the hotel was unfamiliar. I'd not been fully focused when Gwen first pulled me from my home universe – my initial portal trip had induced the jet lag of the gods. But Iestyn seemed to know exactly where he was going. I shuffled over to the girl to attempt a word in private.

'Bide your time, they've given me a gun for self-defence.' I flashed her the rather paltry weapon, concealed beneath my robes.

Gwen was about to answer when her eyes rolled back in her head and she crashed against the corridor wall. Iestyn dragged her to her feet, the torc activation trigger clutched in his hand. 'That was just a tickler. Keep moving – no reason for you lovebirds to chat.' Seemed he was keeping us on a short leash.

We came to a stairwell set behind a pair of glass-fronted doors. Thankfully it seemed deserted and we began our descent. Weapons were drawn; we were getting close to the target. The shaft was soon full of scowling druids, covering each other's progress, from both above and below. These were the trained elite of the Gorsedd's foot soldiers, shock troops of the druidic revolution. I just hoped they didn't turn out to be cannon fodder. I was relying on these psychos to keep Gwen safe while I carried out my part of the deal.

The portal was located in the hotel's basement, deep in the staff quarters not frequented by Joe Public. The stairwell exited onto a long corridor lined with closed doors. Our destination lay at the far end. Room 237 was not all it seemed. Iestyn crouched in the doorway to the corridor and peered down the hall. All was still and silent. I was conscious of the rest of the team stacking up behind me, covering the stairs above with an arsenal of automatic weapons. In such a confined space the smell was intense – stale sweat, adrenaline and gun oil. My heart was thumping as Iestyn gave the signal to the entry team, who peeled off and started down the hallway.

Could it really be this simple? Gwen had told us each Consortium gate was manned by a small security team, a basic level of defence to guard against accidental discovery and maintain the complex apparatus. The hope was that, bereft of leadership since the meteor strike in Virginia, we could catch these grunts napping. Moving briskly in tactical formation we were soon halfway down the passageway. Three hefty druids took the lead, guns raised and at the ready. Gwen glanced back the way we'd come, to the remnant of our squad guarding the stairwell.

'This is too easy, something's wrong.'

I too sensed something amiss – was I developing Gwen's sixth sense for danger? We were sitting ducks in the empty corridor. I didn't think our opponents were ones to skimp on firepower.

Iestyn ground his teeth as he brought up the rear. 'Don't jinx us, girl – we're almost there.'

Prophetic words perhaps. One of the doors ahead opened with a creak. Our squad froze, itchy fingers glued to triggers. Out stepped a vacant looking fellow, a doughnut hanging from his mouth and newspaper under one arm. He was doing up the flies on his hotel uniform and failing. He saw us and did a comic book double-take. For a moment everyone was still, perhaps contemplating the futility of human existence. It was a moment which couldn't last.

Doughnut guy reached for the small of his back, and the gun that lay hidden. He had no chance, but had to try. An avalanche of lead filled the corridor. The unfortunate guard danced a jig of death, bouncing from one wall to the other. Driven backwards he came to rest sprawled atop a fire extinguisher, pinned to the smouldering plaster in a profane crucifixion – not so much a holy Jesus, as a holey Swiss cheese, smoke spiralling from every perforation.

The silence that followed was deafening, or was that just the fearful ringing in my ears? The Gorsedd clearly didn't favour suppressed weapons. Some of us had contributed more to the barrage than others. Still struggling to free the gun from my robes, I felt Iestyn barge past me. 'That's one down, check the target room – CONTACT!'

A scrum of armed druids rushed the door the guard had stepped through, quickly followed by a burst of automatic fire. There was zero chance this mission was still covert. I peered into the room from the hallway. A second uniformed gatekeeper lay bloodied on the bed, a chirping phone clutched in his hand. It squawked a startled one-sided conversation, before Iestyn blasted it to shrapnel. The druid leader stepped back into the corridor.

'Their friends will be on their way. Let's get him through the gate, and pronto!'

Gwen knew the role she'd been brought to play. The portal room itself was next to the one used by the hapless guards – room 237. The girl stood before the door and flexed her nimble fingers. 'There'll be a key on one of the bodies – find it.'

Iestyn's cronies sprung to work. Sure enough the guy who'd never finish his doughnut had what we were looking for.

Iestyn wiped the blood off the keycard and handed it to my companion. Gwen swiped it through the lock, the light blinked green and we were in. Guns drawn, we checked the corners as druids took up defensive positions in the hallway. We had no idea how long before the inevitable counter-attack.

The chamber behind the door was no ordinary bedroom. I'd come through this way before, but I'd been in no fit state to notice my surroundings. I was only a little more composed now. The space was bare of furnishings, just four grey walls and a naked swinging bulb – interior decor clearly wasn't a priority. Iestyn didn't need to shove me, I sprung forward gladly – it looked like I was going home, even if only temporarily. Gwen followed us inside. The girl grabbed my arm and spun me into a fierce embrace, a gesture as unexpected as it was welcome. Instead of a kiss her lips lingered by my ear.

'Someone wants you to go through. This was a set-up all the way.'

Before I could reply Iestyn pulled us apart. 'That's enough of that, you pair of preverts. I would say *get a room*, but we're already in one.'

I reached out for Gwen's outstretched hand. 'Don't worry – I'll be back to save you.'

Her brown eyes locked with mine. 'I know you will. Watch your back.'

Iestyn was having none of it. 'Enough of the smut. Nogood Boyo ere's got a job to do, and so do you, you artificial bitch.' He gestured with his weapon to a numeric keypad mounted on the wall behind us.

Gwen's lip curled but she set about her task. Which reminded me – I checked the instructions she'd written out earlier, the notepad described the button sequence I'd need to punch on the other side once I was done. It wouldn't do to lose it – Gwen's fate depended on my swift return. I also had Taliesin's vial of magic herbs. I was fully equipped and loaded.

Iestyn appeared before me and reached out a shaky hand. I looked at it for a moment, before taking it in a firm grip. The druid leader pumped it up and down, his eyes welling up.

'You might be a soy-boi, but it's a noble thing you do this day. The fate of our nation depends on you. Good luck.' His palm was warm and sweaty; mine was much the same. He and his team faced a challenge every bit as difficult as my own. I just prayed Gwen could stay out of the crossfire.

'Roger that.'

There was no time for further speeches – Gwen's fingers had worked their magic. 'It's done. Gate triggers in twenty seconds – fire in the hole.'

Iestyn threw me a wobbly salute and bundled the others from the room. For the first time in what felt like ages, I was on my own. This was also the first time I'd gone through a gate without the girl by my side; it felt lonely. I would have done anything for one of her mints. The last image I saw before the door slammed shut was Gwen forcing a smile of encouragement as she fingered the golden collar clamped tight around her neck. I resolved not to let her down. The light went out and I experienced that familiar sinking feeling.

28

Sweet Home Aberdare Zero

I came to on a bare metal floor, cold boilerplate dimples pressing against my cheek. Sitting up I wiped the snot from my nose and the spittle from my lips – it tasted like I'd gone a night drinking nothing but economy prosecco. I was in the library service lift I'd last seen the day I met Gwen. That day seemed long ago, in another world – which is weird because it had actually been this world – *the* real world. My head was woozy and my vision blurred, but not as bad as I'd experienced in earlier transitions. Maybe I was getting used to gate travel, just as Gwen had claimed.

I dragged myself to my feet and looked round for the stairwell. There was no chance I was using the lift, even for its normal mundane function. Sure enough I soon found the dusty steps and made my way slowly up to ground level. Good – as usual the place looked deserted. Discreetly I made my way to the exit, letting out a sigh of relief as I caught site of the open front doors. For once it was even sunny outside – a good omen. This had been easier than I could have hoped.

'Ere he is look – Swansea Baywatch is back.'

I pulled up short, an icicle piercing my heart. It was Mrs Abergavenny, the ancient head librarian.

'Where's ewe bin, Kev bach? And with a maxed-out library card, an all.'

Grimacing I turned to face her. 'Oh, you know – here and there – around. Been away with... work.'

I needed this like I needed a hole in the head. The swivel-eyed fossil scuttled from behind her counter and grabbed my cheek between finger and thumb. She had a vice-like grip despite her slight stature. She stank of lavender cough drops and something worse – rumour was she liked nothing better than sucking on a fisherman's friend. I didn't envy the poor guy.

'If ewe's thinking of bunkin off to Rio then think again, buster. I've got contacts.'

I was sure she had Ronnie Biggs on speed dial, but it was hard to talk with her steely fingers clamped around my face. 'Ooourha,' I just about muttered.

My tormentor had a flinty twinkle in her pale grey eyes. 'Some might believe ewe needs *Women in Love* for "research", but I wasn't born yesterday, or even the day before.'

I didn't think she'd been born at all – built in a Soviet tank factory more likely – but wisely kept this observation to myself.

'Bring it back, sunshine, or I'll have ewe in traction down Ysbyty Nye Bevan before ewe can say reconstructive surgery. Reading me loud and clear, are we?'

'Uhu.'

'And the pages better not be stuck together this time, filthy bugger. Comprende vous? Now where's ewe really bin, fuckface?'

Nodding, I tried to extricate myself from her grip, but it was no easy task. It felt like she was giving me whiplash, as she tugged my head back and fore.

'Ooot ov own eesearchin me ook.'

Tilting her head to one side like some sort of demonic crow she considered this for a moment. 'The book, you say?'

'Uhu.'

Mrs Abergavenny made a face like she was chewing a salty wasp. 'Maybe for the best, luv – I don't likes to piss on your parade but Mr Beynon down the chemist said he read *The Windy Ninja* and it was utter shite. Shallow characterisation and weak underlying narrative structure, he said. Plus, ewe got the sociopolitical dynamic of fourteenth century Japan all wrong.'

With a playful slap which left me counting stars, she let me go. I tried to massage some life back into my features but it was a losing battle. I felt sure I'd develop a bruise.

'All feedback much appreciated, Mrs A,' I lied.

My tormentor didn't seem convinced. 'I wouldn't pay much attention to what Mr Beynon says. Don't think there's much in the way of characterisation in those filthy magazines he reads under 'is counter. And as for underlying narrative – plenty of underlying whores, but that's about it. Mochyn bach!'

I nodded my agreement, but she wasn't finished yet.

'Get yourself back home first – your mam's neighbours are worried sick. Threatening to call the police, they is – and we don't wants no fuss, does we? Leave a note explaining ewer both okay. Put what passes for their minds to rest before they get Plod involved.'

I backed out of the doorway and stumbled down the steps. I didn't want this foul-mouthed harridan getting hold of me again. 'Thanks, I'll be sure to do that, Mrs A.'

She waved to me from the entrance. 'Remember – mam first,

or you'll have me up in your grill. And ewe don't wants that twice in one day, believe me!'

Once was more than enough. I didn't run, despite the urge, but instead walked briskly down the deserted street. Just what an irate version of Mrs Abergavenny would look like boggled the mind. I wanted to put as much distance between me and her as possible. I think she watched me go until I was out of sight, maybe through binoculars. Something about her gave me the creeps. She was right about one thing, though – my first stop should be home. Where had Mum got to?

Being back in the old town was messing with my head. I'd only been gone for a week but already it seemed a weirdly alien place. Something here had changed, or was it me? It was like I was in an alternative reality, which was ironic considering what I'd been through. I kept expecting to see a stream of flying cars drifting across the horizon, or bump into one of the ubiquitous robots which bumbled around Aberdare+1, but nothing was doing. No gleaming skyscraper towers thrust up from the valley floor, no garish advertising holograms danced in the air – the skyline was just the low-level jumble of terraced housing I'd grown up with. The hillsides were covered in nothing but trees. I'd only been home five minutes and already I was missing the glamour and excitement of the other side – maybe even the danger.

Mrs Abergavenny might have been a deranged old coot but she had been right about Mum – she'd not heard from me in days. And where the hell was she, anyway? I sometimes went to stay with friends, but I'd always let her know where I was going, and keep her posted with regular updates. My mates thought it hilarious. Now I was in for an almighty bollocking. Bad, but not my biggest concern just then. Still, I could do with heading home, to get a change of clothes and a toothbrush if nothing else. When I'd left with Gwen I didn't get time to pack.

Something was tugging at the back of my mind. Some minor detail about what Mrs A had said. I felt certain it must be significant, but couldn't for the life of me put my finger on it. Never mind, it was probably nothing. I was in high spirits as I strode through the sunshine. This mission was getting done.

I turned the corner at the bottom of our road and ran into a familiar face. It was one of our neighbours, Arwel, who I'd known since childhood. A bumbling galoot of a lad, it was hard not to feel a twang of pity – he was nothing like me – a sad case who still lived with his parents and would be lucky to ever leave home. He did a double take when he saw me and looked me up and down. Perhaps because I was still wearing my Gorsedd robes.

'Kev, lad – how you doing, butt?'

Self-conscious of my bare ankles and sandals, I smoothed the front of my smock. 'Won't lie to you, Ars – I'm on my way back from a book launch in Cardiff. My publishers know how to throw a party. Was quite a night.'

His eyes lit up. 'I bet they do. Fancy dress was it?'

I forced a smile. 'Yeah, cosplay is all the rage with the literary set these days. Should have seen some of the chicks.'

Arwel looked suitably impressed, if a bit confused. No great change there then. 'I thought your book was about ninjas, Kev, not druids? I've heard it's full of smut.' He broke into a grin.

I struggled to retain my patience. The standards of literary criticism around here left a lot to be desired. 'It's true it contains... adult themes. You know me, I've always been one to surf narrative's dark rim. Bit of an edgelord.'

Arwel blinked. 'Tidy. I'll have to take a look, when it comes out, like.' He continued to study me, an odd expression on his vast moon face. 'Something different about you, Kev? And

I don't just mean the clobber. Seems like you've changed somehow, mun.'

He peered at me as if I was some freshly landed alien, and maybe I was. But I had no time for such idle speculation. Sidestepping I squeezed past him up the front of the terrace. 'I'd love to stay and chat, Ars, but I've got a lot to do. Ciao.'

This seemed my day for being accosted by time vampires – just typical. Didn't they know I was on an urgent mission? And the worst offender might be yet to come. Arwel stood aside and watched me go. 'Good luck, Kev! Say elo to your mam, if you find er.'

'You too, Ars. Take care.'

Mum's car was not outside our front door. With luck I could grab what I needed and go, minus the Spanish Inquisition. Our house sat in the middle of a long terrace. My budding instinct for danger told me it best to go for a rear entry – much in keeping with local romantic traditions. I spirited down our rubbish-strewn back lane, where a lot of that rear entry action took place. After bunking over our wall, I was in. My own key was long gone, but the one Mum kept under the flowerpot was in its usual place. Silently I let myself into the kitchen and listened for a moment to the silence – I'd learned to be cautious. All was still. Where on earth was she? Should I be worried? Nah, she was probably fine.

Heart thumping, I padded my way up to my room. It felt smaller somehow, the room of a child. I ran a hand over my collection of pencils and pens next to my drawing board – would I ever get to use them again? My rucksack hung behind the door, I threw a few basics in and changed my clothes. It was good to get out of the foul-smelling bardic robes; jeans and t-shirt were more my thing. A hot shower would have been great, but there was no time.

Tearing a sheet of paper from my sketchbook I composed a

brief note to 'Whoever it may concern', just the basics. I told them I was staying with friends on a writing crunch to get the first draft finished. A thin story perhaps, but with luck it would take the edge off any fears. Didn't want anyone getting the cops involved. I agreed with Mrs A on that. Nice of her to take an interest.

Minutes later I was done. Exiting the same way I'd entered, I put the key back and climbed over the wall into the lane. Paranoid perhaps, but why leave by the front door when it might be watched? In tricky situations some people ask *What would Jesus do?* My version was to ask the same question of Gwen. After turning a few corners I was soon trotting up the road to the hill. Grandad here I come.

29

Gafr Rhywiol Nursing Home

Travelling the familiar path up to the home I mulled over what I was going to say. I had the vial of 'herbs' Taliesin had given me, but I couldn't see how it would make much difference. Grandad had good days and bad – even on the good he struggled to recall details from that morning, let alone seventy years before. As for explaining the intricacies of a zero-point energy device – good luck with that. Isaiah was more likely to sprout wings and fly. This whole jaunt was a long shot, yet I kept thinking back to what Taliesin had said – there was no denying that guy's faith in his visions. This was our only chance at salvation. But I was conscious of the missing presence by my side. I kept thinking of Gwen, and that infernal nerve-frying collar round her neck. For her sake, at least, I had to try.

The nurse at reception didn't look up from her magazine. I signed the visitor's book and checked who else had been in to see Isaiah. He'd had no other guests that week – wherever Mum was, she wasn't keeping Gramps updated on my disappearance. Why didn't that surprise me? Just when I thought I'd be able to slip in, all nice and discreet, I was pinned to the spot by a whining voice from the back office.

'Ah, young Mr Jones! Just the person I wanted to see.' It was Mr Hudson, the home's bumbling duty manager. He was brandishing a thick wad of printed statements. The big red letters 'FINAL DEMAND' were stamped on each one.

Did I know how far behind our payments were? When would we settle our bill? Of course he didn't like *asking guests to leave*, but he left me in no doubt that this was the next step for my grandad, if we didn't come up with some cash, and fast. It took all my skills of negotiation to convince him Mum would stump up the funds before the end of the month. He didn't look all that convinced as I all but bounced up the stairs – and to tell the truth, neither was I. We'd cross that burning bridge when we came to it.

The sterile halls were deserted at this time of day; the old folks couldn't expect much to disturb their peace and quiet. The evenings and weekends were a little busier, but this was basically a warehouse for storing date-expired human beings – a staging area for those shipping out to destinations unknown. I'd once asked Grandad, what was it like growing old? He'd told me it was better than the alternatives, but only just. And this was a nicer place than some, to see out your last days, but still pretty grim when you got down to it.

I found Grandad's door ajar, knocked loudly and went in. He was in his usual place, sitting by the window gazing out at the pleasant view of the forested mountainside. Grandad looked up and smiled a bit groggily. For the briefest of seconds I got a glimpse of the man he'd used to be.

'Kev, bach. Where've you been? I've missed you.'

Although grazed by a harpoon of guilt, I smiled back. 'Hiya Grandad. How you doing?'

'Doing fine, lad. Is it time for another film night? *Terminator* Part Two, next I think.'

'Afraid not, Gramps. I've been away with work.'

He looked surprised. 'Working now, are we? Your mam says the world of work is not for you. Says you take to it like a duck takes to Scrabble – chopsy mare sometimes, your mam.'

I kept smiling, although my teeth were so gritted they could have melted snow. 'It was a research trip for *The Windy Ninja*, I've told you about it.' Just a little off-white lie, not a million miles from the truth, I consoled myself.

Isaiah looked confused. 'Mr Jenkins cross the landing gets ever so windy when they give us cabbage soup, but he's no ninja. At least I don't think so. What's a ninja again?'

These days conversations with Grandad were prone to detours. I tried to focus on the mission at hand. Somehow I had to get Taliesin's potion into him. Inspiration arrived on a tea trolley. 'Can I get you a cuppa?'

'I thought you'd never ask, lad. Shut the door and come in.'

Isaiah's neat room didn't have much in the way of personal possessions. There was a sun-faded sepia photo up on one wall – a pretty girl in a wedding dress stood next to a strapping young man wearing a Clarke Gable moustache and Air Force NCO uniform. Gran and Grandad must have been barely in their twenties when they married. They looked happy enough on their big day, but if you looked closer you could see the uncertainty in their eyes. Mr Hitler's world tour was still building to a crescendo and not every punter was coming back in one piece.

Across the room from the picture stood a sideboard bearing a swarm of smaller photos – Mum and me at progressing stages of life; first days at new schools, Christmas mornings and birthdays, me as I boarded the train to Telford Art School – the punctuation points of life. The only other item of note was the elaborately carved teak box Grandad had brought back from his time in the Far East, containing an assortment of letters, trinkets and medals tarnished with age. Next to these meagre possessions a chipped plastic tray held a travel kettle, an eclectic assortment of mugs and a tiny carton of milk – as succinct a manifestation of the fractured nature of modern living as ever there was one. At least it let Grandad retain some independence.

I filled the kettle from the sink and set it to boil. He'd always told me the RAF was not powered by anything as mundane as kerosene or diesel, but by tea – it's drinking as ritualised as anything you'd find in China or Japan. *The Windy Ninja* would have approved. Grandad saw me inspecting the tiny packet of teabags.

'From the NAAFI is it?'

'Yes Gramps, of course. Only the best.'

'Thank Christ for that. Lucky they've got any left, if you ask me. War ended months ago.'

I nodded. 'Yes, it did. Running down stocks, I expect.'

'Had that Mrs Abergavenny up here again the other day.'

The hairs on the back of my neck stood to attention and saluted. For some slippery reason I couldn't quite put my finger on this revelation troubled me greatly. 'Really – what did she want?'

'Oh, she's up here all the bleedin time. Brings that trolley load of books for the *old people* – very popular, she is.' He gave me a conspiratorial wink.

It seemed I'd been holding my breath; I let out a sigh of relief, panic over. 'Ah I see.' It tickled me how he referred to the other occupants of the home – as if they were minor irritants who he stoically put up with. Gramps was a generation older than some of them. Isaiah hadn't finished yet. He checked both left and right as if worried about eavesdroppers and sank into a conspiratorial whisper.

'There's folk in this place who'd do anything to get their hands on a bit of smut. A well-fingered *Lady Chatterley* is about as close as most get, what with our rubbish Wi-Fi and all. Mrs A has a copy with Post-it notes on all the rude bits – saucy devil.'

I sat down at a small table across from him. 'Isn't that a bit racy for some of the guests? They shouldn't be thinking about things like that at their age. Your age.'

Isaiah shook his head. 'Oh no, bach. We're no strangers to overexcitement up here. Has its uses, though.' He spotted my blank expression. 'Helps free up bed space when it tips flagging inmates over the edge. Sometimes nature needs a little helpin 'and.'

He was a practical man, my grandfather. For once I was very nearly lost for words. 'One way to look at it, I suppose.'

Isaiah scratched his stubbly chin. 'Always makes a big fuss of me, does Mrs Abergavenny. VERY attentive, she is. Reckon she might have the hots for us. If I was just ten years younger –'

'– you'd be...' I did a quick calculation, 'eighty-six, Grandad. Would it make that much difference? On second thoughts, don't answer that.'

He gazed off into the middle distance, drifting away into a world of his own, as he increasingly did these days. I struggled to get the mental image out of my mind – sometimes it's a curse to have too good an imagination. Seemed I needed to jet wash the inside of my skull.

The boiling kettle rescued me from the horror show inside my brain. The device was on the verge of a meltdown, clicking off just in time. It reminded me I had a mission of my own. I got up and strolled over to the sideboard, taking Taliesin's vial from my pocket out of line of sight. How many drops should I use? The swivel-eyed mystic had been as vague as ever with his instructions – I wished now I'd paid more attention up that cursed mountain. I was flirting with the prospect of a comatose geriatric, or worse, on my hands. Carefully I coaxed out a single drop, it hung there for a moment, gleaming in the afternoon light. The slightest shake, and it fell, hitting the surface to bloom like a rainbow supernova. I stirred and stirred but an oily sheen remained on the surface, matching the stain on my heart.

'Here you go Gramps. Don't burn your mouth.'

We sat and talked about nothing in particular – the usual sorts of things. Who amongst the residents was not talking to whom, which of the nurses was pilfering pills. It seemed the internet access had been switched off because Mrs Griffith and her bridge posse had been blowing their pensions via online poker again. When would they learn? Probably never.

I watched closely for signs of the potion taking effect, but nothing happened. If anything Grandad grew drowsy – maybe Taliesin had been talking through his backside about its enlivening effects. I steered the conversation onto a perennial favourite; Grandad always enjoyed telling me what he'd got up to in the RAF. He'd served all over the place in WW2, filling more roles than Swansea's flagship Greggs. Some of the things he'd seen and done were enough to make your hair stand on end. Trouble was I'd heard the stories a thousand times before. At least the one's he was prepared to tell me.

I finished my tea and tried to sound casual. 'So I was thinking, Grandad – I might write up some of your stories – once I've finished *The Windy Ninja*, of course. If that's okay with you.'

The old man raised his eyebrows and stifled a yawn. 'That would be nice. Your mam would like that.'

How to approach this? 'The problem is I need you to fill in the blanks. You've never told me the whole story. Tell me something new.'

He gave this some serious thought. 'Did you know I built the first airfield in Nepal?'

'Yes Grandad. You had nothing but three trucks, a team of Sherpas and a ball of string. Got to meet the king, you did. He gave you the freedom of Kathmandu.'

'And I can drive a flock of sheep through the town any time I bleedin want.'

'That must really come in handy.'

'What about the time me and Ernest Hemingway went drinking in Singapore?'

'He was fine with spirits but couldn't handle the beer. The cops released you on the condition you never came back. You were on antibiotics for months.'

Isaiah got that faraway look in his eyes again. I put a hand on his arm. 'Grandad, are you ever going to tell me the other bits? The parts you never talk about.' He looked at me innocently. Did he really not know what I was driving at?

'I bet you saw some strange things at the end of the war. Why don't you ever talk about that?'

He turned his pale watery eyes on me, the pupils oddly dilated. 'Some terrible things went on, lad – bloody awful.'

I felt bad pressing him, but kept thinking of Gwen in that infernal nerve-frying collar. 'I know, Grandad. But I need you to tell me – for the sake of posterity, at least.'

He let out another sigh, and was silent for a long while. His eyelids drifted shut, I thought perhaps he'd fallen asleep. When at last he spoke he sounded even more tired than before.

'After we landed in Normandy the brass had more pilots that they knew what to do with. The Luftwaffe had been shot from the skies. Those of us who were *only sergeants* had little chance of getting near a Spitfire. Sent us for retraining, they did. Luckily there were plenty of less glamorous jobs going round – less glamorous but a lot more dangerous.'

'What did they make you do?'

Minutes slipped by, with no sound to break the silence but the ticking clock. At last Isaiah rocked forward and mumbled, 'They retrained us as forward air controllers. The silly sods who drove along with the frontline troops and called down air support.'

'Sounds risky.'

'It bloody was. Our own tanks had no chance against a Tiger, too well armoured. All the firepower had to come from the sky. Trouble was Jerry soon got wind that the blokes in the armoured cars bristling with radio gear were orchestrating the show. We were the main threat – had a massive target pinned to us all the way from Caen to the Rhine crossings.'

'Lots of casualties?'

Grandad looked sad. 'Aye, the attrition rate was grim. Lost more mates in those few months than the rest of the war put together.'

This was all news to me. I'd not heard this part of his service history before. Tantalisingly I sensed the final pieces of a jigsaw falling into place. 'So you were in Germany when the war ended?'

Isaiah nodded. 'The arse end of April 1945, a little north of Hanover. Bloody messy it was.'

My imagination had gone into overdrive. 'Must have been quite a time. Bet you saw some stuff.'

He nodded. 'It was like the end of the bloody world. Snow still on the ground and not a leaf on any of the trees, thanks to the constant bombing. Hitler wanted to take the German people down with him, thought they'd been proved unworthy

– silly sod. You don't want to know about some of the places we liberated.' Grandad shuddered and his eyes closed.

It pained me to push him, but I sensed we were approaching some crucial revelation. A thousand closely studied History Channel documentaries ran on fast forward through my brain. I leaned in close. 'Did you ever see any... weird technology? Weren't the Germans doing all sorts of bizarre research – you know, black magic and things?'

I'd played enough *Castle Wolfenstein* to know I was on firm ground. Most serious historians agreed Hitler escaped to Antarctica on a UFO – it all made sense when you thought about it. I could quote entire sections of *Hellboy* chapter and verse. Indiana Jones was practically a relative.

Grandad's eyes flickered open and he took a deep breath. It was a struggle for him to stay awake. I wasn't sure if he was completely rational anymore. 'Rubbish, all rubbish. The only thing the Nazis were researching was how to cover up their crimes. There were... some odd events, though –'

A tingle traversed my spine. 'What... events?'

Isaiah sat bolt upright. 'What I read in that church for starters – the darndest thing!'

'What church, Grandad?'

He looked at me as if I was simple minded. 'The one with the crooked spire, of course. Try to keep up, lad.' He paused for a moment, before reaching forward to grip me with a liver-spotted hands – his skin so transparent I could almost see the bones. 'It was in bloody Welsh, you know – how's about that!'

'What did it say?'

Suddenly he was struggling to keep his eyelids open again. 'And that was before we even reached the castle. That was an accursed place – where I found the second mystery – along with that pair of imposters.'

'What castle, Grandad? What imposters? This is not making much sense.'

'Everything was either burning or getting blown to bits. Had no time to examine what they'd found in the cellar. Bastards knocked me out. Still don't know how I made it out alive.'

I could feel my heart beating faster. 'What was this place called?'

Grandad leant forward, his nose almost touching mine; his eyes closed, as he whispered, 'Schloss Drachenburg, was its name –' His mouth hung open, ready to impart fresh wisdom, further arcane revelations, but all that came out was a loud snore.

Gently I jogged his frail hand. 'Come on Gramps, you need to tell me the rest!'

But that was all I was getting from him today. Grandad's head sank forward till his chin rested on the collar of his cardi. He was out for the count. I eased him back in his chair and slowly regained control of my breathing. I barely knew what to make of it all.

It was all so maddeningly vague I could almost cry, but was it enough? My thoughts returned to Gwen, and the ruthless men holding her captive the other side of the gate. Did I have enough information to placate Llywsiffer?

Surely it was no coincidence the inventor of Anthracite had been stumbling through crumbling Gothic castles, finding weird Nazi technology, in the last days of the Reich? I could see it now – a young Isaiah bathed in the unearthly glow of some profane eldritch artefact not meant to be unearthed by man. Somehow this world's Isaiah had failed to see it through – some 'imposters' had got in his way; in other dimensions he'd had better luck. The future could turn on a sixpence. So much for me being the Chosen One. Came as quite a relief, though I did experience a twinge of disappointment.

Reading between the lines it seemed clear what had gone down – Grandad had stumbled over some freakish experiment which set him on the path to Anthracite. The simplest explanations were often the best, as Grandad himself had always told me. I had no doubt I stood on the brink of the whole shabby truth. But was it going to be enough to save my friend?

I put a blanket over my slumbering Grandad and stood over him chewing my lower lip. The old guy looked so peaceful, his frail chest rising and falling with measured rhythm. Sleeping like a baby, dreaming of who knew what. It was time for me to be decisive. Gripped by a fresh sense of exhilaration I grabbed my things and slipped quietly into the hall. The time had come to head back to the library to rescue the woman of my dreams. Perhaps this visit had raised more questions than answers, but if they were the right questions then at least I was making progress. I might not yet hold the smoking gun, but I sure could smell the cordite. I just prayed the druids would agree.

30

Overdue Charged with Extreme Prejudice

I raced back down the hill towards my date with destiny. I hoped very soon it would lead to an actual *proper date* with Gwen, one involving candles, wine glasses and blow jobs. Never let it be said I'm not an optimist at heart, as well as a romantic. Saving fair maidens from certain death must surely count for something, even in these enlightened times. I told myself not to count my chickens before they hatched, but I could almost hear these babies clucking.

The Aberdare I'd grown up in seemed tame compared to the one I was heading back to. As I jogged past familiar landmarks I was struck by the small scale of the place. People I'd known since childhood shrank before me, their mouths hanging open – perhaps they could sense I was a man on a mission – either that, or it was the mad glint in my eye. I ran past the ramshackle pub at the bottom of the high street, The Bailiff's Arms. Outside old men stood smoking in the sunshine. Inside, the discount meat shoplifted from the Co-op round the corner accounted for most of the trade. I raced past Coin-Wash City, with its flaking sign and banks of empty dryers, my days of watching Mum's socks tumble hypnotically long gone. A blaze of charity shop windows rushed by, a low-rent *Generation Game* conveyor of tat.

As usual the library stood deserted. It struck me as ironic that I'd always used this place as a doorway to other worlds. The books it contained helped me escape the mundanity of my pre-Gwen existence. All the time it had secretly housed an *actual* gate to another dimension – one far beyond the pitiful strainings of my imagination. Who'd have thunk it – one of those little harmonic resonances with which life is peppered.

I bounded up the steps two at a time, and raced through the grandiose front doors. Thank goodness there was no sign of Mrs Abergavenny at the desk. The last thing I needed now was some aimless chatter about the literary merits of my own work in progress. Composing myself I strode through the silent hallways, while checking my pockets for the notepad bearing Gwen's instructions – the button sequence needed to trigger the gate mechanism. I was relieved to find the comforting weight resting against my hip. But something was bothering me, tugging at the back of my mind. I skidded to a halt and, like a demented lederhosen dancer, patted down all my available pockets. But there was no escaping it – I didn't have Taliesin's flask; I'd left the potion next to Grandad's kettle back at the home. It would *probably* be all right, I told myself. What was the worst that could happen? No time to go back now.

Resuming my progress I turned down the corridor leading to the service elevator. Rounding the last corner I pulled up short. Mrs Abergavenny stood, in power stance, sorting through a trolley load of faded books and humming an off-key rendition of 'Calon Lân'. Her butchery interrupted, she peered at me over her bifocals, eyes locking on mine like some predatory wild animal.

'Ah Kevin, back so soon. I trust ewe've got *Women in Love?*'

Flummoxed, I blurted the first words that came into my head. 'Well, I do my best Mrs A, but to be honest results have been patchy thus far.'

Her thin lips pulled back in a sneer and I got a flash of tiny yellowing teeth, slightly pointed. From the back of her throat came a sound like a Dobermann growling, incongruous from such a small old woman. This was a wrinkle I'd not been expecting. Perhaps I could change the subject.

'Lovely day outside.'

She gazed at me with exaggerated wonder. 'Yes, isn't it just LOVELY! So mild for the time of year, don't ewe think?'

I nodded. What fresh insanity was this? It was then that I remembered a minor detail from our earlier conversation – she'd told me to *get yourself back home to Mam first*. First before what? Almost as if she'd…

'BEAUTIFUL how the sunlight glints off the abandoned abattoir. The glue factory has never looked so lush. Just a shame ewe can't score a decent bit of cheese on toast round here, not for love nor money!'

'Mrs A, how did you know –'

'Love's the stench coming off the municipal tip in the morning, I does. Smells of piss and desperation. I's had enough of this mingin dump. By the way, how's your Bampa?'

'He's fine thanks. Wait a minute, how do you –'

She disappeared behind her trolley, only to bob up again much too fast. The gun looked comically large in her frail liver-spotted hand, the other supporting her bony wrist like a pro. I got the feeling she'd done this before. The weapon was pointing at my head – déjà vu all over again – except this time there was no Gwen to bail me out. The impressive piece of hardware trained in my direction had the multi-barrelled, LED-flashing, futuristic look of the ones to which I'd recently become accustomed. It wasn't a weapon from this world.

Something large and bitter seemed stuck in my throat. 'Any chance I can convince you you've got the wrong guy?' I asked, a bit lamely.

Mrs Abergavenny chuckled, and smiled her bittersweet little old lady smile. It was like watching a grey-haired piranha preparing to attack. 'Listen, Billy Big Bollocks – you've got about as much chance of that as you have of ever selling that book of yours. Now, are ewe going to play ball? It will only get harder if I have to blow your kneecaps off first.'

I licked my lips. 'When you put it like that Mrs A, I guess I'll get my shorts and daps on. What's the game you have in mind?'

She looked me up and down like I was a side of prime beef. 'First things ffwcing first. I'm reliably informed you're packing heat.'

Maybe my innate charm would work here. 'Nice of you to notice, but it's just these jeans are a bit tight.'

She wrinkled her nose in disgust. 'Ych a fi! I mean you can dump the artillery, you chopsy bugger. And no funny business, like. I've met some pricks in my time, but you're a whole walking cactus.'

There was no chance I was trying anything even vaguely amusing. I could see she had the drop on me, not to mention the reflexes of a venomous snake and the look of a cold-hearted killer – something to do with the manic glint in her grey eyes and the tone of authority in her reedy voice; that and the enormous gun.

Using finger and thumb I reached round slowly to the back of my waistband and carefully removed the rather feeble excuse for a weapon the druids had given me. Bending at the knee I slid it across the floor. My tormentor trapped it beneath one of her turquoise slingbacks.

'You can keep the notebook – you're going to need that soon enough. Now get in that ruddy lift.'

There were a few details I wanted to clear up first. 'So Mrs A, was it all a big show from the start? You were sent here to spy on me and Grandad?'

She kept the gun trained on me as I shuffled into the elevator. 'Don't get the idea you can pump me for information, boi. I'm not the villain in some daytime cop show. But I can tell you I wasn't entirely putting on an act. When I said *The Windy Ninja* was shite I meant it from the bottom of my black bile-filled heart.'

I forced a smile. 'Thanks. Good to know there's still some honesty left in this world. These worlds.'

She took up position on the other side of the lift, gesturing to the buttons with the gun. 'Get the sequence right first time, you gobby little shite. I don't wants to have to knock you out and do it myself. And trust me, neither do you. I'm not in the mood to be gentle.'

'I wouldn't trust you as far as you could throw me.'

'Ooooh, you'd be surprised how strong am I – commando training, and all that. Now get to work, sonny boi, we don't have all bleedin day.'

With her free hand she slid a tube of cough drops from up her cardi sleeve and stripped one from the top of the stack. She walked it across her knuckles, like a croupier with a poker chip, tossing it into her mouth with practised ease. I guessed this wasn't the first time she'd been through a gate. She didn't offer me one.

I took up position at the lift control panel. Peering down at Gwen's instructions I warmed my fingers up, like I'd seen her do a lifetime ago. When I was ready I took a deep breath and began punching the code with great care. I took my time; I had no desire to find out just how rough this mad old harridan could be. When it was done I paused and held my breath. There was a faint click, followed by a whirring sound.

'Fire in the hole,' my captor cackled.

The gate mechanism was about to trigger. We were heading back to Aberdare +1. Mrs A kept her gun trained on me the whole time. The lights went out and I felt myself falling.

31

Aberdare Part Deux

I regained my senses sprawled on the floor of a bare room. It took me a moment to recognise where I was – I'd been here before. It was room 237 at the Gateway Plaza Hotel in that other Aberdare. It looked like my fingers had not let me down. My recovery was interrupted by the theatrical clearing of a throat behind me. Mrs Abergavenny lounged against the wall, picking her teeth with a long fingernail. She still had her gun pointed at my head. She spat out her cough drop, which skidded across the floor right up to my nose.

'Good of you to join us, bach. There's someone who wants to meet ewe – and he ain't the type to keep waiting. Let's blow this mingin joint.'

I staggered to my feet and lurched through the open doorway. I couldn't help but notice it was leaning askew in the frame. All the while Mrs A kept a wary distance, as well as her shooting iron at the ready. The corridor outside was not as spick and span as I remembered. Bullet holes riddled every surface, scorch marks adorned the walls, brass shell casings littered the floor. They were going to have to get a new carpet – more than one individual had done some serious leaking all over it in the not so distant. We'd messed the place up taking the gate, but this was on a different scale. It looked like this had been the scene of a major battle. Panic gripped my vitals in its icy claws – what had become of Gwen? I was less concerned about Iestyn and the druids.

Before I could ask Mrs Abergavenny shoved me down the hallway. The more mundane elevator doors at the far end looked to have avoided the worst of the destruction. My captor saw me flinch.

'Don't worry, princess snowflake – this one's just a normal lift. You're in no fit state for climbing stairs. We're 'eading to the top floor, penthouse suite. Lucky ewe.'

I didn't feel lucky as I slouched against the buttons. My head felt like it had been kicked in by a belligerent mule high on steroids. 'Who are we meeting upstairs – should I have worn a tie?'

Mrs A ripped off her starched librarian's collar and tossed it away. 'My employer would like a word. More than a few words, as it 'appens. You might need a ffwcing dictionary.'

'And who is this high-rolling charmer? The same jokers Gwen blew out back in Florida? There's nothing I can tell him.'

Mrs Abergavenny looked appalled. 'Don't be ridiclus! You'd do well to shut your cakehole, less ewe wants to be leaving in an amblance.'

Despite stiff competition, maybe the Welshest thing I'd heard in a while. My captor looked me over with an expression halfway between pity and contempt. Before I could reply the lift arrived with a ping and the doors swished open. It looked a little more inviting than the one leading to the Aberdare Library cellar, but that wasn't hard. Why were all my silver linings wrapped in clouds of toxic gas? I hesitated for a second. Mrs A waved me inside.

'For your information I'm on the side of the angels, me – a hatchet-woman for the forces of truth and justice. Cymru am byth, and all that shit. Now get in the ffwcing lift.'

She struck me as more of a battleaxe than a hatchet-woman, but I kept this observation to myself. I was going to discover which side she was on soon enough. I didn't think it would be mine.

The lift was one of those extra fast ones. It did things to my stomach that shouldn't be allowed, even if it didn't take me to another dimension. Despite its speed our ascent lasted several minutes – we must have glided to a halt above the clouds. The doors opened onto a scene of sparkling opulence, quite the contrast to the battered hallway below. Mrs Abergavenny motioned me forward.

'The Boss is waiting. Make sure to mind your manners. Impoliteness grips my shit.'

I stepped out onto a thick white carpet – it was like walking on a flattened yeti. At the far end of the massive room a floor-to-ceiling window overlooked the bustling metropolis which was this world's version of Aberdare. Streams of air-cars drifted past in the middle distance, glinting in the sun. Backlit by the glass I could just make out the silhouette of an enormous desk. Seated behind it was a single figure, a stocky, well-built man smoking a fat cigar. He got to his feet and leaned on the table as we approached.

Mrs Abergavenny holstered her gun. 'Here he is, Boss, safe and sound, like I promised. Mouthy bugger, mind. Want me to give him a fat lip? Slap 'im round a bit? Asking for it, he is.'

She sounded too keen for comfort. Holding up a hand I shielded my eyes against the glare. The guy behind the desk shook his head in silence and came round for a closer look.

There was something about the way he moved, something familiar and chilling. He was like a pit bull crossed with a hobbit, a loaded gun ready to explode. Gradually my eyes adjusted to the brightness and details coalesced into view. It took a moment for his features to register, recognisable yet eerily different from the ones I knew. It was a face which had filled my childhood with terror. I was just able to catch the yelp before it escaped my throat. Standing before me was Uncle Genghis, or at least his richer, meaner local twin.

32

Congealed Blood Is Thicker Than Water

The cigar tumbled to the floor. Genghis spent a long time simply staring at me, his mouth hanging open; it wasn't a good look. He seemed shocked and a little numb at my existence. I knew the feeling. I gave a half-hearted smile.

'Hiya, Uncle.' My voice sounded high and reedy. I wasn't doing a great job of playing it cool. There was a strong chance I'd soon form a molten puddle on the floor.

Genghis didn't return the smile. I fought back an irrational urge to ask how the vaginal steamer business was going, even though I knew full well this version of Uncle G had his stubby fingers in bigger, hotter pies. In this reality Genghis was CEO of the mighty Jones Corporation, the family business Isaiah had left in his grasping, nicotine-stained hands. I was sure his grip was just as steely here as it was in my home universe where, as a child, he'd regularly lifted me by the scruff of the neck and boxed my ears just for fun – unhappy days.

I noticed another figure lurking in the shadows. Shadow guy

cleared his throat. 'Of course, we'll have to run a DNA test. We have to be sure.'

Uncle Genghis looked irritated, but at least the twitching eye had stopped. Along with its twin it remained fixed on mine. He said, 'No need for that, Mordred. Can't you see the resemblance? He's one of us all right. Get a load of the face.'

Mordred didn't sound convinced. 'Still, we can't afford to take any chances. Not with what's at stake.'

Self-consciously I ran my fingers over my features, while Uncle Genghis slowly shook his head. At last he reached out his hand. With a start I realised he was offering to shake. I don't think the Genghis I knew had ever offered me that courtesy, other than as a prelude to a slap. Not wanting to seem rude I held out mine. He took it carefully, as if suspecting I might disappear in a puff of smoke. He didn't even crush my knuckles very hard.

'Hello, Kevin bach,' he said, peering deep into my eyes. I could smell a faint whiff of burning yeti hair rising from the smouldering rug, and see the first tendrils of smoke. 'Good of you to come.'

Keeping his gaze on mine, Genghis bent down and retrieved his cigar.

I was conscious of Mrs Abergavenny standing behind me. No doubt her frail hand was still resting on her gun. 'I didn't have a lot of say in the matter, if I'm honest. I always like to be honest.'

Genghis sat on the edge of his desk and began relighting his cigar. 'Very wise, boi – you're always best being honest with me. Sorry about the reception committee. It was for your own protection.'

It was hard not to show my frustration. 'Protection? Lately everyone's telling me that, usually before putting my life in danger. Gets old fast.'

Genghis blew out a smoke ring. 'Well, in this case it's true. You're going to have to trust me.'

'And I wish people would stop saying that too. Trust is earned rather than given.'

Uncle G regarded me through narrow eyes and a haze of blue-grey fumes. 'You sound just like your grandfather. Look a lot like him too. I suppose you're wondering what this is all about?'

I let out a massive sigh. 'I've wondered little else these past two weeks. Feel free to fill me in any time you like.'

He bounced to his feet, and for a moment I panicked that he'd take my invitation literally. Genghis halted a foot before me and looked up into my face. His breath smelt of tobacco and high-end whisky – another upgrade from home.

'We've recently taken this facility from your friends in the Gorsedd – they couldn't hold it for long, bloody amateurs. But they didn't give up without a fight.'

'Yes, I noticed the bullet holes. And they weren't my friends.'

'Oh really, then how would you describe them?'

I waved smoky eddies in the air. 'Kidnappers, maybe. Blackmailers, at a push. What happened to Gwen, the girl I was travelling with? They were holding her hostage so I'd play along.'

Genghis flicked embers at my feet. 'Your girlfriend is fine – charming young lady, if a little high spirited.'

'Tell me about it. Where is she?'

'You're going to have to trust me she's okay. Good in a firefight, that one. Our counterattack wouldn't have gone so smoothly without her contribution. She'd be up for a medal, but I'm informed she's already got plenty.'

'Is she okay?'

Uncle G weighed his head from side to side in a non-committal fashion. 'She's in a better state that Llywsiffer's assault team. Fanatical thugs the lot of 'em – we had to slot more than a few.' He saw my agitation and did his best to sound reassuring. 'Your friend's getting the best medical care available. Under the doctor, she is. Remember, we've got better facilities by ere than what you're used to at home. She's going to pull through.'

I gulped past the knot in my throat. Genghis couldn't do *reassuring*. 'I can imagine your ICUs get a lot of practice. Can I see her?'

Genghis waved a hand in front of his face. Smoke swirled around him like a craggy mountaintop. 'All in good time, young man. Give your hormones a bloody rest.'

'Believe me, they've had a long holiday.' He didn't seem to hear me.

'First we needs to get you somewhere more... secure. There's many things we need to discuss. Plans to be made. Events are coming to a head. Won't you please step this way.'

There was a snort of derision from the shadows. 'Not this madness again. This is a distraction we don't need.'

Fire flashed in Genghis's eyes. 'Can it, Mordred. I'm still in charge, remember.'

'We'll see about that.'

Genghis's snarl morphed into a crooked smile as he turned back and ushered me towards the lift. 'Still got a few tactical differences to iron out. Won't you step this way, young man.'

It wasn't a request, but an order. This version of Genghis was clearly used to getting his way. Mrs Abergavenny stood aside, but conspicuously kept one hand clamped inside her cardi. It wasn't her big heart that was causing the bulge. Resigned to my fate I shuffled back the way I'd come. Genghis clomped along beside me, staring up at me all the way. Reaching the doors I finally cracked, planting my feet stubbornly and shaking my head.

'I can't take another trip through that gate. My nerves are too frayed.'

Genghis punched the top button on the panel. 'Don't worry about that, boi. We're heading upwards, not down.' The doors glided open with a ping.

'Upwards? I'm not ready to meet St Peter just yet.'

Genghis grinned; somewhere a fairy died. 'No lad – he'd never let me in – too many points on my licence. There's a landing pad on the roof. We're flying you out, not to heaven, but to the next best thing.'

33

Cwtched in the Lap of Luxury

Two days later I was getting bored with my luxurious surroundings. Genghis had been right – it wasn't heaven, but the mansion would have given God's architect a run for their money. If the door to my suite of rooms hadn't been locked I could have convinced myself I was a VIP guest at a swanky spa hotel, rather than a prisoner. One unpleasant thought spoiled what should have been a comfortable stay – was I awaiting trial or execution?

The flight up from the Gateway Plaza Hotel had been brief. Genghis had one of those swanky air-car limos just like Llywsiffer – if anything his was even more extravagant. He'd ordered himself a drink from the automated mini-bar shortly after take-off, but I'd declined – not trusting my nerves to an injection of alcohol. My host seemed to have a lot on his mind. I guessed running an ailing global mega-corporation fast spiralling down the pan was a daunting experience. The dark-glassed windows gave no hint of our course as we left the gleaming spires of Aberdare behind. If I had to guess I'd say we flew north, into the hills.

Even at the speeds the flyer travelled we could not have gone far. Soon we landed and I was ushered out of the gull wing door by a sparkling android butler. Genghis shouted something about having to round up the rest of the board, over the whine of the engines, before taking off in a cloud of dry leaves and stale whisky fumes. I was left standing on the landing pad next to an imposing palace, nestled snugly between a range of forested hills. It looked like the palace of a modest Roman Emperor, maybe Nero or Caligula. Gold inlaid marble columns encased the impressive facade. Were they to be my prison bars?

Without explanation I was shown briskly to my apartment. I could see at once the residents of this facility took their security very seriously. It was luxurious enough, but the thickness of the walls either side of the vault-like front doors told their own story. It looked like the stronghold of some Middle Eastern dictator transported to the mountains of Wales. I was hoping it lacked the torture chamber in the basement. The whole place was a bunker for a gang of paranoid billionaires.

I was escorted down a long, wide corridor, lavishly decorated, to a further set of security doors. C-3PO stuck a long shiny finger into what looked like a USB port on steroids and I was ushered inside. The doors locked behind me with a hiss and my ears popped at the change in pressure. Nothing was getting in or out. I inspected one of the statues – it appeared to be real gold, but somehow still gave off an air of ostentatious tat. I couldn't complain about my accommodation. Each of the rooms had more floor space than the house Mum and I shared. The waterbed was a bit much, but I was so shattered I fell onto it and drifted off into a troubled sleep. I think I dreamt I was on the *Titanic*, frantically rearranging the deck chairs as we slid into the icy depths.

Sometime after midnight I woke in a cold sweat, convinced I'd sprung a leak, but my clamminess was just down to me alone. The low-level lighting came on automatically – it was that sort of place. I dug out a plush bathrobe from the walk-in wardrobe and passed the rest of the night on one of the sofas – I was done with sleeping all at sea.

The next few days passed slowly, with no sign of my host. The food was top notch and plentiful, delivered by a dumb waiter which seemed able to meet any request. Even Mum's family favourites were rendered with uncanny precision. I couldn't rate the communication so highly: I heard nothing from any relatives – my family in a nutshell. Clearly this lot weren't so different from the flock of black sheep I knew back home.

The suite of rooms came with a state-of-the-art entertainment system. All the satellite news channels were blocked – I would have killed to know what was going on in the outside world – but just about every movie ever filmed was at my itchy fingertips. I watched all the *Zulu* remakes, before discovering plenty of biopics telling Grandad's dramatised life story from every angle imaginable. I sat open mouthed through several of the musicals, aghast at who they'd cast to play my relatives. In case there was any doubt, Jason Statham can't do a Welsh accent, let alone sing in one. At least yours truly was spared such cross-eyed aberrations; Isaiah himself was not so lucky. Sean Connery I could accept – at a push – even with his obligatory Scots accent (first Anthracite prototype? '*Shplendid*'). Stephen Segal was more of a struggle. I don't remember Grandad owning that many guns, or foiling so many terrorist plots. Nobody told Hollywood Windsor Davies would have looked the part, and could have nailed the accent too. Oh dear, how sad, never mind.

One lazy afternoon, sat lounging in my underwear, watching the end credits of one such masterpiece roll by, I sensed I was not alone. I let out a strangled yelp behind a cloud of vaporised popcorn. Someone was standing silently watching me. It was Gwen – her arm in a sling, sporting the last traces of a black eye, but other than that, she looked unharmed.

'What's new pussycat – how's it going, Kev?'

I hurdled the sofa and stood before her, checking her over for more lasting damage. 'I'm fine, but how about you? They told me nothing about what happened when I left you at the hotel!'

Gingerly Gwen gave me a hug and smiled at my show of concern. 'I'm fine. Still a bit sore, but it was only a flesh wound. Considering how kinetic things got when they jumped us, that's a minor miracle.'

It was so good to see her again; tears welled up in my eyes. 'What happened to Iestyn and the druids?'

She wrinkled her dainty nose. 'They... weren't so lucky. I'll say this for the Jones Corp strike team – they were very thorough – mostly ex-Special Forces, just like me. When I saw what was going down I rolled with the flow, even caused a bit of a distraction. Those druids won't be holding another barbecue anytime soon. Messy.'

Thoughts of the wicker man made me shudder, but our current predicament was of more pressing concern. 'So Genghis's people patched you up? What are they going to do with us now?'

Gwen stiffly shrugged her shoulders and winced. 'That's the sixty-four million dragon question. But if they were going to do us harm, we'd be dead in a ditch by now. So look on the bright side, kiddo. We might still get out of this yet.'

'Didn't know there was a bright side, but I'll do my best.'

Her gaze wandered round the room. 'You certainly seem to have made yourself at home.'

I have to admit I'd made quite a mess – half-finished takeaway cartons and pizza boxes formed greasy ziggurats on every surface. I hadn't been expecting guests. 'Yeah, a guy could get comfortable round here – a real home from home.' Recent events came back to me with a shudder. 'Did you know the librarian back in Aberdare was working for them? Mrs Abergavenny must have been watching me for years.'

'Really?' Gwen didn't seem all that interested.

'Sure was. That's how she got the drop on me – I could have dealt with a stranger, but I trusted her – sneaky cow.' I made karate hands.

Gwen smiled. 'Yes, I'm sure you could've.'

I was a little offended she didn't seem more convinced, but I was keen to bring her up to speed on my news. 'My mission to the care home was a complete success. I was coming back with vital information pried from Grandad. It wasn't easy, but I struggled through. What I learned would have got you released. So, in a sense, I rescued you after all. Don't I get some credit?' I flashed my best smile.

Her eyes went wide. 'My hero.' Reaching out her good arm she patted my cheek. I tried to nuzzle her hand, but it slipped down my face and pressed a single finger against my puckering lips. Suddenly Gwen looked deadly serious instead of grateful. Her gaze flicked round the room.

'Yes, I think we might have underestimated Genghis. He seems to have been one step ahead all the time. Reasonable guy – as long as your interests align with his. I only wish he'd hired me from the start, rather than those American halfwits. Would have avoided a lot of pain, not to mention wasted ammunition.'

I was confused. 'If he'd hired you I'd be very dead.'

Gwen shot me a look and gave a micro-shake of her head. I was getting the impression I wasn't the only one her speech was intended for. I guess it was naïve to think I'd been on my own this whole time. The walls had ears, if not high-definition video and thermal tracking to boot.

I measured my words carefully. 'So what happens now? Don't get me wrong – I like it here, but there's only so much luxury I can take before going batshit crazy. They can't cage a Spartan like me for long.'

Gwen relaxed and even managed a bit of a chuckle. 'Don't worry, Leonidas. Events are coming to a head. Plenty has been going on we don't know about. All should become clear shortly. I've been asked to tell you you're not the only one they've taken into protective custody.'

I was about to enquire who *they* were, and how she seemed to have such a cosy relationship with them all of a sudden, when my jaw dropped again. Mum was standing in the doorway, watching us, tears welling in her eyes.

'Kevin, my baby! Where did you go?' She closed in and clutched me in a fierce embrace. My mum might not look strong but she's always had a grip like a python where I'm concerned. I struggled to get my breath back. 'It's great to see you too, but what are you doing here?'

Mum tousled my hair with more force than was strictly necessary. 'Oh my goodness, will ewe listen to 'im. Can't a woman visit her cousin's secret mansion without the Spanish Inquisition? We've always been a family that sticks together, even if sometimes we don't speak for years!'

'Mum, Genghis isn't keeping any secrets. He's not –'

'He's a bleedin dark horse, that's what he is.'

Even by my mum's standards of logic this had to be some sort of record. I sensed there was something fundamental she wasn't grasping about our situation. She wittered on, 'He's a real secret squirrel, that Genghis – keeping all this from us, cooped up in that tiny house. But I always said your Uncle would come good in the end. Who knew there was a goldmine buried in vaginal steamers – only 'im. Genius!'

Yes, who knew? 'Mum, the Genghis who brought us here is not the Genghis we know from home.'

She looked at me as if I was a bit *twp*. 'Of course he's not – it's as if he's a new man – more mature, somehow. Fair play to 'im, he's turned hisself round. This mansion is bloody lush, just like my best boy.' There was a fresh round of hugging and dabbing at my face.

I could see I would have to take this one step at a time. Despite having bought me a boxed set of the *Matrix* films last Christmas, Mum was not au fait with the concept of parallel universes. Sadly she was more familiar with the concept of over-the-top displays of affection and scuppering my chances with the ladies. She grabbed my face in her hands and pulled me down for a soppy kiss.

'You're a very naughty boy, Kevin – for running away without telling your old Mam where you were going – but I can forgive you. How long have you known about this place?'

I let out a weary sigh. 'You've been here longer than any of us. Gwen and I have been doing a spot of travelling.'

Mum turned and gazed adoringly at my companion, who seemed to find the entire exchange rather amusing. 'Yes! I've already met Gwendolyn, your *little friend*.' Mum dropped into a stage whisper they could have heard in the next room. 'Lovely, she is. Are you and her... you know, doing the horizontal?'

'Mum! Give it a bloody rest will you.'

My face reddened as Gwen's shoulders lurched up and down with suppressed mirth. With an effort she composed herself. 'Your mam and I have been getting to know each other, Kev.

She's told me so much about you – her special *dwtty* boy. She loves you very much. Touching.'

Mum squeezed me to her side, almost lifting me off my feet. 'Yes, he is very special, but quite the rascal. Sometimes I wonder if I've been too soft with him, but he'll make someone a WONDERFUL husband one day. He's so good round the house.'

At times I think Mum missed her calling as a bricklayer; she has such talent for laying it on with a trowel. All I could do was grin like an idiot as Gwen beamed her most beautiful smile. She rose from the arm of the sofa on which she'd been sitting.

'Such a sweet reunion. You two clearly have a lot of catching up to do – I'll leave you to it.' Gwen turned and made for the door.

I wasn't having that. 'Wait! Is that all the explanation I get? Do they let you come and go as you please? What happens next?'

Gwen looked over her shoulder but didn't slow. 'I'm just down the hallway, Kev. They've put us all in the guest wing together. Genghis is just waiting for some others to fly in. Apparently there's a big meeting planned for tomorrow. Should be fireworks.'

'A meeting with who?' This was exasperating.

Gwen swiped a keycard through the control panel next to the door, which opened with a hiss. 'My best guess would be the full Jones Corporation board. Their problems are stacking up. Rumour has it there's some sort of power play going down. You might get to wave a sparkler.'

I couldn't hide my frustration – could she come and go as she pleased? 'How come you're so chummy with them all of a sudden? Who cares about their problems – what are they going to do with me?' I peeled myself out of Mum's embrace. '... do with us?'

Gwen paused in the doorway. 'You'll want to have a shower and put some trousers on. See you in the morning, kiddo.' She rippled her fingers in my direction. And with that, she was gone. Clearly she was afforded a greater level of trust than some of us, and me a full family member – the cheek of it! I was left to explain the idea of parallel universes to Mum, which was sure to be an uphill struggle. I just prayed this was the toughest challenge which lay ahead.

34

Keeping up with the Joneses

It was a long night. Each time I thought Mum was on the brink of getting it my hopes were cruelly dashed. I don't know how she rationalised the flying cars and clanking robots straight out of *Lost in Space*, but she had an astonishing ability to edit out inconvenient facts that didn't suit her. Mum wouldn't have it that we hadn't rumbled some secret mansion Genghis and the rest of the family had been keeping quiet from us for years.

Round about midnight I gave up and crashed bleary eyed on a sofa – there were plenty to pick from. Mum was escorted back to her rooms by a pair of silent security droids. I don't know what she thought they were – hostess trolleys on steroids, perhaps. I tried to get some sleep; I sensed tomorrow would be a long day. My rest was troubled by nightmares of scheming uncles bent on world domination. I awoke to the sound of a blaring alarm.

One of those computerised female voices meant to put you at your ease, but in reality having the opposite effect, cut across the din. *'Your presence is requested in Conference Room One. Immediately.'*

She repeated this message on a loop, as I swam up through murky layers of consciousness. Bitching Betty had the sort of voice that brooked no argument. Two mechanical guards glided in and didn't look in the mood for debate, all but throwing a bucket of water over me. I pulled on my clothes; the shower would have to wait.

The whirring robots led me through a maze of broad corridors much like the one outside my apartment. It seemed this complex was even bigger than it first looked. At last we came to a halt at a set of high double doors. A tall, slim middle-aged man in military uniform stood waiting, peering at his phone. I had a vague sense I should recognise him, but I couldn't think from where or when. His greying hair was pulled into a tight man-bun, strangely at odds with his military regalia. A bright pink beret was tucked under one arm. I let out a gasp – it was Taliesin.

He looked a lot different from the last time I'd seen him, sprawled in the back of Llywsiffer's limousine. Gone were the frayed rags of a mad prophet, in their place the smart dress uniform of an officer in Welsh Special Forces. The smell was more conventional too – my nose was detecting nothing but spit, polish and the ruthless efficiency of a trained killer. His name badge read Colonel Frank MacIntyre. Next to it was a long row of medals.

'Good morning, young man. I see you managed to drag yourself out of bed before noon. Ready to hit the beaches?'

'But I thought you were –'

'Working for the druids? A lot of people thought that. A lot of people were wrong.' He set the beret on his head at a jaunty angle.

I blinked in confusion. 'But you told them J-Corp can't build any more Anthracite drives.'

'They would have found out soon enough. We've got more leaks than a Saint David's Day choir. We needed to force their hand – bring their treason out into the open. My mission was a complete success.'

'Complete success? You almost got me burned alive at the stake – medium rare!'

The Colonel made a gun with his finger and thumb, miming a shot to my head. 'Always a risk of minor collateral damage in any military operation. Got you out just in the nick of time though, didn't I? Not so much Sun Tzu as Three, Four and Five, that's me.'

'You bloody psycho,' I muttered. But I could see zero ffwcs were given by this nutter, who continued.

'Enough of my tactical genius, lad. All will be made clear in good time. You have a date with destiny, and she's one tart you don't want to keep waiting.'

As if on cue an alert trilled on his phone. Frank/Taliesin pushed open the double doors and ushered me inside. It was like stepping into a pressure cooker – the charged atmosphere at full boil. You'd have needed more than a knife to cut the tension filling the air – an Anthracite-powered chainsaw might have done it; then again, maybe not.

We entered a cavernous hall beneath a high, arching ceiling – a lavishly appointed boardroom. A huge conference table, ringed with grim-faced executives, dominated the chamber. The seated attendees came in all shapes and sizes; there were women and men, ranging from middle-aged right up to geriatric. Several were using oxygen masks. One had been badly cobbled together like a first attempt at Frankenstein's monster, the lower half of his body encased in a space age wheelchair crossed with a tank. Most of the others had a disquieting familiar cast to their features. All heads turned to look at me. They had the same blue-grey eyes I'd seen many times before in another world, the same eyes that looked back at me from a mirror. They were the eyes of my family.

I got the impression this meeting had been going on for some time. Uncle Genghis was on his feet, seemingly mid-rant. He pocketed the device he was holding and stabled a gnarled finger in my direction.

'And this is how we're going to do it!'

There were guffaws of disbelief from the assembled gathering. A row of coloured lights flashed manically along the front grill of the legless cyborg – a one-man roller disco consisting of only half a man. Whatever Uncle G had in mind the rest of the clan didn't seem to think me up to the job, which of course got my back up something rotten. Didn't these jokers know with whom they were dealing? Then again, maybe they did.

Chief amongst the guffawers was the shadowy figure from my meeting with Genghis at the top of the hotel. Mordred didn't look any less shady under the glaring lights than he had back in the hotel. In fact, now that I could see his dour expression, I liked the look of him even less.

'Have you lost your mind, Genghis? Our organisation is facing two existential crises. How is this kid going to help with either one?'

Genghis gritted his remaining teeth. 'You're really boiling my piss today, Mordred. I'm still CEO of this shambles, and I've been hatching us a plan. Stop clucking before I scramble your eggs.'

His antagonist threw his head back and laughed. 'Maybe not CEO for long, Chicken Little. Your *plans* got us into this mess and now the sky really is falling on your heads. This lad's face has been plastered over every news bulletin these past two weeks, ever since that botched hit you organised in Aberdare went south. The Welsh electorate is demanding answers.'

If looks could kill Genghis would have committed homicide. 'And we will supply those answers.'

'How?' Mordred spat. 'You barely understand the questions. It's common knowledge that hit squad leads back to us – we're getting accused of terrorism on our very own doorstep. This shitshow has terrible optics – a total PR disaster!'

An expression formed on Uncle's craggy face that I'd seen before. It was a look usually followed by extreme wanton violence – apart from that time the takeaway got his order wrong, when it'd been extreme wonton violence. But this version of Genghis was made of sterner stuff. He got his breathing back under control with a heroic effort and stretched his corded neck muscles with a loud creak. When he spoke it was with eye-watering patience. 'You know what they call you, Mordred, down in the rarebit dives and laverbread dens of Swansea?'

'Enlighten us, do.'

'*Perineum Jones.*'

Mordred looked unsure where this was heading. 'And why's that, pray tell?'

'Because you're halfway between a cock and an arsehole. Reel your bloody neck in, mun. Our immediate issue – the looming electoral defeat of our friend and colleague President Island here – we will deal with in *Stage One.*' Genghis gestured to the mechanical monstrosity sitting beside him. The row of lights rippled again.

With a gasp I realised this was what was left of the National Leader – Barry Island had seen better days. The President of the Welsh Republic had been put back together, after his close encounter with the drone bomb, as best the doctors could. Advanced as medical engineering was over here in +1, it still had its limitations. The President was a human jigsaw with several pieces missing.

Genghis continued unabashed, 'Once the minor irritation of the Gorsedd is out of the way we can move on to *Stage Two* – the *other matter*.'

Mordred didn't sound impressed. 'Minor irritation? They're about to hijack our country. I'll believe your solution when I see it working. I'm not holding my breath.'

Genghis's piggy eyes narrowed above the first hint of a smile. Perhaps it was the thought of Mordred's face turning blue. 'Then I suggest you take a butchers at this.'

He reached out and punched a button on the console recessed into the desk. With a gentle whir the wall at the far end of the room dilated to reveal a giant screen. It showed a looming image of Gwen and myself, slouched in the back of Llywsiffer's limo, bravely trying to overcome the shock of almost being spit roast. I realised at long last that cerise was not my colour. The dress I'd been wearing was quite revealing.

Genghis had a smile on his face, nonetheless. 'Colonel MacIntyre, why don't you tell the board what we're seeing.'

Beside me, Frank/Taliesin snapped to attention and cleared his throat. 'During my deep recon mission behind enemy lines I was able to obtain footage of the Primary Target.' The video paused, while a ticker tape of text printed out theatrically beneath Llywsiffer's brooding features. *Pendragon, L. Leader of the Gorsedd Nationalist Party, front-running presidential candidate.*

'Over a period I ingratiated myself with the druids and gained their trust. They came to see me as a valuable source of information – some of it legit, some of it black propaganda. They had no idea I was a double agent.' There were gasps from several of those assembled. 'Approximately five days ago my cover was almost blown by the arrival of certain rogue elements.'

The picture paused again as Gwen and myself got the same explanatory treatment. *'Gwendolyn Jones' aka Wanda Sevastopol, et al – mercenary trans–Multiverse operative, Consortium hired gun, ex Special Forces.* Whoever had put this presentation together had found a freeze frame which showed me in the worst possible light, gurning like a troglodyte with both eyes half closed, my face creased in what looked like constipation. *Jones, Kevin G. Alleged family member from primitive alternate dimension. Expendable.*

For once my emotions got the better of me. 'Expendable? The bloody nerve of you people! We're related, don't you know?'

Uncle Genghis shushed me into silence. 'Ignore that bit, lad. It's just a typo.' It didn't stop me quietly fuming as Colonel MacIntyre went on.

'Llywsiffer proceeded to coerce these blunderers into aiding the druids in their nefarious plans. Secretly I filmed the whole exchange. Our Psych-Warfare boffins have come up with an edit that's rather damning for Mr Pendragon. Watch this.'

There followed an 'enhanced' version of our conversation with the Gorsedd leader. It was just a word or two which changed here and there, but the implications were clear.

'We plan to overthrow the globalist elite who've run this country. You're going to help us do it.' These incriminating words were heard tumbling from Llywsiffer's blood-red lips. *'Wales's enemies around the world consider you the key weapon in their plan to halt our domination.'* It went on and on, the Jones Corp board around the table looked on open mouthed. This was some next-level kompromat. Deep fakery which plumbed new subterranean depths.

By the time the video finished Genghis was looking smug. It didn't suit his battle-scarred face. 'All it needs is the right sort of spin. We just need young Kevin here to go on record that he's a foreign agent sent to fund the Gorsedd and subvert Welsh democracy, and we're home and hosed. Interference from foreign powers won't sit well with the voting public.'

There was a stunned silence. Maybe Genghis's plan had legs after all, unlike the unfortunate President Island. Even Mordred couldn't help but look impressed. He mumbled, a man deprived of his moment of glory, 'I suppose this *could* work.'

Genghis regained his usual swagger. 'You bet it will sodding work, sugartits. Llywsiffer and the Gorsedd are going to be stitched up like a cut-price boob job. When I've finished with him he won't get elected dog warden of Bryn, never mind President. His goose will be cooked in our very own napalm oven.'

The speakers built into Barry Island's wheelchair let out an electronic whoop. I think he would have high-fived Genghis, if he could have moved his arms and had possessed the required number of digits. As it was we were treated to a twinkling light show. Uncle G barely glanced sideways at his accomplice.

'Put a lid on it, Davros. You'll soon be serving another five-year term, looking after the best interests of Wales, as well of course as Jones Corps. Which as we all know is the same thing. Battle stations, everyone. Let's get this political party shfarted.'

35

October Surprise

An hour later I found myself in the well-equipped TV studio which served the Jones family compound, their head of media fussing over me like a mother hen. Just why the make-up was necessary I did not know. Apparently I looked 'pastier than a decorator's workbench – perhaps I hadn't been getting enough sun?' The android applying the foundation had more appendages than a Swiss army knife – one slip and I could have lost an eyebrow. I sat very still. At least it was over quickly. I didn't get given a chance to back out.

The autocue held the prepared statement, carefully crafted by J-Corp's Psychological Warfare Division. I found it hard to believe IKEA had an equivalent department, but these days you never knew. Uncle G sat on the edge of the desk, glaring at me intently. I avoided eye contact as much as possible; just looking at him made me giddy. I was already sticky with sweat.

'This isn't going to make me look bad, is it?'

Genghis pulled off a panto-level performance of shock and surprise. 'Noooo, bach – quite the reverse. Ever since we all saw those grainy images of you fleeing the carnage in Aberdare the whole nation's been wondering *Who is this mystery man?* We're going to paint them a picture, and it's gonna be a real beaut.' His gesture encompassed the broad sweep of distant stars.

I wasn't feeling artistic. 'Just so long it's not a picture of Dorian Gray.'

Genghis blinked at me vacantly. 'You can call yourself whatever you bloody well like, mate, just so long as you help me nail Llywsiffer's sorry ass. We'll say you're turned and work for us now – like your hot lady friend. True enough, ain't it?'

I didn't think disagreeing was in my best interests. Uncle Genghis was a man of extreme emotions, I had no desire to test his limits. 'It's just – I'm not much of an actor. I don't know how convincingly I can pull this off.'

Genghis was having none of this defeatist talk. 'What do you mean, you can't act? It's in our blood, lad. Look at all our famous relatives who've trodden the boards – Tommy Lee, Catherine Zeta, James Earl –'

He saw my wince and pulled up short. I said, 'You sure about that last one?'

Genghis shushed me into silence. 'He's what's known as a brother from a different mother. I often wonder how *Star Wars* would have turned out differently if he'd supplied Darth Vader's body and David Prowse had done the voice – maybe in a parallel universe...'

I never had Genghis down as such a philosopher. Did the version back home possess these hidden depths? The thought made me uneasy. Perhaps I was warming to the mad bugger, like a moth flitting round a dangerous open flame. Either way I was on deadly ground. The dreamy faraway look in my host's eye departed as swiftly as it had arrived.

'Let's cut the yap and get you ready to rock and roll. We

need this in the can for the *Six O'Clock News*. I had a word with my mate who runs S4C and he's cleared the decks for this story. When I say "Jump" he asks "How long do you want us hanging mid-air?"'

'Won't the Consortium know where I am after this? Those bastards will be on my case again.'

Genghis shook his head with an evil smirk. 'Since I arranged for that meteor to gatecrash their war council you have nothing to fear from the Yanks. Will take em years to pick through the rubble, never mind recover.'

I gritted my teeth in frustration, there was no getting out of this. I was just going to have to go with the flow and hope it didn't turn into lava. There was just one thing still weighing on my mind.

'Where's Gwen? I thought she'd be at the meeting.'

Genghis's features lurched into what passed for his version of a smile. 'Ah yes – your main squeeze – don't worry, she's fine. Her and the Colonel are already preparing for our next little project. Talented lass.'

I couldn't tell if this was good news or bad. 'That's a relief – I think. Wouldn't want anything to happen to her.'

Uncle G's features were more suited to a leer. 'I bet you wouldn't, boi. Quite the hottie, ain't she? Have you – you know – slipped her a crippler yet?'

I was horrified. 'We're just friends, Unc.'

'Friends with benefits?'

'Well, if you count not being dead in a ditch as a benefit, then I guess we are.'

He gazed at me long and hard. 'Are you sure we're related? I mean, the DNA tests came back positive, but sometimes I wonder. Boffins can get things wrong, same like us mortals.'

Much as I would've liked to deny it, Genghis was my relative – my first cousin once removed, in fact – there was no escaping the awful truth. I wouldn't have minded if he'd been removed a bit further. How the jump across dimensions affected our relationship I didn't like to speculate. The English language needed to do some catching up. Maybe there was a Welshperanto word. I let out a weary sigh.

'No Unc, we're related all right. Growing up on the other side you were around quite a bit – or at least, your doppelganger was. Mum seemed quite taken with you – I mean him.'

Genghis looked fascinated; perhaps it hadn't occurred to him he had a twin back in my universe. His voice dropped to a whisper. 'What's he like – you know – that other version of me?'

I thought, all things considered, the unvarnished truth was best avoided – exiled to Siberia, in fact. This was going to need a thick layer of Ronseal. 'Oh, he's much like you, only… less sophisticated.'

Genghis seemed to like my answer. He grinned and patted me on top the head like a puppy. 'Look straight down the lens. Stick to the script. Pull this off and you'll be rewarded. Cock it up and…'

An intense red light blinked on next to the camera. I didn't need Genghis to spell out the consequences of failure. I pulled myself together and started reading. Seemed I was destined to be Uncle G's performing seal after all – I just hoped I'd end up with a kipper, rather than a brutal clubbing.

I won't bore you with the details; it went on and on. The payload was short and sweet. What it boiled down to was this: I was a highly trained clandestine operative hired by Wales's enemies – all the usual suspects, the shady characters accustomed to running the world – at least before us jumped-up sheep worriers stole the show. The CIA, KGB, Masons, Opus Dei, and the Chinese Communist Party were all thoroughly fingered by yours truly. By the time I finished I wished I'd been wearing latex gloves. The irony was not lost on me – here I was pointing my soiled digits at the same conniving shits who'd hired Gwen to kidnap me in the first place – a case of poetic justice if ever there was one. I told the audience at home how this clandestine cabal had clubbed together with the druids to bring about a more malleable Welsh regime. It had been my job to be the sphincter, to channel dark money to Llywsiffer and help sway the election – collusion in the subversion of our democracy.

Of course, I went on, when the Jones Corporation got wind of the plot, they'd gone to extreme lengths to stop me – culminating in the failed assassination attempt back in Aberdare, and the snatch-and-grab hit in Swansea. J-Corp wished to apologise unreservedly for the damage in both incidents, for which they'd pay generous compensation. Genghis and Co had simply been carrying out their patriotic duty to protect the integrity of the constitution – just like the voting public now had to when they re-elected J-Corp's preferred candidate, in the battle-scarred and heroic figure of Barry Island. It was a political slam dunk, and I was smashing Llywsiffer's severed head through the flaming hoop.

Before it was over I pleaded for forgiveness from my fellow countrymen and women. Fortunately I'd been stopped before this evil plan could come to fruition, and now I'd been turned by the good guys. The heroes at J-Corp had foiled the men in the blacked-out vans, the ones with the contingency plans, and the mirrored glasses, with the mirrors on the inside. Go back to sleep Wales, the grown-ups are back in charge. Good game, Uncle Genghis.

36

The Man from Uncle

The next day Genghis came to see me at the apartment. I should have known something was up as he was all smiles, which made a change from the Genghis I knew, who was all dodgy schemes and Chinese burns. As well as the stained and crumpled suit he was wearing a gap-toothed grin half a mile wide, but his bloodshot eyes seemed haunted. It looked like he'd been up all night.

'Shwmae butt! The first numbers are in. Last night's broadcast was a complete success – the metrics are looking bang tidy. The boyos running our polling operation tell us the Gorsedd's popularity is falling faster than a Llandudno stripper's draws. The election's in two days' time and Barry Island is going to win again. Our opponents stand no chance. When the results roll in Llywsiffer will be spitting blood, as well as teeth.'

Perhaps I should have looked more relieved, but I was too jaded and weary of my Uncle's high-octane exuberance to care. 'That's nice. So I scratched your back, perhaps it's time you scratched mine? Quid pro quo?'

Genghis set about helping himself to my well-stocked fruit bowl. 'You want calamari? We'll get you calamari.' He tossed a grape into his gaping mouth. 'Llywsiffer has had his chips, not to mention his shandy and curry sauce. That ffwcer will be sewing mailbags on Lundy Island before you can say *don't bend over in the shower*. It's going to be like the *Shawshank Redemption*, but without the redemption.' Uncle's round pot belly quivered like a gammony jelly.

Genghis might have been built like a brick privy but this was more like talking to a brick wall, a wall lost in a world of its own. Vainly I tried again to get my point across.

'I'm thrilled to have helped, Unc – you're welcome, by the way. Isn't it possible for you to help me in return?'

But Genghis was busy fiddling with the entertainment system's remote control. 'I won't lie to you, Kev bach. I was trying to have you terminated at first. But my plans changed with the situation – flexible, I am, see. It became clear you were more use to us alive. You should thank your lucky stars I'm the sort of bloke who can think on the fly.'

Calmly I counted to ten under my breath. I couldn't imagine my uncle doing yoga, and clearly empathy wasn't one of his strong points. 'Yeah, I'm a *really* lucky guy. I just want to go home, and live my life in peace, rather than pieces. Can we get that sorted please?'

Genghis's head snapped round quicker than seemed humanly possible. He fixed me with a beady eye, to which the manic twitch had returned with a vengeance. 'My faith in you has grown enormously, Kevin. You've done such a great job – *so far*.'

I didn't like the sound of *so far*, it had an ominously painful ring to it. I fought back the panic rising in my voice. 'It's over, Genghis. I've helped give your enemies a proper shoeing. Can't you just let me and Mum go home?'

Genghis was giving me that look, the one with the cold-dead shark eyes. A bulging vein on his temple joined his eyelid in hammering out a frenzied rhythm. I couldn't help but wonder what part of him would start vibrating next. I reminded myself with whom I was dealing – Tony Soprano minus the laughs. He paused the video, which had started playing on the big screen, and turned to face me.

'It ain't over till the fat lady sings, and she hasn't even started gargling yet. It's so far from over it's not even under.'

Whatever larcenies my uncle had committed in his long and murky career his crimes against language could surely have gotten him locked up and the key blasted into space. I winced at his butchery, as well as the bitter disappointment welling up inside. But this was no man to argue with. I faced one of those momentous turning points in life where you find out who you really are. I didn't like the look of some of the alternatives. Bravely I locked on my sweetest smile and forced the words out one by one.

'What else can I do to help?'

At least I now had Genghis's full attention. 'You remember back in the boardroom I spoke of two problems? Well this is the second one, and it's a biggie.'

'A biggie? The last one was far from trivial.'

He put a hand like a JCB's bucket on my shoulder. 'You see Kev bach, what I'm doin here is maiming two troublesome birds with one stone. And that stone is you. The first is flapping round in a cloud of bloody feathers –'

'That's Llywsiffer?'

'Exactamundo, mi amigo. We solved that proper tidy, like. Now it's time to line you up on the second. Bonnie Tyler might be *Holding out for a Hero* but we're going to have to roll with what we've got, and what we've got is you – warthogs and all.' He prodded me in the chest. 'You up for a challenge, boi?'

Perhaps the most rhetorical question ever asked. I closed my weary eyes, embracing the darkness. The darkness farted and kicked me in the shins. 'And if I help with this *then* I can go home?'

Genghis grabbed hold of my head and shook it, in what he must have considered a friendly manner. It almost gave me concussion. 'Does the Pope shit in the woods? If you fix this, you can have a kiss on the cheek, boi – *and* you can go home. How's that, for starters? We'll even shut down the gate so you won't be troubled again, by us or any Yank or Kremlin ffwcers. Fair dos?'

Despite double vision my face must have registered some emotion. Was this the light at the end of the tunnel, or Ivor the Engine hurtling towards me? Already regretting it I bit the bullet, I just hoped it wouldn't explode.

'What do you need me to do?'

Genghis half turned and pointed to the video screen. It showed an image of this reality's version of Isaiah looking very old and tired. It would have been easy to mistake him for my grandad back in Aberdare, that's if it wasn't for the smart suit and gleaming laboratory full of space age equipment the founder of J-Corp had arrayed behind him.

Uncle G took a deep breath and continued, 'He was a secretive man, Isaiah; such a genius the board afforded him complete control over the Anthracite manufacturing process. Seems we were a bit lax in keeping tabs on the old fella. Turns out it cost us dear.'

My eyes narrowed; I had a sick feeling where this was

heading. Were the rumours true? Genghis looked a bit sick himself, as he continued.

'He was clever about how he did it. His most recent medical said he had years left to live. He led different parts of our organization to believe he'd briefed the others. Operations thought R&D had all the details, R&D were told Production had the plans. Don't know if you've noticed but sometimes this family is not great at communication. Before we knew what had happened he was gone, and he took one vital component with him.'

I could well vouch for my family's communication issues; I was experiencing more than a few of them right now. 'What is it you're telling me? Spell it out, man. Words of one syllable, preferably less.'

Genghis massaged the bridge of his nose and looked almost as old as the man in the freeze frame image. 'All our J-Drives passed through Isaiah's personal workshop at the final stage of manufacture. It was a highly automated process – just him and a bunch of androids. He added his *secret sauce*.'

I could barely believe what I was hearing. 'And you're telling me you've lost the recipe?'

Genghis nodded sadly. 'Before he passed away Isaiah took it from us. But what he took was more of a key than a recipe. Upshot's the same though – we can't build new J-Drives no more.'

So the rumours were true. While still in the guise of Taliesin, the Colonel had told me much the same halfway up Cader Idris, and again outside the board room. And now here it was, straight from the horse's mouth. It beggared belief, but knowing how slipshod my family could be, it didn't surprise me in the slightest. My mouth hung open as I struggled to take it all in.

'A bit lax, on your part. Don't you think?'

Genghis looked like he wanted to punch something. For once I had no fear it might be me. He muttered through gritted teeth, 'We can learn from this. When you've helped us fix it we're going to change our ways. You'll see.'

I tried in vain to contain the manic giggle that escaped my lips. The weird thing was, in his own way, I felt certain Genghis was sincere about changing the family culture. I closed my eyes in weariness. 'I don't know why people keep expecting me to sort this shit out. As I told Tal... I mean Colonel MacIntyre, I'm no engineer. I don't know one end of a spanner from the other.'

Genghis shook his head. 'We're not expecting you to do the science. There's likely only one man who's ever lived who could do that – and his remains are hurtling towards the colony on Alpha Centauri.'

'So how do you expect me to solve this?'

Genghis chewed his lip as if fighting some internal dilemma. 'First, let me show you what your grandfather had to say. You knew him better than most; at least, your local version. Take a seat, lad.' Uncle thumbed the video remote and Isaiah sprang to life.

'Greetings to you, my unworthy family. By the time you hear these words I will be long gone, and so too will your golden goose – which you never appreciated or understood. I'm removing the secret to your fortune and stashing it in a better place, then leaving on my final journey into the stars. Good riddance to both of us, some might say. Ours was never really a marriage made in heaven, and this is the no-fault divorce.'

I jumped to my feet. 'Wait – he stashed what where?'

Genghis was almost sobbing. 'He tried to change us, he really did. But we were too arrogant to listen. Get a load of this.' He pushed me back down into the chair. The camera zoomed in on Isaiah.

'The circumstances surrounding my discovery of Anthracite have troubled me for decades. Yes, it's true, I put in years of hard, patient work, but it wouldn't have happened without one crucial element dropping into my lap. A kind benefactor Paid It Forward. I can't bring myself to do the same for the likes of you.'

'What does he mean *discovery*? Surely it was an invention. What *final element*?' Genghis shushed me again, as Grandad carried on.

'Therefore I can't, in good faith, leave it in the grubby, grasping hands of my unworthy relatives. Another man, better than any of us, judged me worthy – I can't say the same for you. Over the years you've proved yourselves to be nothing but a bunch of dishonest greedy fools. You've corrupted the nation I loved, using our power for your own wicked ends. If it was this bad when I was around to hold you back I shudder to think what it'll be like when I'm gone. That's why it ends – right here and now.'

I think there might have been a tear in Genghis's eye, but when he saw me looking he made a great show of pretending to remove a phantom eyelash. Isaiah lectured on.

'But, of course, there's a possibility I could be wrong. Unlike many of you I'm not so certain in my arrogance. If one of your number can prove themselves worthy, there's a chance you can get it back. A slim chance, as you'll have to face unspeakable danger, just as I did all those years ago. Best get your skates on, as there's a ticking clock – a natural time limit, if you like. Prove me wrong and prove yourself worthy. You'll have to work out where I've put it, first. Go on, I dare you. I won't be holding my breath. Hwyl fawr, and thanks for all the fish.'

The screen faded to black as Genghis stabbed the remote

control in disgust. Red eyed or not, his face could have curdled milk. 'Now you know as much as we do, boi – well, mostly.'

It was hard not to scoff. 'Mostly? There's some gaping holes in this sorry tale. What's this *key* Isaiah was on about? Explaining that would be a start.'

Genghis looked at me long and hard. 'Some members of the board would have me crucified for what I'm about to tell you. But like I said, my faith in you has grown enormously.'

'Flattered, I am sodding sure. Spit it out.'

There was a loud creak, as my Uncle stretched the knotted muscles in his corded neck. 'What Isaiah created was essentially a battery – each Anthracite device a container for vast power. If you want a more technical explanation you'll need to ask the boffins we keep locked in the basement.'

I waved his words away. 'No point, it would all be Greek to me. What puts the energy into this *battery* in the first place?'

Genghis's eyes went wide. 'That's the thing, see. Isaiah had this… this crystal… this lump of rock he'd brought back from the war. I got to see it once. He kept it locked in his laboratory. Glowed all purple it did – like kryptonite in reverse. This thing was the dog's knees, the bee's bollocks.'

'And what did he do with it, this magic talisman?' It seemed I'd stopped breathing.

Genghis's hoarse voice dropped to a whisper. 'In his lab he had this special laser – a massive long thing bolted to a bench. It pointed at the rock. The other side of it ran the J-Drive production line. Each Anthracite unit stopped for a second and the laser fired. Put the *juice* into them, it did. The crystal was the key. Isaiah called it his *tachyon prison*.'

My eyes narrowed. 'Sounds more like a prism to me, Uncle, but I get the point. And Isaiah has hidden this special rock somewhere?'

Genghis looked at me with hope dawning in his eyes. 'I knew you'd get it, lad – you've got a slice of your grandfather's genius about ewe, however thin.'

'Flattery again – good job I'm not the type to let it go to my head. Why do I feel there's some crucial detail coming? Where he stashed this McGuffin, for instance?'

Genghis's face creaked into what might have been a smile. 'You know working J-Drives can be rigged to open gateways to other worlds? You've been through more than a few yourself.'

I nodded and suppressed a shudder. If I never had to go through another gate it wouldn't be too soon – apart from the one that led home. Uncle continued.

'Well, we're opening new portals all the time – only just starting to discover where they lead. Before he died Isaiah made several trips through a new experimental gate he'd just opened – a *special* gate, code name 'Narnia'. It's a doorway that leads to a world seventy-five years out of sync with ours, back into an alternative past. He was visiting a version of 1945 – central Germany to be exact. He hid his precious crystal in the ruins of the collapsing Third Reich.'

My face might have registered a dawning understanding, not that Uncle was the type to notice. I muttered, 'As a young man Grandad finished up in Germany. He was there on the ground, attached to an army unit.'

Genghis nodded. 'The gate opens near the spot where Isaiah's squad ended the war – must have remembered the place – a secluded manor house a little north of Hanover. It's where we think the younger version stumbled across the crystal in the first place. The Nazis were doing all sorts of weird shit. *Our* Isaiah must have hidden his prism in the same spot, returning to the scene of the crime, testing if any of us have the balls to go through what he did to get it back. You might well find two of the bloody things when you arrive – ain't that typical!'

I was fast developing a splitting headache. *When I arrive* – the cheek of the man. 'Wait! Can't you send one of your agents? This mission sounds ideal for the likes of Gwen – a combat courier like no other.' Surely Genghis had thought of this; but Uncle grimly shook his head.

'Isaiah was a sneaky bugger – only a true Jones can access the lock. He was well capable of rigging a genetic scanner to block anyone else. Needless to say we're not snowed under with volunteers. My own useless kids are bottled up in their mansions not returning calls. The rest of our beloved family are pampered and spoiled – not men of action like you and me. If I was only thirty years younger…'

I thought of the extended Jones clan in this world – decadent billionaires to a man and woman, vapid socialites not willing to risk what they already had – *I'm alright Jack, get your hands offa my stash*. I was beginning to see the horrible logic in Uncle's thinking. But something else was gnawing at the back of my brain. 'He was trying to *pay it forward*,' I muttered under my breath.

'What was that?' Genghis was watching me like a hawk.

'Oh, nothing. It sounds risky, but if I do this for you, then we're quits, right?'

Genghis looked me straight in the eye. 'If you pull this off we'll be more than quits, our whole family will be in your debt forever. But there's something else you need to know.'

'Jesus Christ on a pushbike, is there no end to these revelations?'

Genghis's nervous twitch returned. 'There's a hard time factor at play. In a month the war ends on the other side of the gate. Time passes the same rate both sides, just decades out of whack.'

'Thank God for that. Can't we just wait for hostilities to finish and buy our way in with a load of nylons and chewing gum? The locals will be more cooperative once the shooting stops. What's the rush?'

Genghis's face turned sour. 'Three days from now the remnants of an elite Waffen SS Panzer brigade launch their final attack in this area. Isaiah's unit is destined to be on the receiving end.'

'Oh, that's a nice detail. How come they don't – didn't – get wiped out?'

Uncle gulped down another grape, as sweat broke out on his brow. 'Records show our bombers flattened the place to halt the German tanks. Probably on Isaiah's direct orders. You know what his job was by this stage of the war?'

I had a horrible sinking feeling in the pit of my stomach. 'It was calling in the RAF – he was a forward air controller.'

Uncle nodded. 'Bang on, sparky. The ensuing firestorm levelled the chateau. Our Isaiah knew anything planted would get destroyed – any lingering evidence blasted to bits. You'll be up against a ticking clock, as well as an army of suicidal Nazis bent on going out in style. I won't lie to you, boi, it's a risky venture.'

This struck me as perhaps the understatement of this, or any other, century. 'And if I refuse this suicide mission?'

Genghis's expression went blank. 'What I've told you is beyond top secret. We can't have you running around with this information in your pretty little head. You either need to fix the problem, or we need to fix your head – permanently, and with extreme prejudice.' He squashed the grape he'd been toying with between short stubby fingers. Its juice ran down the back of his hairy, calloused hand. Genghis paused to lick it off.

At least Uncle had the good grace to look a bit sad about this revelation, just not very much. Genghis might have been an unscrupulous shitlord of mammoth proportions but you couldn't fault his low cunning. Still, when there's no getting round a problem sometimes you just have to pucker up and face it head on. I let out a weary sigh. 'I guess I'm in. Where do I sign up?'

It shouldn't have surprised me, but the lunatic already had a health and safety waiver printed at the ready. He slid it across the table, along with his fancy monographed pen.

'Good lad, that's the spirit. Sign this and we can get you kitted out. I bet Isaiah would've been proud to see you in uniform.'

37

Obligatory Training Montage

Next morning I was awoken bright and early by that same computerised voice. This time Bitching Betty was a little more polite, if no less persistent. *My presence was requested at Firing Range 3.* (Lol, what? Perhaps I shouldn't have been surprised). *A 'non-organic colleague' would soon arrive to show me the way.* And *what would I like for breakfast?* She advised I have plenty of carbs. Perhaps my status was on the rise round here after all.

Soon I was following R2-D2's retarded cousin down another series of endless corridors, pressurised security doors hissing open and closing in our wake. The decor in this part of the mansion grew less ostentatious – we'd left the Jones family apartments behind and plunged into the working side of the compound. We rode a long airport-style travelator, scores of cryptic, numbered doorways silently rolling by. We traversed huge server rooms filled with banks of Dragon 32s, blinking and whirring as they processed their arcane calculations. Perhaps they were mining the Buttcoin cryptocurrency the family used to hoard its great wealth. Exiting through a wide vehicle loading bay bathed in sunlight we were greeted by an automated golf buggy waiting to take us the rest of the way. Shortly we arrived at the firing range, set back into the forested hillside. I wasn't the first to arrive. Colonel MacIntyre was waiting for me, businesslike as usual. From somewhere in his depths R2 unfolded a mechanical arm holding a clipboard and presented it for signature – seems I was a precious commodity not handed over lightly. My escort beeped and whistled tunelessly before trundling away to headbutt a wall, finally locating the doorway on the fourth attempt. The Colonel looked me up and down.

'Morning soldier, good of you to join us.'

MacIntyre was decked out in camouflage fatigues, bulging ammo pouches hanging from his webbing. What looked like a chunky metal bicycle pump gone wrong hung on a strap round his neck. He looped it over his raspberry beret and greying man-bun.

'Right lad, we need to get you at least passingly familiar with some of the kit you'll encounter on the other side. Know what this is?'

Dubiously I eyed the short stubby weapon. 'Despite my CSGO stats I have to warn you I'm more a lover than a fighter.'

The Colonel snorted. 'Not much of either, if reports are true. Don't go getting ideas – this is not for taking down crazed Nazis – but you need to blend in with Isaiah and his men. Don't want you standing out like a throbbing sore thumb, does we.' He handed me the gun.

'It's a Mk 3 Sten – sod all use at distance, but it can keep an enemy's head down proper tidy. Careful, that's the safety.'

Even with the recent competition there followed perhaps the loudest and scariest half an hour of my life. If Colonel M had heard of Health and Safety, he paid it no heed. After filling the sky with multiple clips of flying lead I began to get some control over the spitting demon snarling in my hands. I might have even got some rounds on target, who knows? The Colonel dryly informed me that any low aircraft stood no chance with me around. Pity, any we encountered were likely to be on our side.

Dazed, and with a ringing in my ears like the very bells of hell, I became aware I was being watched. While I was lost in my cordite haze, we'd been joined by a familiar face. Behind me Gwen leaned casually against a sandbag wall.

'Watch where you're pointing that weapon, hotshot. Don't want it to go off in your hand.'

The Colonel reached over and flipped the safety as I broke into a big grin. 'Where the hell have you been? I was getting worried.'

Gwen strolled over and gave me a hug. She was dressed much like the Colonel, minus the ammo pouches. Camo seemed to suit her. 'There's been a lot of planning to do. This is not your usual cross-reality op.'

A wave of relief washed over me. 'You mean you're coming with me?'

She smiled. 'Wouldn't miss it for the world, kiddo. To be fair, they didn't give me a lot of choice, but yes I'm coming with you.'

I couldn't help but feel my chances of success had just skyrocketed. Gwen looked me up and down. 'Someone's got to keep you out of trouble – I wasn't about to let you do this on your own. Perhaps the only chance we both have of getting out of this alive is if we pull it off. I'll warn you now – ain't gonna be easy.'

'Yeah, that's the impression I'm getting.'

The Colonel gave an impatient cough. 'Sad as it is to have to break up this cosy reunion, we need to be getting a shift on. We've got a lot to get through and the clock is ticking.'

The Colonel summoned up another golf cart and drove us to a small airfield tucked away at the back of the extensive grounds. A strange retro-looking vehicle was parked in front of the biggest hangar. MacIntyre clambered up onto its slabby olive green bonnet and called down to us, 'You're going to need to learn to drive one of these puppies. Isaiah will be herding something similar. You passed your driving test, lad?'

I nodded a bit uncertainly. I felt sure this would be a million miles from my mum's Nissan Micra and the back streets of Aberdare, however mean they'd seemed at the time. 'What the hell is it?'

The vehicle looked like a VW camper van mated with a large rubbish dumpster, one which had received its fair share of incoming fire. Scratched and dented armour plating seemed to have been bolted on in a hurry by a blind mechanic with more hope than sense. It was hard to escape the image of Mr T bearing a welding torch and a scowl. Four oversized tractor tyres held the contraption high off the ground. The Colonel must have seen my dubious expression.

'What we have here is a Humber armoured car – the RAF forward air control units were driving these at the arse end of the war. We can open a gate just big enough to send this one through with you inside.' He tossed me a ring of keys and went on.

'Don't go thinking it's a tank – the armour is only good for defeating small arms fire. Anything bigger will open you up like a can of spam, turning you into minced fritter.'

I could well believe it. A folding roof hatch gave access to a dark, cramped interior – this thing wasn't built for comfort, never mind speed. As we sat surveying the controls, MacIntyre topped us up with diesel. Gwen looked troubled, which I didn't think was a good sign. 'What's up?' I asked.

Her forehead furrowed. 'Never heard of a gate which could push something this big through before – the energy needed must be huge, even if it's a reality in kissing distance to this one.'

I shrugged. 'Genghis said it was seventy-five years out of phase in the past – doesn't sound that close to me.'

Gwen just shook her head. 'There's something fishy about this, mark my words.'

Further speculation was cut short as Colonel MacIntyre stuck his head through the hatch. 'You crazy kids have got a full tank of juice. Take her for a spin, but go easy on the clutch – the grease monkeys tell me it's a bugger sourcing spare parts.'

Gwen and I took turns driving carefully round the test track next to the airfield. The Humber was heavier than I was used to but I did my best, only stalling a few times. MacIntyre rode with us and passed a withering judgement.

'It will have to do. We're pushed for time, but I don't think you're going to win any Grand Prix. Kevin here changes gear like old people do the naughty – slowly, with a lot of grinding and clanking. The inadequate lubrication doesn't help.'

I tried not to sound hurt. 'Mum's car is an automatic – I don't think I did that bad.'

Gwen patted my hand on the steering wheel. 'Don't stress, Boss, we'll get by. I'd best check the equipment lockers – for the want of a nail, and all that.' She vaulted out of the cockpit and busied herself outside, leaving me cooped up with the Colonel.

'You know she volunteered to come with you.' He was looking at me weirdly.

'What's that?'

The wizened old soldier frowned. 'I'm on the payroll of J-Corp – a follower of orders, that's me – but she's a freelancer, could have sat this one out. Instead she signed up for the duration.'

It took a moment for this revelation to sink in. 'She told me unless we get Genghis what he wants our days are numbered. Both of us know too much.'

MacIntyre shrugged his shoulders. 'Maybe you do, lad. But it'll be common knowledge pretty soon. It's been obvious nothing's coming off the Anthracite production lines for months.'

'So our heads aren't on the chopping block after all?' My relief was short lived, as the Colonel shook his.

'Hers isn't. Genghis knows she's a pro, and a valuable asset to boot. You don't kill off talent like that if you know what you're doing. And apart from all his other faults Genghis does know what he's doing. Jones Corp is more likely to buy her off and give her a full-time contract – cheaper that way, and less messy.'

Too much of this situation seemed to be sailing way above my head. 'And what about me?'

MacIntyre chuckled. 'Oh, they'd dump your headless corpse far out to sea without a second thought. Your existence raises too many awkward questions. Isaiah's last will and testament was a tad vague about the Jones family line of succession. Your DNA could get you permanently MIA.'

A wave of nausea washed over me. The Colonel didn't help, heartily slapping me on the back. 'But that's not going to happen, is it lad? Because you're going to get this mission done. Come on, boyo – time for your next briefing.'

38

The Final Countdown

Gwen and I spent the afternoon in a succession of bone-dry lectures, as the Colonel silently looked on. It was all very thorough. This was a man who dotted the i's and didn't so much cross the t's as run them through with a spear. We were given lessons in basic German and a primer on historic British Forces slang. The coffee I'd drunk that morning came in handy, as I don't think my snores would have been appreciated. Halfway through a session on battalion radio procedures, MacIntyre's fist crashed down on the desk beside me.

'Pay attention lad! These are details which just might save your skin. And you need to stay alive to complete my mission, or I'll bloody kill you.'

'I'm doing my best, sir. I'd much rather just get on with it. When do we hit the ground?'

'Time for that soon enough, Andy McFlab. Proper preparation prevents piss poor performance, as Isaiah used to say. You're heading through the gate at 0600 – got to get you ready first. Where's your sense of professionalism?'

This about tipped me over the edge. 'It's sat at home in another universe drawing cartoons of farting ninjas. Maybe I'm not cut out for this shit.'

Gwen put a restraining hand on my arm. 'Kev, it'll be okay.'

The Colonel gave me a withering look. 'There's just one more class – I suggest you pay attention. Your final briefing is with J-Corp's head of intel. Though I doubt even she can whip you into shape.' Muttering to himself MacIntyre clomped off to brood in a corner.

As if on cue our final tutor strode into the hall. She had a face I recognised, though last time I'd seen her she was wearing less gold braid and medals. Mrs Abergavenny seemed to outrank the Colonel by a fair distance – apparently she was some sort of general. Who knew? Aberdare's ex head librarian clapped eyes on me and frowned.

'Here he is look, Mission Improbable.' She slapped her weighty briefcase down on the table and un-handcuffed it from her slender wrist, before opening it up with a clatter.

'Right, it appears the boi is as ready as he'll ever be. Which is not saying ffwcing much.'

At least the swearing had not been part of an act. For some reason that made me feel a little better. 'Nice to have such a vote of confidence. We've already had the *bad cop* routine, no need for *worse cop*.'

Her gaze pinned me to my chair. 'Shut it, you mouthy bugger. You'll need to listen to what I have to say, or you'll be full of holes long before any Nazis get hold of you. We on the same page, are we – or at least matching exercise books?'

Gwen nodded enthusiastically. 'We're listening, Ma'am, aren't we Kev?' I didn't get the impression this was the time for backchat, so I decided it best to keep my views to myself. Mrs

A held up what looked like a small stubby wand, a dull purple fairy light at one end. About halfway along its length a single button sat under a bright red trigger cover.

'This device is how you signal you're ready to come back. It's linked by quantum entanglement to a receiver our end. Experimental as ffwc, so be careful with it.' She tossed the transmitter to Gwen, who caught it deftly, before carrying on.

'We can force open a return doorway, but you'll only get a second or two. The gate will be in a fixed location – the same spot we drop you off –'

Gwen frowned. 'This doesn't sound like any gate I've heard of before.'

Mrs A's lip curled dangerously. 'You can discuss theory with the boffins at YIT when you come back. If you come back. I deal in lead, and hard facts.'

My companion shrugged and inspected the gadget with professional interest. 'Heard rumours you guys were developing something like this – handy bit of kit. How far is the drop from the rendezvous?'

Mrs Abergavenny twirled her fingers over the briefcase and the video screen behind her sprang to life. A map of Germany zoomed in on the area just north of Hanover, between the towns of Schwarmstedt and Celle. Glowing military unit markers were scattered across the display.

'Your LZ is eight clicks from where we estimate you should bump into Isaiah. You won't have time to hang around, but you'll have to move carefully, as there are plenty of enemy soldiers in the area. Things have got pretty chaotic – there's been some desertions but the best of the German units are still fighting hard, even if bereft of higher command.' A pair of snaking, dashed lines marched across the map, intersecting at a third spot. I didn't like the look of the brooding question marks surmounting Nazi flags scattered either side of the route. 'You should be in radio contact with Isaiah before arriving here.'

I held up a hand. 'How are we going to blend in with Isaiah's men? We can't just show up and tag along.'

Mrs A pulled a sheaf of papers from the briefcase. 'Our research geeks tell us Isaiah's platoon's taken casualties – constantly short of warm bodies since crossing the Rhine. We've faked these orders from up the chain of command – you two are a couple of replacements. It's the last days of the war and everything frayed round the edges. No one will inspect you too closely.'

I could see one of this plan's many flaws. 'That's a good job, because I don't know if you noticed but Gwen here will find it hard to fit in as one of the lads.'

Mrs A threw me a withering look. 'Credit me with the brains God gave a weasel, why don't you, bach. Our wardrobe department is your next port of call. You're both going to look the part, at least – even if you might struggle to act it. Your little friend is just going to have to keep out of Isaiah's way. Once you've met up with Sergeant Jones you'll continue on with him to the spot where he ended the war.'

Behind her the map was replaced by a faded photo of a crumbling Gothic ruin. I could well imagine Dracula stepping out of the moss-choked pile, either him or maybe Shaggy and Scooby Doo. Mrs A perched a pair of wire-rimmed spectacles on the bridge of her nose. 'This is the Schloss Drachenburg, as best we can tell the spot Isaiah ends up. We don't know for sure what goes down here, but we think he finds some weird Nazi experiment which leads him to invent Anthracite years later. We also think it's where *our* Isaiah stashed the tachyon prism we need you to retrieve – to get Anthracite production rolling again.'

I kept quiet about my own theories on what we would and

wouldn't find at the castle. I was taken back to my recent conversation with Grandad at the care home. Mrs Abergavenny went on.

'Take a good look at the place – it's the key to the mission.'

I felt the hairs on the back of my neck prickle – the Schloss Drachenburg already gave me the creeps, and all I had to go on was a grainy picture. What would the real thing do to my state of mind? But there was more to it than that – I was having doubts about Isaiah senior's motives. 'So there's two ways we can solve this?'

Colonel MacIntyre nodded. 'Either bring back what Isaiah junior finds, or locate Isaiah senior's magic rock. Either way we'll be cooking on gas again in no time. But remember there's a hard time factor at play – the day after tomorrow, in every time stream our survey teams have checked, the RAF bomb the place to oblivion. Isaiah didn't want his prism falling into the wrong hands, but he did want a thorough test of whoever has the cojones to make the attempt. You need to be long gone before the bombers arrive.'

A sentiment I strongly shared. 'Yeah, not something I want to stick around to watch.'

In a green blur Mrs A shot forward and grabbed me by the lapels, her nose inches from mine. 'But remember this, Sonny Jim – don't bother coming back unless you've completed the mission. A quick, clean death will be preferable to what I'll have in store if you return empty handed. Do we understand each other?'

I was only up to nodding. The foul harridan loosened her grip a little, and peered at me over her bifocals, finally shaking her head in exasperation. 'Dew, dew, dew – sometimes I despair of the younger generation. Not so much Special Forces as Special Needs. Time to get you kitted out.'

With Mrs Abergavenny's words ringing in my ears the Colonel hurried us through to 'Wardrobe'. Yes, the Jones Corporation had a department for everything. MacIntyre left us to oversee preparations at the gate. My astonishment circuits were long since blown, but Gwen saw my expression and felt obliged to bring me up to speed. With new portals opening all the time there was a growing need for operators to get a head start fitting in; inter-universe travel was creating demand for many unusual skills. When I sat down in 'Hair and Make-up' I got another surprise. Juan looked none the worse for the shoot-out at his luxury apartment back in Swansea, where we'd left him valiantly covering our escape. He clearly didn't feel the same way about me, running strong, tanned fingers through the unruly thatch on top of my head, his dark eyes wide with dismay.

'Kevin amigo, it is good to see you again but you neglect your conditioning regime – no?'

'Good to see you too, mate! I thought you were done for up on that balcony in Swansea. Gwen, did you know about this?'

My companion nodded with a rueful smile. 'It takes more than a J-Corp snatch squad to finish old Juan off. He came to see me as soon as I arrived.'

The man himself was peering into my thick hair as if he expected to find something nasty, a look of disdain on his chiselled features. 'My friend, you are a martyr to the split end. Is it not so?'

'If that's all I end up a martyr to I'll count myself lucky. What did they do with you? There was a lot of shooting – stuff blowing up.'

Gwen answered for him. 'It got kind of kinetic back there. We assumed it was the Consortium who tracked us down –

truth was they were too busy picking through the rubble for survivors at CIA HQ – it was Jones Corp who got to us first.'

'So they weren't trying to kill us?'

She shook her head. 'Genghis had changed the orders by then – he wanted us taken alive.'

As realisation dawned I would have nodded in understanding, but Juan had a firm grip on my head, tilting it to his preferred angle. It was all I could do to swivel my eyes in his direction. 'Sorry about your bike.'

He only shrugged his muscled shoulders. 'My guests that day, how you say, turned out to be... not so bad. We came to an understanding. The House of Jones has need of my skills – as, so it seems, do you.'

Inspecting myself in the mirror I didn't think I looked that bad. 'Just a trim please. Maybe a bit off the top.'

Juan pulled a sour face. 'I mean – I am good, but I cannot be performing miracles.' He made the sign of the cross, doing well not to stab himself with his unsheathed scissors.

I could see where this was heading. 'I'm going to have to have one of those train crash *Peaky Blinders* 1940s haircuts, aren't I?'

The coiffeur looked at Gwen for guidance. She sighed. 'You know what you've got to do. Let him have it.'

A few minutes later it was over – at least it had been quick. I felt like a freshly sheared lamb. Juan stood back and admired his handiwork, such as it was. 'Perhaps not my very best, but *ffrrrt* – clients, what is it they know?'

Gwen took my place in the barber's chair. 'When that client is Genghis Jones, best do as he says. He's used to getting his way.'

My scalp felt like it was catching a cold. 'I've noticed that about the mad bugger.'

Juan sighed and got down to work on my friend. A flurry of

clacking scissors and tumbling hair later, it was over. Gwen's cut was just as short as mine, if a little less severe. I didn't think she'd stand up to close inspection – she was still very female in several interesting ways – but then I got the feeling her appearance was far from the sketchiest part of this endeavour. As one of Juan's underlings swept up our sheared locks, I sensed a presence looming in the doorway. Colonel MacIntyre looked on with folded arms, and a worried frown. At last, if a little grudgingly, he nodded with approval.

'Just like the rest of this mission, it'll have to do. Lovely though it's been, watching this reunion, we need to get these two prepped – their uniforms are waiting.'

We said our goodbyes and Juan wished us luck. The solemnity with which this simple ritual was conducted didn't inspire confidence. Obviously Juan thought there was a good chance he'd never see either of us again – a man of experience and fine judgement, who knew how to calculate odds. Gwen patted his cheek and told him not to worry, we'd be back in no time.

Next door was the Wardrobe Department. It was all very thorough. We were handed authentic British Forces dog tags, already stamped with our fake identities – Airmen Smith and Murphy, RAF Forward Air Control Regiment. No detail was considered too small. Perhaps that's when the severity of my plight finally hit home. There was no backing out of this. As we were being measured for our equally authentic khaki uniforms, I mentioned my concerns to Gwen.

'Try to relax, we'll get this done.' She laid a hand on my shoulder. I was a rhapsody in olive drab; the woollen suit was hot and heavy and made me itch like crazy, but it wasn't the only thing making me perspire. I looked deep into her brown eyes, so at odds with her shaven scalp.

'You really think we can do this?'

'Yeah, too right I do,' she said without a moment's hesitation. 'If this is possible, then we're the ones to pull it off.'

'*If* it's possible. I wish I had your faith.'

She only smiled. 'It's not faith, Kev, its confidence. I have confidence in you. You're not the same guy I fast-tracked out of Aberdare Public Library.'

Nearby the Colonel was looking at me long and hard. 'And what's your professional opinion – do we have an Eskimo's chance in hell?'

The old war horse chewed his lip for a while. 'For this mission, I reckon… maybe one in five – too many unknown factors to know for sure.'

I threw my hands up in despair. 'You see – the voice of experience thinks we're done for.'

Gwen just threw back her head and laughed. 'We're all done for in the end, Kevin. It's what you do in between that counts. Grab your webbing, soldier. We've got a big day ahead of us tomorrow.'

39

Off to Narnia in the Morning

I don't think I got a lot of sleep that night. My head was filled with crazy dreams – deranged Nazis chased me through musty castle halls, while an avalanche of bombs demolished the surrounding stonework. When that infuriatingly soothing AI voice roused me from my troubled slumber I almost welcomed the new-found peace. Nothing that lay ahead could be worse than what had been playing through the hours of darkness. I felt more tired than when I'd gone to bed, but when would I get the chance to sleep again?

As instructed I geared up and presented myself at the test track at 0600 precisely. I was greeted by a pale grey dawn – eddies of swirling mist hanging close to the ground, filling every dip and furrow as if they knew danger lurked higher up. A foxhole or nice deep trench struck me as a splendid place to hide. Perhaps it wasn't too late to find one and sit this out.

Gwen and the Colonel were already waiting at the main hangar, standing out in green fatigues amongst the gaggle of assembled lab coats – this place looked like boffin central. Every egghead on the company payroll seemed needed to send us on our way. All eyes turned as I sauntered casually across the tarmac. The Colonel stood next to a pot-bellied bald man, who bobbed from foot to foot in what I took as nervous excitement – either that or he badly needed the loo. He held a clipboard and wore thick glasses, as well as a stained and crumpled white coat. MacIntyre impatiently checked his watch.

'Nice of you to join us, lad. This here is Doc Watkins, our Head of Gate Technology. More degrees than an isosceles triangle. He'll personally supervise the firing. Today we take no chances.'

I tried to keep the tone of bitterness out of my voice. 'Some of us don't have that luxury. Let's get on with it before I change my mind.'

Gwen proffered a friendly fist pump by way of greeting and nodded ascent. 'Howdy, partner. No sense in hanging round. Let's get it on.'

The dumpy scientist held out a clammy hand. 'An honour to meet you, young Mr Jones. Can I just say, on behalf of all our technical staff, how much we admire your courage. You must possess balls of reinforced steel.'

I tried to sound blasé as I wiped my moist palm on a woolly thigh. 'Yeah, it's going to be tough – but *dem's da breaks* for yours truly. Just how risky are we talking exactly, Doc?'

The chief engineer's eyes went wide behind milk bottle lenses as he blew air from his cheeks. 'Hard to say. As you're no doubt aware, this is a highly experimental gate – left to us by the Great Man himself – your dearly departed Grandad. To tell the truth, we barely understand its workings ourselves. Just going through the thing is playing Russian roulette with your molecules. You're a braver man than most, Mr Jones.'

I was finding it hard to swallow past the large ball which had risen in my throat. 'Lovely,' was about all I could stutter. 'You have... tested it, though?'

Doc's laughter rose in pitch to a level which frayed my nerves. 'Tested it? Damn things tested us. *Satan's Sphincter* some are calling it. We've sent drones through and most of them even made it back.'

'Most? What did these drones tell you?'

'Analysis of the telemetry data has thrown up significant anomalies.'

'Uh – what sort of anomalies?'

Doc opened his mouth as if to reply, but pulled up short. You could almost hear the screeching of brakes. He must have caught sight of the dangerous glint in the Colonel's good eye. He continued in a less assured tone. 'Perhaps it's best I stick to the facts. This will be our biggest portal yet – truly one of a kind. Basically what we're doing is ripping this universe an asshole and shoving you through. They say travel broadens the mind; you'll be lucky if this trip doesn't stretch yours to breaking point.'

I was finding the Doc's enthusiasm in no way contagious. Colonel MacIntyre saw my expression and grabbed me by the elbow, ushering us away. 'Thanks for the rundown, Doc. Time for these crazy kids to saddle up and hit the trail. Time's a-wasting, and this is one mission which won't complete itself.'

But Watkins wasn't finished yet, calling after us, 'Whatever happens it'll be spectacular. We're not so much *pushing the envelope*, as shooting it into space. Good luck, you're goyin to bloody well need it!'

To the sound of receding manic laughter the Colonel led us over to our waiting mount – assuring us every aspect of the vintage vehicle had been checked and double-checked twice over. Nobody wanted a mechanical breakdown to jeopardise our mission; there was more than enough else which could go wrong.

But my gaze didn't linger on the idling olive drab truck; a short distance ahead across the concrete a device altogether more impressively sinister grabbed my attention and threatened not to let go – in fact it made me giddy just to look at it. A circular steel frame arched ten metres above the bare floor, the sturdy scaffolding holding it aloft lost beneath a jungle of cables and wires. Spaced evenly around the circumference sat the glowing J-Drives, sixty-four magic black boxes already idling in anticipation of their sphincter-creating moment of glory. At the centre of the infernal ring the air itself danced and shimmered, distorting the image of the dawn-dappled hillsides beyond. Looking into it gave me vertigo, not to mention a sick feeling in the pit of my stomach.

Doc Watkins appeared again by our side, the limpet we couldn't shake off. 'We're not even feeding it power yet. She's a lively one, all right. Almost as if she's got a life of her own.'

Leading up to this deviant contraption stood a sturdy wooden ramp, ending abruptly before crossing the plane of the portal. There was no need for a return the other side – what drove up wasn't long for this world, it would take its chances in the next.

Beside me Gwen's voice had grown hushed. 'This is not like any gate I've seen before. Should it be glowing like that? What will happen when it's switched on?'

On the hangar floor around us a mini Bolshoi ballet of tornadoes formed and reformed in the swirling dawn mist – dust devils straight from hell. Nearby, for no apparent reason, a length of fire hose clanked and banged against the corrugated hangar wall. The hairs on my forearms stood to attention, even those around my privates straightened like they would soon be on parade. Watkins had the decency to look embarrassed as he scuttled over to his troublesome charge. He gave his pride and joy a swift kick, causing a rainbow shower of sparks to cascade down on his bald head. The ethereal glow subsided, if only a little.

'Still a few teething troubles to iron out – minor bugs in the system.'

Beside me Gwen let out a long, slow breath. 'That's good to know. You sure this is just a normal gate?'

In a fit of coughing the Doc seemed distracted by some detail on his clipboard, haranguing a flinching underling into setting it right.

Gwen nudged me in the ribs and pointed with her chin up to a wide gantry suspended from the ceiling. 'Seems the top brass are here to see us off.'

A gaggle of chain-smoking VIPs looked down from on high, worry etched on every face. In their midst stood Uncle Genghis, puffing on a cigar and looking cooler than the rest. Mrs Abergavenny was by his side, and even from this distance I could see the whites of her bony knuckles as she gripped the rail. Genghis tipped his head in my direction when he caught my eye; I was torn between saluting and flipping the Vs; instead I just stood gawping back.

Colonel MacIntyre snapped me out of my stupor, tossing me a set of keys which I juggled but didn't drop. 'She's prepped and full of gas – loaded with all the kit troops like you could expect to carry. Some of it wasn't easy to obtain. Acquisitions wanted to bill you for any breakages, but I told them to take a hike.'

'This organisation is unbelievable,' I muttered.

'Thanks, we do our best.'

The squat armoured car I'd learned to drive the day before was looking a lot less armoured than I remembered. I felt sure it would have a magnetic attraction to German bullets.

MacIntyre turned to my companion. 'You've got the recall transmitter safe and sound?'

Gwen produced what looked like a short chunky baton, topped off with a flip-top lid, protecting a big red button. 'Check. Locked and loaded, Chief.' She stowed the device securely in her tunic.

'Just remember that's your only way back. When you trigger the transponder our boffins will snap open the gate – likely a one-shot deal. You won't have long to get back through.'

Gwen nodded. 'We're ready to roll. Let's get this show on the road.'

The Colonel looked at her for a long time. 'Whatever else goes down over there make sure you bring yourself back in one piece. When this show is over I hope to get the chance to serve with you again, just like old times.' They locked eyes, as some unspoken understanding passed between them. MacIntyre snapped a smart salute.

Gwen returned the gesture. 'I hope so too, sir. It's been an honour.'

The moment was only broken by a self-conscious cough from Doc Watkins. 'You're going to want to go through at approximately 38.62 kmph – that should counteract Coriolis on the other side. Good luck. We're ready when you are.'

There was nothing else for it but to clamber up onto the bonnet; I reached down to give Gwen a hand. I couldn't help but notice she had a tear in her eye, but she smiled up at me all the same. No words passed between us, but we both knew we'd come a long way. The question was, would we get any further – or was this the end of the road?

As I took my place in the driver's seat the crowd of onlookers parted to give us plenty of room. Maybe they didn't trust my driving skills – either that or it was wariness of the still dormant gate. The Humber's antique diesel engine coughed and spluttered, but rumbled into life on the first attempt. We were ready to go.

Doc Watkins waved his clipboard above his head, a signal to some hidden lackey to throw the switch. Probably just a button on a console, but I imagined a spring-loaded affair such as might bring Frankenstein's monster to life – perhaps that's just what this was.

Across the hangar the ring of J-Drives thrummed into life and a neon halo danced around the framework, throwing stark shadows around the hall. The tornado ballet went into overdrive. But that was nothing compared to what happened at the heart of that hellish rig – a glowing mirrored disc of swirling hues dilated to fill the space – a one-way portal into Satan's very own disco. I was conscious I wasn't wearing my dancing shoes. Hairs all over my body stood on end, and I felt my bowels tighten. The causes for this were many and varied. I looked over at Gwen.

'You ready to do this?'

She grinned, a bit sheepishly. 'Ready as I'll ever be, kiddo. How about you?'

I took a moment to examine my feelings. 'Can't lie to you, I'm bricking it. I'm not cut out for this sort of thing.'

She patted my hand on the wheel. 'None of us are, the first time. You'll do just fine–'. She seemed ready to say more, but hesitated.

'What?'

She looked at me long and hard. 'You know Kev, when we first met you were a bit of a dickhead – a right pain in the arse.'

'Thanks.' Not really what I was expecting at a moment like this, but I'd been called worse in my time. 'Perhaps they can chisel that on my gravestone. That's if there's enough of me to bury.'

Gwen's eyes were very large. 'But you've changed a lot since then – just wanted you to know that.'

Neither of us felt the need to fill in the blanks. Instead I put the truck into gear, took my foot off the heavy clutch and we lurched towards the ramp. They say there're no atheists in a foxhole, and I found myself praying to whichever mad gods watched over me for protection – I'm not sure if any of them were listening. I closed my eyes as we passed through.

40

Lower Saxony: April 1945

I don't know how close I got to Doc Watkins' target speed, but we only skidded a little when we reappeared the other side. That wasn't the only pleasant surprise – transit through this singularity felt different to all the others. The nausea barely registered – perhaps it was true you got used to it with time. Either way I only felt a mild dizziness, rather than the gut-wrenching symptoms I'd experienced on each other occasion. When my eyes reopened we were bouncing across barren farmland towards a stand of blasted trees. Gwen was already scanning the cab's armoured vision slits for danger.

'Get into cover fast, don't know who saw us come through. The locals are unlikely to be friendly.'

'They'll be rubbing their eyes if they did – we must have appeared out of thin air.'

I angled towards a clump of trees. The frozen ruts of the ploughed field tested the suspension to the limits, but I had no desire to be caught in the open. Before long we pulled up, nestled in a patch of comfortingly dense undergrowth.

From a pocket in her battledress Gwen produced her trusty smartphone and started flicking through the screens.

'I thought that thing was contraband – they told us no modern tech should be brought through the gate.'

Gwen sniffed. 'What the top brass don't know won't hurt them. Besides, there's something I need to check.'

'I'll be impressed if even you can find a Wi-Fi signal.'

She barely shook her head. 'This app will work just fine.' She was engrossed for a moment, before her brown eyes went wide.

'What's up?'

Gwen tapped the screen in a repeat of the previous pattern, then just stared at it for longer than seemed necessary, before letting out a long and measured sigh. 'Nothing to worry about. Tell you later.'

There was nothing else for it but to break out the compass and maps to get our bearings. To meet up with Isaiah's troop we needed to move towards the village of Schwarmstedt; the gate had dropped us a few miles to the south. After adjusting our watches to local time – 1500 hours – we moved out through the eerily silent landscape.

Soon we were making good progress along a rutted farm track. The sky was low and grey with no hint of mid-afternoon sun. Scattered pillars of dark smoke on the horizon and the dull *crumpf* of distant artillery were the only signs of war – winding down perhaps but still capable of going out with a bang. We saw no sign of civilians, which suited me just fine. After a while I even stopped imagining fanatical Nazis hidden behind every bush. My jangling nerves settled just a little. Gwen directed us south of one silent village, the open fields letting us avoid unnecessary entanglements. I didn't get the feeling congestion would be a major problem – the whole landscape seemed dead and deserted. Colonies of large craters in the ploughed fields bore witness to recent bombing.

My companion got on the radio and dialled into the frequency we'd been briefed Isaiah's unit was using. After some false starts she was able to lock us in. The guy on the other end sounded a little surprised, but accepting enough of our cover story – that we were green replacements sent up from the parent battalion trailing half a dozen miles to the rear. At least Isaiah's men would be expecting us, reducing the risk of getting shot by our own side.

The only moment of drama came when a sudden roar of aero engines sent me swerving off the road and into a hedge. Two fighters went streaking overhead, passing too fast and low to have any chance of spotting us. The markings showed they were ours, but the racks of rockets and bombs slung underneath the broad wings filled me with dread – there was no denying we were heading into a real war zone; this felt nothing like one of my video games back home. Gwen stuck her head out of the top hatch to help direct my efforts to reverse out of the ditch. No serious harm seemed to have been done to our mount, which came as a relief. If anything the added foliage would help us to blend in.

Within the hour we crested a low ridge and spotted a derelict farmyard hunkered down in the valley below – a gaggle of olive green vehicles laagered between its crumbling walls. Through binoculars I spotted several armoured cars, much like our own, a handful of tanks and a couple of canvas-backed trucks. This was the bedraggled troop of airmen we were destined to join. Somewhere down there a younger version of my grandad was in command. I handed Gwen the scopes.

'Seems your navigation skills didn't let us down.'

She looked for herself. 'Never in doubt, mate – never in doubt. Let's go down and meet the great man himself.'

I put the truck in gear and we rolled down the slope. There didn't seem to be a lot of movement around the farm – for whatever reason Isaiah's men were keeping a low profile. As we pulled into the courtyard we were greeted by the sound of a machine gun cocking.

'Hold it! What's the password?'

Someone on the first floor of the barn wasn't in a trusting mood. Panicking I looked over at Gwen for guidance. No one back at J-Corp had thought to brief us on this crucial detail. She held her hands up in dismay, at as much of a loss as I was. A sudden commotion from the barn broke the silence.

'What the hell you doing, you daft bugger – finally we get some replacements and you want to blow their eads off.'

There followed a muffled exchange which might have involved a bit of swearing, maybe an underling getting cuffed around the ears. Either way the large barn doors were soon creaking open. Watching through the vision slits I saw a figure in mud-splatted uniform step from the shadows. Beneath the grime and fatigue I recognised him right away – it was this reality's younger version of Isaiah. It looked for all the world like one of my grandfather's old photos had gained colour and sprung to life. My breath caught in my throat, it was eerie how much he looked... well, like me – a harder, leaner version of myself, but the resemblance was uncanny. Despite being the same age he seemed older somehow, every sinew radiating an unmistakable authority.

'Don't take it personally, some of my boys are a little jumpy. Jerry's all over this area like a case of the clap, and he's up to all sorts of tricks, sneaky bugger.' At least we sounded nothing alike; you could hear the gravel and tobacco in Isaiah's voice. I stuck my head out of the hatch and smiled nervously.

'HQ sent us, sir. We were told to report to Sergeant Jones.'

His eyes narrowed as he studied my features, perhaps wondering why his new recruit was so pale and shaky, perhaps marvelling at my resemblance to the man he saw staring back from the shaving mirror each morning. At last Isaiah grunted, 'I'm Sergeant Jones. Who the hell are you?'

I clambered out of the top hatch and slid down the bonnet, landing in a crumpled heap at his feet. Isaiah was peering curiously at our truck; something about it wasn't right and we were about to be rumbled. In a panic I had visions of us being shot at dawn as imposters. On wobbly legs I stepped into his view line.

'I'm Smith, sir, and that's Private Murphy.' Gwen climbed out and gave a curt nod, before making a big deal of clearing bits of hedgerow from the grill. She kept her head down as much as possible – the dabbed-on stubble wouldn't stand up to scrutiny.

Isaiah looked at me as if I'd slapped him. 'I'm not a bloody officer, lad – I work for a living. *Sergeant* will do just fine, or Sarge.' His pale eyes ranged over me, narrowing to twin chips of smouldering ice. I felt my stomach tighten and had to fight the urge to look away. It took every ounce of effort to maintain eye contact. He knew something was wrong, but couldn't put his trigger finger on just what.

'And you say Battalion sent you? We've not heard a peep from them buggers in days. What the ell's going on back there?'

I struggled to remember our cover story. 'They've got radio issues, sir… I mean Sarge – something to do with the weather. Major Forbes sends his regards.'

Isaiah's gaze seemed to pierce my soul. 'Does he now? Any fresh orders from the sod? Let me guess, he wants us out front again. I'm getting sick of being his rolling tripwire.'

It was all I could do to grin nervously and nod. 'He says to keep heading north-west. There's a fortified manor house he wants secured.'

Isaiah seemed to have heard it all before. 'No change there then. I must be paying for sins in a previous life. A lot of sins.'

'Where do you want us, Sarge?'

Isaiah grunted but seemed convinced, for the time being, gesturing over his shoulder. 'The big fella in the cowshed is Corporal Hicks, he'll get you sorted with a brew and a bite to eat. Have to get your skates on mind – we move out in an hour.'

I thanked him and staggered away, straining not to depart with undue haste. Gwen shuffled after me, coughing loudly into an oily rag – we were hoping our new comrades would keep their distance rather than risk a dose of late winter flu. I was glad to put some yardage between myself and Isaiah. Discreetly I watched him take a slow walk round our steaming truck, all but kicking the tyres.

At least Corporal Hicks seemed pleased to see us. It turned out the troop had been awaiting replacements for weeks. Despite this shortage of manpower Isaiah's RAF team were not alone. They'd been assigned a section of tanks, split from their parent unit to provide a spot of much-needed firepower. In the last chaotic days of the war, organisation on all sides was breaking down. The three Shermans were a welcome addition to the makeshift platoon. As the senior NCO present Isaiah was in charge, but operating with scant instructions from higher command. His small team had been advancing cautiously, wheedling out the last of the enemy resistance and calling in air strikes where needed. There were rumours of peculiar activity in the area, all sorts of mysterious *Wunderwaffen* that would turn the war in the German favour, as well as some sort of prison camp the other side of the forest to the east.

The rest of Isaiah's men seemed weary and battle scarred. All could sense this was the war's final chapter – they just wanted to get it over with and go home in one piece. The brooding airmen and tankers paid us little attention, which suited us just fine. Green replacements had a habit of not lasting long – no point in getting chummy with someone you might be shovelling dirt over in short order. We got given tea so strong it could have powered one of the tanks, and strips of beef jerky that could have doubled as armour plate. I exchanged a few curt words with the others huddled round the camp, but no one seemed keen to chat. When the signal came to mount up we hurriedly finished our brews and made for our waiting vehicles.

I found Corporal Hicks atop the engine deck of our Humber, a can of whitewash in one hand, paintbrush in another, microscopic fag clenched between chapped lips. He was hurriedly daubing an Allied identification star over our paintwork. He grinned around his ciggie.

'Last thing you want is some trigger-happy Yank fly boy using you for target practice – wouldn't be the first time. This should have been done back at the depot. What were those goons thinking?'

This slip reminded me of another which had almost cost us our heads. 'What's the platoon password? No one thought to tell us up at Battalion.'

Hicks jumped down from our truck and retrieved his smoke between thumb and forefinger. It was almost too small to see. 'The lax bastards. At present we're using *Aneurin Bevan.*'

He saw the puzzled way I was looking back at him. 'Don't ask. He's the Sarge's MP back home. Don't get Sarge started on politics – he can go on for bloody hours, he can.'

I was about to tell him not to worry – I was planning on doing as little chatting with Isaiah as possible – when a visible change came over the corporal. His smile slipped and he all but stood to attention. Maybe no surprise, as I found Isaiah standing at my shoulder, the tip of his own roll-up smouldering in the gloom. The Sergeant gave the tiniest flick of his head and Corporal Hicks make himself scarce.

'Everything alright, Sarge?'

'I'm not so sure,' he muttered, blowing smoke.

'Beg pardon?'

He looked me up and down. 'A new bloke shows up, who could be my twin; he's got a reclusive mate who seems to have an advanced case of TB. Just strikes me as odd, that's all. And trust me – since we landed in Normandy I've seen my fair share of odd.'

For some reason I was finding it hard to swallow. 'Just here to do my duty, Sarge, that's all. You know – for King and Country, and all that.'

Isaiah spat. 'My first duty is to my men – to get them home in one piece. You can keep that jingoistic bullshit, fold it sideways and ram it up your arse. When this is over things are going to have to change back home – otherwise our grandkids will be doing this all over again someday, just like our dads did back in the first round of madness.'

Although the air was cold I felt sweat break out all over my body. 'Right,' was about all I could manage to say.

Wearily Sergeant Jones shook his head and seemed to grow older. 'Don't mind me, lad. We've been through a lot, of late. There was this camp we rolled through last week... not pretty.'

I only trusted myself to nod, a bit mechanically. 'We heard the rumours, even back at the depot. I can imagine it would affect anyone.'

Isaiah shot me a withering look. 'None of us will be the same after this is over. Not one. With luck you can patch up bullet holes, and mend broken bones. *This* is another matter entirely.' He tapped the side of his head.

Before I could add my no doubt pertinent insights, Isaiah strolled over to our truck to inspect Hicks's handiwork. Apparently satisfied, he nodded, the glowing stub of his fag once more dangling from his lip. Taking one last drag he flicked it in the mud at my feet.

'We gotta get a shift on. Smith, you and Murphy can take the lead. Not too fast mind, and keep your eyes peeled for danger. This scrap ain't over yet.'

Maybe he didn't totally trust us. Can't say I blamed him – I don't think I trusted us either.

We drove for what seemed like hours with little incident, the rest of the convoy strung out a hundred metres behind. Isaiah kept in radio contact the whole time, ordering corrections if we strayed off his chosen path. The landscape was flat and dreary, the bare skeletons of blasted trees stark against the leaden sky. The scenery wasn't helping my mood. Again I began to see enemies at every turn, more than once taking evasive action at what I thought were hidden German guns. Gwen looked over at me after one such brush with disaster.

'Take it easy, kiddo – the last thing we need is you running us off the road.'

My nerves were already fraying at the edges. I was dismayed to find we'd travelled a fraction of the distance I'd imagined. Just how Isaiah and his men had coped with this unrelenting pressure and tension all the way across northern France I had no clue. As dusk fell a change came over the landscape. The scattered clumps of trees began to form bigger copses, and the fields became smaller. We arrived at the brow of a low hill and looked down on a shallow valley. A bombed-out village lay ahead, brooded over by an ominous wall of dark trees on the far side, a pair of smothering arms beckoning us in.

The radio receiver crackled, relaying Isaiah's gravelly tones. 'This is far enough for today. Give me one sweep of the town then we park up for the night in the forest on the other side.'

41

The Church

I sensed something wasn't right about the village from the start. There was nothing specific I could point to, just the unmistakable din of a hellish klaxon jangling inside my head. Perhaps I'd been around Gwen too long not to have developed some of her instinctive sense for danger. The silent hamlet looked like many others we'd rolled through that long drab day – the husks of shattered buildings burnt, blasted and collapsing into the rubble-littered street – a smattering of ash-blackened snow dusting the scene like Satan's dandruff. But this place was different, something wasn't right. Beside me it was easy to tell Gwen sensed it too. She took another long look through the rangefinder eyepiece and exhaled slowly.

'Let's just take it easy. There's no more sign of the enemy here than anywhere else. Nice and slow.'

Still, I hesitated. Maybe it was that internal klaxon, but in the distance did I hear the peal of some discordant bell? So sure was I that I scanned the rooftops for a glimpse of this town's church tower – and when I found it my pumping blood seemed to freeze. The spire leant at a drunken angle.

Gwen saw my expression. 'What's wrong?'

I spluttered out the words. 'The church steeple – it's the one Grandad told me about back in Aberdare – the one with the crooked spire.'

She wrinkled her nose. 'There're lots of crooked spires in Germany just now. High explosive raining from the sky tends to have that effect.'

'Not like this one. This is different.'

My companion looked glum but nodded, more with fatalism than understanding. 'Perhaps. In any case, I don't think there's any bypassing this place. Take us in.'

Before I could react, Isaiah's craggy voice crackled over the radio. 'What's the delay up there? They're not paying us by the hour. The sooner we get this done the sooner we can all go home.'

I reflected that some of us weren't getting paid at all, but kept this observation to myself. Taking a deep breath Gwen squeezed the microphone transmitter switch. 'No problem, Sarge. Just being careful, that's all. Like you ordered.'

A pregnant interlude of static filled the airwaves. When he spoke Isaiah sounded quieter. 'Take your time. We all want to get through this. I'm sick of writing those letters home.'

There was nothing else for it. I steadied my nerves, gunned the engine, released the handbrake and drove on. The first few derelict homes looked much like any others we'd passed since joining Isaiah's platoon, but something still felt wrong. Every shattered pile of masonry, every fire-blackened brick, every smouldering tree stump seemed to cry out that we were fast approaching some crucial crossroads – an eye in the hurricane of fate. Turning the corner at a dark and shuttered *gasthaus* we rolled into the deserted main square. My attention was drawn to the brooding Gothic churchyard setback behind a row of bare trees, crooked spire stabbing the darkening sky like a broken finger. With hindsight I like to think this distraction played a part in what happened next.

Helpless to resist I stamped my foot on the brake and we skidded to a halt, tyres screeching in protest. Gwen was far from impressed.

'What the hell you doing? We're a sitting duck out here in the open – keep moving!'

I threw my hands up in frustration. 'It's the church Grandad told me about. He read something crucial inside. We have to take a look.'

Gwen was shaking her head in dismay. 'I don't think Sergeant Jones is into detours. He strikes me as the type who does things by the book.'

'We need to think of an excuse to stop!'

She glanced up at the rear-view mirror. 'It better be fast, the rest of them are arriving.'

Sure enough the first of the Shermans had turned the corner and trundled into the square, the unmistakable clatter of tracks on cobbles shattering the eerie silence. Not to be left behind, the radio got in on the act, crackling to life with a burst of static. '*Smith, Murphy – what's the delay?*'

Beads of sweat stood out on Gwen's smudged forehead as she licked her lips. 'He doesn't completely trust us yet – knows something's up. It'll be a stretch selling him a sightseeing excursion. I don't think old German churches are his thing.'

I was all out of ideas but, it seemed, not out of luck. There was a flash and a deafening crash. Simultaneously something long, hot and glowing fizzed past – a molten snake flying at waist height, rending the air mere feet from our olive drab flank. Our truck rocked on its axles. Behind us the lead Sherman exploded in a volcanic shower of sparks, its doomed turret spiralling lazily into the sky. Smoke was already billowing from its interior. As usual Gwen was first to react.

'It's an ambush. Get us out of here!'

Stamping the clutch I fumbled with the gear stick, but my hands seemed encased in boxing gloves. 'Where's the fire from?'

'Dead ahead, twelve o'clock!'

Now the adrenaline had kicked in it wasn't hard to spot what Gwen had seen. Just yards ahead a three-storey town house had taken an earlier direct hit. The structure had collapsed in on itself in a chaotic jumble, filling its cellar and footprint with rubble. Amidst the tangle of roof beams and floorboards a German anti-tank gun had been skilfully hidden, camo netting obscuring its angular form. Like frantic worker ants the grey-clad crew scuttled to reload the cannon, one of them spinning a hand-wheel to traverse the barrel. Its next target was us.

'Do something Kev!'

I couldn't have agreed with her more. Like all the best plans mine was simple; behind us a maze of side streets opened off the square. If I could reverse down one we'd be out of harm's way. But in war the simple things are hard.

'Hurry Kev!'

For once there was a rising note of panic in Gwen's voice. Ahead the gun crew had almost lined us up. Each second took on an elastic quality, stretching like treacle until it could be measured in heartbeats. I gunned the engine into a deafening roar. At last the gears meshed, I looked back over my shoulder, and lifted my foot from the pedal. But like I mentioned, in war the simple things are hard.

I hadn't found reverse; what I'd found was first. As the clutch plates came together with a screech we rocketed forward. I didn't have time to aim, even if I'd been looking in the right direction. The Humber crashed through the crumbling front wall and mounted the rubble scree like a ramp. The gun and crew were exactly in our path; still accelerating we slammed into them and their weapon. There was a sickening screech of metal grinding against metal, followed by a chorus of equally sickening screams. Roof beams and masonry clattered down on the top of our vehicle, choking dust and cries filled the air. I was thrown forward, my head hitting the dashboard with a thunk. A galaxy of stars went supernova, before the blackness rose up to take me.

Some hazy time later I found myself sat on the back step of the medical truck, while an orderly reeking of iodine patched up my face. I had a nose which wouldn't stop bleeding and the world's worst case of tinnitus, but other than that I was okay. Maybe my guardian angel had taken a break from the all-day drinking binges and was back on duty. My new friend had just finished wrapping the last bandage when he looked past me and froze. A brooding figure stood at my shoulder – it was Sergeant Jones. The medic gathered up his kit and hurried away.

'That was good work back there, lad – quick thinking, I like that.' Isaiah forced a smile, but the rest of his face was flinty. I wasn't about to tell him my actions had been more down to ineptitude than courage. Perhaps he was warming to me after all.

'Oh, it was nothing, Sarge. Just trying to do my bit, that's all. You know me.'

He pretended to be taken aback. 'Do I?'

All of a sudden I was sweating, despite the chill night air. Now it was my turn to force a smile, as Isaiah leaned an elbow on the tailgate.

'And don't be so modest, lad. You must be a natural. Not

everyone is so calm, their first time under fire.' He offered me a smoke.

I shook my throbbing head. 'No thanks. Those things will kill you.'

Isaiah snorted without much mirth, before his eyes locked with mine. 'That *was* your first time under fire – wasn't it?'

I came over all light headed, and for once it had nothing to do with the world-class streak of near-death experiences I'd recently been through. 'Yes, Sarge – sent here straight from Battalion, we was – me and Murphs.' I didn't like where this was heading. Putting a hand up to my temple I murmured, 'Feeling faint – might need to lie down.'

Isaiah's tone remained neutral. 'Yes, I bet you do. Lying comes naturally to some. Fill your boots, son.' I swayed a bit and fluttered my eyelids, but Sergeant Jones wasn't finished yet.

'And on the subject of Private Murphy – your shy friend – he also seems to know what he's doing. Guess I struck lucky getting you pair?'

I felt a strong urge to change the subject. 'What happened to the Sherman crew?'

Sergeant Jones looked grim. 'None of them made it out alive. Messy. More good men lost. Jerry is still full of tricks. That's why we all need to be on our guard.'

'I'll keep my eyes peeled.'

Isaiah struck a match on the rusty paintwork, lit up and took a drag. He peered down at me for a long time. 'Good. I will too. Just you remember that.' He blew out an impressive plume of smoke. 'It will take a while to replace the wheel on your Humber. We've done a sweep of the village; there're no more enemies to be found – at least the ones in German uniform. Get yourself a bite to eat, then get your head down for the night – we move out at first light.'

'Will do, Sarge.'

He turned to go, then looked back over his shoulder. 'Just remember – I've got my eye on you.'

'Why's that?'

'Dunno, maybe I want to pick up some soldiering tips. We'll see.'

And with that he strode off into the night, the glowing tip of his smoke dangling from his lip. As I watched him depart I heaved a sigh of relief. Isaiah didn't know what we were up to, but he knew we were up to something. We'd been naïve to think he wasn't savvy enough to spot a couple of fakes. This was one more complication I didn't need right now. At least I wasn't alone with my gloomy thoughts for long. A shadowy figure emerged from the alley behind the truck. It was Gwen. 'Private Murphy' sat down by my side.

'How you doing, sport?'

I was relieved to see her. 'I'm okay. Took a bit of a bang to the head. Missed all my vital bits.'

She smiled. 'Yeah, I noticed. You're going to have a scar. What will your mam say?'

'I'll be grounded till further notice. But that's not the end of our problems. I don't think Sergeant Jones trusts us.'

Gwen snorted. 'I *know* he doesn't trust us. Suspicious types – your family. Not always easy to make them see sense. Now I know where you get it from.'

For a time we both watched Isaiah at work across the square, barking orders and overseeing the recovery of our scout car from the wreckage of the building where it came to rest. Wherever he went the men were galvanised into fresh bouts of action. It was plain he was a natural at giving orders – not a trait I seemed to have inherited.

Gwen got to her feet and reached out a hand to help me up. I staggered upright. 'Where are we going?'

'Where do you think? You managed to wangle that delay you wanted. Since we're here we might as well check out the church.'

In the stress of combat I'd forgotten all about my grandad's words back in the care home. Now that I had a better look at the brooding Gothic pile, crooked spire and all, further investigation didn't seem like such a good idea. The place seemed to glare down at us malevolently from the other side of the street, its shattered windows staring blindly like empty eyes. A shudder ran down my spine as I remembered another abandoned church in the shadow of Cader Idris – I just hoped this one led to a happier end. Before I could raise any misgivings my companion had gone. Full of trepidation I followed Gwen across the scorched cobbles. The steps up to the place were littered with rubble, and the stained glass windows had seen better days, but the structure itself seemed intact. Against all odds it had avoided the worst of the surrounding destruction – divine providence, perhaps.

An ancient oak doorway shod with iron blocked our path; behind it was inky darkness. Ever resourceful Gwen had thought to bring a torch. She switched on the beam and swept it across the nave. Elaborate candelabras hanging from the rafters threw shadows around the hall. Despite the gloom it wasn't hard to find what we were looking for. Whoever had left the message wanted it to be found. Scrawled across the far wall, in what looked suspiciously like very modern aerosol spray paint, were three dripping red words.

It took me a moment to process that they were written in Welsh – not exactly what you'd expect to find daubed in a deserted German church at the arse end of Götterdämmerung. It looked like the tag of some time-travelling graffiti artist, and perhaps that's just what it was.

I found I'd stopped breathing. 'What does it say?'

Gwen stared at it for a long while. 'Gwybodaeth yw Pŵer.'

'I can see that. What does it mean?'

She took an age to answer. 'Knowledge is Power. Mean anything to you?'

There was no doubt who'd left these words. 'Perhaps. It's a message from Isaiah, isn't it? The one from your world.'

She nodded. 'It's more than a message – it's a clue.'

'A clue? Intended for who?'

'Whoever Isaiah wants to find what he's hidden. He's paying it forward.'

'A worthy member of his family,' I murmured. 'We need to beat them to it.'

Before Gwen could reply we both jumped at the sound of the creaking door behind us. Sergeant Jones stood in a shaft of moonlight, staring from us to the writing and back again. He looked confused. I knew just how he felt. In slow motion his cigarette tumbled from his lips and hit the flagstones in a shower of sparks – his mouth moved soundlessly as if he meant to say something, but had run out of words.

Instead he just slowly shook his head, turned on his heels, and slipped back the way he'd come. Gwen and I exchanged a glance, but there was nothing left to say. We both sensed things were coming to a head.

42

The Schloss Drachenburg

The next day we awoke to heavy fog, a pale grey clinging blanket low to the frozen ground intent on keeping secrets. Sergeant Jones avoided us as we brewed our tea, but more than once I caught him watching us from across the busying camp. The other men were surly and uncommunicative. Within the hour we'd packed our gear and were on our way again. It wasn't long before we had reached or destination, and our blind date with destiny.

The convoy moved cautiously out of the trees in a ragged line abreast. The idea was a hidden enemy could only take one of us out. Small comfort for the designated target, but the constant fear for a unit like ours was, travelling in column, a cunning ambush could take out the first and last vehicles, trapping the rest in a killing zone. We'd been lucky the day before; we wouldn't be so lucky again.

We trundled cautiously over a ploughed patch of open ground, maybe a quarter of a mile wide. It's a mark of how quickly I was learning that I immediately recognised the place for what it was – a killing ground, devoid of cover. Crossing it felt dreadfully exposed. Ahead of us was the deserted castle, the Schloss Drachenburg, I recognised from those endless briefings back in another, saner world. The castle reared up from the earth like a broken tooth. Just looking at it gave me the creeps.

Over the radio Isaiah instructed us to make a circuit of the grounds. I got a good look at the imposing outer walls, and the moss-covered gatehouse at the end of the long gravel drive. Gwen steered us between the gnarled trunks of ancient apple trees in the orchard, before pulling up in the cobbled courtyard at the heart of the castle. She sounded no more impressed than I was.

'What a miserable place. Like something dreamt up by Hieronymus Bosch with a hangover.'

I couldn't disagree. So this was the spot Isaiah has been so keen to visit. At first glance I couldn't see the attraction. The former owners had left it in quite a mess. At least we wouldn't be troubled by the casual tourist. As the younger version of my grandad ordered his men to set up a defensive perimeter, I cast a baleful eye over the dank and dreary ruin. It wasn't hard to imagine crazed Nazi scientists conjuring up hellish inventions in its depths.

Off to one side of the courtyard, set back under a Gothic arch, a pair of thick oak doors hung off their hinges. Behind them the musky depths of the castle looked dark and uninviting. I peered inside with trepidation. From behind me Isaiah's voice made me jump out of my skin.

'Smith, where the hell do you think you're going? I need you on the east wall manning the Bren gun. Jump to it.'

I made some lame excuses about needing to relieve myself, while Sergeant Jones peered at me with disdain; he didn't look convinced. 'And you can take your mysterious mate with you,' he said, flicking his head to where 'Private Murphy' was unloading ammunition nearby. 'Try to stay out of trouble this time.'

When he'd gone, Gwen came shuffling over. She was trying to look relaxed but her eyes darted all over the castle, some primordial danger instinct kicking in. There was an unfamiliar skittishness about her which I found unnerving. When she was sure Isaiah was out of earshot she put her head close to mine.

'We need to take a look around. This place is bigger than I thought.'

'Too right it is. You could hide an army in this pile, never mind the doohickey we've been sent to find. Where do we begin?'

Her gaze drifted back to the ominous doorway I'd been investigating before the interruption. We both knew where Isaiah would have stashed his prize – somewhere deep inside this infernal ruin. She checked her watch.

'We have maybe an hour of daylight left. I've got no desire to go stumbling round this place in the dark. Let's get on with it.'

Before I could reply a deafening crash resounded from the castle's north wall. The surrounding air seemed to quiver and shake, a confetti of moss raining down from the ancient stones above. It was impossible to escape the conclusion some joker was firing high explosive shells in our direction. In reply one of our machine guns high in a tower opened up, shooting at a distant target. There were alarmed shouts all around as men went running to find cover. The whip-crack of incoming rounds sounded overhead. The Schloss was under attack; the battle had begun.

Gwen dropped the ammo box she'd been carrying, Bren clips tumbling across the cobbles. 'This is it – now or never. We don't have much time.'

'When did we ever?'

But she was already gone. Not caring if Isaiah watched, I followed her through the archway and crazily tilting doors. It was chill and dark inside the cavernous hall, the air reverberating as the sounds of battle outside drew closer. Whoever was shooting at the Schloss was finding their range. Gwen broke out a torch and pinned it to her lapel; I did the same with mine. We were in the great lobby of the castle, faded tapestries and ancient weapons hanging from the walls. At the far end I could just make out the twin arms of a grand staircase sweeping up to a balustraded first floor gallery. Between these arms was a dark maw, a third stairway descending into an inky abyss. I didn't much like the look of it.

Gwen scanned our surroundings and came to a quick decision. 'You take the upper levels, I'll check downstairs. You know what you're looking for?'

I nodded, trying not to show my relief. 'I'm guessing it will stand out like a sore thumb.'

She patted me on the back. 'That's what I'm hoping too. Keep in touch by radio. We're gonna get this done.'

And so we went our separate ways. Outside, meanwhile, the firing intensified. Curtains of pale dust blossomed from the distant ceiling, each fresh concussion causing me to flinch. I pulled my scarf up around my face to filter out the worst, but the smell of damp and decay was enough to make me gag. Old Isaiah had wanted someone to find what he'd hidden, so how hard could this be? It was just unfortunate that what was left of the German army seemed intent on crashing the party.

Racing along the first floor landings was far from easy. Rotting furniture had been pulled from adjacent rooms, the debris of earlier looting. I stuck my head through each doorway but nothing struck me as out of place. At the end of the landing an arched window looked out over the orchard to the north. Maybe I could at least discover what was happening outside. I'd have been wiser to not let my curiosity get the better of me – what I saw chilled my blood.

A line of grey enemy tanks were pushing towards the castle, firing as they moved. It looked like they were the remains of hastily cobbled together German units. There were all sorts of vehicles, vintage early war models as well as the dreaded Tigers. Several blazing wrecks bore testament to the accuracy of our return fire. But the waves of Panzers just kept coming, dark-clad infantry leapfrogging between the boxy hulks. When a stream of rounds tore past my window I barely got my head down in time. Rolling clear I pressed myself against the clammy wall as I slowed my breathing – there was little I could do to help. I just prayed Gwen was having better luck downstairs. As if on cue my radio crackled to life, a familiar voice ringing in my ears. 'You need to get down here fast. I'm in the cellar.'

'You've found it?'

'It's not that simple.'

Seemed to me it never was. More stray fire hit my position, pinging off the splintering masonry. I needed no further prompt to get moving. Crouching low I went scurrying for the stairs, bounding down two at a time as fresh impacts shook the building. The Schloss had stood for hundreds of years, but how much longer?

As I reached the ground floor the courtyard doors on the other side of the hallway crashed open. A stooped figure came staggering through. It was Isaiah, looking grim and battle scarred but ruthlessly determined. He was limping badly and weighed down by a bulky radio set cradled in his arms. This wasn't one of our handheld walkie-talkies, but the big VHF rig used for talking to higher command. Too late to hide, he spotted me and his eyes went wide.

'Smith – help me with the transmitter. We're running out of time.'

I could relate to that. I floundered on the last step – this was a distraction I didn't need. 'We gotta get out of here, Sarge – Jerry's coming!'

Isaiah collapsed at a mouldy trestle table, panting from his exertions, perspiration clinging to his brow. Tough he might have been but his injuries were clearly getting the better of him. 'Don't you think I bloody know that, lad? We're going to give them the welcome they deserve. Gimme a hand here.'

I helped Isaiah upright as he started turning the radio dial. Static spilled from the headset as he pinned it to his ear. 'Comms was back up briefly, but my truck took a direct hit. Just got to find the air support channel on this piece of junk…'

Isaiah was engrossed in his work, sweat trickling down his bloodied brow. I edged towards the flight of stairs at the back of the room, the one descending to the crypt and whatever mysteries Gwen had found. But my escape wasn't to be that easy.

'Where do you think you're going?' Isaiah's head snapped round. 'Grab this antenna and hold it up high. Almost had em then.'

'But Sarge!'

'Cut the blabber and do your duty, man. Or I'll shoot you long before Jerry does.'

I didn't doubt him for a moment. There was no getting out of this; Gwen would just have to wait. Isaiah threw me the end of a twisted and frayed wire, before breaking into a fit of coughing. I climbed onto the table and held the aerial aloft. I could hear what sounded like artillery impacting in the courtyard outside. The shells were getting nearer.

Much twiddling and cursing ensued. Isaiah only paused to wipe blood-flecked spittle from his lips. At last he found the frequency he was after, the dispatcher's voice coming through loud and clear.

'This is sector air control, where've you been Fox One? Proceed with sit rep.'

Isaiah wasted no time. 'MAYDAY – requesting immediate strike on our position – we're overrun!'

The hall was rocked by a fresh series of explosions. A display of ancient swords and halberds clattered to the floor – they would have made an ironic way to go. Mouldy plaster tumbled from the distant ceiling. My eye was drawn to a large round candelabra swaying ominously overhead, the long chains which held it lost in darkness above. If I balanced on tiptoe maybe I could grab it.

My fingers brushed the black wrought iron. I missed my grip, but I'd slowed it sufficiently so on the next swing I was able to stop it entirely. With a pounding heart I grabbed hold of the candelabra and, straining every sinew, threaded the antenna through the frame. Numb fingers shaking with effort, I tied a makeshift knot in the wire. My aerial hoisting duty done, I considered the options for escape.

I could see Isaiah was distracted, busy calling in the bombing run, reeling off map references like a demented bingo caller. It didn't sound like he had much hope of getting out of this alive, resigned to some fiery Valhalla. And, like it or not, the rest of us would be coming along for the ride. As silently as I was able I slipped down from the table and backed towards the stairs.

43

Into the Crypt

I found Gwen racing up to meet me. For once she looked flustered, beside herself and out of breath. 'Where the hell have you been? I thought you'd got hurt. Sounds like bedlam up there.'

With an effort I regained my composure. 'I had a bit of a detour. It's bad, but things are about to get a whole lot worse. Forecast is for intermittent showers, turning to prolonged heavy bombing. And I haven't brought a mac. Better show me what you've found.'

Gwen led me back down into the darkness, the light from our bobbing torches playing across the glistening walls. The staircase changed from wood to chiselled stone, the treads worn smooth by the ages. The shaft spiralled to our left, corkscrewing its way into the earth. We were descending into the guts of the castle, maybe into the bowels of hell itself. The foot of the stairs opened onto a long and musky tunnel, a low, vaulted ceiling arching overhead. Giant wooden casks nestled in alcoves set back in the walls, their contents long since plundered. It was all I could do to keep up with Gwen, my breath misting in the cold, stale air. We came to a skidding halt at the far end of the chamber, a stout iron door blocking our path. It was age worn but solid enough. It looked like it might guard a bank vault. My heart sank.

'I don't understand. How do we get in?'

Gwen pointed to an alcove tucked away in the shadows. Her torch beam focused on what she'd found. 'Take a look in the corner.'

The computerised panel was glaringly out of place. Blinking red LEDs surrounded a small screen mounted above a glowing pad. At the centre of the luminous button was a tiny black dot.

Gwen ushered me forward. 'It's a genetic lock. The display's asking for a sample of blood. Put your finger on the hole.'

'Blood? Meeting Dracula's the last thing we need right now.'

She gritted her teeth. 'Don't be daft. You just have to be part of the Jones clan to get in. Isaiah wasn't taking any chances.'

I just hoped this was the only blood I'd spill that day. Taking a deep breath I rolled up my sleeve and put my thumb over the pad. Just when I thought nothing would happen a loud click made me flinch and I felt a sharp stab of pain. At least my yelp was drowned out by the whoosh of air as the sample was extracted. For a moment all was still. Then, one by one, the lights around the display started blinking green. From deep within the walls came the rumble of grinding gears. The crypt door unsealed with a hiss.

Gwen was through in a flash. 'We've not got long. This place will be rubble soon. Getting buried alive is no improvement on being shot.'

I stumbled in after her. The chamber was small and round, illuminated by flickering lanterns arranged round the wall like wards guarding a pagan shrine. Ancient manacles dangled from the ceiling. On the far side the glistening floor sloped down towards a gaping chasm covered by a rusted grill. It guarded what looked like a hellish chute, no doubt for the easy disposal of victims' remains. This was a place to give health and safety inspectors nightmares, if not to test their sanity to the limits. A torture chamber so old school it was almost wearing short trousers. But none of these details held my attention for long.

In the middle of the room stood a very modern computer terminal. In fact, by the standards of the place I called home, you could have called it futuristic. One of the frameless holographic displays I'd become used to danced and flickered with a stream of arcane symbols, scrolling by for no good reason other than to show off. Not exactly the sort of device you'd expect to find in the dungeon of a crumbling German castle. But even this wasn't the most eye-catching feature.

Atop the terminal sat a glass box, like a fish tank illuminated by an eerie purple light radiating from what lay within. What little breath I had left caught in my throat. The box's contents looked like a lump of jagged amethyst crystal, glowing with an ethereal inner light. The thing seemed to quiver and throb, struggling against its containment, straining to be let off the leash. You could almost see the energy coming off this thing in waves. This could only be the fabled Anthracite prism Genghis had sent us to find.

Gwen grabbed my arm, her voice hoarse. 'This is what your grandad left behind.'

'Yeah, no shit, Sherlock.' She looked at me askance.

Any sense of achievement was dampened by the muffled thud of fresh explosions impacting above our heads. A fine dust rained down from the cracks in the shadowy ceiling. My heartbeat had gone up a gear; it was now or never. I stepped up to the terminal, more determined than ever, Gwen by my side.

Crossing some invisible threshold, a row of shimmering letters printed out one by one.

Welcome dear relative. You've done well to get this far. Are you ready to play the game of your life?

Two equally holographic buttons pulsated beneath the words. I pushed my finger through 'YES', trying hard not to wince at what might happen next. Above us the explosions were getting louder. With agonising slowness Isaiah's words appeared on the display.

'The power I've locked away is not to be used lightly. So I have the knowledge you're a Jones close to my own heart, I hope you don't mind a few simple questions. I so want to Pay it Forward, but I have to be sure.'

'What's he on about?' My unease was growing fast.

Gwen sounded in no better state than me. 'Haven't got a clue. Look, he's getting to the point.'

'What is the password? You have three guesses. Fail, and this cabinet locks forever. Be sure of your answer – much depends on what you do next.'

A holographic keyboard flickered into view, while on the screen a blinking cursor seemed to mock me. Gwen could offer little help, only shaking her head. 'You'd better come up with something fast, kiddo. We haven't got long.' More explosions above us; more debris raining down from the ceiling.

My mouth had gone dry. Grandad must have thought someone like me (and I was beginning to believe he'd meant it to be me), or the young sergeant wrestling with the radio above, could have guessed the answer. I wracked my memories for some clue – maybe something he'd once said. A thousand conversations ran through my brain. What were his obsessions? What was he forever banging on about?

Gwen stood at my shoulder. 'Maybe it's best you don't overthink it. Use the Force, Luke.'

Inspiration struck like a bullet. My fingers stumbled as I typed.

'ANEURIN BEVAN.' Maybe not my best guess, but I was just getting warmed up. I was hardly surprised when the keyboard pulsed red and a blaring klaxon sounded.

Gwen's voice had gone up an octave. 'Don't think you got that right, sport. Two more goes.'

At least Isaiah was trying to be helpful – words flickered across the screen. '*Not a bad first try, you're on the right track. What you see before you is the key to limitless POWER. To avoid disaster any who wield it must also possess KNOWLEDGE.*'

Gazing at the glowing words in mounting panic I tried to put the collapsing tomb out of my mind – not an easy task with the ceiling raining down. What was Isaiah trying to say? He was trying to give me clues – to give me every chance of succeeding. Almost like he was giving me advice. Fresh insight arrived in a flash, and this time I knew I was nearer the mark. My fingers danced.

'FRANCE IS BACON.'

I was ready to pump the air in triumph, but again the keyboard flashed red. This time the siren sounded louder. My heart sank through subterranean levels, like one of those infernal lifts. Before I could react Gwen all but showed me aside. She took our final turn at the keyboard, her fingers ablur.

She typed 'FRANCIS BACON' and hit return.

The keyboard flashed green. The klaxon changed to a triumphant ovation. Confetti seemed to rain down from the ceiling, but I it might have been chips of stonework. There was a hiss of rushing air, as the seals on the fish tank popped open. Ever so slowly the glass walls sank into the console, revealing the shimmering prize within. The Anthracite prism was ours.

Gwen held open the bag Doc Watkins had given us. 'Grab that thing and let's go!'

As my fingers wrapped around the gleaming crystal it seemed to vibrate and quiver in my hand. I gazed down spellbound as its colour cycled through every hue of the rainbow, and some others beside. My mind was filled with a chorus, as if an angel had struck a chord on some heavenly harp. As so often Gwen dragged me kicking and screaming back to reality.

'Let's move, or we're toast!'

Reluctantly I dropped the crystal into the sack. Gwen pulled the drawstrings and stuffed it in her jacket. I turned back to the doorway. The chamber might have been crumbling around us, but still I pulled up short. A lone figure stood blocking our path.

Sergeant Isaiah Jones eyed us grimly from beneath a bloodied brow, panning his stubby machine gun from one to the other. His lip curled as he growled, 'I'm in the mood for shooting someone, and I'm happy to start with a couple of deserters.' He cocked the gun and jammed the stock against his shoulder. He seemed not to notice the chunks of ceiling collapsing behind him.

It looked like I'd come this far only to be ended by one of my own flesh and blood. The frustration was too much to bear. I tried to sound calm; it wasn't easy.

'We're not deserters, far from it.'

His chuckle turned into a rasping cough. 'Oh, really? Then what the bloody hell are you?'

'It's complicated. We don't have time.'

He didn't seem convinced. 'There was always something odd about you pair from the start. Maybe you're working for the other side – Nazi infiltrators hiding amongst my men. I

318

shoot spies even quicker than I shoot deserters. Close your eyes.'

I took a hesitant step forward; the gun barrel rose up and pointed at my chest. 'Look Isaiah, it's a far from simple story, but you have to trust us.'

He spat out a bloody globule of phlegm. 'Trust you? My men are getting slaughtered upstairs – you pair knew this attack was coming. Don't think there's anything you can say that'll stop me filling you full of holes.'

As he aimed down the sights there was an earthquake-like rumble; I didn't think it was my stomach. 'What if I told you we're from an alternative universe on a secret mission to retrieve the key element in a world-changing invention an older version of you left for one of us to discover that will cause Wales to become a global superpower?'

He paused for only a moment. 'Then I'd say you're talking bollocks. Do you think I was born yesterday?'

'No, you've been born far more times than that, and will be again.'

Isaiah looked confused; can't say I blamed him. There was a fresh rumble and a loud crack. From above us a sizeable chunk of masonry broke loose and plunged from the ceiling. Isaiah looked up, but it was too late, it struck him a glancing blow on the temple and he collapsed like a sack of spuds. His weapon clattered across the flagstones.

Gwen didn't waste any time. As the air filled with debris she grabbed my arm and made for the rusty grill behind us. 'Give me a hand with this thing – it's the only remaining way out.'

I could see she was right. Behind where Isaiah had stood the passage was rapidly filling with rubble. The floor shook and buckled as the castle collapsed above our heads. But there was no way I was leaving Isaiah behind, abortive summary execution or not. Squirming free I stumbled back through the billowing dust to find him half buried under a mound of debris. Grabbing hold of his webbing I dragged him over to where my companion squatted, straining and cursing at the grate.

Gwen had already bent one corner of the grill from its frame. There was a padlock but it had long since rusted shut; brute force was our only hope. Veins throbbed on her temple, almost ready to pop.

'Take hold of this and pull!'

I had to pause and cover my face – the stench rising from the chasm was enough to make me retch. I didn't like to think what was down there. Against the growing din I called over to her, 'Any idea where this leads?'

'Not a clue. But I'd rather take my chances down there than stay and get buried alive. Grab that corner, we're almost done.'

For once Gwen would get no argument from me. There was no chance of digging our way out the way we'd come. As far as escapes went it was this stinking chute or nothing. I grabbed one of the flaking iron bars and pulled for all I was worth. Slowly it started to move. As if in unison, around us so did the glistening walls.

We made a gap just big enough to squeeze through as stonework crashed down. Gwen wriggled under first, taking care to protect the prominent bulge in her tunic. She looked back at me. 'Here goes nothing.' Her fingers let go of the bars and she slid away, swallowed by the darkness.

I didn't have time to hang around. Isaiah was showing no signs of life, a trickle of blood dribbling from his forehead. Considering the state of him I doubted this fresh wound made much difference, but I was relieved to see his chest moving with a steady rhythm. Shimmying under the grate was easy enough, but dragging my sleeping relative was another matter. Hanging onto the bars I somehow managed to pull him after me, onto a level area at the head of the chute.

But as I pushed off and let gravity take hold I realised the flaw in my plan. Isaiah's uniform was criss-crossed with belts and buckles – one of these had snagged on the grill and stuck fast. I was left dangling down the chasm, gripping his legs while the strap strained under our combined weight. Above I could hear the ceiling caving in, a shower of masonry peppering my face. How long before this shaft collapsed too?

With gritted teeth I hauled myself up Isaiah's body. If only I could release the snagged harness. My muscles filled with lava as I strained against the weight, but I hadn't come this far to fail. Blindly my numb fingers found a clasp and snapped it open. A lone ammunition pouch came free and tumbled past me into darkness. But I knew I was close. Finding another buckle I winced as cold steel dug into the flesh of my fingers. This time I'd hit the jackpot. Isaiah slipped free of his harness and we both started to slide, gaining speed at a rate of knots.

44

The Catacombs

It was a terrifying helter-skelter ride through pitch darkness, headlong down an ancient chute slick with slime. I might have thrown up, if I hadn't been so busy screaming. Isaiah didn't seem to notice; he was out for the count. I wasn't destined to be so lucky. Acceleration pinned back my cheeks as a rancid hurricane of air whistled past. Would my torment never end? Just as I teetered on the brink of madness I felt the canted floor drop away beneath – suddenly I was falling through space. Bidding an unfond farewell to this world, and all others, I braced for impact on the craggy rocks of my imagination, but it was an impact which never came. Instead, freezing water hit me like a slap.

The shock ripped away what little breath remained. Coughing and spluttering I kicked for the surface to search frantically for Isaiah. In the darkness I didn't fancy my chances. Just when I was about to give up hope, a hulking shape bobbed next to me in a froth of bubbles. This time my screams at least served a purpose – the echoes suggested we were in a large cavernous chamber. They took an age to die down, reverberating through the blackness. Before I could get my bearings I felt myself taken by a current. I had a firm grip of Isaiah, tilting his head back out of the water, but there was no sign of Gwen. All I could do was hang on and drift – a fitting metaphor for my life to date, perhaps.

We bobbed along for what seemed like an eternity, me shivering in the icy current, Isaiah lolling against my shoulder. I couldn't feel my feet by the time I noticed a smudge of grey in the distance. The light grew as we washed round a sweeping bend, and I fought to temper a surge of hope. The soft radiance suggested the unmistakable hint of daylight. Soon it was clear we were flowing along an underground river, perhaps a sewer running underneath the castle. Above us a glistening arch of stone shimmered in the half light. As we bobbed round the final corner I glimpsed sky ahead. Soon the channel exited a jagged cave mouth set back in a towering cliff. At the horizon the setting sun tinted ragged clouds a fiery orange behind a brooding silhouette of trees. We were out in the open air.

Before I had time to celebrate a hand grabbed me by the collar and pulled me towards the shore – it was Gwen. She hauled me out of the water onto a narrow sandy ledge at the base of the cliff. It didn't take long before she was busting my chattering balls.

'Where the hell have you been? I was beginning to think you weren't coming out. Like it in there, did you?'

I coughed up half a lung of oily water, wrestling Isaiah out after me. 'Not my favourite experience, if I'm honest. We had a bit of a wardrobe malfunction at the top of the chute, but we're alright now. Have you got the prism?'

She patted the bulge in her jacket. 'Safe and sound.'

'What about the recall beacon?'

'Ditto that. Have some faith, I know what I'm doing.'

323

'I'm glad one of us does.'

She regarded Isaiah suspiciously. 'But we need to get out of here – there's another wave of bombers coming in.'

Despite being clogged with water my ears told me Gwen wasn't wrong. The dull drone of aero engines filled the western sky. Somewhere above the clouds yet more Allied planes were on their way. Behind us a column of dark smoke rising from the castle signalled the Schloss had already taken a mighty pounding. It seemed there was more to come.

Gwen used a fallen branch to hack at the undergrowth crowding the back of our ledge. 'I think there might be a way through. Let's get moving.'

'Wait – what about Isaiah?'

'We can't take him with us. Not long ago he was all set to use us for target practice.'

I could see she had a point. The man who was destined to become my grandfather lay flat on his back, out for the count, but showed signs of coming round. I turned him over and checked his airways; his pulse was strong and his breathing steady. He coughed up a stream of muddy water and stirred in his sleep.

Gwen put a hand on my shoulder. 'It's best we're not here when he comes round.' I nodded.

We readied a pack of basic supplies – some of our meagre rations, a roll of bandage, some morphine, and left it by his side. My companion was eager to be on our way. 'He'll have a mighty headache and a fresh set of scars to go with the others, but he'll be safe down here sheltered by the rocks. We've done all we can.'

I knew she was right, but I didn't like leaving him this way. Call me sentimental, but I felt the urge to let him know who'd saved him. As Gwen disappeared into the bushes I reached into my jacket and tore off my dog tags, tossing them next to the pouch. Self-consciously I threw him one last salute, before scrambling after her. I had a strong hunch Sergeant Jones was going to be all right.

When we got to the top of the cliff Gwen hunkered behind an outcrop and unfolded a rather soggy map. Once she'd shaken the water out from her compass it was even up to the job of giving us a bearing. Shivering like a malaria victim I watched as she calculated the heading back to our rendezvous with the portal that would get us home. Satisfied at last she pointed with the folded chart. 'We need to head towards those trees.'

I was relieved she gave the smouldering castle a wide berth. The drone of the next wave of bombers was getting louder and I had no desire to experience the fireworks first hand. Sheltered by the cliff overhang Isaiah would be safe from harm, out in the open we were another matter. I was less than thrilled at the prospect of bumping into any more of those fanatical SS nutters – was it too much to hope they'd been wiped out?

Gwen set out towards the forest, sticking to cover and keeping low. As the shadows grew longer I was glad of the cover of the trees. After what seemed like an eternity, trotting through thickening undergrowth and trying not to trip over logs, my companion paused to check I was keeping up.

'How you doing, kiddo?'

Breathless, I sank to her side in the thickening gloom. 'Well, I'm tired, hungry, and on the point of freezing my nuts off – I've had better days to be honest. But right now most of all I just want to get home.'

She patted my cheek. 'That's the spirit. Can't lie to you – we're in for an uncomfortable evening. This is the last leg, just you remember that.'

'Thanks for your brutal honesty. Just like Colonel MacIntyre I'll hop all the way if I have to.'

Anthracite

Behind us, in the distance, a fresh series of concussions split the night. The Schloss was getting a second visit from the Air Force; hopefully the fly boys were pounding the rubble into dust. Somewhere beneath it all the inconvenient leftovers of Grandad's scheme were being erased from history – he'd picked his spot wisely.

Gwen got to her feet and scanned the dark forest for danger. Content we were on our own she reached down to help me up. 'If we pull an all-nighter we can get back to the portal by morning.'

My heart sank. 'How far is that?'

She shrugged. 'Can't be more than twenty clicks. Just a light training jog.'

I searched my brain for some snappy response, but I was too tired – or perhaps I was learning. It was hard to escape the conclusion I would need every bit of strength to keep up. Silently we set off again through the trees.

45

Back to Reality

Only a hazy recollection of that dreadful night lingers in my memory, and perhaps that's for the best. Gwen set a relentless pace, dragging me in her wake through sheer force of will. We drifted through an endless sea of trees, shadowy ghosts flitting through the darkness. Needless to say she was a lot fitter than me. Despite regular stops to check our heading, by midnight my lungs were bursting, my legs felt like jelly and my pounding heart was ready to explode. Just when I thought I could go no further Gwen pulled up short. We'd arrived at a crumbling stone wall, marking the boundary of that endless forest. Beyond it stretched an open field cloaked in a luminous fog, shot through with the first pale light of dawn. Even to my half-open eyes the landscape had a familiar cast.

Gwen pulled me down behind the stones. 'This is the right place, but it seems we're not alone – look over there.'

Dark shapes moved quietly through the swirling mist. Shielding my eyes against the glare I could make out tanks and trucks laagered up for the night, and the first stirrings of a camp slowly coming back to life.

Gwen let out a weary sigh. 'They're our guys, but this is a complication we didn't need.'

I couldn't have agreed more. 'Just wanna sleep – can't go on any further.'

She could see I wasn't exaggerating. Bundling me up in her jacket she eased me down behind the wall. 'Stay put. I'm off for a look around.'

There was zero chance of me going anywhere I didn't have to. My poor pounding muscles felt like I was still running. As soon as my head hit the dewy grass I was out like a light. Dreaming would have taken energy I didn't have. An ill-defined time later Gwen was shaking me awake.

'This might be our only chance. The longer we leave it the harder this will get.'

I did my best to resist but she wouldn't take no for an answer. Gwen can be rather persistent when she puts her mind to it. The sun was higher in the sky and the bright mist almost cleared. Out in the field the soldiers didn't seem to be departing any time soon. Pale figures milled around, eating breakfast, getting a brew and tinkering with their vehicles.

'So do we sneak in, or what?'

Gwen shook her head as she checked our recall transponder. 'We can't look like we're up to no good. I've not come this far to get shot at the last hurdle by our own side.'

Slumping against the stones I nodded. 'Had enough of that back at the Schloss. So how do we do this?'

Gwen dusted off my jacket and smartened me up. 'We're going to have to brazen it out – just like Milford Haven. You remember the drill?'

'I was afraid you would say that.'

Soon we were marching confidently across the ploughed

field. At least, Gwen marched confidently – I was too busy trying to not look like an imposter, or fall over my poor throbbing feet. Muttering curses, I hurried to catch up.

'Do we know where the portal will open? Can't get my bearings on where we arrived.'

Gwen shrugged without breaking stride. 'I've got a fair idea where it should appear. When it opens we'll be able to see it a mile off – those things are hard to miss.'

'Yeah, we'll see it all right – and so with every other squaddie busy guzzling his body weight in tea around this camp. Must be half the British Army here. A portal to another universe will attract its fair share of attention – inconspicuous, not.'

But Gwen wasn't listening to my moaning, she had other things on her mind. Calmly she produced the recall transmitter from her tunic and snapped open the safety with a nonchalant flick of her wrist.

'Get ready to run when I give the signal,' she said, thumbing the transmit button. There was a loud click, followed by an electronic warble. 'Doc Watkins promised his boffins will have the singularity fired up in less than a minute. We won't have time to hang round.'

I had zero intention of hanging around, and even less of getting left behind; I only hoped the signal worked. 'We're going to have the best part of an armoured division crashing through along with us, if we're not careful. That's going to be embarrassing.'

'We'll cross that pontoon bridge when we come to it. Walk this way.'

We reached the outer ring of trucks, maintaining a steady pace. An overall-clad mechanic wiped his hands on an oily rag and looked us up and down, but that was as far as any challenge went. Maybe this was going to work after all. Moving through the lines of vehicles I could hear the throaty roar of engines warming up for the day's march ahead. Beside me Gwen was scanning the skyline for any sight of the portal. She let out a gasp and her eyes went wide.

'There she blows.' She broke into a dead run. I did my best to keep up, tired muscles creaking into life.

A hundred yards ahead, and a little to our left, something weird was happening above the forest of radio antennae. It looked like reality was coming undone, the air shimmering like the heat haze above a fire pit. I had no desire to toast any marshmallows, I just wanted to get home.

'Stay close – we only get one shot at this.' Gwen accelerated from a jog into a sprint. Wincing with pain I struggled to comply.

A red-faced sergeant major stepped into our path. 'Halt – who goes there!'

But we didn't hang around to chat. Gwen jinked one way, I went the other. We left him in our wake fumbling with his holster. 'Ere, where the bloody ell do you think you two are going?'

Now we could see our prize. Between the lines of flatbed trucks and armoured cars the familiar anomaly was powering into life – a gleaming disc of swirling mercury suspended in mid-air. The portal opened like an iris, beckoning us to sweet oblivion, or maybe back to the world of +1 – perhaps they were the same thing. Doc Watkins hadn't let us down.

The faces that flashed by paid us scant attention. Bemused soldiers stood around agape, hypnotised by what they saw but couldn't understand. I had to admit the gate made a good distraction. Its bottom lip hovered four feet above the mud, iridescent waves of colour rippling across it in the early morning light. It was beautiful and terrifying – a bit like life. Gwen reached out and took my hand. I can't be sure but I think she was smiling as together we dived through. I braced for the less than pleasant sensation of transit, but instead we just kept falling through the light. I don't think I ever felt more alive than at that moment.

46

The Prodigal Nephew Returns

The concrete floor was hard and cold. My head throbbed. My tongue felt coated with radioactive waste, and I don't mean the good kind. This was a place I'd visited before. I guess the falling through the light bit didn't last. Struggling to sit up I found Gwen crouching over me.

'You took your own sweet time. Where've you been, kiddo?' She patted my cheek and smiled. I was beginning to feel better.

'My head hurts, but I think I'll make it. That sure felt different to any normal gate. You sure it was the same as the others?'

Gwen looked ready to elaborate, but was interrupted by a team of paramedics skidding to a halt around us. We were soon being scanned, prodded, examined and tested in ways not entirely in keeping with our new-found heroic status. It seemed we'd come through the portal in an unexpectedly far-flung spot on the extensive J-Corp landing pad, and the retrieval team had to scramble to catch up. Doc Watkins' boffins weren't far behind the medics, their leader red faced and out of breath.

'Bugger me, it worked – sometimes I impress myself!'

But the Doc's moment of triumph was short lived. A gaggle of Jones Corp suits were next to arrive, Uncle Genghis huffing and puffing at their head. 'The Nobel Prizes can wait.' He struggled for breath, hands on knees. 'Well boy, did you get it? If not we can always send you back.'

I was about to give the preening buffoon a piece of my mind, when Gwen pushed me gently back down. 'Cool your jets, Genghis. Rest assured we've not let you down.' She reached into her uniform and brought out the padded bag the Doc had given us what now seemed a lifetime ago.

An expectant hush fell over the assemblage. Gwen tossed the sack to Genghis, who juggled it like a hot potato. Frantically Uncle loosened the ties and reached a shaking hand inside. Reverently he drew forth the contents. The glowing Anthracite gemstone throbbed gently on his outstretched palm, illuminating the circle of gawping faces with its baleful glow. Genghis's tone was hushed. 'Doc, is it – the real thing? Do your stuff.'

Doc Watkins regained his composure, adjusting his thick NHS specs to squint at our prize. He wrinkled his nose for a moment, before unclipping a long pen-like device from the front pocket of his lab coat. The instrument looked much like something a medic might use to check the inside of an ear. He put the eyepiece up against the crystal and peered through the other end.

There was a hushed silence. Everyone was still. Even I found I'd stopped breathing, and I had no doubts about our prize's provenance. After a heart-stopping moment the Doc straightened up, licked his lips and passed judgement.

'It's the real thing all right. Fire up the assembly line.'

333

Genghis looked like he might explode with relief and happiness. 'YEEEESSS – GET IN THERE! We're back in business!' He carefully handed the crystal to Watkins, who placed it in a specially prepared containment chamber, pushed on a trolley by wide-eyed lackeys. The assorted boffins were soon shooed back to their labs, on the double, all the better for minimising their exposure to daylight. No doubt the Anthracite prism would be creating fresh J-Drives within the hour.

Genghis turned back to us. He looked like he wanted to teach the world to sing, if not in perfect harmony then at least in close approximation. 'I knew you pair wouldn't let me down. And to think some doubted you were a chip off the old block – I'll have em fired. Possibly shot.'

'That's nice,' I said, as Gwen helped me to my feet and dusted me down. Uncle G squared up to me, though whether to punch me or give me a hug I couldn't be sure. Somehow he'd retrieved his smouldering cigar – billowing blue smoke stung my eyes. He held out a gnarled hand, which I took with trepidation. It was soon being enthusiastically pumped up and down. 'Bloody proud of you, lad. Well done.'

I slept most of that afternoon and right through the night, back in the comfortable suite of apartments deep within the Jones family compound. My legs felt like they were still running, pounding through an endless forest of dark, brooding trees. Some faceless threat pursued me, forever present, yet never quite catching up. But I never doubted I'd escape the demons on my tail. I was faster and stronger now and had the best motivation to keep running. There was a beautiful light at the end of my dream, a blazing amethyst radiance that shone through the trees. When I burst from the forest into the open I launched myself into the sky and soared. For the first time in a long while I woke fully rested with a smile on my face.

The mood round the villa had changed for the better. Even the buzzing service robots seemed perky and upbeat. Was it my imagination or had the AI announcer's voice taken on a more soothing, sultry tone? There was another welcome development – my room was unlocked and I could come and go as I pleased. Not that I needed to go anywhere; I had a steady stream of visitors.

Mum came to see me not long after I awoke. She seemed to think I'd been out of town at *'one of my comic book convections'* – playing at fancy dress, mixing with the wrong crowd and probably staying up much too late. God knows what Genghis had told her. I didn't have the heart to tell her the stormtroopers I'd been dodging had been the straight-shooting, far more deadly kind – she'd only worry; sometimes you can know too much. At least Mum was in good spirits.

'Your uncle tells me it's all sorted and we'll soon be back at home. Your grandad must be missing us something rotten – worried sick I imagine, up in that madhouse.'

I wanted to tell her our version of Isaiah was probably having a whale of a time – Taliesin's potion I'd left behind likely taking him places few of us ever visited. 'Don't worry Mum, I'm sure he'll understand. I'll go see him, first chance I get.' Truth was I couldn't wait to see him again. Perhaps I now had a better understanding of some of the things he'd been through. Going home couldn't come soon enough.

Mum wasn't the only visitor I had that day. Doc Watkins dropped by for an informative chat. When he wasn't ramming you head first through unstable portals to alternate dimensions packed with psychotic Nazis, he seemed a decent bloke – at first, anyway. We sat drinking tea on the sunny balcony

Anthracite

outside the apartment, while he filled me in on recent developments.

'So we were able to get the J-Drive production line spinning up to full capacity almost straight away. Seamless, it was. And all thanks to you. Genghis is running around like a kid at Christmas.'

'That's nice for him.' As a boss I could well imagine what a pain in the neck my uncle would be.

Doc leaned closer. 'That's why I've come to see you – some of us senior staff need you to have a word with the bugger.'

It was hard not to snort in derision. 'What makes you think he'd listen to me?'

The Doc blinked. 'Thinks the sun shines out of your jacksie, he does. Not like his usual self at all – to him you're the hero of the hour.'

It was impossible not to roll my eyes in exasperation. Was there no end to my travails? 'I didn't ask for any of this. What do you want me to say to him?'

Watkins' voice dropped into a conspiratorial whisper. 'Keeps talking about us *changing our ways*, he does. Raving about a *gentler, kinder J-Corp* – as if such a thing's possible. Well some of us did very nicely out of the old ways, thank you very much. The board sent me to ask if you could get him to rein it in a notch. The shareholders are jittery.'

This revelation bothered me not one jot. But maybe there was a way I could play this situation to my advantage. 'I *could* have a word with him, if there was something in it for me.'

The Doc's eyes went wide. 'You scratch my back –'

'– I'll massage yours.'

'What do you want?'

'Information – and I don't want to have to lock you away in Portmeirion to get it. This hero still has plenty of questions of his own.'

Watkins nodded cautiously. 'I'll… see what I can do. What do you want to know?'

Now it was my turn to lean close. 'Let me get this straight; the all-singing, all-dancing version of Isaiah from this world was looking to help a kindred spirit – to *pay it forward*? That's why he travelled through the gate back to '45 to hide the prism?'

Doc Watkins checked both left and right. I didn't like to tell him about the bugs I felt certain ringed the apartment. 'That's right. Isaiah wanted a fellow Jones to benefit from his invention – some like-minded prodigy rather than the corrupt types he saw over here. Must have been getting soft in his old age – paranoid in the head, if you ask me.'

I frowned. 'But that video message he left – he tipped Genghis off about what he'd done.'

Watkins nodded sagely. 'He was a wise man, your grandfather. Prepared to entertain the possibility one of his existing relatives might have the gumption to get to it first – some distant cousin, perhaps. Seems he was right after all – though I doubt he was thinking of you.'

I considered this for a moment. It had been troubling my weary brain ever since getting back that I'd not exactly helped carry out Isaiah's final mortal wish. 'So what would he make of what I've done? I've just won Anthracite back for Genghis – not exactly what Isaiah had in mind.'

Doc Watkins shrugged. 'Who's to say, lad. Your grandad wanted to help one of his relatives – someone worthy, more like himself – seems to me that's just what he's done. He'd be happy you've won your freedom.'

Maybe that would have to do. Despite what the board wanted to happen maybe Genghis was capable of real change. I wandered, lost in my thoughts for a while. But there was something else even more troubling eating at the back of my mind. It made my head hurt just thinking about it.

'So the version of Isaiah from this world – the one who couldn't have kids – where did he get the Anthracite prism from? Who *passed it on* to him?'

Doc Watkins looked at me long and hard. It seemed he might squeeze out a glowing amethyst gemstone of his own, his expression hovering somewhere between consternation and constipation. When it arrived his reply was hoarse and stuttered.

'We've had a top team of analysts at Ystradgynlais Institute of Technology brainstorming that very question since the cach hit the ffan. The Trans-Multiverse Forecasting Department gets only our brightest and best. You might not like their conclusions.'

'Recent improvements in my levels of resilience might surprise you. What did the boffins down at YIT say? Theory me up, Doc.'

Watkins licked his lips. 'As far as they can tell – though this is mostly conjecture, mind – our Isaiah, *the real Isaiah*, got the crystal at the end of the war... from another version of himself. It was left for him in a locked genetic vault underneath the Schloss Drachenburg, the details of which might be familiar to you.'

It took a while for the implications of this idea to sink in. I did a lot of blinking. I'm not sure it helped. 'Right. I had a bad feeling you were going to say something like that.'

For a man of science the Doc looked mightily embarrassed. 'They think maybe, in a world without World War Two, the local Isaiah had the peace and quiet to develop the crystal and J-Drive from scratch. There's still a lot we don't understand.'

'Maybe the understatement of the century,' I muttered vacantly, as I struggled to get my head round the bigger concept. 'So we still don't know where the motherlode originates from? Somewhere up the line there's a *Keystone Isaiah* seeding all the other Universes, reflections of a reflection *paying it forward* into infinity. Maybe we should get in touch for a chat.'

Watkins tapped the side of his prominent nose. 'Have no fear, bach. We're briefing a top operative for that very mission as we speak. Keystone Isaiah – I like that phrase – needs to be protected from any dark forces out to wreck us. He's doing the Lord's work.'

Doc Watkins stood up. 'Perhaps I've already said too much. You'll remember to have a word with your uncle? The share price might depend on it.'

'Oh, I have plenty to say to Genghis, don't you worry.'

Doc patted me on the shoulder. 'Good lad. Ironic really – the Consortium who hired your young lady friend to kidnap you at the start of all this – remember them?'

'Yeah, those "dark forces". How could I ever forget?'

'They believed you were the key to preventing Wales developing the J-Drive and coming to dominate the world – in a way they were right.'

I must have looked more bemused than usual. 'How so?'

'Think about what you recently did back in '45. That's one universe where Isaiah never gets Anthracite, so doesn't build the J-Drive. No drive, no Pax Cambria there. You've created a world where the Consortium gets their way. A small victory for them perhaps, but a victory all the same.'

My mouth must have hung open, as Doc turned to go. 'But don't let it bother you, lad. Plenty more realities out there. We're not greedy, we can spare them a few. After all, the Multiverse is a big place.'

Uncle Genghis seemed a decade younger, as if a vast weight had lifted from his shoulders. This had the eerie effect of making the pocket psycho look even more like the version I knew from home. He'd arrived bearing a sturdy metal tube, the sort which, in days of old, might have contained a rolled-up treasure map. Now the Jones Corp CEO stood in a power stance, centre stage in my apartment, dripping cigar ash and beaming like the Cheshire Cat who'd got the cream, and possibly the canary too.

'Cheer up, lad – the sun is shining, our factories are running full tilt, life is good!'

It wasn't just the resumption of production which had put him in high spirits. Turns out the presidential election had gone our way too. Barry Island had won by a huge majority, with Llywsiffer swept away on a landslide of public scorn. Apparently my broadcast had tipped the balance. Turns out the Welsh public didn't take kindly to outside interference from enemies of the state. Coupled with the resumption of manufacturing, the future looked bright for the once beleaguered Jones clan. Genghis seemed a little disappointed I didn't share his enthusiasm.

'What's eating you? We've won so hard we've given our enemies splinters. Llywsiffer goes on trial for treason next week, and the judge is a friend of mine. Why've you got a face like the back end of a bus?'

I struggled to express myself diplomatically, finally giving up. 'Isaiah put the skids under you fuckwits for good reason. He wanted things to change. I'm not sure how pleased he'd be that I've helped you get back in business.'

Genghis spat out his cigar and had the grace to look shocked. 'Have no fear lad – Jones Corps has learned a harsh lesson.

We've gazed into the abyss and seen what stared back. Not something any of us can forget in a hurry.'

'You sure about that? I've already had one of your underlings bending my ear to talk you down from the ceiling. They're worried you're turning into some sort of tree-hugger.'

Genghis's grey eyes went wide. 'Rest assured I won't be humping any foliage. But there's going to be some real change around here. It'll be business, but not business as usual.'

'Really?'

'Yes, really. We're going to turn this organisation off and on again – a hard reset. Should do the buggers good. Doc Watkins and the rest of the board need to toe the line, or it will be off to the re-education camp for them.'

'Lovely. And if that fails?'

Uncle weighed it up for a moment. 'Might have to shoot some of them in the face, but only a few.'

Have to admit I didn't know what to make of this new happy-clappy Genghis, even if he did run to a nifty line in hipster gulags. The guy seemed sincere, but I'd learnt the hard way appearances could be deceptive. Whatever the true state of play it wouldn't do any harm to ram my message home. Brimming with righteous indignation I squared up to Uncle G.

'I hope so – for your sake. Just remember, Isaiah was the brains of this operation, in more than just the technical department. He was the heart too. Ignore his advice at your peril.'

Genghis blinked and took a step backwards as I prodded him in the chest. 'Stay true to Grandad's legacy, or you'll have me to answer to. Do I make myself clear?'

'Crystal, Kev. Pure Waterford.'

'Just remember I know where you live.'

I was close enough to see the sweat standing out on his

brow. Whatever else he was faking Genghis wasn't faking that. He stuttered and stammered for a moment. 'Give us a chance Kev, I'll bust every available bollock to regain your trust. Even a few of my own.'

'The first step is to send us home in peace – keep your side of the bargain. You up to that?'

Genghis nodded furiously. 'But of course lad, we'll send you and Mam home safe and sound, that goes without saying.'

I closed the gap between us further. 'And the rest of it.'

He looked genuinely unnerved. It felt good to intimidate him for once. My uncle flinched as I backed him into a chair, babbling. 'We've got the Aberdare gate locked down tight. Nothing goes through without our say-so. It's the only portal to your world and we'll guard it to the death. You have my word on that. Scouts honour. You'll be left alone in peace.'

'I'm not certain you were ever a Scout, Genghis – possibly a Girl Guide.'

'Those allegations were never proven.'

I studied him closely. 'So this means we're quits?'

He nodded a bit too fast. 'Yes, yes. More than quits – I owe you big time. Perhaps this small token of my appreciation will help regain your trust.' Arms hemmed in, he inclined his head towards the sturdy metal tube squashed between us. I'd forgotten about that.

My eyes narrowed as I took the heavy cylinder from his hands. Genghis motioned for me to unscrew the cap. It was full to the brim with clinky, weighty discs. I slid the first onto my palm and marvelled at the sight. Genghis seemed pleased with my reaction.

'Should make life easier on the other side. No point giving you cash – ours would only get you locked up, or thrown in the loony bin. You and Mam need never worry about money again.'

I held one of the coins up to the light. Have to admit it made a pretty sight. Likely more wealth than I'd ever held in my hand before. They were stamped with the seal of the Welsh Republic – a golden dragon shfarting a rainbow, powering its way to the stars. There were quite a lot of them.

My host continued his commentary. 'Twenty-four carat gold sovereigns, straight from the National Vault in Llantrisant. When melted down they should fetch a tidy sum, in this world or the next.'

Trust Genghis to see cold hard cash as the solution to any problem. Still, I had to admit, as peace offerings went this one would come in handy. On reflection maybe I did trust Uncle Genghis a little more after all. He put a gnarled hand out and smiled up at me.

'Son, you'll soon be going home.'

I got the distinct impression he'd be relieved to see the back of me.

47

Not So Local Hero

Next day Mum and I made our way to the mansion's landing pad – our scant belongings carried by a beeping service droid. All except the tube of gold coins which I had stuffed down the leg of my new suit – no way was I coming out of this nightmare empty trousered. Scores of household staff and Jones Corp underlings lined our route to wish us well. Seems Genghis hadn't exaggerated how far my fame had spread – I was the battle-scarred hero, making his way home to Valhalla, or at least to Aberdare. More than one pretty young lady darted from the crowd to drape a garland of daffodils round my neck and steal a kiss. It was all a bit much to take. Many shouted get-well messages when they saw my limping stiff-legged gait. I kept looking for the one face I wanted to see, but she was nowhere to be found – the story of my life.

Arriving at the departure lounge I spotted some people I did recognise. Colonel MacIntyre stood at ease, flanked by Juan and Mrs Abergavenny. Even though she held the title of general, my former tormentor was still outranked by the

Colonel in some complex manner I'd given up trying to understand. All three had come to see me off. They were in full dress uniform, cutting dashing figures – between them sporting an impressive swathe of gold braid and medals. The Colonel smiled when he caught sight of us.

'Hello young man. We've all read the report – damn fine performance the other side of the gate. You should be very proud of him, Mrs Jones.'

Mum was more than happy to lap up the praise on my behalf – she was welcome to it. She batted her eyelids at MacIntyre in a frankly nauseating fashion. 'Oh yes, he's such a good boy, my little Kevin. Just need to get him home for his tea and some proper rest.' With speed that would have impressed a striking cobra she reached up to squeeze my cheek between finger and thumb, in a move Mrs Abergavenny seemed to find highly amusing. The Colonel hadn't finished yet.

'No more than Kevin deserves. He's a real credit to you, Ma'am.'

Mum's eyes went wide. 'Yes – amazing how well he turned out, isn't it. What with no father figure at home during his upbringing – me a single mother, and all.' Any more eyelash fluttering and she was in danger of taking off, Dumbo-style. The Colonel might have been brave, but this was clearly a bridge too far even for him. Startled, he turned back to me.

'You carried out the mission flawlessly, and got yourself back in one piece. Can't ask for much more than that. How you feeling about it, bach?'

I wasn't going to lie. 'Still got sleep I need to catch up on, sir. The night we spent tabbing to the rendezvous isn't one I'd want to repeat in a hurry – pretty tough.'

The Colonel clapped me on the arm so hard it nearly knocked me off my feet. '*Pretty tough* is what you're all about, son.'

Anthracite

'I couldn't have done it on my own. I was taking orders from the best.'

MacIntyre grinned. 'You're too modest, lad. Teamwork's what it's all about. You've got to be able to take orders as well as dish them out. You know... if you ever want a job in my outfit –'

Mum grabbed my other arm, pulling me away. 'He's 'ad quite enough excitement, thank you very much! Just want to get him home where I can keep an eye on 'im. Don't reckon some types he's been mixing with are the best influence on the poor boy.'

The Colonel gave me a quizzical look, but all I could do was shrug in resignation – see what I have to deal with.

Juan reached out a big hand to shake mine. 'Well done, mi amigo. We knew you could do it.'

'That's not what you thought when we first met.'

He shrugged his massive shoulders. 'What do I know? I am just a humble hair-wrangler. The fact I possess godlike talent has no bearing on my skills at judging character. Our mutual friend's faith in you was not misguided.'

I did my best to sound casual. 'Which reminds me – where is Gwen? I was hoping to see her before I left.'

Mrs Abergavenny flashed a smile – seemed she had her best teeth in. 'Oh, that slip of a girl is around ere somewhere. Last I heard she was running the clean-up operation other side of the gate. Everyone's doing their best to respect your wishes. There'll be no more visitors, from us or anyone else. We'll lock down your world tighter than a shark's bum at forty fathoms. That is what you want, isn't it?'

I still found it hard to believe this geriatric commando had been deep cover monitoring my progress for years. For quite a while I stood there, doing no more than puffing out my cheeks. At last I managed a rather feeble nod. Truth was there were

346

some people I'd be gladder to see the back of than others. Case in point: this diminutive psychopath. For what I hoped was the last time, Mrs A cast a beady, jaundiced eye over me. 'I won't lie to you Kev, always had you down as a proper bell-end, but I'm glad to say you proved me wrong. Put it there, butt.'

She held out a bony hand, which all but crushed mine in its vice-like grip. I blinked back tears of pain, rather than sadness.

'All the best – and remember, the Colonel's offer stands. If you ever wants a job I'm sure someone as resourceful as you will find a way to get in touch. You know where to find us.'

I wasn't so sure about that – it was hard to imagine being desperate enough to risk my neck for these nutters again. My heroing days were over. I longed for the comforting embrace of my familiar Aberdare – the proper Aberdare – the one filled with decent people. Boredom wasn't so bad when you get used to it – certainly better than some of the alternatives. The moment was broken by the sight of the corporate limo landing on the tarmac. We said our final goodbyes and Mum and yours truly made our way out into the sunlight. We were on our way home.

The shuttle dropped us on the roof of the Gateway Plaza Hotel high above downtown Aberdare. We were helped from the aircraft by the beaming manager, who couldn't do enough for us. *Did we want a complimentary stay in the Presidential Suite? Drinks at the bar? The company of enthusiastic young ladies, or gentlemen?* Nothing was too much trouble. It was all very different to my previous visits. It seemed Jones Corp would do a better job of running the place than the Consortium. Declining politely I took the chance to take in that view one last time. It remained as impressive as ever, a long line of freighters waiting to dock at the space terminal further down the valley. But if I'm honest I was already itching to clap eyes on a more familiar skyline.

The doting manager led us to the waiting express elevator and ushered us in; the guy was intent on escorting us all the way to the basement. It seemed I was slowly becoming okay with the concept of lifts, but, just like a fart after a particularly violent stomach bug, it would be a while before I could completely trust one again. As the doors closed Mum saw my distress and reached out to squeeze my hand. Goodness knows where she thought we were heading. I'd given up trying to guess how she rationalised all that'd gone down. As far as I could tell she still thought we'd been in the real world, with Genghis and the family keeping secret their great wealth – some sort of tax dodge, no doubt. Maybe this was for the best. If ignorance was bliss I knew what I'd been through also proved the opposite. For the first time in a long while I realised I'd missed my mum. Maybe it takes a life-threatening ordeal to fully appreciate the mundane comforts of home. I resolved to appreciate her more when we got back.

We arrived to find the basement a hive of activity. J-Corp workmen in hi-viz and hard hats busied themselves closing down the much fought-over Aberdare Gate – a venue which had changed hands more times than Captain Hook. It seemed Genghis was keeping his side of the bargain. A harried-looking corporate suit was waiting to usher us down that short corridor packed with painful memories. The bullet holes had been painted over, and the scorch marks wiped clean, but I could have sworn I still smelt a hint of cordite lingering in the air. We soon arrived outside Room 237, as empty and bare as ever. We were destined to be the gate's final travellers.

Mum entered first, bending the corporate suit's ear about what a clever baby I'd been – sooo advanced for my age. As if the poor sod hadn't looked harried enough. I paused at the threshold, one hand on the jamb, to gaze at the bare chamber where all my misadventures had begun.

'Weren't you going to say goodbye, Kev?'

My heart skipped several beats, then made up for it by going into overdrive. I had the presence of mind to fix a wry smile on my lips, as I slowly turned. 'Of all the libraries in all the worlds, you had to walk into mine.'

Gwen wrinkled her petite nose. 'Well, it was *you* I was specifically looking for, so perhaps not that much of a stretch after all.'

A million emotions surged through my bosom. How best to put my feelings into words? 'Beside the point. You can argue with fate all you like, but in the end it will club you into submission. Our paths were always meant to cross.'

'Maybe they were. Make sure you take good care of your mam when you get back, as well as your grandad.'

'I'll do that.'

My one-time kidnapper looked bright and alert as usual, decked out in her mission gear, a packet of mints resting lightly in one fingerless-gloved hand. 'That's good to hear. I just wanted to see you before you left us for good. You give any thought to the Colonel's proposal?'

I'd thought about MacIntyre's job offer all right, but I knew it was an idea that didn't have the full set of legs, much like the man himself. Sure, I'd done okay back at the Schloss Drachenburg, but if I was honest I knew long term I wasn't cut out for Gwen's line of work. I could see I would have to let the poor girl down gently.

'Listen babes –' she did a double take, perhaps surprised by how suave I could be when I turned on the charm, '– if that gate closes and I'm not through it, you'll regret it, maybe not today, maybe not tomorrow, but soon and for the rest of your life.'

Gwen put on a show of bafflement. I shouldn't have been surprised – her acting skills were as sharp as her reflexes. 'Don't think so mate. I reckon we made a pretty good team.'

'Gareth and Phil,' I nodded. 'SuperTed and Spottyman.'

Even her winces were things of beauty. 'More Sam Tân and Norman Price, if you ask me. You were a bit of a div at first, truth be told, but we rounded off most of the rough edges. I've had *worse* partners.'

High praise indeed. Gwen hid it well but I sensed a flood of tears were just around the corner; time to be masterful. 'Now you listen to me, honey. Do you have any idea what you'd have to look forward to if I stayed? We both know what would happen – nine chances out of ten we'd wind up hitting the sack pretty hard, and that's one impact neither of us would walk away from, at least not in a straight line – not good for either of our careers.'

She did quite a bit of blinking. 'Most of the rough edges, anyway.'

'Pardon me?'

'I'm glad you've given it so much forethought, Kev. I'm confident we could keep it purely professional. But I guess it's down to you in the end. No worries, no hard feelings.'

The poor girl was clearly in bits, but hiding it well – maybe too well. I thought it best not to point out there had been some hard feelings, kept under control with regular cold showers. I mopped my eyes. 'We'll always have Aberdare.'

She brightened. 'Aberdare and the Schloss Drachenburg. Couldn't have done it without you, sport.'

I turned my head to show my best side. 'I'm no good at being noble, but it doesn't take much to see the problems of two people don't amount to a hill of cheese in these crazy worlds.'

She smiled at me, brave girl. 'Someday I'll understand, but not now. Here's looking at you, kiddo.'

All the dust hanging in the air must have caused my eyes to well up as I held out a hand for her to shake. Gwen looked at it as if I were offering her month-old porridge.

'Don't be soft, you daft muppet. Come here and give us a proper cwtch.' Before I could protest she'd locked me in a fierce embrace – I'd forgotten how strong she was. Her hair smelt of wild flowers, undercut with the ozone tang of the gate. I tolerated this ordeal heroically and thought noble thoughts. Luckily no cold showers were needed. At last Gwen pulled away. Taking hold of my arms she gazed at me intently with those big brown eyes. 'You know Kev, you've changed a lot in the short time I've known you.'

I blinked my eyes back into focus. 'You really think so? For the better, I hope.'

She nodded enthusiastically. 'Definitely for the better. Hope you don't mind me saying, but you could be a total plank when we first met, at least some of the time.'

'Yeah, maybe most of the time. I used to think I was a tragic hero, but perhaps I was exactly half right.'

Smiling, she gave my arms a pat. 'Maybe you've swapped those around. It's funny how things work out, don't you think.'

'I'm not sure if funny's the word I'd use.'

'I mean – if I hadn't accepted the mission to fetch you I never would have put things right with the Colonel. I'll always be grateful for that. Wouldn't have happened without you.'

I forced a smile. 'Glad to have helped. It's good to feel you belong.'

'Maybe we're both heading back where we belong.' She offered me a sweet. 'For the journey, like.'

I took one and popped it in my mouth. Would I ever be able to eat a mint again without thinking of this moment, and my dear factory-built ninja kidnapper? In life we all have crosses to bear; maybe this would be mine.

'There's just one thing I don't understand.'

'Just the one?'

Perhaps it was my growing maturity, but I let that slide. 'When we crossed over to '45 you ran a test on your handheld – seemed to rattle your cage. What was that about?'

Gwen paused, as if trawling through her flawless memory. 'Oh, nothing much – just ran a local pi test, that's all. Standard procedure when making a new jump in the field.'

I wasn't letting her off that lightly. 'Come off it. Nothing about that op was standard procedure. What did it tell you?'

Gwen sighed and gazed at me. 'Nothing you needed to know at the time.'

'Nothing I needed to know *at the time*. Spill it – you owe me that much after what we've been through.'

Gwen suddenly took a great interest in the details of my suit lapel, picking off flecks of invisible fluff. 'The pi test confirmed what I already suspected – that we weren't in a parallel universe at all, we'd gone back in time to yours.'

Jaw and stomach dropped in unison. 'But that's not possible. What happened to *all theory suggests time travel's not a thing*? Paradoxes turning the universe inside out, grandchildren winking out of existence, all that jizz?'

Gwen puffed out her cheeks. 'That's just it – all theory. We're finding new angles on this stuff every day. Don't imagine for a moment the boffins have got a perfect picture, maybe they never will. You live and you learn, aye.'

'Or you don't live long,' I was just about able to mutter.

There was a lot to unpack here, the implications slowly sinking in. I could feel the mother of all migraines coming on. 'So we were interacting with my world's past all along? What if I'd got Isaiah killed? Or even not pulled him from the rubble? How could I have been born?'

Gwen's smile looked too much like a grimace. 'Wouldn't have been great, no. That's why I didn't think it best to burden you with that information. We had enough on our plates.'

I could well attest to the fullness of our tableware amidst the crumbling Third Reich – more sauerkraut than I ever wanted to see in one go.

'Still – all worked out for the best in the end,' Gwen continued breezily.

There was not any good answer to that, so I kept my mouth shut. Perhaps I really had changed after all.

The poignant silence was broken by a shout from the technician in the room behind. 'Portal's ready to go in five. Last call for Dark Age Aberdare. Duty-free will not be sold. Thank you for flying Jones Air.'

Gwen glanced over my shoulder. 'Your mam's waiting. Better go, she'll only fuss.'

She would indeed. 'Goodbye Gwen. Maybe I'll see you around.'

'Maybe you will.' She leant forward, stood ever so slightly on tiptoe, and kissed me on the cheek. The warmth from her lips blossomed on my skin, before sending veins of electric lava racing down my spine. I was sure it was a feeling that would stay with me forever – I certainly hoped so. Gwen looked at me with those big brown eyes one last time. 'Just remember Kev, life begins where your comfort zone ends.'

Wasn't that the truth. I turned and headed back to the awaiting gate. I was finally going home.

48

Aberdare Zero

And so that's how I found myself back where it all began. The old home town certainly *looked* the same, as I didn't so much step down from the train as stumble bleary eyed from the library, but this Aberdare felt different somehow. I think Mam sensed it too. We stood on the library steps, blinking in the sunlight, drinking it all in – hair of the dog for a pair of recovering alcoholics. The mountains ringing the valley slouched in their old familiar fashion; the same wonky skyline poked its broken nose above the rows of houses, as if fearful of what the day might bring; but something was different, something had changed. Maybe it was us. Whatever had happened we were home at last, and home had never felt so good.

I got Mam settled back at the house. No need to cook my tea – I promised her a slap-up fish supper from the chippy to celebrate being back. After I stashed my trouser-load of gold under my bed I went up the hill to see Grandad. The nurse on duty at the front desk did a double-take when she saw me come in, quickly scurrying into the back office to fetch her boss. Mr Hudson, the duty manager, came stomping out, his face like thunder, before all but screeching to a halt, wide eyed. I was getting used to this reaction from people I knew.

'Ah, young Mr Jones. Forgive me but I barely recognised you. Nice suit.' The fool seemed ridiculously impressed.

'Just the same old me underneath,' I said. 'We'll have your invoice paid by the end of the week, you have my word on that. I'd like to see my grandad, please.'

Mr Hudson looked briefly jubilant at the talk of invoices, before regaining his composure and putting on his best stern face, the one he reserved for relatives of incalcitrant guests. Apparently he'd been trying to call me for days. I didn't like to tell him my old phone was still hitching a ride in a tacsi, buzzing around another version of Aberdare – one with more in common with Mos Eisley than this one. Some ideas just don't translate.

Hudson bent my ear for a good ten minutes on the subject of Isaiah's behaviour. It *couldn't go on*, he said. There needed to be *changes*, or we'd have to make *other arrangements* for Grandad's care, never mind if we settled the bill. I was left in no doubt that I 'needed to have a word' with him. Despite these pronouncements of doom I found the old guy up in his room, sitting calmly in his favourite chair overlooking the hillside. He looked up when he heard me approach, and his face lit up.

'Kev bach, where've you bin, boi? Missed our little chats I ave.'

'Sorry Grandad, missed you too. I've been away on business. There were a few things I needed to take care of, but I got them sorted out. I'm back now.'

'Good lad. Back for good?'

'I think so, yes.'

His watery eyes danced over me. 'Something different about you? Look taller; hint of a tan, maybe.'

He might have been deep into his nineties but Gramps didn't miss much. 'I got a new haircut, Grandad. Came free with the job.'

He looked suitably impressed. 'Nice and short, could be forces – I can't keep up with these modern fashions.'

'What goes around, comes around, Grandad. I think you told me that.'

'Aye, lad, pretty sure I did. One of those fancy places down Cardiff way? All hair gel and posh coffee, no doubt.'

It was hard not to smile. 'Something like that, yes.'

'Well, whatever the reason you're looking good on it. Perhaps you should get away more often – does a boy good to see the world.'

'Just like you did, Gramps?'

He threw me a wry look, which turned into a smile. 'Well, some parts of it, at least.'

Grandad was right about that. He was clearly having one of his good days – which reminded me of the small problem I'd been asked by Hudson to address. Isaiah liked it here and it was the only care home in the valley. Now that our money worries were over there was no reason he couldn't see out his days here in peace, just so long as I could smooth this little issue with his landlord.

'Listen Grandad, the walking rugby has got to stop. Mrs Beynon's hips aren't up to it. Not all the other guests are as hardcore as you. There've been complaints, and several hospitalisations. Hudson is having kittens.'

Isaiah looked dubious. 'Complaints? Not from the inmates, there haven't been. Most of em are more than up for it. It's just their whining kids who've complained. When you're stuck by ere you need your distractions. You'd think them that visit would be more understanding.'

'The families are just concerned, that's all.'

The old guy huffed and puffed. 'Maybe if they were so concerned they'd come to visit more often. Not all are as good as you and your mam. Some wrinklies only see their folks birthdays and Christmases if they're lucky. Criminal, it is.'

Despite his words I felt a stab of guilt at my recent absence. 'Maybe you're right, Gramps, but do you think you could dial it down a bit? Perhaps get back to the online poker – less hazardous to everyone's health.'

A spot of pro-level muttering ensued. 'But not to their wealth. That Mrs Griffiths cheats like a baboon, counts cards she does – banned from every casino in Vegas, she was, back in the day.'

I'd met Mrs Griffiths, and for her, *back in the day* must have been sometime in 1973. Then I had an idea. 'We could always open up our film nights. Hook up that big flat screen Hudson bought for the lounge.'

Grandad brightened at this suggestion. 'Aye, the crusties would like that. What flics did you have in mind? Could do with broadening some horizons.'

I thought for a moment. 'Well, I've recently developed a strong urge to watch *Blade Runner* one more time. You up for that, Gramps?'

This seemed to meet with his approval. But suddenly he sat up with a jolt, as if remembering some vital piece of information. 'Never mind Saturday Night at the Movies, boi. That stuff you left me – you have any more of it knocking about?'

'Any more of what left?'

He leant forward, affecting an elaborate stage whisper. 'That little bottle. The Water of Life we called it. Dynamite in a flask.'

A moment of confusion, then I remembered. When I'd last come to visit, looking for clues at Llywsiffer's behest, I'd left Taliesin's potion behind. The small vial of druidic herbs had helped spark Isaiah's brain into recalling the past – seems it had done more than just that. The geriatric rugby was beginning to make sense.

I licked my dry lips. 'Grandad, did you give any of that stuff to any of the other inmates… I mean, any other guests?'

Isaiah got a faraway look in his pale eyes. 'Mrs Richards makes a lovely urn of tea every day at four, bloody lovely, it is.'

'Grandad, what are you trying to say?'

His gaze drifted to some distant horizon. 'Lovely it might be, but that brew only gets better with a little addition.'

'Gramps, what did you put in it?'

'It was only a tiny bottle. We had to really stretch it out to get it to last all week.'

I found some small measure of comfort by the simple act of energetically massaging my temples. If I pressed hard I could almost get the images out of my head. Almost. 'But the potion's all gone now, right?'

'Yes,' he said sadly. A long pause ensued. 'Any chance you can get some more of the stuff?'

'Not a chance, Grandad. No chance at all.'

He sighed deeply. 'Oh well, perhaps it's for the best.'

This took me by surprise. 'Really, what do you mean?'

He got that faraway look again. 'It was making Mrs Beynon frisky as hell. If I'm honest, I could do with the rest.'

I didn't press him for details, I knew they'd only make me wake screaming in the night. Some aspects of the lives of those we're close to are best kept out of sight. I knew Grandad was happy, just like I knew somewhere deep inside that carved teak box on his sideboard, amongst the old photos and medals, was a set of dog tags belonging to 'Private Smith', the man who'd saved him back in 1945. Just knowing these things was enough for me.

Later that evening, when I brought Mam up to speed on Grandad's situation, I thought it best to skip talk of magic potions and geriatric gang bangs. She would only worry, and the worst of the danger seemed past. Next day I took a trip down to Cardiff to exchange part of the gold I'd brought back into cold hard cash – it came to quite a sum. Not enough to retire on but plenty to pay Grandad's care home fees for years to come and still leave us with a tidy nest egg. In time I'd research getting a better price on the rest of the haul, but it was a start. I invested some of my windfall in a shiny new state-of-the-art laptop, for which I had a specific use in mind.

We hadn't been back long when an all-too familiar face came a-calling. The features might have been the same, but this version of Uncle Genghis was missing the designer suit and triple-A teeth. Of course when Mam made reference to his hidden millions and secret mansions, tapping the side of her nose conspiratorially, Uncle G looked at her as if she were bonkers. For some less than logical reason this immediately set my back on edge. Who the hell did he think he was, treating her like that?

Genghis wanted to know if I'd finished drawing up plans for his foot spa conversion project – The Vaginator 5000. He had a mate over in Treorchy ready to start banging them out from his body repair shop once the blueprints were complete. *Didn't I understand this time next year we could be millionaires?* Hats off to him for his optimism, but I thought even *milliners* might be pushing it.

Instead I told the mad fool I'd had other things on my mind, bigger fish to fry – fact was I'd been sautéing Moby Dick.

His reaction was much as you'd expect. Genghis gazed at me in mounting fury, steam all but whistling from his perforated ears. There followed a good deal of screaming and gnashing of crooked teeth, stumpy limbs flailed round our kitchen – it was quite a show.

I watched him calmly, Mam cowering behind me, as his rage subsided. The whole spectacle put me in mind of a spoiled toddler – how had I ever been scared of this silly little man? Genghis had lost any terror he'd once held for me. Bored with his ravings I got hold of the scruff of his neck and frogmarched him to the door. Mam was a little concerned, but she seemed to enjoy the spectacle of me throwing him out of our house. I told Genghis not to come back until he'd smartened up his ideas and learned a bit of respect. He went stumbling off down our street, pinballing into parked cars and looking over his shoulder at me with something close to fear.

The next day I got down to work. Re-reading *The Windy Ninja* was not an easy experience. It felt like something written by somebody else, someone smaller and hopelessly out of touch with reality, ironic as that may seem. I resolved to start anew, to create something more honest and from the heart – but what? They say it's best to write what you know.

I powered up my new laptop and stared at the flashing cursor for the best part of an hour, examining my feelings. What conclusions could I draw? I felt a whole lot better for having had the chance to say goodbye to Gwen, my mind was at peace. At last I felt ready to move on with the next stage of my life. So what had I learned on my travels? Next time your life flashes before your eyes make sure you've got something to watch. Perhaps I knew what to write after all, I needed to begin paying it forward. I started typing.

I've seen things you people wouldn't believe. Fishing ships on fire off Caldey Island. I've watched Anthracite power beams glitter in the dark around the Aberdare Gate. When I'm gone these moments will be lost in time, like… tears in the rain. And it's just started pissing down.

The End

Acknowledgements

Thank you to all the people who supported this book and helped to make it happen. *Anthracite* was a lot of fun to write, but what helped make it such an enjoyable experience was the positive feedback I got along the way. Huge thanks to my beta readers Barbara Thomas, Gillian Cranston, Paul Vickers, Steve and Lucy Corley, Daniel and Luke Thomas – this is a better book for your invaluable advice and encouragement. Thank you to the team at Unbound who were incredibly professional and easy to deal with throughout – Andrew, Anna and Cassie helped the whole process go remarkably smoothly. Big thank you to Philip Purser-Hallard who did a superb job on the structural edit and came up with some great suggestions. Thank you to my Dad, Allan Thomas, who would have loved this book but sadly isn't around to read it – so many of the books I read in my formative years were down to you. Last and by no means least, thank you to Lisa and Jacob, whose love and support makes it all worthwhile.

And finally, I'd like to express my deepest thanks to everyone on the list of patrons. It takes a lot to stump up cold hard cash on the promise of an outlandish project such as this. There would be no paperback edition of this book without you.

Each and every one of you is a true hero of the revolution. From the bottom of my heart, diolch yn fawr. I'd love to hear what you think of Anthracite. You can find me on Twitter at @MattT_Author. I'm looking forward to hearing from you.

A final note

There's been a twenty-year gap between my last books and this one. While I can't promise anything concrete, I don't get the feeling there's be a twenty-year gap between this one and the next. Apart from anything else there are too many interesting characters in *Anthracite* who I don't feel I've finished exploring yet. My mind keeps getting drawn back to this one crazy world in particular, and what really lies sleeping beneath Swansea Bay.

Unbound is the world's first crowdfunding publisher, established in 2011.

We believe that wonderful things can happen when you clear a path for people who share a passion. That's why we've built a platform that brings together readers and authors to crowdfund books they believe in – and give fresh ideas that don't fit the traditional mould the chance they deserve.

This book is in your hands because readers made it possible. Everyone who pledged their support is listed at the front of the book and below. Join them by visiting unbound.com and supporting a book today.

Dan Abramovich
Caspar Addyman
Jannette Berends
Stephen Bowden
Geoff Bowler
Lisa Branford
Nia Burgess
Laura Burkinshaw
Lazlo Burns
Jane Campbell
Brandon Clauser
Steve Clough
Helen Coles
Mark Crosby
Tony Cross
William Daniel
Nicholas James Davey
Rebecca Davidson
Don Davies

Joshua Davies
Kate and Hugh Davies
Rhian Davies
Trevor Down
Ruhi Habib Edwards-Behi
Paul Elliot
Matthew Evans
Theresa Evans
Tom Evans
Lou Fasulo
Matthew Gabrielli
Susan Godfrey
Peter Hale
Mike Harford
Gary Haskins
Umair Hassan
Lucy Henzell-Thomas
Sonja Hochgeschurz
Ken Hollan

Lin Hornby
Amy Hudson
S Hudson
Richard Hughes
Robert Hughes
Myrthe Hultermans
Michael Humphries
Gary James
Gwyn James
Mike James
Paul Jeorrett
Callum Jessamine
Roger Jones
Jeannette Juricic
Dan Kieran
Stefanie Kudla
Rupert Lang
Félice Le Poer
Darren Lester
Alain Lewis
Anastasia Lewis
Gavin Lewis
Kirsty Lewis
Jane Loveday
Catherine Makin
Philippa Manasseh
Sarah Maximiek
Carol McCollough
Zitah McMillan-Ward
John Mitchinson
Diego Montoyer
James Morrison
David Murphy
Rhel ná DecVandé
Linda Nathan
Carlo Navato
Kay Nettle
Par Olsson
Elaine Orchard
Paula Page

Sophie Parker
Lisa Pearce Collins
Katrina Pecina
Dan Peters
Katherine Petersen
Tom Plank
Justin Pollard
The Pondy-Upton family
Philip Raab
Colette Reap
Christopher Rees
Louise Reid
Pat Richards
Toby Rodgers
Arthur Schiller
Janette Schubert
Gemma Scott
Colin Sheasby
Isobel Sheene
Colin Simpson
Karen Smith
Roy Stilling
The many way to
Edward Thomas
Les Thomas
Wendy Thoms
Barbara Thorne
James Tobin
Gareth Tregidon
Donna Trett
Susan Turner
Rosemarie van Leeuwen
Mark Vent
Jack Weeland
Clancy Wendt
Katie Weston
Richard Whitaker
Derek Wilson
Adam Wynne
Esme Young